PRIVATE WARS

PRIVATE WARS

A Queen & Country Novel

GREG RUCKA

BANTAM BOOKS

Ruc

PRIVATE WARS
A Bantam Book / November 2005

Published by
Bantam Dell
A Division of Random House, Inc.
New York, New York

Book design by Glen Edelstein

Bantam Books is a registered trademark of Random House, Inc., and the colophon is a trademark of Random House, Inc.

Library of Congress Cataloging-in-Publication Data
Rucka, Greg.
Private wars / Greg Rucka.
p. cm.
ISBN-13: 978-0-553-80277-1
ISBN-10: 0-553-80277-1
1. Women spies—Fiction. 2. Americans—Uzbekistan—Fiction.
3. Illegal arms transfers—Fiction. 4. Uzbekistan—Fiction. I. Title.

PS3568.U2968P75 2005
813'.54—dc22
2005050115

Printed in the United States of America
Published simultaneously in Canada

www.bantamdell.com

10 9 8 7 6 5 4 3 2 1
BVG

For my brother,
Nick

ACKNOWLEDGMENTS

A thank-you is owed to the following for their assistance in bringing this work to life.

Ben Moeling, for giving freely of his time, insight, and experience. All things considered, the late hit really wasn't that bad.

In London, gratitude to Andrew Wheeler, Alasdair Watson, and Ade Brown; in Barnoldswick, to Antony Johnston and Marcia Allas. Thanks to all for giving me the lay of the land, the turn of the phrase, and the occasional couch to sleep on.

At Oni Press, where *Queen & Country* continues to thrive, thanks to James Lucas Jones, Randal C. Jarrell, and Joe Nozemack, not solely for their wonderful friendship, but for their continued support as well.

As before, I am indebted to all of the gifted artists who have worked on *Queen & Country* thus far—Steve Rolston, Tim Sale, Brian Hurtt, Durwin Talon, Christine Norrie, Bryan O'Malley, Leandro Fernandez, Jason Alexander, Carla "Speed" McNeil, Mike Hawthorne, Mike Norton, Rick Burchett, and Chris Mitten.

Once again, to Gerard V. Hennely, who spends a lot of time thinking about the kind of things the rest of us don't want to spend a lot of time thinking about. As always, your help has been invaluable.

To David Hale Smith at DHS Literary, and Angela Cheng Kaplan at the Cheng-Kaplan Company, who continue to represent me with diligence, passion, and only the barest hints of annoyance. Additional gratitude to Maggie Griffen.

Thanks again to the real Tara F. Chace, who would always rather be carried; to Ian Mackintosh, for creating a world where a fictional Tara F. Chace *could* be carried; and to Lawrie Mackintosh, who is truly one of the most profoundly generous men it has ever been my pleasure to know.

Finally, to Elliot, Dashiell, and Jennifer, who make the hard things easy.

The police repeatedly tortured prisoners, State Department officials wrote, noting that the most common techniques were "beating, often with blunt weapons, and asphyxiation with a gas mask." Separately, international human rights groups had reported that torture in Uzbek jails included boiling of body parts, using electroshock on genitals and plucking off fingernails and toenails with pliers. Two prisoners were boiled to death, the groups reported. The February 2001 State Department report stated bluntly, "Uzbekistan is an authoritarian state with limited civil rights."

—From "U.S. Recruits a Rough Ally to Be Jailer," by Hans Rudolf Oeser, for the *New York Times,* May 1, 2005

c. Torture and Other Cruel, Inhuman, or Degrading Treatment or Punishment

The law prohibits such practices; however, police and the NSS routinely tortured, beat, and otherwise mistreated detainees to obtain confessions or incriminating information. Police, prison officials, and the NSS allegedly used suffocation, electric shock, rape, and other sexual abuse. . . . In February 2003, the U.N. Special Rapporteur on Torture issued a report that concluded that torture or similar ill-treatment was systematic.

—From "Uzbekistan," in *Country Reports on Human Rights Practices,* published by the U.S. Department of State, February 25, 2005

The government claims its efforts serve as part of the global campaign against terrorism. Yet in the overwhelming majority of cases, those imprisoned have not been accused or convicted of terrorism or charged with any other violent act. Human Rights Watch has documented the torture of many of those detained in the context of this compaign, including several who that [sic] died as a result of torture . . . including beatings by fist and with truncheons or metal rods, rape and sexual violence, electric shock, use of lit cigarettes or newspapers to burn the detainee, and asphyxiation with plastic bags or gas masks. A doctor who examined the body of a detainee who died in custody in 2002 described burns consistent with immersion in boiling water.

—From "Torture World Wide," published by Human Rights Watch, April 27, 2005

GLOSSARY

Article Five   Referring to NATO signatories; Article Five declares that an attack against any one of the member nations is an attack against all of the signatories; further, that member nations shall, in the instance of such attack, render assistance and aid to fellow members.

BOX   Used to refer to the Security Services, more commonly known as MI-5 (U.K.)

C   Head of SIS; also Chief of Service

CAO   Cultural Affairs Officer

CENTCOM   United States Central Command, oversees U.S. security interests in 25 Middle Eastern and Arab nations

Chancery   The principal office of an Embassy, housing the Ambassador's office

CIA   Central Intelligence Agency (U.S.)

CIS   Confederacy of Independent States

COB   "Close of Business"

COM   Chief of Mission (U.S. State Department); generally refers to the Ambassador

conops   Concept of Operations—official document describing parameters and goals assigned to a prospective operation, and securing necessary permissions to pursue the undertaking

COS   Chief of Station (CIA)

CQC   Close Quarters Combat

D	Deputy Secretary of State (U.S.)
D-Int	Director of Operations (SIS); sometimes Director Intelligence
D-Ops	Director of Operations (SIS); sometimes Director Operations
DC	Deputy Chief of Service (SIS); also Deputy Chief
DCM	Deputy Chief of Mission (U.S. State Department)
DOO	Duty Operations Officer
DPM	Deputy Prime Minister, DPMs plural
EIJ	Egyptian Islamic Jihad, *Al-Jihad al-Islami*; founded late 1970s, merged with al-Qaeda in June 2001. Dr. Ayman al-Zawahiri one of its founders.
FCO	Foreign and Commonwealth Office (U.K.)
FSB	Forward Support Base (U.K. Military)
FSO	Foreign Service Officer (also FO); indicates a career State Department Officer (U.S. State Department)
GSPC	*Groupe Salafiste pour la Predication et la Combat* (The Salafist Group for Call and Combat); violent religious extremist group based in Algeria
GWOT	Global War on Terror
Hizb-ut-Tahir	The Islamic Party of Liberation, a banned Uzbek opposition party seeking greater religious freedom in Uzbekistan
HOS	Head of Station; also Station Number One (SIS)
IMU	Islamic Movement of Uzbekistan; terrorist organization with ties to al-Qaeda, responsible for terror attacks in Uzbekistan. Often confused with *Hizb-ut-Tahir*
JI	*Jemaah Islamiyah* (Islamic Community);

	extremist terror organization operating in Indonesia, Malaysia, Singapore, and the Philippines. Has ties to al-Qaeda.
JIC	Joint Intelligence Committee (U.K.)
LNG	Liquefied Natural Gas
LS	Landing site
MANPAD	Man-portable air defense system; a surface-to-air missile capable of being launched by a lone individual
MCO	Mission Control Officer (SIS); Ops Room post responsible for oversight of actual mission execution; also Main Communications Officer (SIS); responsible for recording and coordinating communications between the Ops Room and the field
Mission	Generic term used interchangeably with "post" or "embassy," referring to the entirety of the official representation made to a host country (U.S. State Department)
MOD	Ministry of Defense (U.K.)
NCTC	National Center for Counterterrorism (U.S.)
NVG	Night-vision goggles
PA	Personal Assistant
PRC	People's Republic of China
PUS	Permanent Undersecretary
RSO	Regional Security Officer (U.S. State Department)
RV	Rendezvous
S	Office of Secretary, Department of State; Secretary of State (U.S.)
SAS	Special Air Service (U.K.)
SIS	Secret Intelligence Service (U.K.)

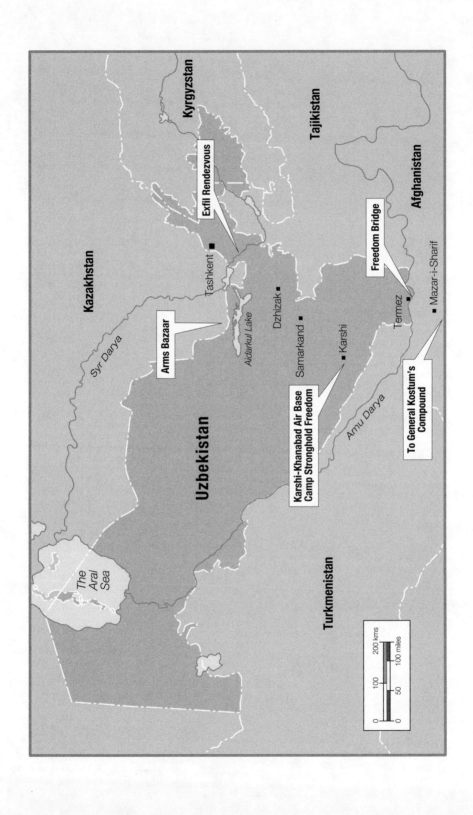

PRIVATE WARS

Preoperational Background
Chace, Tara F.

As far as Tara Chace was concerned, she died in Saudi Arabia, in Tabuk province, on the rock-hard earth of the Wadi-as-Sirhan.

She died when Tom Wallace died, when she heard the chain of gunshots from the Kalashnikov, saw the spastic strobe of the muzzle-flash from across the wadi, one man, unnamed and unknown, lighting the other with gunfire even as he killed him. There were nights when she still heard her own howl of anguish, and she knew the sound for what it was, the little life within her stealing away into the desert air.

Tom was dead, and as far as Tara Chace was concerned, she was, too.

She'd been wounded in the Wadi-as-Sirhan, had fought hand-to-hand with the man who had murdered Tom. He'd tried to split her skull with the butt of his rifle, and when that had failed, tried to choke her to death with his bare hands. Chace had used her knife, and opened his lungs to the outside air, and at the School they would have called that winning. She might have called it that, too, if she'd felt there was anything left to win.

She was still numb from it all when she came off the plane at Heathrow to discover her Director of Operations, Paul Crocker, waiting for her at the gate itself. It was unheard of for D-Ops to greet a returning agent, and the surprise managed to penetrate the fogginess she now traveled in, and she had cause to wonder at it, but not for long. With Crocker as her escort she avoided Customs, winding through endless switchback corridors and through baggage claim until emerging into the drizzle of an early autumn morning.

Crocker guided her to a waiting Bentley, climbed in beside her, and the driver pulled out as soon as the door closed, and that was when Chace finally understood what was happening, and where she was being taken. Her mission in Saudi Arabia had been entirely unsanctioned, and Chace had gone AWOL to do the job. Even if they did still trust her, she had to be debriefed, and that debriefing would take place away from London, at a secure facility hidden in the Cotswolds, called the Farm.

The drive was long, and held in silence. Crocker knew better than to try to engage her in conversation, and for her part, Chace was sitting beside a man whose living guts she now hated.

When she'd fled London some ten days earlier, the boys from Box hot on her heels, she'd been a Special Operations Officer in Her Majesty's Secret Intelligence Service. She'd been the Head of the Section, in fact, code-named Minder One, with two other Minders under her command and tutelage. Along with Minder Two, Nicky Poole, and Minder Three, Chris Lankford, she had provided HMG with covert action capability, as directed and supervised by D-Ops, Paul Crocker. He was their Lord and Master, their protection against the vagaries of government and the whims of politicians who saw agents as disposable as Bic pens, as nothing more or less than small cogs in a very large machine.

Stolen documents needed retrieving in Oslo? Send a Minder to get them back and hush the whole thing up. Potential defection in progress in Hong Kong? Send a Minder to evaluate the defector's worth, to then either facilitate the lift or boomerang the poor bastard back into the PRC as a double agent. Islamofascist terrorist assembling a dirty bomb in Damascus? Send a Minder to kill the son of a bitch before he can deliver the device to Downing Street.

Tara Chace had left London knowing that she was one of the best—if not the best—Special Operations Officers working for any intelligence service anywhere in the world today.

She had no idea what she had returned as, but a trip to the Farm made at least one thing clear.

Tara Chace was *not* being welcomed home with open arms.

The Farm wasn't, really, though from a distance, if people didn't know what they were looking at or looking for, they could perhaps take it as such. From the lane, a single road wended through a gap in the dry stone wall, disappearing beyond a wall of trees that concealed cameras and sensors designed to keep people out as much as to keep people in. After another mile came another fence, this one more serious, of metal and chain, guarded by a gatehouse and walking patrols, and past that, one could glimpse the manor house concealed beyond further trees. Into the compound, one found the dormitories, as they were euphemistically called, bungalows constructed in the early sixties that demonstrated all of the architectural grace of the period, lined up side by side along a paved walkway, surrounded by yet another chain-link fence, this one topped with razor wire.

As far as prisons went, Chace thought that this one wasn't half bad. Her bungalow was simple and comfortable enough, and when she wasn't being interrogated by the likes of David Kinney and his Inquisitors from Box, or being evaluated by the head SIS psychiatrist, Dr. Eleanor Callard, or submitting to yet another physical by yet another physician she'd never met before in her life, she was left alone. She could take walks with an escort, read books from the manor library, exercise in the gym. There were no clocks anywhere she could see, and she was forbidden access to television, radio, newspapers, or the internet.

The supply of scotch and cigarettes, however, was generous, and Chace availed herself of both.

She'd been at the Farm a week when Crocker returned. The Director of Operations came to her bungalow, let in by a guard, to find Chace vomiting into the toilet, and he waited until she was finished, until she had used the sink to rinse out her mouth and slop water onto her face, before saying, "It's time to come back to work."

Chace dried her face on a hand towel, refolded it, and replaced it on its bar, before asking, "And what if I don't want to?"

"Of course you want to," Crocker said. "You're a Minder, Tara. You don't know how to be anyone else. You can't be anyone else."

It was what she'd feared the most since arriving at the Farm, the question she'd taken to bed with her every night. Not wondering what would happen if they threw her out on her ear, if they discharged her dishonorably, if they sent her packing. No, that would have made it easy; they would have made the decision for her. Shunted off with a reminder of the Official Secrets Act and an admonishment to keep her nose clean, she could have left and blamed it all on them, on Crocker and Weldon and Barclay, on politicians and analysts in London and DC who felt Tara Chace was a world more trouble than she was worth.

That would have made it so easy.

Instead, her worst fear realized, manifested now by Crocker, telling her that all was forgiven.

Telling her what they both knew.

So she went with him, back to London, and back to work.

Six weeks later, she and Minder Two went to Iraq on Operation: Red Panda, to assassinate a member of the new government who had been passing defense information to the insurgency. Things got bloody.

Things got very bloody.

Perhaps bloodier than they needed to get.

When they returned to London and had been debriefed, Chace was ordered to see Dr. Callard a second time.

"How are you feeling?"

"Fine. Some trouble sleeping, but fine."

"Are you still drinking?"

"I eat, too."

Callard's mouth twitched with a smile, and she scribbled something on the pad resting on the desk in front of her. She asked Chace more questions, and Chace answered them with requisite evasion. The whole process lasted an hour, and when Chace again descended to the Pit, the basement office she shared with Lankford and Poole, she knew what the Madwoman of the Second Floor would report to D-Ops.

Chace wasn't a fool, and she knew herself well. She was drinking too much and sleeping too little. More often than not she started her mornings by being ill into the toilet. She was sore, and plagued by bad dreams when she could sleep. She was prone to irrational anger and sudden sorrows.

Even if she hadn't been able to read Callard's notes upside down, even if she hadn't seen the words *post-traumatic stress,* Chace would have made the diagnosis herself. Either that or assumed she was premenstrual, but she'd already missed two periods since Saudi Arabia. That wasn't unique in her life; there had been times of high stress in the past when she'd missed her cycle more than once.

All the same, she stopped at the Boots nearest her home in Camden on her way back from work that day, just to be certain. She read the instructions on the box, followed them, waited.

And found herself staring at two pink lines, which, according to the instructions, indicated a positive.

She left her home, returned to the Boots, bought another test, and repeated the procedure, with the same result.

Two pink lines.

"Bloody fucking hell," she said.

The hard copy of the Minder personnel files—past and present—were held by D-Ops, or more precisely, held in the secure safe in his outer office. Keys to the safe were in the possession of Crocker; the Deputy Chief of Service, Donald Weldon; and the Head of Service, C, known outside of the building as Sir Frances Barclay. Duplicates were stored on the in-house computer network, but access to those files in particular required a password that was altered every twenty-four hours, and even then, only supplied to the aforementioned holders of the keys.

Plus one other person, Kate Cooke, who manned the desk in Crocker's outer office, serving as his personal assistant. Not only did she have access to the password, but she had her own set of keys. After worrying the problem all night, it was Kate that Chace finally decided she stood the best chances with. First, they shared minority female status in the Firm; second, they bore a common cross, most clearly embodied in the form of D-Ops, but readily recognizable in the guise of any of the other Department Heads. That Chace was Head of Section for the Minders didn't change this; Minders were considered in SIS to be more or less pariahs, closer to working-class thugs than to the more refined agents posted to stations around the world.

Finally, she and Kate had known one another some four years, and, in that time, managed a weak kind of professional friendship, one that began when each entered Vauxhall Cross at the start of the day, and ended when they departed again for home.

All the same, it took Chace some cajoling, and more deft lying, before she was able to get Kate to hand over the file on Wallace, Thomas S. (deceased). She scanned it quickly, and learned that

Wallace was survived by his mother, Valerie, and that she lived in a town in Lancashire called Barnoldswick.

The following morning, Chace delivered her request for a leave of absence to Crocker, by hand. He read it at his desk, scowling, while she stood opposite him. When he'd finished he lit a cigarette, leaned back in his chair, and glared at her.

"Don't be a damn fool," Crocker said. "You can't possibly keep it."

It was more anger than humiliation that colored Chace's cheeks. Of course Crocker had known. They'd given her a complete workup at the Farm; they'd have done bloodwork as well.

Which meant Crocker had sent her to Iraq knowing she was pregnant.

"I am taking a leave of absence." She was more than a little surprised at the sound of her own voice. It was surprisingly calm.

"Is it Tom's?" Crocker demanded. "Is that it?"

"Twelve months," she said.

"You can't do it, Tara, not on your life. You can't have a child and be in the Section, it's not possible."

"Ariel and Sabrina," Chace countered, using the names of Crocker's daughters.

"Jennie." The name of his wife.

"Twelve months' leave. Sir."

"Not on your life."

"Then I quit," Chace said, and walked out.

She caught an early train out of King's Cross the next morning, bound for Leeds, riding in a nonsmoking carriage that reeked of stale cigarettes. The ride took some two and a half hours, and once in Leeds she changed to a local connection, taking it as far as Skipton, where she hired a car and bought a copy of *Lancashire A* *to* Z. She took a room at the Hanover International Hotel, stowed her things, and, famished, ate a late lunch while going over the maps. She went to bed early.

In the still-dark hours the next morning, Chace made the fifteen-minute drive from Skipton to Barnoldswick. She parked the car near the town square, and after a seventy-minute reconnoiter, had found four positions ideal for static surveillance of number 17 Moor View Road, the home of Valerie Wallace.

It was light surveillance, the best Chace could manage without giving herself away, the best she could manage working alone. As a result, she was careful, trailing Valerie Wallace at a distance as the older woman went about her business in the town, working at the local charity shop, meeting friends for lunch or tea at this or that house, visiting the local surgery to see her GP. Autumn brought an already cold wind that promised a fiercer chill come winter, and most of the widow Wallace's activities were thus confined to the indoors, which made getting close difficult.

Shortly after midnight on her third day of surveillance, Chace broke into the surgery, curious as to the reason for Wallace's visit. She spent an hour with a penlight in a darkened file office, reading Valerie Wallace's medical history. When she was finished, she replaced everything as she had found it, and managed to relock the door on her way out.

In the afternoon of the sixth day, while Wallace was having her regular luncheon with friends at the tea shop off the square, Chace picked the lock on the back door of 17 Moor View Road, and worked her way in careful silence through the older woman's home. If her schedule held true to form, Wallace would go from lunch to the local hospice for volunteer work that would stretch until almost the evening, and so Chace took her time. She searched in cabinets and closets, beneath the beds and in drawers, even going so far as to examine the contents of the kitchen, just to gain some insight into the older woman's diet.

In Valerie Wallace's small bedroom, smelling of lavender and laundry soap, Chace discovered a collection of framed photographs carefully arranged atop the dresser. There were pictures of a younger Valerie and, presumably, her late husband. Gordon Samuel Wallace had been a career soldier, and in two of the pictures stood in uniform, looking proud to be wearing it, if vaguely uncomfortable to be photographed while doing so. A third showed Valerie holding a newborn, and the remaining two were of Tom exclusively. One of them mimicked the portrait of his father, perhaps intentionally, wearing the dress uniform of a Royal Marine; the last, more recent, was taken in the sitting room of this very house, the branch of a Christmas tree reaching into the frame as Tom looked out the front window at the moor.

Wedged beneath the last was a folded letter, and Chace freed it, opened it, already knowing what it was.

Dear Mrs. Wallace: It is with great sadness that I must inform you of the passing of your son, Tom, in service to his country. . . .

Chace replaced the letter as she had found it, and departed as silently as she had come.

On the tenth day, a freezing November Tuesday, at nine o'clock exactly, Tara Chace knocked on the front door of Valerie Wallace's home.

"My name is Tara Chace," she said. "I worked with Tom."

Valerie Wallace, standing in the half-opened doorway, frowned slightly, squinting up at her. She was a small woman, easily a foot shorter than Chace, with hair more gray than black, and not so much heavy as thickened by age and gravity. She let her frown deepen, and didn't answer.

And Chace found herself at a loss, the speech she'd so carefully rehearsed abruptly gone, disappearing like the vapor from her breath. She tried to retrieve it, found only bits and pieces, incoherent and useless.

Valerie Wallace shifted, one hand holding the door, still staring at her.

"We were lovers," Chace finally managed. "Before he died. We were friends and we were lovers, and I'm pregnant, and it's his. It's ours."

She thought it would garner some reaction, at least; if not the words, at least the clumsiness of them. And it did, because, after another second, Valerie Wallace blinked, and then opened the door more fully, inviting her inside.

"Perhaps you'd like to come in for a cup of tea, Tara Chace," Valerie Wallace said. "And you can tell me why you're here."

On the twenty-eighth of May, at seventeen past nine in the morning, at Airedale General Hospital in Keighley, with Valerie Wallace holding her hand as she screamed through the final surge of labor, Tara Chace gave birth to a daughter. The baby was healthy, twenty-two inches long, weighing seven pounds, eleven ounces.

She named the child Tamsin.

There were nights when, despite exhaustion, Chace found she could not sleep.

Staring out the window that overlooked Valerie Wallace's well-tended and now fully in-bloom garden at Weets Moor, holding Tamsin in her arms as the baby slept, Chace would sit and stare at nothing. She could feel her daughter's heartbeat, the rustle of her breath, the heat of her small body.

And Tara Chace would wonder how she could feel all of that, and still feel nothing at all.

CHAPTER 1

9 February, 0929 Hours (GMT+5:00)

They gave it an hour after the husband left, just to be certain he hadn't forgotten anything, that he wouldn't be coming back, before they knocked on the door. Four of them went to do it, while another two waited in the second car, the engine idling.

The two who waited were jealous of the four who went. They thought they were missing the fun.

All were men, and all wore business suits of the latest style, acquired for them in Moscow and Paris and Switzerland, then altered by tailors here in Tashkent, men who were paid pennies to adjust clothing worth thousands. All six finished their look with neckties of silk and shoes of Italian leather and cashmere-lined kidskin gloves. A few wore overcoats as stylish as the suits they covered, to ward off the howling chill that blew down out of the mountains in Kazakhstan to the north.

The only thing that marred the line of their clothing, each in turn, was the slight bump at hip or beneath an armpit, where they carried their guns.

Back before Uzbekistan had declared its independence from the creaking and cracking Soviet Union, before the failed hard-liner coup in August of 1991, when they were still called the KGB, none of them would have dreamed of wearing—let alone owning—such finery. Signs of Western excess, such garments would have flown in the face of Communism. Certainly they would have made a mockery of the subtleties required for their work.

But those days were long past, and fewer and fewer of them remembered a time when orders came from Dzerzhinsky Square. They weren't KGB, and they weren't Communists. They called themselves the National Security Service now, the NSS, and if they believed in anything anymore, it was in power and money, in that order. They were the secret police, and they didn't care who knew it. They were beholden to—depending upon whom you spoke to— one of two people. Either they marched to the tune played by their nation's leader, President Mihail Izmaylovich Malikov, the man who had led the country since he declared its independence in August 1991, or they danced to the music played by his elder child, his daughter, Sevara Malikov-Ganiev. That's where the true power was. While President Malikov's other child—his only son— Ruslan, had influence and friends of his own, they paled in comparison to that held by both his father and his sister.

This was why the four NSS men who entered Ruslan Mihailovich Malikov's house at half past nine on a frigid February morning had no hesitation whatsoever in arresting his wife, Dina, for espionage and treason. This is why they did not hesitate to beat her in front of her two-year-old son when she tried to keep their hands from her body. This is why they did not hesitate when they had to drag her, flailing and screaming, down the stairs and out onto the street.

And this was why they did not hesitate at all when it came time to torture her.

They hooded her once they had her in the car, and they bound her hands, and when she made a noise, they struck her, telling her to be quiet. Best as Dina Malikov could tell, they didn't drive for long or very far, and when the car stopped, she was dragged from the vehicle, and felt the instant bite of winter on her skin. They propelled her down echoing corridors, yanking and shoving her, sometimes pulling her hair, sometimes her shirt. There was the cold sound of heavy metal sliding on concrete, and someone shoved her so hard then that she couldn't keep her feet, falling to the floor. Red light exploded across her vision as she was hit in the head again, and when she could see once more, the hood had been removed.

She'd seen this room before, but never in person. It was larger than she'd thought it, lit by a string of naked bulbs that dangled from the ceiling, shining too bright, banishing all shadows and all illusions of the safety to be found in them. The floor was cold, poured concrete, the walls of gray cinder block. The odors of urine and mildew and cigarette smoke combined, still not strong enough to obscure the scent of feces.

There was a table, wooden and stained, and three chairs, also wooden. A video camera stood on a tripod in one corner, and beside it, on the floor, a red metal toolbox. Other tools lay nearby, devices designed for one purpose that could be redirected to another, far crueler. Against the opposite wall, a claw-footed old bathtub sat, anchored by two pipes, one to fill it, one to drain it.

Three men stood staring at her. Two of them she didn't know, didn't recognize, but the third she did, and that terrified her more than any of what had come before, because it drove home to her exactly how bad things were going to get. As they had taken her from her home, as they had dragged her and beat her, she had allowed herself the illusion of hope, that Ruslan would return, that her marriage would offer her some protection, that she might survive. But looking at Ahtam Zahidov as he removed his suit jacket and carefully draped it over the back of one of the chairs, for the first time, Dina Malikov thought she was going to die.

"Dina," Zahidov said, and he gestured to her with his left hand, absently, and the two other men took this cue to move forward, and they began to strip her. She struggled, alternately cursing and pleading with them, with Zahidov, and Zahidov merely watched, and the other two hit her in the back and the belly until she had no air, until she couldn't struggle any longer. The two men tore the clothes away from her, mocking her, mocking her husband, and when she was finally naked they forced her to the table. Again, she tried to fight them, and again they beat her until she could not, and they laid her across the tabletop, and they held her down.

Ahtam Semyonovich Zahidov moved behind her, and put one hand on the back of her neck, and with his other forced himself inside her.

"Where did you get the tape?" Zahidov asked. "Who gave it to you?"

She tried not to sob, shaking on the floor, tears and blood mingling on her face.

"Who gave it to you?" Zahidov asked.

She drew a long inhale, feeling the air burn her torn lips. "My husband—"

"Is in Khanabad for the day, making nice with the Americans at their air base, and will not be home until evening." Zahidov canted his head to one side, as if seeing her for the first time. "Tell us what we want to know, and you will be home before he returns. Back with your boy. He needn't ever know what happened here."

She spat at him.

"We can blame the extremists, Dina," Zahidov said, his voice soothing with reason. "He doesn't ever have to know."

The sob escaped her without her meaning it to, the shame scorching through her, hurting more than her body itself. Ruslan would believe it, if she told him, if she blamed the Islamic extremists, if she blamed Hizb-ut-Tahir, he would believe it. She could be home, she could hold Styopa again, hold her baby again, and Ruslan would come home. So easily he would believe it, he would want to believe that she had been taken, had been kidnapped, that it was the Islamic extremists who had wanted her as a hostage, but she had escaped, somehow, some way, and she could tell him, and he wouldn't know, he wouldn't ever have to know what had happened, what had really happened, what Zahidov had done, had let the others do, all it took was a name, one name—

"Just tell me who, Dina," Zahidov said. "Tell me, and this will all end."

She blinked through her tears, through the glare of the lights at him, sitting in the chair, looking at her like he was her friend.

Dina Malikov shuddered, and closed her eyes, and said, "I can't."

She heard him sigh, a sound of mild disappointment almost lost in the size of the room, and then she heard the rasp of metal on metal, as the toolbox was opened.

In the end, she told Zahidov everything.

She told him the name of the NSS officer who had given her the videotape documenting the torture of Shovroq Anamov's sons while the old man watched, helpless to ease the suffering of his children. The tape that recorded the obviously false confession of the old man as he swore up and down that, yes, he had been south to Afghanistan, yes, he had met with the terrorists, yes, he had helped arrange the bombings that had struck the market in Tashkent in the spring. The tape that showed the tears running down the old man's face and captured his keening when his eldest boy, shocked one time too many, stopped moving the way a human being moved, and instead jerked like a fish on the end of a line.

She told Zahidov how she arranged to get the tape out of the country, how she'd made contact with a junior political officer at the American Embassy by the name of Charles Riess, how it had happened at the embassy holiday party this past December, hosted by Ambassador Kenneth Garret at his residence, just outside of town. How it had been Riess she'd been passing information to, so Riess could in turn pass it on to the State Department. How it was her fault that the White House was withholding another eighteen million dollars in aid to their ally Uzbekistan.

She told Zahidov everything.

In the end, though, it wasn't enough.

In the end, they put her in the tub and filled it with boiling water.

The NSS officer who had served as her informant was arrested before nightfall, and shot before midnight.

Zahidov would have done it himself, but he was too busy arranging the arrests of the extremists responsible for the kidnapping, rape, and murder of Dina Malikov. One of them was a schoolteacher in Chirchik who had continued to try to incorporate passages from the Qur'an into his lessons. The other two had also insisted on practicing their religion outside the manner permitted by the state, and one of them, a woman, had led a group of forty in signing a petition to be presented to President Mihail Malikov demanding their right to worship as Muslims. All three were arrested by midmorning the next day.

Near the home of the schoolteacher, half buried beneath rocks, was discovered the body of the missing Dina Malikov. She had been horribly beaten and burned, her teeth shattered and the nails of her fingers and toes torn from their digits.

She was so disfigured, in fact, that Ahtam Zahidov had to send a request to Ruslan Mihailovich asking that he come at once, to identify his wife's body.

CHAPTER 2

London—Vauxhall Cross, Operations Room

10 February, 1829 Hours GMT

Paul Crocker had known Operation: Candlelight was a bad idea the moment it crossed his desk.

He'd known it the same way he'd known his elder daughter had become sexually active, long before he'd heard the fact from his wife, Jennie. He'd known it the way he'd known that he'd been passed over for promotion to Deputy Chief, long before his C, Sir Frances Barclay, had smugly confirmed it for him. He'd known it the way he'd known he was losing Chace when she came off the plane at Heathrow eighteen months earlier, and he knew it the way he knew that Andrew Fincher would be a poor replacement for her when Donald Weldon, in his last act as Deputy Chief of Service, railroaded Crocker into taking the agent on as his new Head of the Special Section.

Part of it was instinct, part of it was experience, honed from almost twenty-five years in Her Majesty's Secret Intelligence Service, through countless operations all over the globe. Jobs he'd worked, jobs he'd planned, jobs he'd overseen. The successes, and more important, the failures.

Candlelight had been bad news from the start, and what Paul Crocker saw now on the main plasma screen of the Ops Room wall—or more precisely, what he wasn't seeing—only drove the point home.

He should have been looking at a live satellite transmission. from Kuala Lumpur, where, according to the callout on the world map on the wall, Operation: Candlelight was "Running," and the local time was two-thirty in the morning. He should have been seeing what Minder One, Andrew Fincher, was seeing, as the Head of the Special Section made his way along the harbor to the target site. He should have been hearing it as well, the susurration of the water, the hushed transmissions relayed between Fincher and Minder Two, Nicky Poole, stationed at the ready point with the SAS brick, waiting for Fincher's go signal.

But no, instead, Crocker got static. Static to look at on the plasma wall, in the box above Southeast Asia where the feed should have been coming through, and static to listen to on the speakers, instead of the low calm of the voices of men, preparing to do work.

Julian Seale, seated at the map table to the left of where Crocker now stood, glaring at the garbled screen, coughed politely.

"Might want to do something about that," Seale said.

"You think?" Crocker snapped, not bothering to look at him. Instead, he strode forward, to the Mission Control Desk, where William Teagle was frantically attacking his keyboard with his fingers. "Bill, what the hell's happened to the feed?"

"Checking now, sir." Teagle twisted in his chair, turning to another of the consoles surrounding him at the MCO station. Teagle was new on the desk, only three months in, and Candlelight was his first major operation, and Crocker thought the stress of it showed on the man's face, the perspiration shining on his forehead. If he'd been inclined to it, Crocker might've been sympathetic. As it was, he didn't have the time.

"Is it the upgrades?" Seale asked Crocker.

Crocker frowned at the plasma wall. "Possibly."

The entirety of the Ops Room had seen a renovation in the past year, from the plasma screens to the computers to the secure communication arrays that kept the SIS headquarters here in London in touch with stations and agents around the world. It had been long overdue, and when it had happened, Crocker had believed it to be a good thing, and it had given him hope for his new Deputy Chief of Service, Alison Gordon-Palmer. It had been Gordon-Palmer who had forced the proposal through the FCO, it had been Gordon-Palmer who had bullied C into securing the necessary funding, and it had been Gordon-Palmer who had gone out of her way to consult with Crocker as to just what the upgrades should entail. By the end of the process, Crocker had come to believe two things about the new DC.

First, that even without a background in operations, Alison Gordon-Palmer understood the Ops Directorate's importance in the grand scheme of SIS, and as such, Crocker could count her as an ally; and second, he wanted to maintain that relationship, because he now had no doubt how difficult his life would become if she decided he was her enemy.

Crocker turned back to Seale, calling across the room. "They don't know we're coming? You're certain?"

Seale shook his head. "Our intel puts the cell in place and standing by until the morning, when they're supposed to meet their friends in the Straits. They're being careful, but they've got no reason to think we're on to them, Paul, none at all. Not unless something's happened on your end. But nobody from the Company's tipped the Malaysians."

"I've half a mind to send an abort, call the whole thing off." Crocker looked back to the wall, at the static, fighting the urge to grind his teeth. "If we let them slip, any chance we can catch them on the water before they try to take the tanker?"

"How?" Seale asked. "They get into the Straits of Malacca, we're going to lose them."

Crocker nodded quickly, as if to say that yes, he got the point. "Dammit, Bill, what's happening with the fucking feed?"

"Lost the signal, sir," Teagle said, turning to another screen.

"There's a tracking error on the CVT-30, I think. I can't bring it back up."

Behind him, Crocker heard Seale mutter a curse. He turned, covered the distance to the Duty Operations Desk and Ronald Hodgson in three long strides, saying, "Ron, get onto the MOD, now. Tell them we need to piggyback their link to Candlelight, and we need it five minutes ago."

Ronald Hodgson nodded, already reaching for one of the four telephones arrayed around his station.

Crocker turned to Seale, said, "You're certain we can't abort? Try to take them at sea instead?"

"Be a totally different op."

"I know."

Seale unfolded his ankles, rose from his slouch in the chair to his feet, one hand brushing down his necktie. One of perhaps two handfuls of African Americans holding senior postings in the CIA, Seale had come to London as COS only four months prior, filling the post vacated by his predecessor and Crocker's friend, Angela Cheng. Where Crocker ran to lean, even lanky, Seale went broader, exhibiting perhaps more strength than speed. The two men were roughly the same age, each sneaking up on fifty within the next year, each married, each with two children. Viewed together, they formed a strange complement, both physically as much as professionally.

"God, they try for the tanker and it goes wrong, Paul," Seale said. "We'll have the G-77 screaming at us like we were selling naked pictures of their mothers. And if the JI takes the *Mawi Dawn*, they'll be sitting on two hundred thousand gallons of liquefied natural gas. That blows up, windows will be shattering all the way to Bangkok. It'll be the Revenge of Krakatoa."

"I know that, too."

"Worse if they plow the ship into Singapore Harbor."

Crocker grunted, shoving a cigarette into his mouth, not wishing to contemplate the scenario any further, nor to imagine the destruction. Bad enough that the Straits of Malacca were perhaps the most dangerous waters in the world, rife with piracy. Bad enough that Jemaah Islamiyah made its home in Malaysia, with a government filled with its sympathizers and supporters. Put the two together, add one supertanker filled with LNG and one box of disposable lighters, and, yes, perhaps Seale was overstating the potential damage.

But only slightly.

From the MCO Desk, Bill Teagle uttered a small cry of triumph. "Signal, sir! Audio only, but better than nothing."

"Let's hear it."

There was a shriek of static from the speakers on the plasma wall, and then the voice of Andrew Fincher, Minder One, came through, choppy and littered with squeaks and pops from the satellite. Crocker could make out the sound of Fincher's movement, the rustle of his clothing beneath his words.

"—on approach now . . . see lights on the second floor, no signs of movement . . . hold on . . ."

Crocker's scowl deepened. It might have been the radio and the patch, but to his ears, Fincher sounded beyond nervous. When he glanced to Seale, now standing beside him, he saw from the other man's expression that he'd heard the same thing.

There was another crackle, then Minder Two's voice, as Poole transmitted. "Songbird, this is Nightowl. We're at stage one, taking position, please stand by."

"Nightowl, Songbird. Confirmed. Let's make this fast, right? I've got a bad feeling here. I don't want to be out here any longer than I have to."

"Songbird, understood. Moving to position one, stand by."

Silence from the radios.

"Your man Fincher sounds like he's about three steps ahead of panic," Seale murmured softly. "You want to tell me why he's taking the lead and not Poole?"

"Fincher's Minder One, he worked as the KL Number Two before coming into the Special Section. He knows the ground."

"Four years ago he knew the ground. Poole's ex-SAS, he knows the drill."

"Which is why Poole's the liaison with the brick and not Fincher."

"Yeah, but Fincher—"

"I don't have anyone else, Julian," Crocker snapped. "Lankford's in Gibraltar, and Fincher is Head of Section. If it was KL, I had to send Fincher with Poole. I couldn't hold him here in reserve."

From the corner of his eye, Crocker saw Seale frowning at him.

"Fincher's a tool, Paul," Seale said. "You can hear it in his voice—he's not made for this."

Crocker didn't respond, instead fishing out his lighter and finally giving flame to the cigarette that had been waiting for the last three minutes. The fact was, he agreed with Seale, not that Fincher was a "tool" per se, but that he was wrong for the job.

A year and a half ago, after Chace had left, Crocker had scrambled to find a replacement, spending six weeks poring through personnel files. The traditional method of advancement among the Minders was promotion through attrition; Minder Three became Minder Two as Minder Two became Minder One and on and on, each agent replacing the next as his or her predecessor was promoted out of the Section, retired, or perished. The problem was that when Chace departed, she'd taken the lion's share of operational experience with her. When she'd left, Poole had just under a year as a Minder, and Lankford less than half that.

Under those circumstances, Crocker had been unable, and in fact unwilling, to promote either of the remaining Minders. They simply didn't have enough experience, let alone enough seniority.

It was Weldon who'd proposed Fincher, and it had been the second time the former Deputy Chief had tried to get Crocker to take the man into the section. The first time, Crocker still had Tom Wallace as Minder One, and Chace as Minder Two, and it had been a relatively simple matter to find an agent in training at the School who wanted to join the Special Section. This time, though, the board had shifted to Weldon's favor, and Crocker had found himself powerless to block the move. SIS employed roughly two thousand officers, and of those two thousand, very few had what it took to be a Minder. To Crocker's eyes, that included Fincher.

There was simply nobody else, and with the Deputy Chief championing him to C, Crocker had been left with no other choice but to accept Fincher as his new Head of Section.

It wasn't that Andrew Fincher was a bad agent. He'd served three tours prior to coming aboard as a Minder, the first in KL, the second in London, on the Central Asian Desk, his third in Panama. He'd distinguished himself in both KL and Panama, resourceful and capable, but, in Crocker's view, overly concerned with avoiding risk. What had helped Fincher more than anything was his penchant for making the right friends inside the Firm. Starting with his second tour, he'd begun to make it known that he'd very much like to come to work in the Special Section, and that had made Crocker suspicious. Once he was aboard, the suspicions were confirmed.

Fincher wasn't a bad agent, but he was station-oriented and excessively cautious, two things that translated to a lack of initiative, something that a Minder, in Crocker's view, had to have in abundance. He couldn't send a Minder into the field on a job only to have the agent hesitate and dither before deciding on a course of action, or, worse, repeatedly clear his intentions with both Station and London. In a Special Operation, there just wasn't the luxury of time. Worse, though, was the fact that Fincher didn't see anything wrong with his caution, and in fact, Crocker suspected the man believed he was a better agent than he actually was. As far as Paul Crocker was concerned, all other factors aside, that alone made Andrew Fincher absolutely wrong for the work. He wanted his Minders to think they weren't good enough.

In fact, it was what he needed them to believe for them to do their job.

Chace had been the shining example of the principle, marrying ambition, passion, and self-loathing in a seamless blend.

"Video, sir," Ronald Hodgson said.

"Put it up, for God's sake."

The empty rectangle on the plasma screen flickered, then filled with a grainy image, dark enough that it took Crocker a moment before he could begin to discern details. He was looking at three men, all of them in plain clothes, all with their torsos clad in body armor, sitting in what he presumed was the back of the van they'd acquired for the operation. Two of the men held MP-5 submachine guns, fitted with flash suppressors. The third was Nicky Poole, wearing a radio headset, crouched by the side door, one hand to his ear, straining to listen.

"Where's the audio?" Crocker demanded.

"Switching to the MOD stream now, sir."

There was another crackle from the speakers.

"Songbird, Nightowl. Status?"

No response.

"Songbird, Nightowl, respond please."

On the plasma wall, in its rectangle, Crocker watched as Poole adjusted his position, shifting on his haunches, checking the radio in his hand. He could make out the frown of concentration on Poole's face.

"What the fuck is going on?" Seale muttered. "Where is he?"

"Songbird, Nightowl, respond."

Nothing.

Oh, sweet Jesus, no, thought Crocker.

Over the speakers came the sound of a rattle, something striking the side of the van. Crocker heard one of the SAS swearing softly, watched as Poole pulled away from the door as three MP-5s came up, and then the side door slid back, and the camera flared as its aperture tried to adjust to the abrupt change in light sources.

"Friendly!" Crocker heard Poole hissing. *"Jesus, friendly, don't fucking shoot him!"*

The image resolved again, and Crocker watched as Poole yanked Fincher into the van, one hand on his shoulder, more concerned with efficiency in the move than comfort. The camera readjusted as the SAS trooper wearing the rig moved back. The view canted at an angle, and over the speakers came the bang of the door sliding closed again.

Poole leaned in on Fincher. *"What the fuck happened, what are you doing here?"*

Fincher shook his head, trying to catch his breath. Poole, still with his hand on Fincher's shoulder, shook the other man.

"What the fucking hell happened? Dammit, Andrew!"

Fincher coughed, pulling himself away from Poole's grip. *"They made me. I had to withdraw. We've got to abort."*

Crocker cursed, hearing Seale echoing him. He swung toward the Duty Ops Desk. "Ron, MOD, now! Get me a patch to Candlelight, they *cannot* abort!"

"Open line, sir." Ron handed Crocker the telephone handset.

Crocker put the phone to his ear, could hear the sounds of consternation coming from the Ministry of Defense's operational command post. "D-Ops, who am I talking to?"

"Lance Corporal Richard Moth, sir."

"Put Colonel Dawson on the line."

"Yes, sir."

From the speakers, Crocker could hear Poole cursing at Fincher. *"You've fucking blown us, you fool!"*

"They made me, dammit! What was I supposed to do?"

On the screen, Crocker watched as Poole sat back, yanking the headset from his head. The expression he was seeing on Minder Two's face was much like the one Crocker imagined was now gracing his own.

In his ear, from the telephone, Crocker heard, "Paul? James. What the hell is your man playing at?"

"God only knows. Listen, Colonel, you've got to give them the go order."

"If they've been blown—"

"I understand the risk. They've got to move now, Colonel, there's no choice."

"Hold on."

Crocker looked back to the video feed, watching. After a second's pause, a squawk came over the speakers, and he watched as Poole hastily put his headset back into place.

"Nightowl, go."

From the telephone, Crocker heard Dawson's voice, distant, relaying the go, repeating the order twice, to make it clear.

On the screen, through the speakers, Poole said, *"Nightowl confirms, we are go, repeat, we are go."*

Crocker was sure he saw Fincher blanch.

There was a rush of movement then, Poole reaching for the MP-5 that had been waiting for him as the camera jerked, heading to the doors of the van. The screen flared again, resolved, and now the view was jumping up and down, and Crocker could see Poole and the other two SAS troopers racing along the street, turning now between buildings, running hard, then slowing. They reached the door, two of the troopers taking entry positions, and the one wearing the camera made the breach, and Poole tossed the first grenade, and the sound of the explosion came back at them in the Ops Room, muffled by the speakers.

Then the shooting started.

CHAPTER 3

11 February, 1213 Hours (GMT+5:00)

If he hadn't been so focused on chasing the hare, Charles Riess supposed he'd have seen the car coming. But then again, if he'd seen the car coming, Ruslan Mihailovich Malikov might never have made contact with him, so all in all, Riess figured it more than made up for the scraped knee and sprained ankle.

They'd started the run up on the northeast edge of Tashkent, about ten in the morning, just north of the Salor Canal, setting off in pursuit of a particularly sneaky son of a bitch from the Embassy's Consular Division named Bradley Walker. Turned out his surname was more than a little misleading, and with the fifteen-minute head start that Riess and the twenty-seven other Hash House Harriers had given to Walker, he'd led them on a merry chase. Most times, you could count on the run being completed in about an hour, so everyone could get to the more serious business of drinking.

Most times.

Walker had been given the go, running with a bag of flour to lay trail—or more precisely, to lay false trail—and Riess and the others had stood in the freezing morning, stamping their feet and blowing on their hands. In another two weeks the winter would be over, and Uzbekistan's traditionally temperate climate would return, but for now it was cold enough that Riess seriously considered forfeiting his participation altogether, just so he could return to his home on Raktaboshi Avenue and crawl back into bed. Another of the Harriers, joining them from the German Embassy, had seemed to read his mind, making a joke about calling the run on account of the weather. Riess had looked north, into Kazakhstan, and seen snow on the mountains.

The chase began, the pack setting off in pursuit of the hare, heading first toward the Botanical Gardens. Riess had run long distance in college but quit upon entering the State Department, only to pick it up again after he'd met Rebecca. They'd met early in his first posting, Tanzania, and it had been part of their courtship, what Riess had supposed was some Darwinian hardwired leftover proof-of-virility ritual. He'd gotten as far as picking out a ring and preparing a speech, had scouted locations in Dar es Salaam, just to find the right place to propose.

Then the Embassy had been bombed and eighty people had been wounded, and eleven had died, and Rebecca had been one of those eleven.

Now when he ran, Riess sometimes imagined Rebecca was running alongside him, and that was how he remembered her, and it made the going easy, despite the cold. Today, he soon found himself leading the pack. He stood five ten when his shoes were off, and one-seventy-eight on the bathroom scale after a shower, wearing nothing but his towel, with long legs Rebecca had described as spindly. If his German/English heritage had given Riess anything, it was a runner's body.

He ran, eyes open for the trail, and just before the zoo, he saw what he was certain, at the time, was a smudged arrow of flour, pointing him toward the northwest. He pressed on, crossing the Jahon Obidova, heading northwest now, down along the Bozsu Canal. Splotches of flour appeared every hundred meters or so, keeping him on track, and behind him, he could hear the singing and laughter of the pack. Riess felt the warmth of his own breath as he ran through the clouds of condensation he was making.

It was when he saw trail indicating that Walker had crossed the canal that it occurred to Riess that this chase wasn't going to be as easy as he'd thought it was.

It was an hour later, circling the TV tower along northern Amir Temur, that he realized that Walker had been planning this run for days, if not weeks, and had been laying false trails for it as well. He doubled back, heading south down Amir Temur, in the direction of the square, and it was as he crossed Husniddin Asomov that the BMW shot through the intersection, its horn blaring, and like an idiot, Riess looked to find the source of the sound rather than getting out of the way.

And it sure as hell looked like the car was going to hit him, so Riess did what people normally do in such circumstances: he dove, trying to reverse his direction, off the street. He was certain he could feel the front fender of the car brushing his sneaker as he tumbled, and then he was on the ground, trying to roll back to his feet, and that was when he twisted his ankle, and went down again, this time harder, and losing a few layers of skin off his knee as a bonus.

Riess rolled onto his back, sitting up, pulling his right knee to his chest with both hands, hearing himself curse. He was dimly pleased to realize that he was swearing in Uzbek. He'd have to drop a line later to the folks at Arlington who'd spent forty-four weeks beating the tongue into his head.

The BMW had come to a stop, and Riess saw it was an older model, maybe ten years old, and the driver's door opened, and a man came out from behind the wheel, looking concerned, asking if he was all right. Riess' first thought was that it was funny that he'd been hit by a man who looked just like President Malikov's son.

"Are you all right, can you stand?" the man asked him, reaching down to take hold of Riess by the upper arms. "Can you stand?"

"It's all right," Riess said. "I'm all right."

"I didn't see you running like that, I'm very sorry. Are you sure you're okay?"

Riess nodded, trying to figure out what to say next. He wasn't a spook, he wasn't one of Tower's cadre of case officers, he was the Deputy Chief Political Officer for the U.S. Mission to Uzbekistan, most often referred to as a poloff. He'd had some basic training in tradecraft, mostly security, ways to keep himself safe, ways to determine if he was being targeted. But when it came time for cloaks and daggers to be handed out, Riess' job was to stay at the embassy and well out of the way. Even working with Dina Malikov had been a stretch, a job he'd only undertaken at the request of his ambassador.

He wasn't a spook, but he knew what this was, and he was quick enough to know that if Ruslan Malikov was trying to make contact with him covertly the day after his wife's body had been found outside of Chirchik, the odds were that they were both being watched.

Riess let Malikov help him to his feet, wincing as he tried to place some of his weight on his ankle. The pain ran around the top of his foot like barbed wire, and he hissed. Malikov put one arm at the small of his back to support him.

"Do you need a hospital? I can take you to the hospital."

"No, I think I'll be okay." Riess tried it again, stepping gingerly and gritting his teeth, and found that if he turned his foot inward slightly, the pain wasn't quite so intense. Malikov's hands came off him, and Riess hobbled experimentally.

"You're certain?"

"It's okay," Riess said. "Really, it'll be fine. Just needs some ice. I'll handle it when I get home."

Malikov studied him, as if trying to discern the truth of the statement, then nodded and moved around the BMW, back to the driver's side. Without another word, he climbed behind the wheel, slammed the door, and pulled away, back into the thin traffic on the avenue.

Riess grimaced, swore again, louder, mostly for the benefit of anyone who might have been listening. He had to assume he was being watched now, even if he couldn't see the watchers, even if he was, just perhaps, being paranoid rather than prudent. It took him a few seconds to realize that what he needed to do next was exactly what he'd been doing before, and he hobbled back toward the street, and spent the next three minutes trying to hail a cab to take him to the Meridien Hotel, near Amir Temur Square.

Once in the taxi and in traffic, Riess leaned back in his seat and reached around, behind his back, to where Malikov had slipped the note into the waistband of his sweats. It was a small square of paper, folded over several times, and easy to conceal in his palm, and so Riess did as he bent forward to check his sore ankle. He slipped the paper into his sock.

The cab dropped him at the hotel, and he hobbled up the steps and into the lobby to find that the others were already there, in the bar, with the hare, who was now drunk almost beyond all comprehension. Lydia Straight, the press attaché at the Embassy, saw him and thus initiated the first round of heckling.

"Chuck! You made it!"

Jeers followed.

Riess showed Lydia his middle finger and took the offered beer from Walker's somewhat unfocused grip. He drank it while leading a rendition of "The Real Story of Gilligan's Island," then started a second while joining in on the traditional version of Elton John's "Rocket Man," before excusing himself to the restroom. He used the sink first, running water to wipe the sweat from his face and the grime from his hands, then wet a paper towel to use in cleaning his skinned knee. When he finished, the only other patron in the men's room had departed, and Riess moved to the toilet stall, where he dropped his sweats, sat on the toilet, and only then retrieved the note.

It was written in English, which surprised him, all in careful block capitals, painstakingly laid onto the paper.

CHARLES—

I KNOW WHAT MY DINA WAS DOING FOR YOU AND YOUR AMBAS-
SADOR, AND FOR THIS MY SISTER HAVE HER MURDER.

MY FATHER IS SICK AND NOT FOR LAST LONG. IT WILL BE BE-
TWEEN MY SISTER AND MYSELF THAT IS TO RULE. I AM YOUR MAN
NOW. I WANT FOR MY COUNTRY MORE TO BE LIKE YOURS. I WILL DO
WHAT EVER IT WILL TAKES.

MY SISTER KNOWS THIS AND WILL TRY TO HAVE ME MURDER
SOON.

I WILL DO WHAT EVER IT TAKES.

The note was unsigned, and Riess figured that was because a
signature didn't much matter. He read it again, slower, just to be
sure he understood what was being said, then got to his feet,
pulling up his sweats. He flushed the toilet, and used the rush of
water to hide the noise of the tearing paper. He waited until the
toilet refilled, dropped the fragments into the bowl, and flushed a
second time. When the bowl refilled again with nothing but dirty
water, he left the stall, relieved to see that he was still alone in the
bathroom.

Riess returned to the bar in time for another drink and the second chorus of "Put Your Thighs on My Shoulders," then sang the
raunchiest version of "Rawhide" he knew as a duet with Lydia.
They were on the third verse when the management asked them,
politely, to leave.

He took a cab home, showered, changed, and then called the
Residence using the house phone. The line had been checked by
the Embassy's security staff only three weeks ago as part of their
standard evaluation, and Riess was as certain as he could be that it
wasn't bugged. Even so, when the Ambassador came on the line,
he kept things vague, asking when would be a good time to come
see him.

"This what I think it is?" Ambassador Garret asked him.

"Yes, sir."

"DCM is hosting a dinner tonight at his residence for a couple of the DPMs, including that bastard from the Ministry of the Interior, Ganiev. Come late, Chuck. Come very late. Hour of the wolf."

"Hour of the wolf," Riess agreed.

"How?" Ambassador Garret asked.

"They boiled her to death," Riess answered. He tried to make the declaration merely factual. He failed.

"Jesus Christ." Garret passed a broad hand over his face, wiping the sleep away from his eyes. "Jesus Christ, she's his daughter-in-law, she's married to Ruslan, and Malikov let the NSS lobster-pot her?"

"The Ministry of the Interior is claiming it was Hizb-ut-Tahir."

"I know what they're claiming. Jesus Christ."

"Yes, sir."

The Ambassador closed his eyes, then opened them again. "She gave you up. If they tortured her, she gave you up."

"I think it's a safe assumption, yes, sir."

"When was the last time you met with her?"

"On the second, so that's nine days ago now. That's where I got the videotape."

Garret frowned, remembering the recording. "Why'd they kill her?"

"It might have gotten out of control. They're not terribly gentle about these things."

"But they can be, Chuck, they can be. They could have fixed it so they got what they wanted and then sent her back home."

"She would have told her husband."

Garret looked at him, his brow creasing, thinking. "Maybe."

"You think there's something else to it?"

"I think that Dina Malikov was alive on Thursday, dead by Friday, and today, Saturday, her husband arranged a meeting with you to say that he wants to play ball. The timing makes me nervous."

"I got the impression from his note that he'd been looking for an opportunity for a while, sir," Riess said. "Dina's death may have been the impetus he needed to make the move."

"Which may be why they killed her in the first place. If it was the old man who did it."

Riess heard the doubt in his voice. "You think it was Sevara?"

"I think Sevara wants the crown, Chuck. And if Malikov really is coming up on his last legs, she may be trying to clear the way for a run at the throne."

Riess considered, watching as Garret looked away from him to the grandfather clock ticking solidly in the corner study's corner. The Ambassador's mouth tightened to a line, and then he used his broad hands on the broader armrests of his easy chair to push himself to his feet.

"Four in the fucking morning," he said. "Let's go to the kitchen. I need some coffee."

The house was silent and dark. The trip from Riess' house downtown to the Residence on the outskirts of Tashkent normally took half an hour, but at three in the morning, Riess had been able to make it in half that time. The roads had been almost entirely vacant, and he'd driven quickly, in an attempt to flush any possible tails. He hadn't seen any, but that didn't give him much confidence that he'd gone undetected. It didn't really matter; he was known in the Embassy as the Ambassador's legman, much to the annoyance of his immediate superior, Political Counselor T. Lindsay McColl. If Riess was called out to the Residence at half past three in the morning, then it was unusual, but not unheard of.

Riess followed the Ambassador through the house, Garret alternately switching on lights to illuminate their way, turning off others as they no longer needed them. Riess wondered if it was a security measure or a habit. Maybe he did it to keep from disturbing his wife. Whatever it was, Riess was certain there was a purpose to it. In his experience, there was very little that Kenneth

Garret, the United States Ambassador to Uzbekistan, did without a very good reason.

Riess' immediate superior in the Mission, McColl, as uptight and self-righteous a Europeanist as Riess had ever met in the Foreign Service, consistently referred to Garret as "the Grizzly," though never while in earshot of the Ambassador. McColl did a poor job of hiding his resentment of Garret, a resentment born, Riess supposed, more of envy than of anything else. Both men shared the same political rank at State, and McColl not only had seniority, but a pedigree, and felt that Garret had robbed him of his rightful ambassadorship. The nickname was meant, therefore, as an insult of the highest order.

But limping after Garret through the Residence, Riess thought it was anything but. Six foot three and easily two hundred and forty pounds, everything on Garret had that ursine sense of scale and restrained power, from the breadth of his chest and the strength in his shoulders down to the thickness of each of his fingers. In all the time Riess had known him, first serving as a junior political officer at the embassy in St. Petersburg where Garret had been posted as Deputy Chief of Mission, and now, six years later, serving as his legman in Tashkent, he'd never once seen Garret exhibit anything but an absolute, controlled calm. No matter what he did, if he laughed, if he despaired, it was all with the same gravitas.

People underestimated the Ambassador to their peril, and while Riess himself had never heard Garret talk about it, it was well known among the Mission staffers just how tall the man could stand. No new arrival to the Chancery in Uzbekistan could make it more than a week before hearing the infamous "Fuck Off, Senator" story.

It went something like this:

Seems that Kenneth Garret had spent a year at CENTCOM as a political adviser after one of his DCM stints. His job had been primarily to offer political insight and counsel to General Anthony

Zinni. After CENTCOM, Garret had rotated back to State, and then, the following year, had been nominated as Ambassador to Kuwait by the Clinton White House. It was a done deal as far as the White House was concerned, and even the Senate Foreign Relations Committee had looked to be smooth sailing, a rubber-stamp proceeding.

Except that the Committee in question was chaired by Senator Jesse Helms, and Helms' history with Zinni was, as one of Riess' colleagues had described it, "defined by white-hot hatred," as a result of a particularly harsh facing Zinni had delivered to the Senator following the Gulf War. After the war, Helms had gotten the not-very-bright idea of turning the Iraqi army-in-exile around on Saddam with CIA backing, in an attempt to overthrow the dictator. It was a plan that suffered from a legion of problems, small and large, so many in fact that General Zinni, in a public hearing, had referred to the idea as a "Bay of Goats."

The Senator was not well pleased.

Garret, so the story went, was approached by one of Helms' staffers prior to confirmation. The staffer informed the Ambassador-in-waiting that his confirmation would positively sail on through, but that, during the closed hearing, the Chairman would ask Mr. Garret some pointed questions about General Zinni. And if Mr. Garret then took it upon himself to perhaps criticize the General's judgment and leadership, well, it would be appreciated. Certainly such comments in a closed hearing would be a small price to pay for Mr. Garret to finally achieve a posting of importance and prestige, one he'd been pursuing throughout his professional career.

According to the story, Garret embarked on one of his infamous pauses, lasting—depending on who was recounting the tale—anywhere from fifteen seconds to an ungodly two and a half minutes, before offering his answer.

"Fuck off."

When the staffer regained his ability to speak, he informed Garret that any confirmation hearing would not occur until the Chairman moved for the nomination to be considered by the

Committee, something that Mr. Garret, by his answer, had just guaranteed would never happen. Not just this job lost, no sir. No position requiring a Senate confirmation. Ever.

Nice knowing you, Mr. Garret.

The Clinton White House, on the other hand, upon hearing of what had transpired, rewarded Garret for his loyalty with a position on the National Security Council. And it was on the NSC that Garret remained until Colin Powell came aboard as S and heard the story himself. Didn't hurt that Powell and Zinni were tight, and so Garret found himself back at the State Department, working in Counterterrorism . . . a position that became the epicenter of the policy universe only a few months later.

Riess liked the story for a number of reasons, but mostly because it had a happy ending. Helms and his winged monkeys on the SFRC left the Hill, and the moment they were gone, Powell pushed for Garret to get the Uzbekistan job. This was pre-Iraq but post-9/11, and the posting was second in importance only to the Mission in Islamabad, given the situation in Afghanistan. More, it was a reward for loyalty, for a job well done that put Garret in line for even greater things. After Uzbekistan, the Ambassador could expect his next posting to be in Turkey, or Australia, or Moscow, wherever he damn well pleased.

This was, in part, why what Garret was undertaking was so potentially dangerous. If it failed, it could end the Ambassador's career.

And Riess didn't even want to think about what it would do to his.

"I want Ruslan in charge," Garret told Riess. "He's the best bet we have going to turn this country into something resembling a free society."

"I agree."

"Problem is, Ruslan doesn't have the muscle to take over when his old man kicks it. And right now, everyone back in Washington likes the looks of his sister. They think Sevara's their girl. She's made some overtures already, she's indicated her willingness to play ball. As far as the old guard back at State are concerned, she's already halfway into power."

"She's as corrupt as her father is," Riess said. "She's just more subtle about it."

"You don't have to tell me," Garret said. "It's the Kissinger legacy, Chuck. The realists are looking at her as someone who can get the job done, who'll hold the line against the extremists, and who'll continue to support the war. And we can't lose Uzbekistan, we need the conduit into northern Afghanistan."

"We'd get all those things from Ruslan. If we supported him, we'd get all those things, and it'd be better for the country, to boot."

Garret studied him thoughtfully, not speaking for several seconds, and Riess wondered if he'd perhaps stepped over some unknown line. If it had been McColl he was speaking to, he'd never say these things, but the Ambassador had always encouraged him to speak his mind. Even so, Riess worried that he'd gone too far.

"You're going to have those ex-KGB bastards crawling all over you, you know that?" Garret asked, finally. "Even if Dina didn't give you up, Ruslan's contact with you today guarantees it."

"Yes, sir."

The Ambassador gave him a small, paternal smile, then turned to the coffeemaker and proceeded to fill two cups. He handed Riess one, then asked, "You ever meet Ruslan? Before today, I mean?"

"At the Independence Day party—theirs, not ours. That's it."

"According to Tower, Malikov wants control of the country to stay in the family when he kicks it. Hasn't chosen one kid over the other, as far as the CIA can tell. God knows, if he doesn't designate a clear successor before he kicks it, all hell will break loose. Might break loose anyway, even if he does. The DPMs would eat their own young if they thought it would put them in charge."

"Sevara's married to Ganiev—"

"Yeah, the Deputy Prime Minister of the Interior, though it's an open secret that she's the one running the Ministry."

"That's not all she's doing," Riess said. "There've been reports of her selling girls into the UAE, that she's formed and armed her own militia. We know she's got her own secret police force, her own courts. And we're not even discussing her legitimate—and I use the word in the loosest possible sense—business interests, from her wireless communications company to owning something like three spas and a movie studio."

"Whereas Ruslan has a two-year-old son and has just become a widower."

"Ruslan's the Chairman of the Constitutional Court, which means he's responsible for writing the laws that his father wants written. He's got some people, but it's nothing like what Sevara's assembled. That's never been how he does business."

Garret drained his cup and again looked to the clock, this one hung on the wall beside the refrigerator. He frowned, and Riess knew from the expression on his face that the Ambassador was doing time-zone math, most likely calculating the hour in Washington.

"Have to start with my calls."

"What do you want me to do?"

"Nothing for the time being."

Riess tried to keep the confusion off his face. "Sir?"

"Nothing. Don't try to contact Ruslan, don't go near him. Just do your job, keep McColl happy. He already thinks you spend too much time with me as it is."

"Ruslan believes his life is in danger, sir. If we don't do something—"

"Easy, Charles. I didn't say I wasn't going to do anything, I just told you to steer clear for the time being." Garret looked at the clock again, frowning. "What's London, five hours behind us?"

"Uh . . . five or six, I think."

"He won't be in yet," Garret said, more to himself than to Riess, then sighed. "I've had enough, Chuck. Thirty years in high diplomacy and not enough time actually spent keeping the people on the ground from being tortured to death. Realpolitik be damned, I've had enough. Malikov goes. One way or another, he goes. We're staging a coup, Chuck. A nice, quiet coup, and when it's over the White House gets to say we did the right thing, even if they'd rather we hadn't done it at all."

"If it works," Riess murmured.

"If it works."

They left it at that, neither of them wishing to say what would happen if it didn't.

CHAPTER 4

**London—Spice Quay,
Residence of Poole, Nicholas**

12 February, 1748 Hours GMT

"Thought you were bringing Tamsin," Nicky Poole said after he'd let Chace inside and taken her coat. "Didn't leave her on the train, did you?"

Chace smacked her forehead with her palm, just hard enough to make an audible impact.

"Oh, damn," she said. "I wondered what that bloody racket was."

She shrugged and grinned, and Poole laughed and asked her if she'd like a glass of wine before dinner, saying that he'd opened a passable French Syrah that he thought she might enjoy. Chace followed him through the flat, past the windows overlooking the Thames, at the rain that was falling hard enough to hide the view of Tower Bridge. She took the glass he offered, raised it to his, and each took a sip to the other's health, before Poole set his back down and returned his attention to the salad he was preparing as a starter.

"You're looking good," Poole remarked. "Thought you'd have gone all dumpy with motherhood by now."

"Nursing is a wonderful thing," Chace said. "I think I'm back to my fighting weight, so to speak. You look like hell, incidentally."

"Didn't get much sleep last night."

"Job?"

He shook his head slightly, not so much as an answer, but rather to warn her off as he added a handful of goat cheese to the salad. "You know I can't talk about it."

Chace nodded, took another sip of her wine, hoping it would soothe her curiosity. It surprised her how much she wanted to know the details, where he'd been, what he'd done, why he'd done it.

"So," Poole said, changing the subject, "where is the little precious?"

"I told you, I left her on the train. Should be in Dover by now, I'd think."

Poole arched an eyebrow at her, then scattered chopped figs on the salad before sprinkling the mixture with a vinaigrette he'd apparently prepared himself. He picked up the salad bowl, snapping his wrist forward, then back, catching the greens as they flipped into the air.

"Very fancy," Chace said. "Tam's fine, she's in Barlick, Val's watching her. We're weaning, and it's easier if I'm not there for it."

"I was worried." Poole set the bowl down, began dishing the salad onto plates. "For a moment I was beginning to wonder if you *had* abandoned her."

"Nice to know you think so very highly of me, Nicky."

"I do think very highly of you, Tara." He handed her a plate, then picked up his own, taking his wineglass in his free hand. "To the table, please. We need to eat it before it wilts."

"Words to live by if ever I've heard them," she said, and followed him to her seat.

They ate well, Gressingham duck served with rosemary potatoes and freshly minted peas. The conversation was easy at first, and each laughed more often than not. Twice Chace tried to steer the conversation around to SIS and happenings at Vauxhall Cross, and the first time, Poole let it continue, going so far as to share the few pieces of information that were harmless, or at least considered open secrets. He liked their new Deputy Chief; Kate still guarded the door to Crocker's office; Lankford had gotten himself a girl; Barclay continued to make life miserable. After he'd served the apple crumble and coffee, Chace tried a second time, asking pointedly how her replacement was working out, and Poole set down his utensils and stopped just short of glaring at her.

"I can't talk about it, and I can't talk about him, and you know that, Tara. So leave it be, right? Enjoy the meal, tell me about your little girl, talk about religion, sex, and politics, if you like. But please, don't ask me questions you know I'm not allowed to answer."

Chastened, Chace nodded. "I'm sorry."

"You miss it so much, reapply. Crocker would take you back in an instant."

"Crocker can burn in hell."

"Fine, then. Shall we talk about the weather?"

Chace shook her head, and let it go, lapsing into silence as she started on her dessert. The dinner marked the third time she and Poole had gotten together since she'd quit SIS eighteen months prior. The first time, he'd come to visit shortly after Tamsin's birth, while Chace was still in the hospital, with flowers and good wishes from both him and Lankford, saying only that he'd heard there were now two of her, and he had to see it himself before he could believe it. Chace suspected that Crocker had let him know about the birth, though how he'd found out, she couldn't guess. It wouldn't have been that hard.

The second visit had been just before Christmas. Poole had come to Barnoldswick bearing gifts for Tamsin and Valerie, and had stayed with them overnight, even going so far as to cook dinner for the three of them. When he'd left in the midafternoon the next day, Valerie had told Chace that, if she was smart, she'd get her grip on that Mr. Poole right quick, before some other lady beat her to the punch, as he'd be a wonderful father to her baby. Chace had smiled and explained that such an arrangement was unlikely to happen, as Mr. Poole preferred the romantic company of other men to that of women. Valerie had digested that, frowning.

"Homosexual?" she'd asked, for clarification.

"Devout."

"No wonder he's so good in the kitchen, then," Valerie had mused, and then gone off to continue wrapping Christmas presents.

They finished the meal just after eight in the evening, and Chace stayed to help with the dishes, clearing the table. By the time all was dry and back in its proper place, Chace could tell Poole was halfway to sleep. Whatever he'd done, wherever it had been, it had taken a physical toll, she could read it in his movements, in his expression when he thought she was looking away. He was angry, too, and she was certain it was related.

He gave her a kiss on the cheek before she went out the door, saying that he hoped they'd get together again soon, and she echoed the sentiment, slipping into her coat and wrapping her scarf around her neck as she went down the hall, catching the lift back to the street. Once outside, though, walking through the rain, she admitted that she probably wouldn't see him again at all, in fact, that this had most likely been the last time they would ever come together for a social visit.

The gulf was too wide, she realized as she walked toward the tube stop to catch the train back to Camden, and each time they got together, it only made the distance between them that much wider. It had nothing to do with friendship, nothing to do with the respect or fondness that either had for the other.

He lived in another world now, one she'd departed of her own choosing.

Riding the tube, looking with contempt at the other passengers pursuing their minor lives, it struck her that she was just like them now.

She was just like everyone else.

CHAPTER 5

London—Vauxhall Cross, Office of D-Ops

13 February 0922 GMT

Crocker's day, when he could rely on that mythical creature called a "routine," normally began at half past five in the morning, with the cruel blare of his alarm as it dutifully roused him from the four or so hours of sleep he'd managed to steal. He would tumble from his bed, and, on days like today, curse the draftiness of the old house as the cold radiated through the rug on the floor. He would lurch more than walk to the bathroom, and let the shower finish what the alarm had begun. He suffered from regular headaches and regular muscle aches, both the result of tension, and depending on how sorry his state, would remain under the water for anywhere from five to fifteen minutes in an attempt to lessen the impact of both, before emerging to shave and dress.

Lately, his showers ran to the long side.

Once in his suit, always three pieces, always gray or navy, he would descend to the kitchen to find Jennie already there, and she would hand him his first cup of coffee for the day, and he would drink it while they shared a quick breakfast, cereal if there was time, a piece of fruit stuffed into a pocket if there wasn't. Crocker would use the telephone, and call the Ops Room, to inform the Duty Ops Officer that he was on his way into the office. He would kiss his wife, promise that he'd be home by dinner, grab his government case, and make his way to the train. If the commute was easy, he could count on reaching Vauxhall Cross by half past seven; if it was hard, it could take him until half past eight, or longer.

On a normal day, Kate Cooke would have arrived before him, early enough that she could present Crocker with his second cup of coffee as he entered his office, taking his government case in trade. While Crocker hung his coat from the rickety stand in the corner of his office, Kate would unlock the case using one of the keys that hung from the chain at her waist, and begin removing and sorting those files and papers that had accompanied Crocker home the previous night. Throughout this, she would provide a continuous commentary, informing Crocker of any matters outstanding that required his immediate attention, or in fact of anything that she thought might be of interest to him at all.

Crocker would settle behind his desk, light his first cigarette, and then begin the necessary but tedious process of vetting the stack of reports as Kate departed, leaving the door open to the outer office so she could remain within earshot. Crocker would scan the files, circulars, and memorandums that had arrived while he'd been away, initialing each as he went, to signify that he had, in fact, seen and reviewed its contents. The stack was always prepared in the same fashion, with those items marked "Immediate" at the top, down to those graded "Routine" at the bottom.

More often than not, Crocker would discover multiple items requiring his attention, and bellow for Kate to return. Dictation would follow, or directions, or curses, or any combination thereof, and Kate would again return to her desk to carry out the latest series of instructions. Crocker would then direct his attention to the Daily Intelligence Brief, as prepared by his opposite number, the Director of Intelligence, Simon Rayburn. This, in turn, would lead to more instructions to Kate, and frequently, those instructions would require the Minders in some fashion or another to join him in his office, more frequently using the house phone to inform the Head of Section of D-Ops' wishes.

On a good day, it would be nine in the morning by the time this particular regimen was completed. On a bad day, it could last well into the late morning.

What happened next depended on a variety of different variables. Should the world appear to be behaving itself, Crocker would move to the Deputy Chief's office, joined by D-Int, and together, sitting opposite the DC, the three would review the events of the day before, and plan for the events of the day ahead. The DC would then excuse them, and depart to carry that briefing up to C, leaving Crocker and Rayburn to return to their offices to oversee their respective domains. If an operation was in the offing, Crocker would make a visit to the Ops Room first to check on the status of the mission, and to make certain that the Operations Room staff was appropriately briefed. He would then return to his office, and continue to attend to matters there, both political and operational. Letters would be drafted, phone calls made, and always more meetings. The minutiae of Intelligence in all of its tedious glory, from budget allocations to changes in security protocols to correspondence sent in response to this department or that ministry.

And so it would go until, inevitably, the red phone on Crocker's desk would ring, and the Duty Ops Officer would be on the line, his voice soft, efficient, controlled, informing D-Ops that something, somewhere, had happened, requiring his attention. The Paris Number One had been arrested for soliciting a prostitute, for instance, or a journalist for the BBC had been arrested in Darfur, accused of espionage, or a car bomb had exploded in Moscow, or the Director of Global Issues at the FCO had been spotted at the airport in São Paulo, when in point of fact she was supposed to be vacationing in California, or Operation: Fill-in-the-Blank had hit a snag.

And Crocker would respond, depending on what was needed, giving his orders, rushing to brief the DC and C, struggling to secure the approval required to do whatever it was that would be needed next. Politics would rear its ugly head, and arguments would ensue, and somewhere, someplace in the world, time would be running out to do whatever it was that needed to be done.

Crises, and more, dealing with crises, was, after all, his line of work.

If things went well, the crisis would resolve in short order, but of course, things rarely went well. Assuming the crisis resolved, Crocker could count on leaving Vauxhall Cross at six in the evening, to negotiate his morning commute once more, this time in reverse, carrying his government case, loaded and locked by Kate before he'd sent her home. If he was fortunate, he'd arrive to find that Jennie had held dinner for him, and if he was extraordinarily lucky, he'd find his daughters at the table as well, Ariel, thirteen, and Sabrina, sixteen. He would use the telephone, and inform the Duty Ops Officer that he was now at home, then sit down to dine and enjoy what little time he could with his family.

Later in the evening, after the children had gone to bed, Crocker would unlock his case, and go through the papers he'd brought home with him. He'd make notes, draft responses, and inevitably fall asleep while reviewing the papers, only to be awoken by Jennie, and redirected to his bed. Sometimes, they even managed to make love before he fell asleep again.

That was the routine.

Monday morning, the routine lasted until he reached his office, and then it went all to hell, pretty much as Crocker had expected it would.

"C wants you in his office right away," Kate informed him as she followed Crocker from the outer office to the inner, taking his case.

"Is Fincher in the Pit?"

"Not yet, sir, no. Poole and Lankford."

Crocker shrugged out of his overcoat, placed it on the stand. "How many times has he called down?"

"Just the twice. Deputy Chief as well, only once."

"We have Minder One's after-action?"

"It's on top of the stack." Kate closed the now-empty case, setting it beside the document safe that stood just inside Crocker's office, to the left of the door. "KL went badly, I presume?"

"Fincher bollixed it up."

"Hardly surprising," Kate murmured.

Crocker stopped moving long enough to glare at her. "What was that?"

"It seems surprising," Kate said, sweetly, adjusting her grip on the stack she'd taken from the case. "Shall I inform Sir Frances that you're on the way up?"

"If it wouldn't be too much of a bother. And perhaps you'd like to inform the Deputy Chief as well?"

"I would be delighted."

He waited until she was out of the room before starting a cigarette, taking the first folder off of the top of the stack sitting on his desk. The folder was red, indicating that its contents were operational in nature, and a tracking sheet was affixed to its front, along with a bar code. It was stamped "Most Secret," and the tab on the side read "Candlelight." According to the tracking sheet, the contents had most recently been received by the Deputy Chief's office at 0818 that morning, and by C's at 0844. Kate had signed for possession at 0902.

Crocker blew smoke, and, still standing, opened the folder. The contents detailed all aspects of Operation: Candlelight, from conops to implementation, everything that had any bearing on the mission. He flipped through the pages quickly, looking for Fincher's after-action. It should have been at the top, the most recent addition to the file aside from Crocker's own assessment, written in the small hours on Saturday morning, after Candlelight had wrapped up. Instead, he found Fincher's report at the bottom, two double-spaced pages clipped together, as if shoved into the folder at the last moment.

He read, and when he was finished reading, he swore, closed the folder, and all but threw it down on his desk. Then he stormed into the outer office, making for the door onto the hallway.

"Get on to the Pit," Crocker told Kate. "Tell Poole I want his after-action on Candlelight, and I want it right away. I'll be in C's office."

He was out the door before she could respond.

"I think you owe us an explanation, Crocker." Sir Frances Barclay was seated behind his very large desk, in his very large chair, his hands resting side by side almost on the desktop, his thin fingers barely touching one another. His voice was placid, friendly, and he blinked slowly at Crocker from behind the thin lenses of his glasses, and he even managed a thin smile.

Seated to the left of where Crocker stood facing the desk, Alison Gordon-Palmer uncrossed and then recrossed her ankles, smoothing her long skirt.

"It's in my report," Crocker said.

"Your report and the report of your Head of Section seem to be at odds."

"Head of Section's covering himself."

Barclay's left eyebrow hitched itself higher a fraction. "Or you are."

"Colonel Dawson will confirm what I'm saying."

"He certainly confirms the firefight," Barclay said. "He certainly confirms that his troopers followed your orders to engage the JI cell after you ignored Minder One's recommendation to abort."

"Respectfully, sir, Minder One doesn't have the authority to send an abort," Crocker responded. "I do."

"It's one of your responsibilities, yes."

"Yes, sir."

"Which in turn would make you responsible for what happened as a result," Barclay said, and his smile vanished. "Six dead, another two wounded on the exfil, and the Malaysians screaming bloody murder about us interfering in their sovereign affairs. The G-77 have rallied around, and are making strenuous protest in New York and Geneva. Downing Street is embarrassed, the cousins are washing their hands of it all, and we look like a bunch of imperialist fools roaming Southeast Asia, spilling blood wherever we can find it."

"It was a Jemaah Islamiyah cell, sir," Crocker replied, tightly. "That's been confirmed. We have further confirmation, including radio and internet intercepts, that the same cell intended to hijack the *Mawi Dawn* as it entered the Straits of Malacca this morning, and then to drive the supertanker into Singapore Harbor."

"I don't dispute any of that."

Crocker almost shook his head, trying to conceal his surprise. "Sir?"

"D-Int, as well as CIA, confirms everything you've said. That is not at issue."

"Then I'm afraid I don't follow you, sir."

Barclay sighed, glancing over toward the Deputy Chief. From the corner of his eye, Crocker watched Alison Gordon-Palmer again smooth her skirt. She was frowning.

Barclay moved his gaze back to Crocker, and the smile reappeared. "How long have you been D-Ops now, Paul?"

Crocker saw it then, saw it all unfurling like a banner into a breeze. He forced his jaw and his hands to relax. "Seven years."

"That's quite a long time."

"I've had predecessors who remained for longer."

Barclay nodded sagely, accepting this. "Many of them too long, I daresay."

"Fincher had no authority to call for an abort, sir, and his actions jeopardized not only Minder Two and the troopers with him, but the entire mission as well. My response was appropriate, and necessary."

"Your response generated a political and diplomatic mess, Paul." Barclay smiled again, thinly. "I find it rather ironic that, with all of the gamesmanship and arrogance you have exhibited in your time as D-Ops, what has finally brought you to your knees is nothing of your own devising, but rather an unfortunate sequence of events that could have happened to anyone in your position. I find that most ironic, I must admit."

Crocker glanced to Gordon-Palmer, saw that the woman was studiously looking away from Barclay, trying to conceal her scowl. Crocker felt perspiration rising to his palms, but was somewhat surprised to find that was the only physical response he seemed to be exhibiting, especially considering his now-burning desire to reach across the desk and strangle Sir Frances.

He resisted the urge. He even managed to keep his voice civil, if not pleasant, when he asked, "What do you intend?"

"I'm going to replace you, Paul," Barclay said. "Colin Forsythe, I think, though I may tap Dominick Barnett—I haven't truly decided yet. Both are capable, and neither will have me worrying that my D-Ops is skulking around behind my back. Honestly, it's only a question of which of them I'd rather.

"As for you, you will remain on as acting Director Operations until the end of the month, at which point your successor will be named, and you will vacate your office. If at that time you wish to continue in SIS, I'm certain we'll be able to find an appropriate position for you somewhere in Whitehall. If you play your cards right and make this easy on me, I might even go so far as to see you posted to the States. There's a JIC advisory position coming open at the Embassy in Washington. You would do quite well in the position, I think."

Crocker kept his mouth closed, concealing the fact that, for an instant, he'd had to bite his own tongue to keep himself silent. But even if he'd managed to keep his voice still, he had no doubts that Barclay was reading everything on his face.

In return, Barclay's smile grew a fraction.

"I told you I would see you gone," he said. "It took longer than I had anticipated, but here we are, at the end, and I have kept my word. More than you can say you've ever done for me."

"Not quite at the end."

"Two weeks from it, then. And don't think for a minute that I shall let my attention wander from you, Crocker. No, my eye will be on you up until the moment you leave this building for the very last time, of that you can be certain. You may leave now."

Crocker left the office without another word.

Alison Gordon-Palmer caught him just as he was stepping into the elevator, preparing to ride back down to the sixth floor.

"Paul!"

What he truly wanted then was to be alone, at least for a moment, so he could indulge the rage that was now roaring inside him. But the Deputy Chief was almost running, trying to catch him before the doors closed, and at the last moment Crocker thrust out his hand, so that she could enter and ride the lift down with him.

"I'm sorry. You must know I tried everything to talk him out of it," Gordon-Palmer told him after the doors had closed. "He's had it in for you from the start, Paul. This thing in KL was the opportunity he'd been waiting for."

Crocker grunted in agreement. His history with Barclay stretched back to his days in the field, to when he'd been a young Minder Two during the twilight days of the Cold War. He'd gone to Prague to lift a KGB defector named Valeriy Karpin, and it had gone wrong, and Crocker had barely escaped with his life. Karpin hadn't been as lucky, shot to death as he hung in the barbed wire on the border with Austria. Barclay had been Head of Station–Prague at the time, and it was Crocker's belief, even now, that Karpin's death was Barclay's fault. Like Fincher, he'd lost his nerve when it had been needed most, and like Fincher, Frances Barclay had done an expert job of passing the blame for the failed operation onto another's shoulders.

Barclay, like so many other civil servants in countless bureaucracies around the world, had gone on to survive and even to thrive. When Sir Wilson Stanton-Davies, the previous C, had been forced into premature retirement as the result of a stroke, Barclay had assumed the position as head of SIS with a sense of entitlement that had made Crocker's stomach turn. Barclay had also made it abundantly clear that he would do everything in his power to convince Crocker to step down.

But before he had been D-Ops, Crocker had been a Minder, and more of that remained in his blood than Barclay had anticipated. Crocker had entrenched himself. While Barclay headed the Firm, Crocker knew his opportunities for advancement were limited, if not nonexistent. His intent had been to wait Barclay out. Eventually, he was certain, the current C would retire, and the sun would once more shine down upon the Ops Directorate. All he'd needed to do was outlast him.

"Paul?"

Crocker brought himself back to the moment, looking at the Deputy Chief.

"What are you going to do?" she asked.

"I'm thinking of firing Fincher, to begin with."

"He'll file a grievance, say it's politically motivated."

"He's been a disaster since he started. He's all but crippled the Section. If the job hadn't been in KL, I would never have sent him."

"All the same, you fire him, you'll lose. Which means that you'll depart, but Fincher will still be here. Bad for the Service, certainly."

"Maybe I can find a job in Iraq that needs doing," Crocker said. "Somewhere in the Sunni Triangle, perhaps."

Alison Gordon-Palmer allowed a soft laugh to escape her before shaking her head, amused. She was in her early fifties, slender, with shoulder-length brown hair that had about as much life to it as the bristles found on the average broom. She favored suits of brown or, rarely, a deep burgundy, and she avoided the use of makeup unless forced to walk the corridors of Whitehall on SIS business. As far as Crocker was concerned, she was the second smartest person in the building—the first being Simon Rayburn, the Director of Intelligence—and, unlike the man she had replaced as Deputy Chief, Donald Weldon, appropriately aggressive for the job. Weldon had been, by his nature, cautious, and disinclined to the risks inherent in intelligence work. Alison Gordon-Palmer, on the other hand, understood that risk came with the territory.

Crocker wondered again, not for the first time, how it was that Frances Barclay had settled upon her as Deputy Chief. He'd been certain the job would go to Rayburn, and had been surprised when she'd been named as DC instead.

It was one of the very few decisions Barclay had made that Paul Crocker could find no fault with.

The lift came to a halt, the doors opened, and Crocker and Gordon-Palmer stepped out, walking through a cluster of junior officers who parted hastily to let them pass. Their offices shared the same floor, and they walked through the maze of white corridors in silence. When Crocker made the turn toward his office, she stuck with him.

"Do you want to stay?" she asked him suddenly.

The question was unexpected, and Crocker responded before thinking. "Of course I bloody want to stay."

Gordon-Palmer nodded slightly, her lips tightening in thought. She waited until he had his hand on the doorknob to his outer office, then said softly, "Seccombe is going to call you."

Crocker stopped, looked at her curiously, waiting for further explanation. She shook her head.

"I recommend you see what you can do for him when he calls, Paul," the Deputy Chief said, and then turned away, heading to her own office.

Leaving Paul Crocker to wonder what it was the PUS at the FCO could possibly want with him, and why the Deputy Chief seemed so certain he would be able to deliver.

CHAPTER 6

London—Whitehall. Office of Sir Walter Seccombe, Permanent Undersecretary and Head of the Diplomatic Service (FCO)

13 February, 1559 Hours GMT

Sir Walter Seccombe's smile was wide and genuine, and he shook Crocker's hand firmly, pumping it twice before releasing his grip.

"Paul, good of you to come," Seccombe said. "I'm afraid we'll need to make this fast—I have to join my Minister for a Cabinet meeting at half past."

"I could hardly refuse the invitation," Crocker said. "Certainly not after the Deputy Chief let me know it was coming."

"I trust she said no more?"

"Only to expect your call."

"I'm grateful that you're willing to indulge me."

Crocker shook his head slightly, bemused by the inversion. He didn't know what Seccombe wanted from him, but he was certain there was very little he could offer the PUS in return. Seccombe smiled again, a second time, grandfatherly in his care, then motioned for Crocker to step farther into the office.

It was a large room, and of a kind that Crocker had seen many times before, most recently that morning, in Barclay's office. The décor, even the feel, of the space was designed to conjure the Britain of a century before, when *empire* was spelled with a capital *E* be-

neath a sun that never set. But where Barclay's office was more effect than truth, Seccombe had the real thing, from the seventeenth-
century globe resting in its mahogany stand to the floor-to-ceiling
bookshelves, all loaded with leatherbound volumes with spines let-
tered in gold leaf. The carpet beneath his feet was certainly silk, certainly over two hundred years old, and Crocker became painfully
aware that his shoes were still wet from the rain outside.

Seccombe continued without looking back, motioning with his
right hand toward the couch and chairs that marked the more social area of the office, indicating where he wanted Crocker to sit.
As Crocker removed his overcoat, Seccombe moved to his desk,
gathering a selection of papers there before returning to join him.
Crocker took a position on the couch, and Seccombe one of the
high-backed chairs opposite.

"Would you like a drink, Paul?"

"No, thank you."

"You're certain you wouldn't indulge in a whiskey? Not after
the morning I'm sure you've had?"

Crocker shook his head. It didn't surprise him that Seccombe
knew what had transpired at Vauxhall Cross that morning. There
was a very good chance that Seccombe had seen it coming well before Barclay himself had. As PUS, Seccombe tracked all aspects of
the Foreign and Commonwealth Office's operations, overseeing
the work of no less than five Director Generals, who, in turn,
guided everything from general defense and intelligence to political interaction and consular services. If the Foreign Secretary, as
appointed by the Prime Minister, was the brains of the FCO, then
Seccombe, in his position as the Permanent Undersecretary—em-
phasis here on *permanent*—was its nervous system. Quite literally,
nothing happened in the FCO without Seccombe knowing about
it, more often than not before it came to pass.

Crocker knew him as brilliant, both as a politician and as a
diplomat, as ruthless and calculating. He could hardly be otherwise and have survived in his position.

Very few people frightened Paul Crocker. Certainly, Frances

Barclay didn't, not even with what had transpired this very day. But if someone came close, Crocker had to admit it would be Sir Walter Seccombe. It didn't matter how friendly he appeared, how many drinks he offered, how many times he might invite Crocker to dine with him at his club, Crocker would always remain wary of the man. As an ally, Seccombe was priceless.

As an enemy, he would be terrifying.

Seccombe settled in his chair, rustling the papers he'd taken from his desk, and gave Crocker the smile for a third time before finally putting it away.

"So Barclay's finally going to get his wish," Seccombe said. "No more Paul Crocker at his back."

"So it would appear."

"Do you think you could adjust to life in Washington?"

"If that's where I land."

"There's a certain prestige to be found in a posting with the Americans. That holds no appeal? I could try to arrange things so that you were put to good use."

"I'm put to better use here."

"So you are." Seccombe paused, tilting his chin upward, his eyes narrowing as he looked at Crocker. "I haven't forgotten that business about Zimbabwe, Paul. You did me a good turn, and I appreciate it."

Crocker nodded. Roughly around the time Barclay had ascended to C, Seccombe had reached out to Crocker to vet a man named Daniel Mwama, who—according to Seccombe—had approached the U.K. seeking assistance in ousting Robert Mugabe, with an eye to taking his place. Seccombe had wanted Mwama checked quickly, and quietly, and had called upon Crocker to do it. Crocker, in turn, had tasked the Minders, at that time Tom Wallace as Minder One and Tara Chace as Minder Two, for the job. It had been a politically dangerous job for Crocker, not only because it had come during a changing of the guard at SIS, but also because it had required him to have agents active in England, something Crocker was strictly forbidden from doing. In the end, he had given Seccombe the information the PUS had required, and Daniel Mwama had been sent packing.

Seccombe had gained the result he'd desired, and in return, had sheltered Crocker from Barclay's initial onslaught. That protection had lasted until this morning.

"I'm sure Alison asked you this, but for my own purposes, I'm asking again," Seccombe said. "You wish to stay D-Ops?"

"I had hoped to become Deputy Chief at some point."

"I don't think Alison is quite ready to move on."

"No chance that Barclay is going to resign?"

"Hmm." Seccombe ran a finger across his mustache, smoothing it. "Not willingly, no."

"Then, yes, I'd say I'd like to remain as Director of Operations, Sir Walter."

This time Seccombe didn't smile. He nodded once, slowly, and Crocker sensed a change in his manner, something felt rather than seen. Whatever trap had been laid here, Crocker had just avoided it.

"Then I have a proposition for you, Paul," Sir Walter Seccombe said. "One that I recommend you think quite seriously about accepting."

To: DIRECTOR OF OPERATIONS
        CROCKER, PAUL
CC: DEPUTY CHIEF OF SERVICE
        GORDON-PALMER, ALISON
From: DR. ELEANOR CALLARD
Date: 15 OCTOBER 2004
Re: MINDER ONE

Dear Paul,

I have had opportunity to review the test results and interview data taken in examination of Tara Chace during her debriefing phase at the Farm and her return to active duty, as per your request. Attached you will find detailed analysis and scoring, for inclusion in her personnel jacket.

The following battery of psychological tests were administered:

1.   Neurobehavioral Cognitive Status Exam.
2.   Shipley Institute of Living Scale.
3.   Beck Depression Inventory-II Scale.
4.   Wahler Physical Symptom Inventory

SUMMARY
Between our initial meeting at the Farm following her return from Saudi Arabia and her release by your directive placing her back to active status, I met with Chace four times for a total of 9.50 hours; since her return to duty, we have met a further two times, for 2.15 hours total. In each of these sessions, Chace has been uncharacteristically subdued and has evidenced a sincere disinterest in the proceedings and outcome of the examinations. This is a marked change from previous evaluations (attached), in particular her exam following Operation: Broken Ground.

When asked about her relationship with Tom Wallace, Chace exhibits anger and visible emotional distress. While she is forthcoming about the nature of their physical relationship, she is less so when questioned about their emotional relationship. She is evasive when asked how she feels about his death, and claims that it is "bitter" but that it isn't the first time someone she had worked with had been killed in the line of duty. When asked if she sees any difference between her current situation and those in the past, she refuses to answer.

Chace confirms that she has difficulty sleeping four or more nights a week, and that she drinks, by her own admission, "regularly." She is suffering from a lack of appetite. She has difficulty focusing and is experiencing lapses in memory. Her energy level and drive are subdued. She denies any social contact or interactions outside of SIS and the Minders. She admits to having nightmares, though qualifies this by saying, "no more than you'd expect." When pressed about the substance of these nightmares, she further admits that, in the main, they concern the death of Wallace. She cites physical symptoms, including vomiting and body ache.

She denies feelings of impending doom, but confirms feelings of detachment.

Based on these findings, it is my recommendation that Chace be removed from the Active Duty Roster immediately and placed on Medical Leave. It is further recommended that Chace be encouraged to attend some form of grief counseling, as well as begin treatment for post-traumatic stress.

Sincerely,

E. Callard, M.D.

Attachments

CHAPTER 7

**Lancashire—Barnoldswick,
Residence of Wallace, Valerie**

14 February, 1414 Hours GMT

She was changing Tamsin when the call came, her daughter screaming in protest at either the discomfort or the indignity of it all, and
Chace felt again the incredible frustration of trying to use reason
on someone who has no use, nor need, of such things.

It didn't matter that Tamsin's struggling made the whole procedure take five times as long as it should have; it didn't matter that
what Chace was trying to do, for God's sake, was to help the little
noisemaker. No, Tamsin didn't want to be on her back on the changing table and she didn't want to be put in a nappy and she was damn
certain it was her right, her obligation, even, to make sure that
everyone from Weets Moor to the town square knew it.

The telephone, then, with its jangling bell, was just insult added
to injury, and Chace heard it, acknowledged it, and then discarded
the information just as quickly, because she was certain the call
wouldn't be—couldn't be—for her. No one called Valerie Wallace
to speak to Tara Chace. Not on Valentine's Day, or on any other
day for that matter.

It wasn't that Chace hadn't tried to fit in with town life. She
had, she truly had. She'd attended the church services and the teas

and the social get-togethers, she'd worn the stoic face and said all the right things, as much as for Valerie's peace of mind as her own. And it wasn't that people were unkind, certainly not once Valerie had explained that Chace's baby was her grandchild, that her son had died before he'd even learned that Tara was pregnant. That particular tragedy had earned her a unique respect, even, with Valerie's friends and neighbors clucking in placid concern.

"Eeee, the poor dear, having to raise the wee thing alone."

"Ooo, all alone, but it's good she's come back here, raise the child right."

"Oh yes, raise a good Lancashire girl, among her own people."

And so on, and on, and ever on.

But there was a pity to it as well, and Chace couldn't stomach that. She didn't want to be pitied, nor did she wish to become prey to self-pity, and so she had come to avoid people, describing an orbit to her life that included Tamsin and Valerie, and not much more. When she went out, she went out pushing the pram, walking alone. She carried out her business around town with the barest of interactions, the most minimal of required pleasantries. She avoided conversation and contact; she steered clear of people when she saw them coming.

She was that poor girl who'd lost her baby's father. A little distant, a little odd, not unpleasant, but best to leave her alone for now, you know how it is. She'll speak when she's ready, when her daughter's out and about, the wee thing will lead the mother back into the world, and the mother will follow, to be sure. Just you wait and see.

When Valerie stuck her head into the bedroom, then, as Chace was snapping Tamsin back into her clothes, she'd already forgotten that the telephone had rung at all.

"It's for you, Tara," Valerie said.

"What is? Dammit, Tam, stop fidgeting!"

"The phone, dear. I'll take Tam, you go and answer it."

Chace looked at Valerie with a mixture of confusion and suspicion, hoisting Tamsin to her shoulder, stroking her daughter's hair. It was coming in faster now, soft as silk and so blond as to be almost white, and whenever Chace found her patience running short with her daughter, she would stroke Tamsin's hair, amazed by the feel of it, always surprised by the way her baby would nestle against her in response.

"I'm not making it up, dear, it really is for you," Valerie said again, almost laughing at her expression.

"Who?"

"Didn't get his name. But he asked for you straightaway, quite polite."

Chace frowned, and Tamsin shifted, responding to the tension suddenly coming from her mother, pushing her face against her shoulder with a soft whimper. If it had been Poole calling, he'd have said as much, and Valerie would have shared it. So it wasn't Poole on the phone, and there was only one other person Chace could think of who knew where to find her.

"Shall I tell him to ring again later?"

Chace shook her head, then reluctantly handed Tamsin over to Valerie. The baby resisted, taking hold of Chace's hair, and she had to free her daughter's fingers before she could slip out of the room down the narrow flight of stairs back to the ground floor, to the telephone in the hall. Behind and above, she heard Tamsin cry again, then go quiet.

Chace picked up the handset and said, "What do you want?"

"I'm in Colne," Crocker said. "I'll be there in fifteen minutes. You can meet me outside."

"I don't want to meet you at all."

"Fifteen minutes," Crocker repeated, and hung up.

Chace replaced the handset in its cradle, slowly, then stared at the phone for several seconds, thinking.

From the top of the stairs, Valerie asked, "Who was that, Tara?"

"Nobody," Chace said, and then added, "I have to go out for a while."

Valerie adjusted her grip on the baby, repositioning her at her hip, fixing Chace with a stare from above, her expression draining, the corners of her mouth tightening. It had been well over a year now that Chace had shared her home, and in that time they'd talked about Tom only a little, and about the work they'd done together even less. But Valerie Wallace wasn't stupid, and Chace was certain she'd long ago deduced at least the broad strokes of the job Chace had shared with her son, if not the specifics.

"You go on," Valerie told her. "We'll be fine here without you for a while."

Crocker surprised her, not because he was on time, but because he was driving a red Volvo wagon, and the car was at least ten years old. She didn't know why, but it seemed an absurd choice for him, and as she climbed into the front passenger seat beside him, she told him as much.

"It's my wife's," Crocker replied. "We're going someplace we can talk. Where's someplace we can talk?"

"The Yorkshire Dales aren't too terribly far," Chace responded, belting herself in. "Though I'm not certain you want to take me anyplace away from witnesses."

"You're going to murder me?"

"I haven't decided yet, to tell the truth."

"Then let's hope what I have to say doesn't push you over the edge," Crocker said.

Crocker waited until he'd found his way onto the Skipton Road before speaking.

"You think I sent you to Iraq knowing you were knocked up."

"You did send me to Iraq knowing I was knocked up," Chace retorted.

Crocker shook his head, flicking the indicator, turning onto one of the narrower lanes. It was a clear day, cold, windy, and out the car windows Chace could see the rolling Lancashire hills, the beautiful houses and the winter-stripped trees, smoke rising from occasional chimneys. The heat was on in the Volvo, the hot, dry air blowing hard from the vents, and both of them had to raise their voices to be sure they were heard.

"When I got to the Farm, I was given a complete workup," Chace said after another mile. "A complete workup, and that included a fucking blood draw."

"And the blood work showed you were pregnant," Crocker confirmed.

"Yes," Chace said, emphatic. He'd made her point.

"I didn't see the results until after you'd come back from Red Panda."

"That's the best you can come up with? You had the entire drive up from London, and that's the best lie you could come up with?"

"Which should tell you that I'm not lying at all."

"Or that you don't think terribly highly of me."

"If that were the case, I wouldn't have made the drive in the first place."

Crocker signaled again, turning them onto an alarmingly narrow strip of road that curled along one of the hillsides. Dry stone walls bordered the way on both sides, and Chace wondered what Crocker would do if they encountered an oncoming car.

"Do you really believe that I'm that much of a bastard?" Crocker asked. "That I'd not only keep that information from you, but then put you into harm's way besides?"

"Yes," she answered immediately.

"Well, at least we're being honest with each other."

"It wasn't always that way, Paul," Chace said. "Don't misunderstand. I mean, I always knew you were a bastard, from the moment you brought me into the Section. But I believed you were, at least, our bastard. That was the rule, wasn't it? D-Ops says 'frog' and the Minders jump, never mind how high, all with the understanding that you'll be there to catch us when we come down. That was the agreement. You broke the trust, and Tom died for it."

Crocker shook his head angrily. "No, that one's not mine. I have more than my share of ghosts, but Tom Wallace is not one of them. He is not one of them, and I won't let you put that blame on me. You brought him into it, not me. You went to Tom for help, not me."

"Of course I went to Tom for help! What else was I supposed to do? You'd fucking abandoned me! You were supposed to protect me, damn you!"

"I did! For God's sake, I did everything in my power to keep you safe!"

"Safe? You were going to sell me to the Saudis!"

"It wasn't me!"

A blue Ford, a squat and square little car, came around the bend ahead of them, and Crocker braked hard, turning the wheel, and Chace heard the tires on the Volvo leave the tarmac, felt the vehicle vibrate as it slid onto gravel. The Ford passed by, hitting its horn, and Chace winced in expectation of the inevitable sound of scraping metal, but it never came.

"It wasn't me," Crocker insisted.

She ended up giving him directions around Pendleside, through Foulridge and then the villages of Blacko and Roughlee, finally pointing him to Newchurch-in-Pendle. Crocker parked them on a steep incline, and they walked uphill another hundred meters or so, to the Church of St. Mary. Chace opened the gate, descended onto the grounds, surrounded by ancient gravestones and slabs. The first recorded construction on the site dated back to 1250, though the current building, a small stone nave and chapel with a squat tower, was most likely built four centuries later. The church and its grounds served as a minor tourist attraction, purportedly linked to the infamous Pendle Witches. Nine women had been hanged in 1612, and one had died in her prison cell. Two of the dead were said to be buried in the yard. Chace suspected it was utter nonsense; the women in question had both been convicted of witchcraft, and, thus declared to be in league with devil, would never have been interred on holy ground.

Etched into the stone tower was a small, odd oval. Called the Eye of God, it was said to have been added as a ward against the witches who had once roamed the nearby hills. Now it overlooked the steps down from the road, the trees, and the distant Forest of Trawden, part of the larger Forest of Pendle.

Chace walked down past the church, finally stopping on the grass beside one of the weathered grave slabs. The wind snapped at her coat and trousers, making the temperature feel even colder. From behind her came the ring of Crocker's lighter opening, closing, and the scent of his tobacco whipped past her, torn through the air in the wind. She'd given up smoking as soon as she'd learned she was pregnant, just as she had given up alcohol, and it pleased her to discover that the proximity of Crocker's cigarettes failed to entice. She'd had a few drinks since Tamsin had been born, wine at dinner, whiskey on occasion, but thus far, that was the only vice of hers to have returned home.

"There's a job," Crocker said.

"I don't want a job. I have a job, I'm Tamsin's mother." She turned, looking up the slope at him, her expression daring him to call her a liar.

Crocker squinted past her, into the wind, into the distance, and decided to continue as if he hadn't heard. "It's in Uzbekistan, and it needs to happen soon, within the week. Have you been following the news?"

Chace refused to answer.

"You know the strategic importance," Crocker said. "You know that Uzbekistan is considered a crucial ally. The Americans have been using the country as a staging ground for their operations, working with the Uzbeks to gather intelligence on al-Qaeda, on what's happening in northern Afghanistan. They've built air bases, put troops on the ground, all manner of infrastructure and support for personnel and operations.

"You know the human rights angle. What happened with Ambassador McInnes."

She simply stared at him, trying to resist his attempt to draw her in. Robert McInnes had been the U.K.'s Ambassador to Uzbekistan, recalled in late 2004 because of his insistence on publicizing Uzbekistan's appalling record on human rights. He'd made the papers, in particular the *Guardian,* with his descriptions of the NSS' use of torture. McInnes had openly condemned both the U.K. and the U.S. for its tacit complicity in such crimes.

It had stuck in Chace's memory because, among his targets, McInnes had pointed a finger directly at SIS, accusing the Firm of profiting from the questionable intelligence gained from these torture sessions. McInnes had been recalled to London following his final outburst and forced out of the Foreign Service within a week of his return home. The last she'd read, the former Ambassador had retained an attorney and was planning on suing the Government.

"President Malikov is not long for this world, Tara," Crocker said. "The old man's got two kids, and it's anyone's guess which one of them will take over when he goes. There's a daughter—"

"Sevara Mihailovna Malikov-Ganiev." She shook her head, angry that she'd taken the bait, unsure whether or not he was testing her, or if he was expecting a faulty memory. Whichever, it was galling. "The son's name is Ruslam Mihailovich Malikov."

"Ruslan Mihailovich," Crocker corrected. "Roughly four days ago, Ruslan's wife was arrested, tortured, and murdered, most likely by the NSS, possibly by Sevara's agents. We think Ruslan may be next on Sevara's hit list, that she's preparing to clear the way for a run at her father's position."

"Ruslan should probably leave, then."

"Yes, well, what you don't know is that Ruslan Mihailovich also has a two-year-old son, Stepan Ruslanovich."

Chace folded her arms across her chest. "So he should take the boy with him."

"Your job is to get them out of the country," Crocker said. "Both of them. Get them out, and bring them safely back to England."

She stared at him.

"We've been told that Ruslan is pro-West, that he's a reformer in the making. If you can confirm that as well, so much the better. We get him here, we can discuss the viability of a coup, either against his father or against his sister, whomever, depending on the situation. Since you'll already have a working relationship with Ruslan, you'll be expected to help facilitate and implement that also."

Chace continued to stare at him.

Crocker drew a last time from his cigarette, then dropped the butt, watching as the cinder died in the wet grass. From inside his overcoat he withdrew a large gray envelope, creased lengthwise from where he'd carried it, folded, in an inside pocket. He held the envelope out to Chace, who made no move to take it.

"There's one hundred and fifty thousand pounds in an account at HSBC," Crocker said. "It should cover expenses for the operation, anything that might arise. I've included contact protocols as well; you're to report directly to me on this, and not through official channels. The documents enclosed, and the account, are in the name of Carlisle, Tracy Elizabeth, the same identity you used during Dandelion, you remember."

"You're recycling a cover?" She looked at him, now even more suspicious.

"There's no reason to believe it was compromised. It's still current, all the paper, right up to the passport."

"It was used. That's what compromises it."

"Would you take the damn envelope, please?"

"I don't want the envelope, Paul. I don't want what's inside it. I don't want the job."

Crocker lowered his hand, the wind catching the envelope in his grip, bending it skyward, as if trying to make it into a kite. Chace saw his eyes flick along the fence that bordered the lane, as paranoid as she was that they might be observed. Somewhere, from farther below on the hillside, they heard a child's laughter.

"There's nobody else," he said. "It has to be you."

"There should be three others else," Chace responded. "Unless you've managed to kill all of them, too, and as I saw Nicky only Sunday last, you'd have been working damn quick at it."

"I can't use the Minders."

"Go to Cheng."

"Cheng's in Washington, and that's beside the point. I've been asked to keep the involved parties to a minimum."

"How minimum?"

"Barclay and the CIA are not included on the distribution list, shall we say."

A gust caught her hair, sent strands across her eyes, and Chace pushed them clear with her finger, tucking the strays back behind her ear. "So it's unsanctioned. You're trying to sell me an unsanctioned lift from a hostile theater, and you want me to do it without alerting either our people or the Americans."

"Ideally. Though I'm told there's the possibility of limited American support once you're on the ground in Tashkent. What form that support will take, I can't say."

"You're out of your mind."

"It's not unsanctioned, it's unofficial. I have permission for the operation, just not through the traditional channels."

"How high?"

"I can't say."

"Intelligence and Security Committee? FCO? Cabinet level? Ministerial?"

"I can't say, Tara."

"But you're telling me that you've secured approval at either C's level or higher, is that it?"

"Yes."

"You understand why I ask, don't you? Because I'd hate to take a job only to discover that I'm going to be sold out again upon completion. Once was enough for me, you understand."

She saw Crocker's mouth twist slightly, his approximation of a smile.

"I didn't say I'd do it, Paul," she warned. "Don't get excited."

"You want to do it."

"So I can become Whitehall's bitch again? No, thank you."

"I'll protect you."

"You did it so well last time."

"I'll protect you," Crocker repeated, more insistent. "You do the job, I'll bring you home, Tara. You'll be Minder One again, you'll be Head of Section again, back where you belong. Where you should be right now."

"I should be back in Barlick right now, with Tamsin."

"I hope you're convincing yourself with that line, because you're sure as hell not convincing me."

"Don't tell me—"

"This isn't about love," Crocker interrupted. "Of course you love her, you're her mother. But you're dying by inches out here. You hate it, and you hate yourself for wishing you were back in London, and back on the job. But you *need* to be back on the job, and we both know it, so perhaps it's time you stopped pretending."

Chace shook her head again.

"I know, Tara." He lowered his voice, speaking more slowly, picking the words more carefully. "I understand, I really do. I was Minder One with a wife and two children; trust me, I know. You're not abandoning her, you're not betraying her."

Chace swallowed, turned away. To the northeast, clouds were sweeping in over the summit of the hill, dragging a curtain of rain along with them.

"She's not even a year old."

"She'll be all right."

Chace heard the rustle of Crocker's coat, knew that he was offering her the envelope again, could imagine the contents. The papers and the passport, the file photos of Ruslam—correction, Ruslan—Mihailovich Malikov and his two-year-old son. Maybe a map, certainly a two- or three-page briefing paper, culled from the Intelligence Directorate, of what to expect from Uzbekistan, from Tashkent. Options and suggestions and Tracy Elizabeth Carlisle, a nice single girl from Oxfordshire who was quite possibly already known to the world as a tissue of lies.

"She'll be fine, Tara," Crocker said. "And so will you."

"I was right," Chace said. "You are a bastard."

She took the envelope.

Preoperational Background
Zahidov, Ahtam Semyonovich

So the Old Man was finally dying, and the irony was, of course, that now was not the time. Had his body chosen to begin failing him even six months earlier, things would have been different, before Ruslan's self-righteous cunt of a wife had started playing at spy. But no, as much as President Mihail Malikov walked and talked and spoke and dressed as a post-Soviet statesman, he had the heart and soul of an old Communist bastard, the kind who would go on living out of sheer will, out of sheer spite, refusing death with pure outrage born of the unthinkable. Death, in the final estimation, was the ultimate relinquishment of all the power Mihail Malikov had spent a lifetime greedily accumulating.

But death didn't really give a damn, and the President's third heart attack in as many years made that abundantly clear. Death was coming for Mihail Malikov, and when it claimed him, then all hell would break loose.

Unless Zahidov could get the pieces in place. Unless he and Sevara could make not only the President but the DPMs and the Americans see the benefits to an orderly succession. And if Sevara could convince her father to state, publicly, that she must assume control in the event of his passing, the battle would be all but won before it started.

The appropriate gestures would have to be made, of course, but nothing out of the ordinary, nothing that hadn't been done before in one fashion or another. Sevara's assumption of power would have to be accompanied by the requisite statements of regret and humility, and the immediate declaration that she would call for a general election at the end of her term, the term that she completed now only at her father's specific behest. They most likely would have an election, too, to appease the Americans and the British, but that was no matter. Like the two elections President Malikov had won already, this, too, would be a formality.

This time, Zahidov mused, perhaps they would give Sevara a little less of the vote. The last time President Malikov had run, he'd "won" office with over ninety-six percent of the vote in his favor, and that after having outlawed the opposition parties.

Sometimes, Zahidov wondered why the President hadn't just claimed ninety-nine percent of the vote. If he was going to be that obvious, what was another three percent? Or even four?

If Sevara won with, say, sixty-five percent, that would be more than enough. And if they arranged it right, it might even look moderately legitimate, too.

So that was the first part, getting the President aboard, and Ahtam Zahidov had to admit that his handling of Dina Malikov had gone a good distance toward bringing that to pass. It had been tricky to negotiate, and Sevara had warned him as much.

"One thing to remove an extremist," she'd told him, watching Zahidov as he dressed at the foot of her bed. "Another thing entirely to kill the mother of his only grandchild."

"You should have children," Zahidov had responded. "Show him that his dynasty can spring from you as easily as from your brother."

"That would require Deniska's cock. Which, unfortunately, would also require the rest of him."

"Put a bag over his head."

Sevara had laughed at the thought, then pulled back the bedsheet and come toward him on her hands and knees. Zahidov had
stopped dressing, watching her approach, drinking in the sight of
her. Sevara Malikov-Ganiev would have been beautiful even if she
didn't work at it, even if she didn't use spas and personal trainers
and stylists. Under the warm light of the chandelier her skin
seemed lustrous, her hair as rich a red as the petals on a rose, her
eyes shining. They'd made love twice already, and watching her
coming toward him, the smile playing at her mouth, her tongue
touching her lower lip, he wanted her again.

When she reached him, he took her in his arms, fastened his
mouth to hers, kissing her with all the passion, all the love he had,
feeling each returned. She touched his cheek when their lips
parted, stroked a lacquered nail over his mouth.

"Our children," she'd promised. "Our dynasty. In time."

"In time," he'd echoed. After she was President, when Malikov
was gone, and beyond caring about things like marriage and divorce and paternity.

She was his biggest weakness, and each of them knew it. It gave
Zahidov shallow comfort to know that he was hers, too.

Sex was so easy to come by at the worst of times, and in
Uzbekistan even the lowest official could slake that thirst. But
whores did nothing for Zahidov, no matter how beautiful, how
willing, how young, how expensive. Even the rape of Ruslan's
wife had done nothing for him; it was just another method of interrogation, a way to break the bitch's will, to demonstrate his absolute power over her. In truth, he wouldn't have even bothered,
instead leaving it to two or three of his men to have their way
with her.

But Dina had threatened Sevara, and that had angered Zahidov.
More, Dina had feared him, and so Zahidov had felt it was important that he take her, just to set the proper direction to the interrogation.

When he'd brought the video of the interrogation to Sevara, she asked him to stay and watch it with her. It had aroused her, and that had in turn aroused him. She'd taken him then and there, in her husband's office at the Interior Ministry, bending over the desk, looking back at him over her shoulder.

"Like Dina," Sevara had commanded.

It wasn't as if the Americans didn't know how business was done in Uzbekistan, the same way it hadn't bothered anyone—at least, not anyone who mattered—when Ambassador McInnes had gone weeping and wailing to the press. Certainly, President Malikov had felt the displeasure from each country, had felt the pressure to loosen his grip, but in the end, everyone involved understood the stakes. There was a war on, after all, a Global War on Terror, a conflict that now raged around the world, and one that required new rules. The Coalition might not approve of how the NSS acquired its intelligence, but disapproval didn't stop the FBI or the CIA or the SIS from using it all the same.

But McInnes, and Dina, and now that new American Ambassador, Garret—they could make things difficult for President Malikov. Every time a tape was released, every time a new report of so-called human rights abuses was filed, the pressure built and kept building until someone, either U.S. or U.K., decided something had to be done. If not to actually redress the perceived problem, to at least appear to be doing so.

This redress took the form of sanctions, more often than not, and that, in turn, meant the withholding of promised aid. In the last four years alone, the U.S. had held back over fifty million dollars in promised funds, all in the name of encouraging President Malikov to improve his record on human rights. The hypocrisy of it made Zahidov want to spit. As if the Americans weren't just the same, as if the British weren't just the same. Abu Ghraib and Camp X-Ray and countless other facilities, Zahidov was certain they were all the same. But when someone pointed a finger at America or at Britain, who sanctioned them?

Just like the rape of Dina Malikov, it was an exercise in power, nothing more.

In the end, the money would come again. Uzbekistan was just too important to the war.

And everyone knew it.

But that didn't keep President Malikov's ego from being bruised each time he was pilloried in the eyes of the world. When the Old Man saw the proof that it was Dina Malikov who had been responsible for the latest round of editorials, angry letters, and sanctions, when he heard her talking about just how much she had given the Americans, it made the loss of his grandson's mother that much easier to bear.

It was a small thing, then, to suggest that perhaps his son had known all along what his wife was doing. That he had perhaps if not encouraged it, certainly permitted it. And if Ruslan had encouraged it, well, the reasons behind such treachery were easy enough to see.

Sevara, the dutiful daughter, devoted to her father, found it hard to say the words.

"He wishes to replace you, Father."

If only it were that simple, and that easy. But Zahidov knew from experience that Mihail Malikov wasn't a fool. The Old Man wouldn't have survived for this long if he were. He knew the ulterior motives in bringing this incident to his attention. He knew that Sevara coveted his power just as greedily as Ruslan did.

It would take more than simple suspicion to fix the ascension.

But this was a start, Zahidov had to admit, and a strong one. Before Dina's confession, Ruslan had been the clear choice, his father's favorite, and male, to boot.

Now, at least, Sevara stood a chance at gaining her father's blessing.

The rest, Zahidov was certain, would come in time.

President Malikov was the first part. The second, more easily handled in a fashion Zahidov preferred, were the Deputy Prime Ministers of the various and sundry offices who held power throughout the country. If they opposed Sevara's ascension, it would make things difficult.

Fortunately, there were three easy ways to deal with the DPMs. Threats, which, Zahidov knew from experience, worked remarkably well when properly delivered. These could be delivered by himself or by his agents. He preferred video for this tactic, because he felt the moving image provided much more immediacy, and thus a greater sense of peril. Played for a recalcitrant DPM in a darkened room, two or three minutes of footage showing a loved one, spouse or lover or child, as the person went about his or her daily business, oblivious, could be all it took. If more pressure was needed, some physical evidence, perhaps, a particular piece of jewelry, or— Zahidov found this particularly effective if there was a romantic attachment—an undergarment of some sort. Presented to make the point perfectly clear: see how close we can get, see how you cannot protect your son/daughter/wife/mother/lover/friend.

It was not the first choice, but should it be required, he had no doubt of its efficacy.

The second option was money, of course, and this was likely to be the most successful tactic. President Malikov had, for obvious reasons, filled the posts of the DPMs with men of like mind, and thus, like the President, their greed was abundant. Payoffs in cash, transfers to Swiss or Cayman Islands bank accounts, these things could be easily arranged, and Sevara had the money to spare. This would not be a wasted expenditure for her, but rather an investment on future gains. In the last two years alone, she had cleared something in the neighborhood of three hundred million dollars American by using the Interior Ministry to facilitate the transport of heroin from Afghanistan into the ever-hungry veins of Moscow.

The poppy had returned with a vengeance with the fall of the *taleban* to the south, and all that was needed was a way to bring it to market. Uzbekistan, with its unique position bordering no less than five other countries, was an ideal transfer point. Unlike her father, Sevara had no qualms about moving the drugs through the country, and Zahidov had no doubt she would continue to work with the drug lords in Afghanistan when her ascension came to pass.

There was but one rule when dealing with the heroin, and it was inviolate, and Zahidov himself had proposed it to Sevara, who instantly saw the wisdom in it. The rule was this: heroin could enter Uzbekistan, and it could leave Uzbekistan, but it could never be sold in Uzbekistan. This was done for no reason associated with the health and well-being of the Uzbeks, but rather out of sheer self-preservation and protection. Should the heroin find its way into the arms of the American soldiers stationed in the country, the Americans would respond with a vengeance, a headache Sevara most certainly didn't want, or for that matter, need.

Which, in its way, brought about the third method of dealing with the DPMs. This was by far the most cost effective, and the most efficient, but also the hardest to achieve.

If the Americans supported Sevara Malikov-Ganiev as the next President of Uzbekistan, the DPMs would fall into line like eager soldiers on a parade ground. If the White House backed Sevara, that would be all it took.

If.

This was why, on the morning of February, Ahtam Zahidov found the surveillance report he was reading so very alarming. After demanding why it had taken four days—four days!—for it to reach him, he had the officer responsible for the report brought in to speak with him. It took another forty-seven minutes to locate the man, but only three minutes after that to get a positive identification from a photograph.

Concerned, Zahidov left his office in the Ministry of the Interior on Yunus Rajabiy, quickly making his way across town to the Oily Majlis, the Parliament Building, on the west side of Alisher Navoi National Park, named after the famed Uzbek humanist and artist who had died over five hundred years ago. It took Zahidov another twenty minutes of searching before he found Sevara, locked in a meeting with the State Customs Committee. He interrupted, knocking twice on the conference room door before entering, and Sevara, seated at the head of the table, her papers around her, an aide standing to the side, turned sharply at the unprecedented interruption.

When she saw it was him, though, she smiled, and despite the message he was bearing, the smile lifted him as well.

"Excuse me, please," Sevara said, and rose from the table, the committee members all sliding their seats back in response, getting to their feet. "No, sit—we'll continue in just a moment."

Zahidov held the door for her as she stepped past, into the corridor. The carpet had been replaced recently, a deep blood-red color, still new enough that it gave slightly beneath his feet. When she was out and beside him, he put a hand on her elbow, taking her another few feet down the hall, making certain they would not be overheard.

"Ahtam? What is it?" The concern in her expression and her voice made it clear her first thought was for him.

"Ruslan is reaching out to the Americans."

The concern on Sevara's face dissipated, replaced by a sharper intensity. "How do you know this?"

"He had an automobile accident on Saturday, and it wasn't an accident. He nearly ran over one of the men from the American Mission."

Her brow creased. "The same man?"

Zahidov nodded. "Charles Riess."

"They spoke?"

"According to my man's report, not more than a few words. But I am certain it was no accident, not the day after his wife's body was found."

"You think he passed a message?"

"He must have."

Sevara made a noise, sucking on her lower lip for a moment as she thought, and Zahidov cursed himself silently, because it made him desire her there and then, even with this problem, even with what it could mean for them. She seemed to know it, too, because she met his eyes, and her smile was sudden and pleased.

"You look so worried, Ahtam. But my brother's given us just what we need. We bring proof that he's trying to move things along with the Americans to my father, my position will be secured."

"Unless he's gone to the Americans to secure his own position."

"With what? What does he have?"

"He won't need much if the Americans support him."

Her smile faded as she considered his response. "You're still watching him?"

"Three men. They're old KGB, so they know what they're doing."

"Dina was one thing," Sevara said softly, and he could tell from her tone that she was still thinking, albeit aloud. "My father could accept that. But removing Ruslan . . . that would be much harder."

"Not that much harder."

"No?"

"Not if the extremists set off another bomb in the marketplace."

"Something to consider."

"I can arrange it."

She shook her head. "No, not yet."

"Sevya," Zahidov said, using the diminutive of her name, "if Ruslan gains the support of the White House, we will not be able to oppose him."

"But he can't have it yet, and he has nothing to offer them but his good word. And the Americans no longer support rulers on the basis of the promises they make, alone. If Ruslan wants their support, it will take time to arrange it."

"And while he is arranging his support?"

"We arrange ours." She paused. "You deal with the Embassy, the CIA. Talk to your contact, make sure he knows how well I can fill my father's shoes. Make it clear that we are the other option, that Ruslan is only one choice."

"And if, having done that, the Americans decide they prefer your brother?"

Sevara shrugged, then pushed up on her toes, to brush Zahidov's cheek with her lips.

"Then you can have your bomb," she said, and returned to her meeting.

CHAPTER 8

15 February, 1553 Hours GMT

It turned out that Crocker wasn't a total bastard, in that, aside from the documents and the account at HSBC, he'd also been kind enough to kick-start the op by providing Chace with the name of a pilot, one Geoffrey Porter, and contact information for the same. The background on Porter that he'd included in the envelope had been terse but serviceable, and Chace supposed it was Crocker's way of trying to prove himself to her, this token offering, as if he was saying, *Yes, I screwed you once, but this time, you see, I'm giving you an escape route up front.*

Getting into Uzbekistan, into Tashkent, wasn't going to be the hard part. There were regular commercial flights, and if Tracy Carlisle couldn't get Chace that far, then the identity was absolutely of no use whatsoever. Getting in, then, that wasn't the problem.

Getting out again, with a grieving widower and his two-year-old son and God only knew who in hot pursuit, that was the trick. Chace had known the moment—the absolute *moment*—that Crocker had presented her with the op that the exfil would be the hardest part. It was some comfort that he'd anticipated it himself, and offered Geoffrey Porter as the solution.

They'd stayed in Newchurch for most of the afternoon, in the churchyard for another hour, then walking the narrow, steep streets of the little village, talking it over. Crocker had stressed—repeatedly—that Chace was to stay below the radar until she had Ruslan and son back in England. As to the method of extraction, he was leaving that to her discretion.

"Quiet?" Chace asked him. "Noisy? Do you even care?"

"If you can do it quiet, that's always preferable. But I doubt you'll have the luxury."

They returned to the Volvo just after four, as it began to rain, and he dropped her back in Barlick, two blocks from the house, at ten of five, telling her that he'd expect contact at completion of the op, once she was back in-country. Otherwise, there was to be no communication between them at all.

"Good luck," he said.

"There's a room in hell waiting for you, you know that, don't you?"

"It's a flat, actually," Crocker said. "The one below yours, I believe."

The Volvo pulled away, leaving Chace standing in the rain and the dark and the cold at the edge of the town square. She watched his taillights disappear around the bend, then turned and walked the three minutes to Val's house, letting herself in the back, through the kitchen, expecting to hear Tamsin screaming and Val trying to soothe the baby.

Instead, the house was quiet, Val sitting in the front room, looking out the window that overlooked her now-fallow garden. She had a cup of tea in her hand, and Chace could see the steam rising from it. She wondered how many Val had gone through already, how long she'd been waiting.

"Tam's sleeping," Val said without prompting.

"A minor miracle."

"She squawked for a bit after you left, then settled." Valerie

Wallace turned her head, rather than her body. There was a single lamp burning in the corner past her shoulder, and the light gave the older woman's skin a warm glow, turned the silver in her hair to bronze, and made the lines of worry on her face seem more like canyons than valleys.

"When do you leave?" Val asked.

Chace hesitated. "First thing in the morning."

"Is it what you did before? What you and my Tom did, is that it?"

Chace shook her head.

"I'm not asking for particulars. I know it's government work—I know that, I'm not daft—and I know it's secret as well. I'm asking if it's the same work, that's all I'm asking."

"I can't say, Val."

Val made a soft clucking noise and turned back to look out at her dead garden, raising her cup of tea.

"I shouldn't be gone too long. One week, maybe two, at the most."

"Was this the plan, then, Tara?" Val asked without looking at her. "You'd come to me and have the baby, and when the time was right and all of that, you'd just go back and leave me to care for my granddaughter? Was this the plan all along?"

"God, no, Val! Never, not at all." Chace crouched, dropping onto her haunches, extending one hand, first to touch Val's own, and then, thinking better of it, feeling guilty, settling for the chair's armrest. "Please don't think that. Please don't."

"I don't know what to think, Tara."

"It's something I have to do, that's all it is. Then I'll return."

"Is it the same work, Tara?"

She needed a second before answering. "Yes, it's the same work."

"Then you can't really promise that you'll be coming back, can you, dear?" Val turned then and looked down at her, and the canyons had eroded, smoothed, and her expression now was the same open, understanding look she'd worn almost two years before, when she'd found Chace tongue-tied and terrified on her front doorstep. "I mean, really, you can't promise that at all, I know that much. Let's be honest about that, at least."

Chace tried to find something to say, some way to answer that wasn't a lie, wasn't more of a lie than the ones she'd already made, but couldn't. In the old house, listening to the rainfall outside, the creak of the radiator in the hall, in the warmth and the darkness, there was only the truth of what Val was saying, and the guilt that came with it. That, and the emotion of the day, the impotent anger and the regret and the hurt, and again, the guilt, all of it now swelling in her chest like some cancer.

She started to cry.

After a moment, Valerie Wallace put her hand in Chace's hair, and Chace rested her face against the older woman's leg, and she sobbed and she sobbed, and upstairs, in her crib, Tamsin, too, began to cry.

She'd called Geoffrey Porter from the train station in Leeds the next morning, and after two rings the phone was answered by a woman with an American accent, somewhere from the South.

"I'm trying to reach Geoffrey Porter," Chace said.

"Just a moment," the woman said, and then Chace heard her muffled shout, and there was more rustling, and then Porter came on the line.

"Can I help you?"

"My name's Carlisle," Chace said. "You've been recommended to me for a charter."

"Recommended? By whom?"

"Someone who knew you in Sandline."

She heard Porter's hesitation over the line at the mention of the company. "Sandline folded."

"Yes, I am aware of that."

"What kind of charter are we talking about?"

"I'd rather not give particulars over the phone. Would it be possible to meet? This afternoon, perhaps?"

"Could do, I suppose. You know the Cittie of Yorke? It's a pub, on High Holborn."

"I can find it."

"I'll be in the main room at sixteen hundred, the one with all the wine butts on the scaffolding, the bloody things look like they're going to tumble down on you. I'll be at the back."

"How will I recognize you?"

"Ask your friend from Sandline," Porter said, and hung up.

There'd been a pub of one sort or another at 22 High Holborn since 1430, though it had obviously seen several changes over the centuries. One of its later incarnations had been as a coffee shop in the late 1690s, and a partial demolition and renovation in the late 1890s had somehow managed to preserve elements of the original façade. Within, the main room was more evocative of a church than a pub, with high ceilings and an oddly shaped stove positioned in the center of the floor to provide heating, something it apparently managed to do without the aid of any obvious chimney. A long bar ran along the left-hand side upon entry, and above it, positioned on scaffolding, were several wine butts, each of them easily capable of holding up to one thousand gallons at a time.

At seven minutes to four in the afternoon, the pub was experiencing the calm before the storm. In just over an hour, solicitors and attorneys and their clients would pour from the nearby Criminal Courts, to fill the pub and wash down the remains of the day with Samuel Smith's selection of beers. But for now, as Chace entered, it was quiet and warm, and she thought it was the kind of pub she'd probably have wanted to spend a lot of time in, once upon a time.

Chace stopped at the bar, ordered a lager, and adjusted the strap on her shoulder bag as she looked around the room, waiting for her drink to arrive. She counted a baker's dozen of patrons, nine of them men, and seated at one of the cloisterlike tables, she saw a man who was most likely named Geoffrey Porter, nursing a pint of his own. He was slight, and shorter than she'd imagined, though it was difficult to be certain with him seated. His hair was straight, brown, receding slightly, and he sported a neatly trimmed beard and mustache, wearing a black leather jacket over a black T-shirt. He caught her looking, met her stare for a fraction, then went back to peering into his drink. Chace didn't mind that he'd made her, because his reaction confirmed it. She'd found her pilot.

She paid for her lager, took the pint, and settled at the table opposite him, shrugging the bag off her shoulder onto the bench beside her.

"Mr. Porter?" she asked. "Tracy Carlisle."

"Suppose if I didn't want you to find me, I'd have worn a suit, hmm?"

"It would have been a start, yes."

Porter nodded slowly, looking her over. A pack of cigarettes rested on the table beside an enormous ashtray, and Porter's fingers idly traced a line around it.

"You know me from Sandline?"

"I know you through a man who knows you through Sandline," Chace said. "Though I understand you're running your own service now, International Charter Express?"

"ICE, yes. Not the same work."

"No. Fortunately, I'm not looking for a mercenary."

Porter didn't try to hide his scowl. "We weren't mercs. We weren't one of those 'civilian contractor' fly-by-nights, nor a bunch of washouts who got their kicks fondling SA-80s and playing at soldier, Ms. Carlisle. Sandline was a private military company. We were the real thing."

"I meant no offense," Chace said, as sincerely as she could manage, even though the slight had been intended, to gauge his reaction.

So far, she liked what she was seeing.

Porter ran his finger around the packet of cigarettes again, slower, looking at her, thoughtful. "So tell me about this charter."

"It's in Uzbekistan."

Porter nodded, his expression remaining neutral. "How many passengers?"

"Three, exfil only."

"Hot or cold?"

"Most likely hot."

"How hot? MANPAD hot?"

"I shouldn't think so, but it's a possibility."

"How much of a possibility?"

Chace shook her head, not so much refusing to answer as to indicate she was unwilling to hazard a guess. "You've flown under fire before."

"Iraq, Bosnia, Sierra Leone." Porter stopped playing with the pack long enough to free a cigarette and light it. "But if you know me through a man who knows me through Sandline, you know that, too."

Chace smiled.

"Where in Uzbekistan?"

"I don't know."

"I'm going to need some details. Tashkent?"

"Unlikely."

"Am I picking up at an airport, what?"

"No, it won't be an airport, of that I'm certain."

"So a helicopter."

"At the start, though I doubt one will get us back to England."

Porter shook his head, annoyed. "Perhaps you better just lay this out for me straight, and I'll tell *you* what we'll need. Unless you're a pilot yourself and have already worked out the particulars?"

"I've worked out some of them." Chace hefted her shoulder bag onto her lap, opening it. She removed a small pager, molded black plastic, and set it on the table between the cigarettes and the oversized and much-used ashtray. "It's a satellite pager. You flip down the faceplate, you'll find a little keyboard, it'll send messages as well as receive them. Today is the fifteenth. You turn it on as of the eighteenth, and it stays on until the twenty-fifth. That's the operational window. When I'm ready, I will page you with the GPS coordinates for the pickup, somewhere in Uzbekistan. You make the RV, take on myself and two other passengers, and bring us back to England."

"Not in a helo I won't."

"I'm not the pilot," Chace said. "I'll leave the particulars to you. Can you do it?"

Porter pulled again from his cigarette, then followed it with a pull from his pint, and Chace saw the sequence for what it was, buying time to think. He needn't have bothered; if he was the sort to agree to the job without considering the angles, he was the wrong sort for the job to begin with.

"If I don't hear from you by the twenty-fifth?"

"If you don't hear from me by the twenty-fifth, the job's off, and you can head home." Chace leaned forward slightly. "But I reserve the right to extend the window if necessary."

"And you'll contact me if that's the case."

"Of course."

Porter frowned, still thinking it over, looking past Chace at the rest of the pub. "What if I need to contact you?"

"You won't be able to."

"If it goes bad on my end?"

"I'm optimistic that it won't," Chace said. "You get the aircraft on station, you wait. I'm sure this isn't the first time you've done this kind of job, Mr. Porter."

"These passengers," Porter said, "I mean, aside from yourself. They're coming willingly?"

"I'm not certain how that's relevant."

"It's relevant to my fee."

"Give me a quote."

"Seventy-five thousand."

"We're talking pounds?"

"Do I look American to you?"

"Fifty."

"I have to cover expenses—most of it will go to the aircraft, Ms. Carlisle. I'll need a helicopter for the RV and the exfil. I'll need to have it maintained, ready, and fueled. I'll need to then fly you and your . . . guests to another location, where we'll need to switch to a private plane. I'll need that plane fueled, permitted, and ready as well, and I won't be able to sit on it if I'm at a make-ready station waiting for a go signal from you. It gets expensive. Can't do it for less than seventy."

"Sixty."

"We're not in a bloody *suq,* Ms. Carlisle. Seventy or you find another pilot."

Chace made a show of wrestling with the number, furrowing her brow. "Seventy, then. Half up front, half on completion."

"No, three-quarters up front, the rest on completion, and that's not counting my incidentals."

"For seventy, you can cover your own incidentals, Mr. Porter."

He crushed out his cigarette, drained the rest of the beer from his glass. "Deal."

"Give me the account information and I'll have the funds wired to you first thing tomorrow. How long will it take you to get to the theater, set up a staging position?"

"I can be in place and ready by the eighteenth, don't worry about that." Porter scooped up the package of cigarettes, dropped them into an inside pocket of his jacket, then produced a pen from the same pocket. He moved his empty glass, then flipped over the cardboard coaster it had been resting upon, and scribbled down a sequence of letters and numbers. Finished, he slid it across to Chace, taking hold of the pager on the return trip.

"I don't move until I confirm the funds have been deposited," he said, pocketing the pager.

"I wouldn't expect you to do otherwise."

Porter nodded curtly, then got to his feet, offering his hand.

Chace rose, and confirmed that he was, in fact, smaller than she'd expected, no more than five foot eight. His handshake was firm and businesslike, and she liked that he didn't muscle the grip, nor did he soften it because he was dealing with a woman.

"See you in Uzbekistan, then," Geoffrey Porter said.

CHAPTER 9

15 February, 1611 Hours GMT

When he'd left for Barnoldswick early the previous morning, the only person who knew where Crocker was going was Kate Cooke. He'd told her for two reasons, the first being that, should all hell break loose, she would know where to contact him; the second was that, as far as Crocker was concerned, Kate was almost as facile a liar as he was, and he needed her to cover for him. She wasn't as experienced at it as he was, but she played the part of a dutiful servant well, and if push came to shove, Crocker had great faith in her ability to look C in the eye, smile prettily, and say, "I honestly don't know, sir."

Which would ideally have been enough, except that when Crocker returned to the office on Wednesday morning, the first thing Kate told him was "C wanted to know where you were yesterday."

"What'd you tell him?"

"Simple wage slave, aren't I? I told him you'd had a family emergency."

Crocker looked at the memo in front of him, for the moment not seeing it. "Nothing more specific?"

"I thought it best to leave it vague, so you could fill in the details."

Crocker grunted. "Good."

Kate scooped up the pile of files Crocker had already vetted, then paused. "DC didn't know where you were, did she?"

"The only person who knew where I was yesterday was you, Kate." Crocker looked at her suspiciously. "Why?"

"Only it was C who asked where you were, not DC. I'd have thought it would come from the DC in the first instance, that she'd be the one doing the asking."

"Don't worry about it."

Kate shrugged. "Simple wage slave. Why should I worry?"

Crocker watched her leave his office, closing the door as she went, and again turned his attention to the memo open before him, then abandoned it, turning his chair to look out the window. It was triple-paned glass, coated on the outside so that, from the street, the windows took on a slight verdigris tinge. The spaces between the panes were filled with argon, to prevent eavesdropping through the use of directional laser microphones. The blinds themselves were similarly treated and lined with lead, to further deter surveillance. But through the slats in the blinds, there was just enough space to see, and from Crocker's office, if the weather permitted, he had a view across the Thames, to the Tate Britain. Farther north, blocked by the angle and intervening structures, stood Westminster Abbey and the Houses of Parliament, and then, continuing along, the offices of Whitehall, the land of Seccombe.

Kate was correct: it should have been Gordon-Palmer who'd been asking after Crocker, not C. As Deputy Chief, it was Gordon-Palmer's job, in part, to attend the day-to-day running of SIS, leaving Barclay free to deal with the more time-consuming and arguably more important work of liaising with the rest of HMG. That it had been C and not Gordon-Palmer who had come looking for him was troubling. It meant C was keeping the promised close eye on Crocker.

But that didn't explain why Barclay had come calling and not Gordon-Palmer. It was possible, Crocker supposed, that, occupied elsewhere in the building or Whitehall, Gordon-Palmer simply hadn't known that Crocker was away. Yet even as he considered it, he discarded the idea. It wasn't the kind of thing she was liable to miss.

The only answer to it that Crocker could see, in fact, was that Gordon-Palmer had known he was away, and had known why. And as it had been Gordon-Palmer who had pointed Crocker to Seccombe, the conclusion therefore was that, whatever game Sir Walter Seccombe, PUS at the FCO, was playing, Gordon-Palmer was playing it with him.

The intercom on his desk buzzed and Crocker reflexively reached back to the telephone, hitting the button without looking. "What?"

"Minder One to see you, sir," Kate said.

Crocker thought about refusing Fincher, telling him to return to the Pit, but it would simply postpone the inevitable. "Roll him in."

The intercom clicked off, and Crocker swiveled around in time to watch Kate open the door for Andrew Fincher. She withdrew silently, closing the door after her.

"Sir," Fincher said.

"Andrew." Crocker rifled through the stack in his inbox and pulled the Candlelight after-action from where he'd been keeping it at the bottom of the pile, holding it up to show to Fincher before dropping it once again. The file landed on his desk with a soft but significant slap. "Explain this."

Fincher hesitated, stiffening, as if coming to military attention. He stood five nine, average build, with ginger hair and the faded memory of freckles on his face, wearing the same dark blue Marks & Sparks suit he always wore to work. Crocker didn't hold that against him; at the wages the Minders earned, if Fincher owned more than three suits, Crocker would have been surprised. Today's shirt was ivory, the tie the same navy as his trousers.

"I'd been blown, sir," Fincher said. "When I approached as advance for the strike team, I noted activity at the site and several lights burning, as well as sentries posted, including one on the rooftop. I . . . I determined that the strike was not feasible at that time, and withdrew to Holding One to inform London of my recommendation that we abort—"

"I've yet to hear anything indicating that you'd actually been blown, Andrew," Crocker interrupted.

"Sir, as I state in my report, the sentries—"

"In which case you should have given the go signal immediately. Instead, you withdrew and further exposed yourself."

"If I had done so, sir, I would have remained in the open until the Strike Team arrived."

Crocker stood up, bathing Fincher in his glare. "Minder Two's after-action differs from yours."

"Respectfully, sir, Minder Two wasn't responsible for the recce."

"They had no reason to know we were coming. There should have been little to no resistance during the strike. As it was, the Strike Team encountered stiff resistance, and was forced to overcome it, with the result that local police responded to the firefight, and witnessed your withdrawal."

"I am aware of that, sir." Fincher wasn't looking at him, instead focusing past Crocker's shoulder, at the Chinese dragon print on the wall.

"You tipped them," Crocker said. "They made you on the withdrawal."

"Respectfully, sir—"

"You lost your nerve."

Fincher went silent, and from his expression, Crocker knew he was right, and that Fincher knew it as well.

"You're suspended from active duty at this time," Crocker told him. "Administrative duties only. You're expected to remain in the Pit in case I need you."

"I'm Head of the Special Section, sir."

"And for the time being, you can still call yourself that."

Crocker came around his desk, passing Fincher and heading for the door.

"Am I fired, sir?"

"If I had anyone to replace you with, Andrew, you would be." Crocker pulled open the door to the outer office, and from the corner of his eye saw Kate, at her desk, look immediately up. "Now get out of my sight."

Fincher remained motionless for a fraction longer, then nodded slightly. Crocker watched him go, waited until the door to the hall had shut again, then turned to head back into his office.

"Sir?" Kate said.

"What?" He put the glare he'd been using on Fincher on her.

"C wants you."

"Where were you yesterday?"

"Family emergency, sir. Ariel took a fall, broke her leg."

Barclay blinked at him, and Crocker could see him trying to penetrate the lie. It wouldn't be that difficult to verify, Crocker knew, but he doubted that Barclay would take the time to have his assistant call his home, to speak to Crocker's wife. Even if he did, it was covered. Crocker had told Jennie that, should anyone ask, Ariel had broken her leg in a bicycle accident the previous morning.

"I'm sorry to hear that," Barclay said, after a moment. "Your daughter will be all right?"

"We had a scare, sir, but she's enjoying the crutches for the moment."

"A ready means of sympathy."

"Exactly, sir."

Barclay nodded slightly, as if satisfying himself. Crocker waited, and after another second Barclay motioned to the chairs in front of the desk. It surprised Crocker. He'd expected to be dismissed, rather than invited to stay longer. He took the chair.

"There's been another MANPAD alert," Barclay said, after a second. "Coming out of Chechnya this time."

Crocker frowned. Man-portable air defense systems—MANPADs—stood in a place of pride at the top of the counterterror nightmare list, mostly because they were an embarrassment to the West in addition to their obvious destructive potential. While the media focused on the more dramatic scenarios of bioterror and dirty bombs, every Western intelligence agency ranked the MANPAD threat much higher, both because it was easier to execute and because, should it come to pass, it would be beyond embarrassing to the governments in question.

Stinger missiles were a MANPAD. And Stinger missiles had been rather liberally handed out to onetime U.S. allies in Southeast Asia and the Middle East, long before the Global War on Terror had begun. The GWOT had happened, and CT analysts in Langley and London had sat up straight in their uncomfortable chairs and begun firing off insistent memos and shrilly worded reports, describing in detail what a single member of Jemaah Islamiyah or the EIJ or any other al-Qaeda-associated terror cell could do with but one of the missiles to, say, a Boeing 777 taking off from Heathrow.

Or, for that matter, to a C-130 Hercules delivering troops into Baghdad.

The Americans had given the world the Stinger, but it was not the only MANPAD system out there. The Russians had the Grouse and the Gremlin; the French, the Mistral; the Israelis, the Barak. There were countless others, of varying efficacy and availability.

And England had first the Javelin, then the Starburst, and now, more recently—and much more effective—the Starstreak.

"I didn't see anything in the daily brief," Crocker said.

"No, Simon just brought it to my attention," Barclay replied. "Nothing hard yet, just a whisper that something might be coming."

"Someone should inform the Russians."

"If they don't know already." Barclay shook his head slightly, as if dismissing the conversation. "That's not what I wanted to talk to you about."

"No, sir?"

"You've been meeting with Sir Walter Seccombe."

"I've had *a* meeting with him, yes, sir."

"Why is a junior director from SIS meeting with the Permanent Undersecretary at the FCO, Paul?"

"He wanted an explanation for the disaster in Kuala Lumpur."

"I briefed the Cabinet myself, including the Foreign Secretary and the PM."

Crocker resisted the urge to shrug. "Sir Walter asked to see me, sir. I'm hardly in a position to refuse him."

"Indeed. You're hardly in much of a position at all, at the moment."

Crocker didn't say anything.

"We discussed, earlier, your future prospects. I'm willing to appoint you as Washington liaison, to move you to the States. It's not a terminal posting, Paul, and it will preserve your future prospects. You could find yourself back here within two or three years."

"I understand."

"But the posting is conditional on your behavior and performance until your replacement arrives. As I said, if you make this transition difficult, I'll have you manning a station in Outer Mongolia. Somehow I doubt your wife or your daughters would appreciate that."

"No, sir, I don't think they would."

Barclay leveled a glare at him. "Then consider this. If you're playing a game with me, if you're withholding information from me, if you're cooking something—anything—of which I would not approve, not only will you end up in Outer Mongolia, but you'll end your career there as well."

"I understand," said Crocker.

Barclay shook his head, as if to say that he doubted Crocker was capable of even that much, then waved his hand, flicking his fingers as if trying to brush him away like so much lint. Crocker got to his feet once more, murmuring a thank-you, and made for the door.

As he reached it, Barclay said, "If Seccombe contacts you again, I want to know about it."

"Of course, sir," Crocker answered, and left C's office to return to his own.

He'd been at his desk for less than two minutes when Kate buzzed him to say that Sir Walter Seccombe's PA had just called, and that the PUS was hopeful that D-Ops would indulge him for a few minutes at his office at his earliest convenience. Hopeful enough that he was willing to send his car and driver around to fetch him.

A hearse might be better, Crocker thought.

Seccombe began with the pleasantries and the customary offer of whiskey, which Crocker again declined.

"So, where are we, Paul?" Seccombe fixed himself a drink, splashing water into his lowball glass to mix with his scotch.

"I should have someone on the ground in Tashkent by tomorrow forenoon," Crocker answered. "Once there, she'll locate Ruslan and begin planning the lift."

"She?" Seccombe turned, the glass halfway to his lips. "Chace?"

"You remember her."

"You used her for the Zimbabwe check, if I recall."

"Yes."

Seccombe took a seat in his easy chair. "She quit."

"A little over eighteen months ago. You're very well informed."

"One tries to keep abreast of things. Andrew Fincher replaced her. You've been struggling ever since."

"I wouldn't say struggling."

"Your Deputy Chief would disagree."

Second time she's come up in this room, Crocker thought.

"How long until Chace tries for the lift?"

"She'll need at least two days on the ground just for surveillance, and that's after she locates Ruslan. If she moves quickly and everything goes her way, she could try for a lift as soon as the nineteenth, Sunday. But I wouldn't hold my breath."

"Sooner would be better than later."

"She is aware of that."

"You briefed her yourself?"

"You made it very clear that this was to be between you and me," Crocker said.

"I did."

"And the Deputy Chief."

Seccombe smiled, draining his whiskey and then setting the glass on the bookstand at his elbow. The stand was an antique, mahogany, its surface covered in green felt, and the lamp on Seccombe's desk shot rainbows through the crystal glass.

"How much does she know?" Crocker asked.

"You may consider the DC an ally, Paul."

"Not much of an answer."

"But enough of one, I think, for the moment."

Crocker thought for a second, then said, "Barclay called me into his office this afternoon, ostensibly to find out where I was yesterday."

"Ostensibly?"

"He hedged, wanted to talk about a MANPAD alert that D-Int had passed along. But he knew I'd met with you, and he doesn't like it. He feels communication between you and SIS should go through him."

"In almost every instance, it does."

"Which is why he's growing suspicious."

"Hmm," Seccombe said. "Then I suppose this should be our last meeting until Chace is back from Uzbekistan."

"That's probably for the best."

"Very good, then."

Crocker rose, saying, "So if I need to pass anything along to you, I should go through the Deputy Chief?"

Seccombe laughed.

"Don't push your luck, Paul," he said. "You have less of it than you think."

CHAPTER 10

Uzbekistan—Tashkent—U.S. Chancery, Office of the Political Counselor

16 February, 0929 Hours (GMT+5:00)

"Where are you going?" Political Counselor T. Lindsay McColl demanded when he caught Riess halfway out the door.

"The Ambassador wants to see me," Riess said.

"Why?"

"Didn't say."

McColl's face compressed, as if squeezing in upon itself with displeasure, and it made his cheeks color, and Riess had the thought that it made the man look like a giant lollipop in a suit, lanky, lean, with a big red head.

"You're spending far too much time with him," McColl said. "You've got work to do here."

Riess nodded, but said nothing, waiting for McColl to realize that was because there was nothing else *to* say, and no way that McColl could justify keeping the Ambassador waiting. It took McColl four seconds to reach the same conclusion, whereupon his face seemed to tighten even further before relaxing.

"Go," McColl said. "But you've got work to do here, don't you forget. You need to deliver that démarche on the U.S. candidate to the Agency for Cotton Project Implementation by the end of the day."

"I thought it might be useful if I sent over a copy of the resume along with the talking points," Riess replied. "Then suggest that I could make myself available if they had any questions."

"We want to be responsive to Washington, Charles." The condescension in his voice was cloying. "And make sure you have the reporting cable about the meeting on the Ambassador's desk by COB."

"Yes, sir," Riess said, and slipped out the door, shutting it behind him and hearing the lock snap in place. He went the fifteen feet down the hallway to the security checkpoint and the Marine standing guard there, swiped his pass in the reader, listened as the locks snapped back in the access door. He pushed through, out of the Political/Economic Section, turning through the Public Affairs Section and nearly bumping into Lydia Straight as she emerged from Cultural Affairs Office with Emily Cachet, the CAO. He hit a second checkpoint, swiped through again, deeper into the building, passing the Warden's office and yet more guards and another access door, which led to Tower's domain of spooks and spies. He'd never been through that door, and never expected to be, either.

The last time he'd been home, he'd gone to the movies, seen some thriller where a secret agent had led the Marines on a merry chase through the halls of one U.S. embassy or another. He'd laughed so hard tears had run down his face at the ridiculousness of it all. Forget the fact that the Marines in question had been armed to the teeth with M-16s and M-89s, body-armored and laden with grenades—to Riess' knowledge, there were perhaps a half-dozen weapons available to the Marines on post, and if even one of them needed to be drawn for active use, the Gunney in question would have demanded written permission from everyone up to and including the Ambassador himself—not even the Vice President of the United States could move through an embassy with such freedom. There were places in the building that Riess had never seen and never would see, and that was called security, and that was the way it was.

A last checkpoint, this time with two more Marines, and he was in the office of the Chief of Mission, waiting in the secretarial pool. He didn't wait long.

The door of Garret's office opened within a minute of his arrival, and the Ambassador emerged with Aaron Tower, both men looking grim. Tower, like Garret, was a big man, perhaps ten years younger, in his mid-forties, blond, and perpetually slouched. Tower acknowledged Riess with a nod, then turned back to the Ambassador.

"I should know more in the next few hours," Tower said.

"Keep me posted."

"Oh, I will, believe me." Tower turned toward Riess. "Chuck."

"Sir."

Riess followed the Ambassador into his office. It was, as far as Riess knew, the biggest office in the building, with a view of the garden from the three windows that overlooked the chancery grounds. The desk was large enough to handle a computer, credenza, telephones, and an endless supply of papers, with a leather-backed executive chair for the Ambassador to park himself in while working. A round table, currently bare, was positioned off in the corner. The couch and four chairs in the center of the room were for more informal meetings. From a flagpole in the far corner hung an American flag, anchoring the requisite glory wall of photographs, the History of Kenneth Garret, spanning a career of thirty-plus years and five presidents. Shots of the Ambassador with Zinni at CENTCOM and Yeltsin at the Kremlin and with the President on Air Force One, and others, the faces of people less famous but no less important in Garret's life. On the desk were an additional two framed photographs, one of Garret's daughter at her wedding, the second of his son's family, including Garret's two grandchildren.

Garret moved behind his desk, pressed a blinking light on his phone, killing a waiting call, then looked up at Riess.

"Malikov's been hospitalized," he said. "They're saying he had a stroke in the small hours this morning, but we don't have confirmation yet."

Riess stopped himself from swearing. "Can he speak?"

"We don't know, but I'd be damn surprised if he could."

"Ruslan can't take it. If Malikov goes, Ruslan doesn't have the backing."

"I know."

"If he tries for it, it'll get ugly. That's if Sevara doesn't try to remove him preemptively."

Garret looked at him patiently, waiting for Riess to stop stating the obvious.

"Is it natural?" Riess asked. "I mean, the stroke?"

"It's possible, but it's just as possible the old man was helped along." Garret hesitated, then added, "That's not why I wanted to see you."

That was even more of a surprise. "Sir?"

"There's a woman arriving sometime today, name of Carlisle. She's here to lift Ruslan. Starting tonight, you need to hit the hotels. The Meridien, the InterContinental. Make contact with Carlisle, find out what she needs, if we can help. And it goes without saying that we don't want the NSS knowing what you're up to. For that matter, we don't want Tower or McColl finding it out, either."

Riess shook his head, trying, and failing, to hide his confusion. "This woman . . . who is she?"

"She's a Brit, she's here to get Ruslan and his kid out, that's all you need to worry about."

"She's SIS?"

"It doesn't matter." Garret stopped, reading Riess' expression, then sighed. "I'm sorry, I can't even remember who I'm lying to anymore. Sit down."

Riess sat, looking at the Ambassador, bewildered. Garret sighed a second time, now regarding him more kindly, then came around the big desk and took the seat beside him, turning his chair so they could sit face to face. He kept his voice low when he spoke.

"After we talked about Ruslan, I floated a query back to State about Malikov's replacement. And the situation is exactly what we knew it would be—it's the Kissinger realists, and they think they can work with Sevara. We're getting no backing there, nothing, and you can bet your ass that Tower's already informed Langley that Malikov is circling the drain, and Langley'll pass that on to POTUS first thing in the morning, and we're going to be right back where we started.

"So I reached out to a friend at the FCO. Upshot is, the British are willing to aid in the transition: they'll back Ruslan. Hence the presence of this operative."

Riess thought, and all he had immediately were questions, so he began voicing them. "Then why isn't she going through their Station? Why involve me?"

"It's got to be done quietly, and that means she's here outside of channels. Figure the FCO is rowing the same direction as the crew at State—they're looking at the realist solution. But my guy, he's got a green light from the Prime Minister as long as we can pull this off quietly."

"How quietly?"

"The White House doesn't find out until after the fact. Their Prime Minister sure as hell isn't going to want to get into a knife fight with POTUS over Uzbekistan. Not during a time of war."

Riess shook his head. "I don't know how much help I'm going to be to her."

"Neither do I," Garret said. "But if the NSS and/or Sevara has Ruslan in their sights, they're sure not going to let him just hop on a jet and fly to London. And this agent, she's hitting the ground naked. You need to provide her with some clothes, so to speak."

Riess didn't speak. One agent, without support, coming to lift Ruslan and his son. He couldn't begin to imagine how she would pull it off.

But sitting in the office, his Ambassador fixing him with a gaze as heavy and serious as stone, he had to believe it was possible. Certainly Garret believed it.

Riess nodded. "All right. I'll hit the Meridien first. You want me to come by after I make contact?"

"If it's pressing. Otherwise, it can wait until the morning. You've still got the NSS on you?"

"Yeah, ever since Sunday. They're not trying to be subtle about it."

"Then contact *only* if it's pressing. They see you rushing out to my place in the middle of the night, they'll be asking a lot of questions."

Riess thought about the way the NSS asked questions, and said nothing.

He ran into Aaron Tower, coming out of Lydia Straight's office.

"Have a good talk with the Ambassador?"

"I suppose, yeah."

"He told you about Malikov?"

"Asked what I thought the DPM response would be."

"Feeding frenzy."

"Feeding frenzy," Riess agreed.

Tower tucked his hands into his trouser pockets, straightening up to his full height, grinning, as if they were sharing some private joke. It made Riess nervous, and suddenly he found himself wondering if they'd crossed paths by accident, if Tower wasn't already aware of what the Ambassador was planning.

It was an open secret at the Embassy—and at the NSS, and probably in downtown Tashkent, and possibly as far south as Kabul—that Aaron Tower was the Uzbek COS, Chief of Station, for the CIA, though there was no official confirmation of that fact, nor was there likely ever to be. On paper, Tower was listed as the Mission's Special Adviser to the Ambassador on Matters of Counterterrorism, a title that defied easy abbreviation or acronymizing, and consequently was never used, except by the handful of personnel who hadn't actually figured out what Tower really did.

What he really did was run CIA operations in Uzbekistan. Which meant he had what the Company liked to refer to as "assets" inside the military and the NSS and the Oliy Majlis and God only knew where else. Sometimes Riess wondered why they were called "assets," as opposed to, say, sources, or even contacts. He supposed it was a holdover from the Cold War, when Communism versus Capitalism had defined the ideological battle, rather than Communism versus Democracy.

So Tower had assets, and he also had agents, some undetermined number of officers in play throughout the country. They took their orders from him, brought their findings to him. Who they were, where they were, what they were doing at any given time, Riess didn't know. He never asked. He wasn't supposed to.

But it occurred to him then that Tower most certainly had either an asset or an officer in both of the hotels Garret had told him to check for Carlisle, and that however he was going to proceed come nightfall, he'd better do it carefully.

"You're the Deputy Pol Chief, Chuck," Tower said. "What's your guess?"

"I'm sorry, for what?"

"Malikov's successor."

"You mean until they hold an election?"

Tower's grin expanded. "Yeah, before that."

"Ganiev."

"You mean Sevara."

"Right, that's what I meant." Riess laughed. "If you'll excuse me, sir, I've got to get back to my desk."

"Ah, yeah, McColl. Tightass. You make sure he remembers who we're working for, okay?"

"I'll make sure he knows the Ambassador's in charge."

"Not the Amb, Chuck. The President. We work for the President." Tower's grin dropped a fraction. "Don't ever forget that."

"I won't."

"Good man," Tower said, and he flashed the grin one last time, then moved out of the way, and Riess continued on, past the Marines and the locked doors, to the relative safety of his desk.

Where he sat and wondered if Aaron Tower didn't already know about a British agent named Carlisle, and why she was coming to Uzbekistan.

CHAPTER 11

Uzbekistan—Tashkent—Hotel InterContinental

16 February, 1924 Hours (GMT+5:00)

It was a nice room, recently renovated, with new carpet and modern furnishings and a sleigh-backed king-size bed, and it reeked of a scent that Chace was certain came advertised as smelling like "Spring" or "Flowers" or some other nonsense printed on the bottle. She locked the door after her, threw the deadbolt, fixed the security bar in place, then dumped her duffel on the bed and pulled back the curtains, looking out at Tashkent at night. Lights glittered off a body of water in the near distance, some artificial lake in the nearby park, and she watched as headlights drifted along the road to the south—Husniddin Asomov, she remembered—and winked in the windows of the nearby apartments.

She was tired and sore, and it made her feel acutely aware of how long she'd been out of the game. She'd been unable to sleep on the flight, despite her best efforts, and that bothered her, too. In the past, she'd always managed to steal sleep on the way to a job, with the knowledge that once things started rolling on the ground, rest would be hard to come by. This time, as often as she had closed her eyes and repositioned herself in the too-narrow-and-not-enough-legroom seat on the plane, sleep evaded her.

She watched the lights flicker on the lake, and wondered what Tamsin was doing. She wondered just what she was doing.

She closed the drapes, and brought out the guidebook and map she had purchased at the airport after she'd cleared Customs. The guidebook was rife with typos and misspellings, badly translated from Uzbek, and full of useless advice about the sort of things she absolutely *must* do before leaving Tashkent. Apparently, seeing a ballet at the Alisher Navoi Opera House topped the list, followed closely by enjoying a traditional meal of *samsa*—a meat-and-onion pie—and *plov*—a pilau rice dish.

She tossed the book into a corner, then unfolded the map, and was heartened to see that it, at least, looked to be more useful. After studying it for several minutes, orienting herself in the city, Chace refolded it and placed the map aside on the desk. Then she opened her duffel, digging out first a GPS unit she'd bought in London, then the satellite phone she had purchased when she'd bought the pager she'd given to Porter, and finally, its charger.

The GPS unit was nothing out of the ordinary, and Chace switched it on, making certain the battery was still charged and that it still functioned as it should. The LCD lit up, and she moved to the window, canting the device to capture an uninterrupted signal. She took a reading, read the numbers, then cleared the screen and took a second reading, seeing that the figures matched the first set. Satisfied, she switched the GPS off and replaced it in the duffel, then picked up the satellite phone.

At first blush, it looked like nothing more than a slightly out-of-date mobile, and could be easily mistaken for such, until one extended the antenna. Stowed against the back of the unit, it swung out and away from the phone, a thick, black baton. Chace deployed the antenna, switched the power to on, then punched in her access code. For several seconds, there was nothing on the display but the luminous green glow, and she'd just begun to think something had gone wrong with the device when it beeped in her hand, and the word "Iridium" appeared on the screen. The bars marking signal strength expanded, then settled, and Chase released the breath she'd been holding, relieved. If the phone failed, the exfil would go all to hell—she'd have to find a way to procure another, and in Tashkent, she doubted that would be easy.

But the phone was working, and that, at least, meant that she had a way to get home.

Chace switched the phone off, collapsed the antenna, then plugged the charger into the outlet by the desk, grateful that the hotel sockets didn't require an adapter. She hooked the phone to the charger, waited until she was certain it was drawing power, then turned once more to the bed.

The telephone on the nightstand rang.

Chace started, stared at it as it jangled a second time, its message light shimmering in time with the noise, and she felt her stomach contract with sudden vertigo.

She hadn't been made at the airport; she was creaky, she knew that, she was maybe off her game, but she was sure of at least that much. There'd been no surveillance in the lobby that she'd seen when she'd checked in, no one casually disinterested in her business, nobody carefully avoiding her gaze.

No one knew she was here. No one was supposed to know.

But her phone was ringing, and unless it was a wrong number, unless it was the front desk calling, it meant that she was wrong, that she *had* been made. She had the sickening fear that it was someone from the U.K. Embassy on the other end of the line, someone from the Station who wanted to know why Tara Chace was in Tashkent, and what she was planning on doing here.

The phone rang a fourth time, and finally Chace answered.

"Ms. Carlisle?" The voice was male, American.

"Yes? Who is this?"

"I heard from a mutual friend that you were coming to town," the voice said. "I thought maybe I could show you around?"

"I didn't catch your name."

"I'm sorry, it's Charles. Chuck."

"Tracy," Chace said. "A guide would be wonderful, Charles. Is there anything in particular you'd like to show me? I've heard the performances at the Alisher Navoi are not to be missed."

He laughed. "If you'd like to see ballet, sure. There's a lot to see in town. Would you like to get together, so we can discuss it?"

"I'm a little tired after my trip, I don't much feel like going out."

"I can come there, if you like."

"Would you?"

"Take me about an hour and a half."

"Call me from the lobby when you arrive," Chace said, and hung up.

Charles called from the lobby one hour and fifty minutes later, and four minutes after that, knocked on the door of Chace's room. She loosed the security bar and the deadbolt, turned the knob just enough to free the latch from the wall, and stepped away, putting her back to the wall.

"It's open," Chace said.

The door swung in, and a man stood on the threshold, slender, perhaps an inch or two shorter than Chace, brown curly hair, wearing a black wool coat and heavy trousers. He entered in a lean, one hand at his side, the other still on the doorknob, looking around as he said, "Tracy?" and from the posture and the motion, she knew he wasn't, at least, an immediate threat, and she felt the tension go from her shoulders and back, felt her stomach settle a fraction.

She waited until he was through before she said, "Charles."

He turned, smiled, and Chace didn't return it, closing the door and then locking it once again, as she had done before. He was still standing exactly as he had been when she turned back, so this time Chace did smile.

Then she grabbed his crotch with her left hand, and shoved him back against the wall.

"Hey—"

"Shut the fuck up," Chace said, and tightened her grip, feeling the heat and weight of his testicles in her hand. He was wearing boxers, which made the holding of him easier. He grimaced but didn't move. As far as immobilization manuevers went, it was entirely inadequate, and Chace knew it; it kept his hands free, and it absolutely allowed for a counterattack, even if she were to bear down with all of her might. As a psychological move, however, it had no equal, and for the moment, it seemed to be doing its job quite well.

Maintaining her grip, Chace began patting him down with her right. She found a wallet in an inside jacket pocket, and a small digital camera in an outer one. She tossed both onto the bed. She ran her free hand through his hair, then along his neck, front, and back, then over the front of his chest, working lower until she had to crouch to check his legs.

"This might be fun if you loosened your grip," Charles said.

Chace ignored him, working upward again, this time feeling along the backs of his legs, over his buttocks, checking the waistband of his pants, untucking his shirt, sliding her hand up over his back.

Satisfied, she let him go.

"Do I get a turn now?" Charles asked.

She continued to ignore him, moving to the desk, pulling out the chair there. She motioned for him to sit in it, and after a second, he complied. From the bed, she picked up the wallet and searched through it.

"Charles Riess?" Chace asked.

"Yeah. But I would have told you that if you asked."

Chace tossed the wallet back to him, picked up the camera. "Why this?"

"I thought you might like to see some faces."

Chace considered, then tossed the camera to him as well. He caught it as he had the first, but with a little more distress.

"Easy!"

"Show me."

Charles Riess stared at her, then turned his attention to the camera in his hands, switching it on and then turning it, showing Chace the display window, offering it back to her.

"First picture is of Ruslan Malikov," he said.

Chace took the camera again, peering at the tiny screen. The color and resolution were both good, the image clear, if small. The picture of Ruslan Malikov was a headshot, apparently taken from another document, rather than of the man in his actual life. It gave no sense of scale, no hint of the man's height, but based on his face alone, Chace knew she would recognize him if she saw him. He was rectangular-faced, brown eyes, black hair cut short but well styled, with a strong jaw and a strong nose. Chace read him as more Russian than Uzbek, with no obvious Asian influence to his features.

"The next one is his son, Stepan," Charles Riess said.

Chace pressed the button beside the screen, scrolling from one image to the next. Unlike the first one, the shot of the boy was of poor quality. The best Chace could tell from it was that Stepan was a toddler, with dark hair and dark eyes, and he owned a T-shirt with a happy bulldog printed on its front.

"Anything else?" Chace asked.

"Yeah, two others. Sevara and her heavy, Zahidov."

The third headshot was of a beautiful young woman, her hair immaculately styled, her eyes almond-shaped and so green that Chace suspected contact lenses. In the picture, Sevara had her hands steepled, and her nails were long and lacquered a light tan. She wore jewelry, a necklace of precious stones, and earrings that matched. Unlike with her brother, Chace could see the Uzbek influence in her features.

"Same mother as her brother?"

"So we've been led to believe. Ruslan looks more like his father, obviously."

Chace nodded, and scrolled to the last picture, the man named Zahidov. Like the pictures of Ruslan and Sevara, this one, too, was taken from a file shot, and was another headshot. Perhaps because

Riess had described him as Sevara's "heavy," Chace had expected someone who appeared bigger and older, and it surprised her that the man she was looking at seemed to be no older than his early thirties, and, at least from his features, quite slight. His hair was brown, brushed back over a high forehead, and he wore glasses, and behind the lenses his eyes were brown as well. His mouth was small, his lips thin.

Chace looked at the picture of Zahidov for several seconds, then scrolled back, slowly, taking her time with each face, before handing the camera back to Riess.

"On the map." Chace pointed to it on the desk behind Riess, and Riess turned in his chair to see what she meant. "Find Ruslan's house and mark it. Mark Sevara's as well, and this Zahidov fellow's."

Riess nodded and turned around in the seat. Chace took the complimentary hotel pen from the complimentary hotel notepad on her nightstand and handed both to him, then stepped back, watching. Riess unfolded the map and quickly marked four locations, then, using the pen, pointed each out to her in turn. She was pleased to see that he'd only circled the locations, making no other notation.

"Ruslan lives here, on Uzbekiston Street, number fourteen." Riess moved the pen. "Sevara's house is here, on Glinka; it overlooks Babur Park. She shares it with her husband, Denis Ganiev— Ganiev is the DPM in charge of the Interior Ministry. The marriage is for show, she's rarely there." He moved the pen again. "Mostly, you can find her here, on Sulaymonova—she's got the penthouse suite." He moved the pen a final time. "And Zahidov has an apartment here, on Chimkent, but as I understand it, he's *never* there."

"Why not?"

"He's screwing Sevara, so mostly you can find him at the suite on Sulaymonova. Either that or at the Interior Ministry, where Zahidov seems to do his best work."

"He's NSS?"

Riess set down the pen. "Yeah, inasmuch as he uses his position at the NSS to support Sevara. It's one of the things that's made her so powerful. She's got the secret police on her side."

Chace nodded, picked up the map from the desk, studying the locations.

"There's something else you should know," Riess said.

"Hmm?"

"Malikov's dying."

Chace lowered the map. "What?"

"He had what appears to be a stroke before dawn this morning. He's in the hospital, and the prognosis isn't looking good."

"A stroke? Is that likely?"

"I'd have thought a heart attack, but a stroke seems reasonable."

"What was he doing when he had the stroke, do you know?"

Riess shook his head, raising an eyebrow at her.

"Was he alone?" Chace asked.

"There's a rumor that he was with one of his mistresses."

"He's sixty-seven?"

"Sixty-eight, officially. Maybe as old as seventy-two."

"There you go." Chace refolded the map, dropping it back onto the desk. "It was an assassination attempt. Someone upped his Viagra dose, tried to give him another heart attack. Got a stroke instead. Messy."

"And difficult to prove, if you're right."

Chace shrugged, turning back to the bed and sitting on the edge. The fatigue of the trip returned, sliding down her shoulders like oil.

Riess was looking at her, trying his best to not appear curious.

"I'm going to need weapons," Chace told him.

The curiosity vanished into something close to mild panic. "That's not my thing, I'm sorry—"

"No, not from you," she interrupted, annoyed. "I'll get them myself. Just tell me where I can make the buy."

She watched his eyes widen slightly with understanding. His eyes were green.

"There's a place west of here, about one hundred and fifty kilometers, north of Lake Aidarkul." Riess hesitated, whether because he was uncertain or simply trying to recall, Chace couldn't tell. "You go north from there, there's a little village just south of the border with Kazakhstan. It's all frontier, there's nothing out there. I was out that way about three months ago, before the *chilla* hit. We were getting reports of a market, I flew out with some of the CT guys."

"The *chilla*?"

Riess grinned, apologetic. "Uzbekistan doesn't get that much weather, but in the winter, there's about six weeks of fucking cold, called the *chilla*."

"Ah."

"Yeah, sorry. Anyway, this market, it was anything goes. Weapons, drugs, livestock. Other things."

"Sounds ideal."

Riess grimaced, showing his teeth. "I don't know. Western woman heading out there alone, they may try to put you up for sale."

"They might." Chace gave him her best smile. "Last question, Charles. Where can I get a car?"

"Rentals are hard to come by. You could go back out to the airport—"

"No. I'll need to buy it."

"Yeah? Huh. Best bet, then, I'd find a car you like on the street and ask the owner how much he wants for it. You've got cash, I assume?"

"Enough to cover expenses."

"That's what I'd do. That way, you'd be sure to get one that runs."

"Very well."

Riess opened his mouth to add something, then closed it, then opened it once more. "Is that all?"

"For now."

"I'm not sure meeting a second time would be that wise."

"No?"

"The NSS has been watching me."

Chace stared at him.

"Not tonight, I made a point of losing them tonight," Riess added quickly.

"You're certain?"

"Yes. Absolutely."

"How'd you come here tonight?"

"Metro."

"How many times did you change trains?"

"Six. Why do you think it took me two hours to get here?"

"You're State Department?"

Riess hesitated, then nodded.

"You've had basic tradecraft, then?"

"I'm not supposed to talk about that."

Chace looked at him, for a moment unable to believe what she'd just heard. "I'm sorry?"

"We're not supposed to talk about that kind of thing."

"You know who I am?"

"Well, I know why you're here, if that's what you mean, yes."

She shook her head, amused, then looked him over a second time, reappraising. He was charming, in a way, and reasonably handsome.

"I don't know if you're naïve or cute or both," Chace said.

"With those choices, I'd rather cute, if you don't mind."

Chace stared at him a moment longer, recognizing a desire she hadn't felt in what seemed like a very long time. She hadn't had sex since she had been with Tom, and thinking of it, it seemed both ages ago and only yesterday.

She got up from the bed, crossed over to where he was sitting, and took his chin in her hand. She kissed him, and after he recovered from his surprise, he returned it.

She broke it off.

"I'm going down to the gift shop," Chace said, "where I hope they will sell me a package of condoms. If you like the sound of that, be in the bed when I get back."

She took her key and headed out of the room, riding the elevator down to the lobby. The gift shop was still open. After she made her purchase, she stepped back into the lobby, then crossed it to the restaurant, a small café called the Brasserie. She ordered a glass of beer, drank it sitting alone at a table, watching the lobby, and by the time she'd emptied the glass, she was as certain as she could be that Charles Riess had not been followed to the Hotel InterContinental.

He was waiting in the bed when she got back.

CHAPTER 12

**Uzbekistan—Tashkent—182 Sulaymonova,
Penthouse of Sevara Malikov-Ganiev**

17 February, 0008 Hours (GMT+5:00)

Zahidov collapsed onto Sevara, breathless, spent, and as happy as
he had been in weeks. He kissed her neck and tasted the perspiration there, moved his mouth along her shoulder, drinking her
sweetness with his tongue, feeling the warmth and smoothness of
her skin, the life of her. She shuddered again around him, ran her
nails up his back, and then let out a long sigh of contentment, giving voice to everything he was feeling.

For a while then, he drifted in languid thought, feeling Sevara's
heartbeat slowing, feeling his own matching pace. She kissed his
shoulder and his neck and then his mouth, each tenderly, then let
her leg slip away from him, freeing him. Zahidov took the cue, reluctantly rolling off her, the bedsheet clinging to him. When he was
on his back, she curled against him, resting her head on his chest.

"Do you think he's dead yet?"

"No." The stroke had been unexpected, not the result they'd
been after, and it complicated things, though not as much as he
had first feared. "The doctors say he's stabilized."

Sevara readjusted her position, making herself more comfortable. Zahidov felt her nails traveling lightly over his belly, up his
chest.

"You're disappointed," she said softly. "Don't be, Ahtya."

"I don't like him lingering."

"But it doesn't hurt us. I saw him at the hospital this evening. The whole side of his body is useless, his face is sagging like melted wax. I talked to him for almost half an hour, holding his hand. He couldn't even move his fingers, he couldn't even speak. The doctors say it's unlikely he'll ever be able to again."

"Unlikely isn't the same as certain."

Sevara rolled, propping herself up on her side, smiling down at him, reassuring. "It doesn't matter. He won't be recovered by tomorrow, love. He won't be recovered in a week, or even a month. It gives us time. He remains President in name, and you and I, we simply move in and take control. We can keep working on the Deputies, making certain they know how things are going to be. And when everything is right and in place, we announce my father's illness, his subsequent retirement, and that I will be acting in his stead until elections can be held."

Zahidov stared at the ceiling, the shadows cast by the candles · burning on the bureau beyond the foot of the bed.

"Time is to our advantage," Sevara told him.

"To your brother as well." He turned to look at her, brushing hair from her cheek with the back of his hand. "It's to his advantage as well, Sevya, and he will do exactly what you are doing."

"Ruslan's got no support from the Americans, you said so yourself. They know he's not strong enough to hold the country together."

"He might be able to change their minds."

Sevara laughed, kissed his hand. "When has Washington *ever* changed its mind, Ahtya, especially with the current American President? No, Ruslan will try, but he'll need the DPMs, and the DPMs will already belong to us. I've spoken to Urdushevich and Tursunova already, and they've told me what I'll hear from all of the rest. Not one of them wishes to lose what they have. And they know that should Ruslan become President, the first thing he'll do is get rid of them all and claim he's fighting corruption. None of them will ever lift a finger to support him."

"It makes me uncomfortable," Zahidov insisted, and he met her eyes, but didn't say the rest.

Sevara threw back the covers and swung herself out of the bed, cursing him. The candlelight turned her skin to gold and shadow. He watched as she opened the closet, pulled on her robe. It was silk, green and black, one he had purchased for her on his last trip to Moscow, and he liked the way it clung to her, and he thought it made her even more desirable than when she wore nothing at all.

"I know what you're thinking, Ahtya," Sevara said. "The answer is no."

"Why not? Because he's your brother?"

"Precisely because he's my brother. Think of how it will look, if nothing else. First his wife, then Papa, then my brother?"

He sat up in the bed. "It can be done with subtlety."

"No, it can't, my love, really, it can't. Even were he to die of natural causes tomorrow it would not be subtle enough, not so soon on the heels of the others. It becomes overt—worse, it becomes obvious, and that *would* force Washington's hand, because the media would report upon it, and they would have to respond to that pressure. Right now, they can suspect, they can even know in their hearts we're responsible for Papa's illness. But if we kill Ruslan, it takes things too far."

"It's not like you to be sentimental about family."

Sevara returned to the foot of the bed, tying the sash of the robe about her waist with a jerk, and Zahidov knew he'd made her angry, even without seeing the expression on her face.

"He's my brother," she said quietly. "He is the father of my nephew. We helped my father along because it was his time to go, because his end was inevitable, and because he blocked our way. Ruslan has no power, Ahtam. He has *nothing*. No support, no funding, no connections, no allies, nothing. We don't have to be savages."

Zahidov leaned forward, matching her tone, speaking just as softly. "As long as he is alive, he will oppose you, Sevya. That makes him your enemy, and that makes him dangerous. You and I have enough to worry about already. Why allow for one more factor we cannot control?"

"If that is your concern, then control him. But that does not require killing him, Ahtam, and I will not allow it." She ran a hand through her hair, pulling the strands in frustration. "Put him under guard, under house arrest, whatever you want to call it."

"For how long? A week? A month? The rest of his natural life?"

She glared at him. "Until the announcement. Keep him in his home for the next two, three weeks, that will be long enough. By then, it will be too late."

"Assuming everything is in place by then."

"Everything will be."

"I don't like it."

Sevara mounted the bed once more, walking to him on her knees, straddling him over the sheets. She put her hands on his shoulders, and he felt the thrill of her touch again, and again wondered how it was she could make him feel that way every single time her skin touched his own.

"You don't have to like it," Sevara told him. "It's what I want. It's what is best for us, Ahtya. Just like you, everything I'm doing, I'm doing it for us."

If the words had come from any other woman, he'd have dismissed them utterly as fiction. But from this woman, he knew it was the truth, and Zahidov put his hands on her hips, feeling the warmth of her skin through the silk, pulling her down on him more firmly.

"I worry," he said. "Because I love you."

She smiled, her upper lip curling with mischief, and unfastened her robe.

"Show me," she said.

CHAPTER 13

London—Hyde Park—Lover's Walk, Park Lane Entrance

17 February, 1114 Hours GMT

Julian Seale was waiting for him, the CIA Station Chief holding a black umbrella large enough to shelter a family of three. Crocker saw him, stepped across a puddle, and offered his hand. Seale shook it firmly once, then released, and Crocker wondered how many more times they'd begin their meetings with a handshake before they were comfortable enough with each other to dispense with the pleasantry.

"Sorry to keep you waiting," Crocker said.

"No, I like standing around in the rain." Seale turned toward the west, then hesitated. "Which way?"

"South, then right. It'll take us into the park."

They began walking, Seale shifting the umbrella to his other hand to avoid hitting Crocker with the canopy.

"You and Angela did this a lot?"

Crocker finished lighting his cigarette, stowed his lighter, nodding as he exhaled. "She used to say she liked the exercise, but I think it appealed to the traditionalist in her."

"Oh, the plots that have been hatched in this park."

"And those are the ones we know about," Crocker agreed. "You wanted to see me?"

"About two things, actually. One is a favor, the other is more an FYI point."

"Is the FYI in exchange for the favor?"

Seale chuckled, a low rumble not unlike the sounds of traffic coming from the road behind them. "The FYI is free, actually."

"Now I'm nervous."

Seale chuckled again.

"What do you need?" Crocker asked.

"Wondering if you can offer any Special Section support for an operation in Casablanca."

"Supporting what?"

"We've located two members of a GSPC cell we'd like to bring in for further questioning. Problem is, all of our Executive Action staff is tasked elsewhere at the moment. The soonest we'd be able to free up an agent would be tomorrow late, putting him in theater late on Sunday at the earliest."

"By which time they will have jumped?"

"Or worse, gone and done whatever it is they're planning to do."

"Which members?"

"Mohammud Belkadem and Hamed Hamouche."

Crocker raised an eyebrow. "Confirmed?"

"I wouldn't be asking for your help if it wasn't confirmed. We just need someone who knows the drill to help our Station with the snatch."

"Moroccan authorities are aiding?"

"We're leaving them out for the moment." Seale flashed Crocker a grin. "You know how the Moroccans feel about the Algerians. We don't want them getting overexcited."

"No, I can see why not." Crocker pulled on his cigarette again, squinting into the rain, considering. "All right, I'll bring it to the Deputy Chief. She should approve it before close of play. One Minder should do it."

"Poole or Lankford, if you don't mind."

"You don't want Fincher?"

"Paul, *you* don't want Fincher."

Crocker didn't bother to argue. "What do we get in trade?"

"Our continued goodwill in the spirit of cooperation during the Global War on Terror."

"That's nice, but it won't sell it to the DC."

"The goody bag is pretty much open on this one, Paul. Tell the DC to make her list, I'll see what I can do."

"You've gotten that from Langley?"

Seale nodded. "We really want these guys."

"I'll tell the DC."

"Lankford or Poole, not Fincher."

"I'll tell her that, too."

"I'm serious, Paul, you can't give this to Fincher. That's part of our deal."

They reached a fork in the path, where it branched in three separate directions. Seale stopped, and Crocker pointed them to the northwestern path, and they resumed walking.

"Give me a couple more meetings, I'll have this down," Seale said.

"I half expected you'd want me to come to Grosvenor Square. You haven't seemed very much like a walk-in-the-park fellow."

"Angela said it was how you preferred to do business. I guess you're as much of a traditionalist as she is."

Crocker flicked his cigarette into the grass, watched the smoke vanish in the rain. "Have you heard from her?"

"Talked to her today. She's still at the NCTC, playing counter-terror expert."

"Let's hope she's doing more than just playing." The National Center for Counterterrorism was one of the by-products of the recent restructuring of the American intelligence apparatus. In theory, the office oversaw all civilian and military counterterrorist operations, and served as both a clearinghouse and a main communications center for intelligence gathered on the same. The Center was directed by the National Intelligence Director, a new post created at the time of the restructuring, and the highest intelligence office in the U.S. Government, outranking even the Director at the

CIA. Angela Cheng's appointment to the Center had been a promotion, in every sense of the word.

"Amen," Seale agreed. "She's actually the source on the FYI. She asked me to bring it to you personally."

Crocker glanced to Seale, mildly surprised, and beginning to suspect that he wasn't much going to like what he was about to hear next.

"We've got some information on some of your missing MANPADs," Seale explained.

"Some?"

"Four of them, actually. Starstreaks."

"Jesus Christ," Crocker muttered. Four Starstreaks were a lot of Starstreaks, especially considering it would take but one of them to bring down an airliner during landing, or, worse still, takeoff. If all four of the MANPADs were in the same hands, it was a substantial potential threat.

Seale reached into his overcoat pocket, then opened his hand to Crocker, revealing a folded piece of white notepaper, almost surreally bright against the darker skin of his palm. "Serial numbers."

Crocker took the paper, tucked it into his own pocket. There was no point in looking at it now. When he got back to the office, he'd run the numbers past D-Int, to see what they turned up. But he did have a question.

"Tell me," Crocker said. "These Starstreaks didn't turn up in Chechnya, by any chance?"

Seale shook his head and came to a stop, looking at him quizzically. "You're in the right region. We think they're in Uzstan."

That's one hell of a coincidence, he thought, *which means it's not a bloody coincidence at all.*

"You think?"

"Our man in Tashkent isn't a slouch, Paul, not with the strategic importance that Uzbekistan holds in the war. He's got an asset who claims that he witnessed the sale of four Starstreaks by some Afghan warlord to an Uzbek national in Surkhan Darya province last month. Said the whole deal went down for sixty grand, American."

"Who bought them?"

"We don't know."

"But they're in Uzbekistan?"

"Hell, they could be anywhere by now. But as of a month ago, they came over the border from Afghanistan into Uzstan, yes."

Crocker scowled, fishing out a second cigarette.

"Is there something you want to tell me?" Seale asked.

The flame from Crocker's lighter quavered in the breeze and the rain. We shook his head and lit his smoke. "No. Not yet, at least."

"You have something going on in Chechnya?"

"Not at the moment."

Seale stared at him, frankly curious. Crocker shook his head a second time, then offered Seale his hand.

"Thank you," he said. "And thank Angela when you speak to her next. I appreciate the courtesy."

They shook hands.

"We'll be interested to know what you find," Seale said.

"You're not the only one," Crocker told him.

Back in his office, Crocker had Kate ring the Deputy Chief to see if she had five minutes to discuss a favor to the Americans. She did, and before Crocker headed up to see her, he handed Kate the piece of notepaper he'd received from Seale.

"Run this over to Simon, tell him it's the numbers of four Starstreaks, he'll know what that means."

"I know what that means," Kate replied mildly. "I do more than just make the coffee."

"But nothing quite as well. Tell him CIA thinks the missiles were sold in Uzbekistan within the last month. The question I have for him is how those missiles got there in the first place."

"I hear and I obey," Kate said.

"The first part is true enough," Crocker snapped, and headed upstairs to see Alison Gordon-Palmer.

"Will one Minder be enough?" the Deputy Chief wanted to know.

"To help with the snatch? Seale seemed to think one would suffice."

"You'll send Poole?"

"I was thinking Lankford, actually. He did a grab last March in Frankfurt, pulled it off quite well. And he hasn't been to Casablanca. Poole has."

"Fincher hasn't been there, either."

"Fincher is locked at his desk for the moment, as you well know."

Alison Gordon-Palmer paused, thinking, then said, "Andrew Fincher isn't a bad officer, Paul. Confining him to his desk is a waste of manpower."

"He may be a fine officer, but he's a bad Minder. And if you're proposing that I send him instead of Lankford, the Americans made it clear that's not an option. This was given to us on condition that we *didn't* use Fincher, in fact."

"His reputation is that bad?"

"Seale doesn't trust him, certainly. Whether the command is from Langley, I can't speculate."

"And Seale's promising the whole line of sweets, is he?"

"He assures me that we'll get just about anything we could ask for."

"Is there anything we should be asking for, Paul?"

The question surprised Crocker, mostly because it was exactly the kind of question that Donald Weldon, the DC's predecessor, *never* would have asked.

"Not at the moment. I'm sure something will come up."

"I have no doubt. All right, then, I'll sell it to C. You task Lankford, run him over to Grosvenor Square for the briefing. If we're quick about it, we could have him in Morocco before dark."

"We'll have to be very quick about it," Crocker said.

Gordon-Palmer smiled at him, as if she knew every last one of his secrets.

"Then why are you still here talking to me, Paul?"

He'd finished briefing Lankford and had called Seale to tell him the loan had been approved when Kate buzzed him from her desk to say that Director Intelligence was outside.

"Send him in," Crocker told the intercom, and got to his feet as Simon Rayburn pushed through the door. Crocker smiled, pleased to see him, and Rayburn returned it. There were few people in the building that Crocker genuinely got on with, but his opposite number was one of those few, and Rayburn, for his part, both knew and appreciated that fact. There had been times in the history of the Firm when the Director of Intelligence and the Director of Operations had scarcely tolerated the sight of each other, to the obvious detriment of SIS. Both Crocker and Rayburn knew how fortunate they were that they did not live and work in those times.

"Interesting set of numbers, Paul," Rayburn commented.

"Thought you might say something like that." Crocker gestured to one of the chairs away from the desk, then went to his door, opening it again, and asking Kate to bring coffee. When he'd turned back, Rayburn was seated. He was a smaller man than Crocker, and even more slender of build, and in all manner quieter as well. He smiled as Crocker pulled up a chair opposite him, staying out from behind his desk, so they could speak as equals.

Kate entered with two cups of coffee, black for Crocker, light and sweetened for Rayburn, then stepped out again without a word, shutting the door behind her.

"Those four missiles have a history," Rayburn said.

"They've certainly traveled."

"More than you know. I did some digging, then checked at the MOD with a source there. With help, I was able to retrace their journey, or at least a portion of it."

"Enlighten me."

Rayburn sipped his coffee, made a face. He set his cup back in its saucer, and set the saucer down on the edge of the small coffee table in front of them.

"The four missiles entered service in July of 1998, and were stored at Her Majesty's Naval Base Devonport. On 11 January 2002, the four missiles in question were transferred, with other material, to RAF Brize Norton. Brize Norton was flying supplies and equipment to the operation in Afghanistan."

"I'm aware how it works, Simon."

"I know you are, Paul, but there's a point to this. The Americans worked long and hard to arrange overflight and the use of two bases in Pakistan. The transport from Brize Norton ends up there, offloading. At which point Islamabad Station takes possession of the missiles."

Crocker almost choked on his coffee. "What?"

Rayburn nodded in sympathy. "You didn't know."

"You're telling me I could have just rung Islamabad Station, they would have told me *they* had these missiles?"

"If you had done so in February of 2002, perhaps. As it is, the Station only held them for a few weeks, at the most. It seems the four Starstreaks made their way rather quickly over the border into Afghanistan, to be delivered to the Northern Alliance."

Crocker suppressed a growl. "They weren't?"

"I couldn't find any report nor any record of their successful delivery. Nor could I find any report nor any record of their use. If the CIA intelligence is correct, they were held and somehow acquired by one of the warlords in the north, and then sold. They very well could have been sold two or three or four times in the interim before ending up across the border again and in Uzbekistan."

Rayburn went silent, giving Crocker a second look of pained sympathy. He risked a second sip of the coffee, and made the same face he had the first time.

"Oh, that is just awful," he murmured.

Crocker ignored him, thinking. In 2002, the Station Number One in Islamabad had been a man named Derek Moss. Moss had been intimately involved in operations in Afghanistan at the time, by necessity—SIS had no working stations in the country, nor any reliable intelligence on the ground at the time of the Coalition action. In the wake of 9/11, Moss and his Number Two, Richard Barton, had spent more and more time crossing the border, a dangerous pursuit even during a time of peace. In a time of war, it had proved fatal.

Both men had been killed in the same ambush in March of 2002. Crocker had been D-Ops at the time, Weldon had been the Deputy Chief, and C had been Sir Wilson Stanton-Davies, Barclay's immediate predecessor.

"You didn't authorize it?" Rayburn asked.

Crocker refocused his attention, putting it back in the present and on Rayburn. "Simon."

"You've been known to play fast and loose with the rules in the past, Paul."

"Not *that* fast and loose. Even if I wanted to, I couldn't have authorized the transfer of four Starstreak missiles."

"Someone did. The DC? C?"

"I can't see Sir Wilson doing it, not without informing either one of us. And Weldon would barely change his tie without clearing it with both C and the FCO first."

"Someone outside the Firm, then."

"Would have to be, and someone fairly senior, at that. Derek Moss knew his job. He would never have undertaken an operation without informing me, not an operation like that."

"Pity you can't ask him about it."

Crocker nodded, lapsing into silence and thought once again.

"One more thing for you, tangential, really, but it just came in from the Station in Tashkent."

Oh, Christ, they've made Chace, Crocker thought. "Oh?"

"Craig Gillard is reporting that President Malikov suffered a cerebral vascular accident yesterday. He's in hospital, and it looks severe. Word is, he's lost all function along one side, and that he's nonverbal."

The relief Crocker felt was short-lived. Chace hadn't been blown, but if Malikov was about to check out, it meant she had even less time than any of them had imagined to get Ruslan out of the country. He only hoped that Chace knew about Malikov's condition.

"Media reported it?" Crocker asked.

"Nothing as yet. I suspect they're trying to keep it hushed up until they get the succession details worked out."

"Most likely."

"It'll be Sevara," Rayburn said. "She'll need two or three weeks to get the DPMs aboard, as well as backing from the White House."

"There's the brother."

"Be serious, Paul. The brother has about as much influence as his father does at this point."

Crocker didn't say anything. Rayburn set down his coffee again and got to his feet.

"Sorry I couldn't be of more help about the Starstreaks. If I dig up anything more, I'll pass it along."

"Simon?"

"Hmm?"

"Who else knows you're looking at this?"

Rayburn shrugged. "Nancy. My contact at MOD. Why?"

"I'm not worried about your PA, but your contact at the Ministry of Defense, will he keep his mouth closed?"

"My contact at the MOD is a she, Paul," Rayburn corrected mildly. "And she understands the necessity of discretion."

"Good."

"You don't want anyone to know you're looking into this?"

"Not yet."

Rayburn shrugged a second time, as if the whole cloak-and-dagger aspect of their business was beyond boredom to him. It was Crocker's suspicion that to Rayburn, that was indeed the case. He was more interested in solving the acrostic than in solving the murder, so to speak.

"Won't breathe a word of it," Rayburn said.

Crocker escorted him to the door, letting him out, then closing it once more and returning to his desk. He lit a cigarette, and turned to look out at the river and the rain.

Before he'd become C, Frances Barclay had chaired the Joint Intelligence Committee. It was a position of power, and one that allowed him to liaise with personnel in both the Foreign and Home Offices, as well as the Ministry of Defense. It was an associated SIS position, with constant and regular access to the business of the Firm.

It was exactly the kind of position, in fact, that would allow for the authorization and transfer of four Starstreak MANPADs to Islamabad Station, and with enough clout to require the Station's silence in the process.

Crocker wondered if he wasn't manufacturing the theory wholly, rather than tailoring it to fit the known facts. After all, the only thing he truly knew was that Barclay had asked him about a MANPAD alert coming out of Chechnya, an alert of which Crocker himself had been unaware. It was circumstantial in the extreme.

But Barclay did have both means and opportunity to initiate the transfer, and to do so at a time when taking such a risk wasn't beyond the realm of possibility. Motive remained the question.

Crocker crushed out his cigarette, feeling the beginnings of a new headache.

He didn't know why Barclay had done it. He doubted he could prove it, even if he did.

But the more he thought about it, the more certain he became.

Somewhere in Central Asia, someone was in possession of four surface-to-air missiles.

And Frances Barclay—C—had been the one to send them there.

CHAPTER 14

17 February, 1343 Hours (GMT+5:00)

The day was clear and cold and bright, and Chace pulled off her sunglasses to get a better look at the boy at the side of the road.

She put him around thirteen, maybe a little older, too thin, wearing the quirky combination of traditional-meets-West clothing she'd seen so much of before leaving Tashkent that morning. The boy wore tan trousers, his pant legs tucked into the tops of his calf-high boots, coated with dust, scuffed and scratched, with a pair of slippers on over them that could be easily removed upon entering a private home or a mosque. His T-shirt was red, just visible beneath the striped wraparound cloak he wore, belted with a sash at his waist. His black hair was mostly hidden beneath the fleeced *tilpak* atop his head, its flaps dangling at his cheeks. Unlike what she'd seen in Tashkent, though, this boy's clothing showed obvious wear, and she could see where both the cloak and the trousers had been repeatedly repaired.

There'd been a mining town some twelve kilometers back, built around an enormous plant constructed to heat-leach gold from the low-grade ore brought up by miners. The plant and, Chace supposed, the mines as well were foreign-operated, most likely by some concern out of the E.U. She'd wondered idly what the kickback to the Uzbek Government had been. She'd imagined it to be substantial, and wondered if the return in gold was worth the cost.

The boy was likely from that community, though what he was doing out here alone she had no idea, and saw no sign of a ready explanation. He had no herd of goats or other livestock requiring attention, and carried nothing but a ratty fabric bag slung over his shoulder. The bag, like his T-shirt, was red, but faded almost pink.

He stood and stared as she slowed the car to a stop, then rolled down her window. The car was a Range Rover, left-hand drive, and at least twenty years old. Chace had purchased it from a middle-aged man she'd met at the Art Center in Tashkent early that morning. She'd paid him five thousand dollars for it, in cash, and he'd been so delighted he'd offered to sell her his brother's motorcycle as well. Chace had, for a moment, entertained the idea; a second vehicle, stashed in Tashkent, might come in useful. But her plan ultimately required moving not just her, but two others, and a motorcycle would be inadequate to that task.

"*Assalom aleikum,*" Chace said.

The boy grinned at her accent. "*Waleikum assalom.*"

"*Siz Ingliz tilida gapirasizmi?*"

He shook his head. "*Yoq, Uzbekcha. Uzbekcha, ha?*"

Chace shook her head, bringing up a grin to match the boy's own.

"*Men Ingliz bilmayman,*" the boy said. "*Russki?*"

Chace switched to Russian, answering, "A little."

"I have a little Russian, too," the boy said, answering in the same. "You are American?"

"English."

"You are lost?"

"A little, I think. I'm looking for the market."

He reappraised her, his look clearly questioning her sanity. "No market."

"Across the border. For guns."

"Oh, yes, there is that market."

"How far?"

"It moves. Not know where now."

"You help me find it?"

The look that doubted Chace's sanity returned, more amused. "Why you go there?"

"I need guns," Chace answered simply.

The boy considered that, then, seeing no flaw in the logic, nodded. "They have guns. More than guns, also. Drugs. Girls."

"I will pay. You be my guide, I will pay." She reached into her coat, freeing one of the bills from the bundle in the inner pocket, showing him an American twenty-dollar bill. "For you."

The boy stuck out his hand, and Chace extended the bill, letting him take it. He examined it with deep suspicion, drawing the paper taut between both hands, holding it up to the sunlight. Chace doubted he could tell a forgery from the real thing, and the whole affectation struck her as vaguely charming. She fought back a smile.

Once the boy was satisfied, he tucked the bill into his trousers, beneath the folds of his cloak, then walked around the Range Rover, coming from behind it. Chace tracked him in the mirrors, and this time she did smile as she watched the boy rise on tiptoe at the rear of the vehicle, to peer into the back. Seeing nothing that alarmed him, he continued around to the right-hand side.

Chace leaned across the seat and unlocked the door, shoving it open, and the boy climbed in, looking around at the interior of the vehicle. Then he closed the door, sighed, stretched, and leaned back in the front passenger seat. Chace fought the urge to laugh.

The boy straightened again, then indicated himself with his right thumb. "Javlon."

Chace indicated herself. "Tracy."

"Tracy," the boy echoed, then pointed out the windscreen, down the narrow dirt road. "Tracy, that way."

At some point early on they must have crossed the border into Kazakhstan, but there was nothing to mark it, and Chace knew that, at least in this part of the country, such designations were meaningless. Calling the border porous was generous. To the south, of course, the situation was different; the border into Afghanistan was watched, if not by Uzbekistan's forces, then by the United States.

They stopped three times, in three separate villages, the first shortly after Javlon had climbed aboard, which he explained to her was his home. There were a handful of houses, and a small mosque, serving as the community center as much as the heart of worship. Javlon sprang from the car upon their arrival, without explanation, and for several minutes Chace waited, wondering if he was going to come back. No one emerged from any of the buildings, not even the mosque.

After five minutes, though, Javlon returned, climbing in, and after him came a handful of others, children and women, all silently watching his departure. Chace saw no men in the community.

Javlon pointed her north again, then, shortly thereafter, west, until they hit a second village. He again leaped from the car, all but accosting an older man drawing water from a well that had been dropped in the center of the square. She heard a hasty conversation in what she supposed was Uzbek, but could just have easily been one of the other half-dozen regional dialects. Returning, Javlon gave her new directions, still heading west, and at the third village, he repeated the process once more.

"Close," he informed her upon returning this time. "Very close. They move always."

"How close?"

The boy thought, then held up his left hand, splaying his fingers.

"Five kilometers?"

"Five, yes."

She watched the odometer then, and after three and a half came to a stop. Javlon looked at her in confusion, and then, when she killed the engine, in something approaching alarm.

"I want you to do something," Chace told him.

He looked at her with open suspicion, his right hand moving with almost comical stillness to the handle of the door.

"Nothing bad," she assured him, and then, very deliberately, still smiling at him, reached again into her coat and freed two more bills from her roll. She was drawing blind, mostly because she didn't want to reveal exactly how much cash she was carrying, and was therefore relieved to see that she had pulled another two twenties, and not any of the larger denominations. She handed the bills to Javlon.

He took them, but the suspicion remained on his face.

Chace pointed out the windshield, over the front of the car. "It's that way?"

"Yes, that way."

"I want you to go first," Chace said carefully. "You understand? You go first, with the money. You buy—"

"Buy?"

Chace gestured, miming the exchange of money. "Buy, yes?"

Javlon nodded.

"You buy a gun, please." Chace raised her right hand, turning it sideways, extending her index finger, making the shape of a pistol, careful to not point at the boy. "A gun. And bullets. You bring them back to me here."

Javlon's face scrunched in confusion, and Chace was unsure if he was trying to fathom her directions or the logic behind them.

"Gun for you?" he asked.

"Yes, but you get it for me first, yes?"

"Then you go buy more guns?"

Chace nodded.

He thought about that for several more seconds, then suddenly let loose with a long "Ohh!" and began nodding.

"You have no gun," he deduced.

"That's right."

"Oh!" He touched his forehead, grinning. "Smart."

Chace gestured out the windshield once more. "You go. I wait here."

She watched as he walked up the road, over a rise, then down and out of sight. She checked her watch, and wished, passionately, that she had bought cigarettes before leaving Tashkent.

After ten minutes, she opened her door and got out of the vehicle. This part of the country—countries, Chace corrected herself—was desert, hard dusty earth and a paucity of greenery. Chilly during the day, it would become freezing at night. But if she was still out here after sunset, the weather would be the least of her problems. She had no desire to walk into an open-air gun show in the middle of nowhere at sundown; it seemed like a very good way to make sure she wouldn't walk out again, even if she was armed when she did it.

It was why she'd sent Javlon ahead, after all. A Western woman with a lot of cash on a shopping trip was going to be seen as an easy mark, and she knew it. Before any actual business could take place, she'd have to prove to the vendors that she wasn't a valid target.

A wind came up, swirling dust off the ground, providing the only noise. She resisted the urge to check her watch again, then surrendered.

Twenty-one minutes.

Then thirty.

And then, coming back over the rise, Javlon, grinning from ear to ear, holding a pistol in one hand and a box of ammunition in the other. When he saw her, he began jogging toward her.

"Tracy! Look!"

Alarmingly, he pointed the pistol at her, and for an awful second, Chace wondered if she would have to kill him, if he didn't kill her first. But the triumphant grin remained on his thin face as he closed the distance, the pride of a job well done, and when he reached her, she took the pistol from his grip quickly, and without any resistance.

"Good, yes?" he asked her, breathless. "Good gun?"

Chace examined the pistol, releasing the magazine, checking to see that it was, in fact, unloaded, before sliding back the breech and holding up the weapon, to cast sunlight into the chamber. She checked the barrel, saw nothing obstructing it, then turned the pistol and examined the firing pin. She'd expected the boy to bring

roximity to Russia and the former
n—but instead he'd brought her a
, the Sarsilmaz M2000.

ave chosen for herself, but Javlon
tisfied that the gun would function,
f the Range Rover. The box of am-
cardboard cracked and peeling.
d it held only sixteen rounds. She
, discovering that only half were the
, she trusted five of them enough to
The rest she left in the box.

"Good," Chace agreed, slapping the magazine into place. She racked the slide, cocking the pistol, then checked the safety. Then she untucked her shirt and slid the gun into her pants, at the front. Javlon watched, his eyes growing wider.

"Okay," Chace told him after she had smoothed her shirt back into place. "All done now."

"All done?"

"You can go."

Javlon shook his head. "I come with."

Chace shook her head. "No."

"But I come."

"No. Dangerous."

The boy shrugged.

Chace pointed at the ground. "Wait here."

"I come."

"No, you wait here," Chace said, growing frustrated. She pointed at the ground beneath her feet again, more insistently. "Wait here. I come back."

Javlon folded his arms across his chest, giving her a look that seemed to say she was both stupid and unreasonable.

"Wait here," Chace said a last time, and climbed back into the Rover.

She left him at the side of the road.

It was closer to three kilometers than one and a half, and she ended up off the road entirely, finally parking at the edge of a gulley. She could see smoke from cooking fires rising from below, and as soon as she stopped the engine, she heard the din of livestock and voices and music. She got out of the car, locked it, pocketing the keys, then removing her sunglasses. She counted six other vehicles, all of them dusty, rusted, and at least as old as her own, parked around the edges of the market. The scent of roasting meat, fuel, and manure mixed in the dry, cold air.

She approached the edge of the gulley, hopped down into the dry creek bed, and made her way toward the noise. The livestock came first, goats tethered in groups of three or four to stakes driven into the ground, chickens in too-small metal cages lined up around them, dropping feathers every time they tried to flap their wings. A couple of dogs were similarly tied.

Past the livestock, the market, such as it was, began in earnest, where the gulley grew wider and more shallow. Chace experienced a painful déjà vu, because she had been here before, not here, but almost here, in Saudi Arabia, a place called the Wadi-as-Sirhan. It had been night then, and Tom had died there, and for a moment the memory assailed her, and she had to stop to fight it off.

A large tent anchored the center of the bazaar, Soviet Army surplus, and framing the approach to its entrance, along both sides, stood pitted and bent metal folding tables, with companion benches. Three separate cooking fires burned nearby, meat sizzling over the flames, fat spitting on the grills. A ragged mutt prowled between the tables, looking for scraps. Music from three separate boom boxes competed with each other, crackling from burst speakers, country-and-western and Europop.

Spreading out, filling the rest of the gulley around the tent, were the vendors, most of them with their wares displayed on dirty blankets or rugs, a few having gone so far as to raise canopies of one sort or another on sticks, to provide shelter and an illusion of privacy.

Chace saw bootleg cassettes and CDs, old magazines, bits and pieces of machinery salvaged from who knew what, and piles upon piles of army surplus equipment. There were flashlights and entrenching tools and MREs and radios that she suspected would never be made to transmit or receive again. Most of the surplus was Soviet-era, but among them she spied bits and pieces of more modern equipment, matériel either bought or stolen from Coalition forces, even what appeared to be a set of NVGs. Three separate vendors were selling drugs, pot and hash and opium and their big brother, heroin.

And there were weapons, so many weapons. Not counting the ones being carried by the vendors and the shoppers, stacked precariously in makeshift displays, arrayed on their blankets, piled one upon the other. The collections spanned the ages, it seemed, weapons that had migrated throughout Eastern Europe and Central Asia over the last sixty-plus years. From the Second World War through Korea and Vietnam, the tools of war that had survived and been passed on from one set of hands to another, with varying degrees of care. There were pistols from Vietnam and rifles from the Soviet invasion of Afghanistan, revolvers from Korea and knives from the Second World War. There were swords and spears and axes of indeterminate origin and provenance, and a wide selection of knives that at first glance seemed to be of local manufacture, and fairly high quality. Ammunition boxes formed makeshift barriers between stalls, labeled in Cyrillic and Mandarin and Uzbek and English. She saw grenades, she saw flak jackets, she saw collapsible batons, she saw submachine guns.

She stopped again, this time to orient herself, aware that she was drawing eyes. It didn't alarm her; it was expected. There were perhaps some thirty to forty people around, either selling or buying. Almost all of them looked to be ethnic Uzbeks, though there were no doubt Kazakhs and Kyrgyzs among them.

And all were men, to the last of them, with the exception of the only other woman Chace could discern, standing at the closed flap of the tent. The men ranged in age from late teens to perhaps mid-fifties, most dressed in the traditional mix of cloaks and boots, a few in the post-Soviet work fashion, the majority with their heads covered. The woman—or girl—looked to be fifteen at the oldest, wearing a filthy robe. Her legs were bare, and Chace suspected that, beneath the robe, she wore nothing else. If she was cold, she did a good job of hiding it.

While Chace watched, the tent flap parted, and a squat man emerged, bearded, pulling up his trousers. Past him, inside, Chace could see two other girls, each naked, moving to cover themselves. The squat man exchanged words with another, seated at the table near the entrance, then stopped, looking her way. Another man, seated at one of the tables, rose and headed into the tent.

Chace heard movement behind her, ignored it for the moment. They still didn't know what to make of her. No one would try anything, not yet.

She tried to put a cap on what she was feeling, forced herself to look away from the tent and back to the vendors, began walking around the circle, looking at the items on each blanket as she passed. She stopped briefly at a display of knives, seeing a bone-handled blade that caught her fancy, thinking that she would need one of her own. In her periphery, she counted three men following her as a group, staying perhaps fifteen feet back. Two of them carried Kalashnikovs on straps at the shoulders. The third, the eldest of the three, wore a pistol in a holster around his waist.

Chace continued working her way around the market, finally completing her counterclockwise circuit at the largest collection of weapons for sale, to the left of the tent entrance. A grumpy-looking Uzbek in overalls and a work shirt watched over the wares, eyeing her with an expression that seemed caught between suspicion and amusement, yet undecided. Chace passed his wares, which seemed to be grouped without rhyme or reason, then stopped and doubled back, her eye snagging on a pistol half buried in a stack near the back of the makeshift stall. It was a semiauto, what looked to be a Smith & Wesson Mk 39, but at this distance, she couldn't be sure. The men following her stopped when she did.

Chace pointed. "Can I see that?" she asked in Russian.

"You're not Russian," the vendor said. It wasn't quite accusatory, but it came close.

"That one," Chace said, indicating the pistol again. "The Smith and Wesson."

"You have money?"

She smiled.

"You come here alone?"

She let her smile grow a fraction.

The man smiled in return, revealing the fact that he was missing his upper two front teeth. "You should not come alone."

"That one," Chace repeated.

The man hesitated, and Chace saw his eyes flick past her, to her left, to the three men who had been following, and she knew what was coming, and she knew what the cue would be.

The vendor nodded, shrugged, and started to turn away from her, toward the indicated stack of weapons. As he did, she heard the movement, caught the motion in her periphery, the Kalashnikovs coming off of the shoulders of both men. There was no haste in their movement, and it gave her all the time she needed. Chace swept her right hand up, over her belly, and brought out the pistol Javlon had bought for her. She struck down the safety with her thumb as she freed the weapon, had her finger settled well on the trigger by the time she put her sights on the vendor's back.

Everyone stopped, the men with the rifles and the ones shuffling at their blankets and the ones eating their meals.

"Alone," Chace said. "Not stupid."

The vendor turned around to face her slowly, and when he saw the pistol pointed at him, raised his hands, showing her his palms.

"They lower the guns," Chace told him. "Or I shoot."

The vendor nodded and spoke in Uzbek. Chace risked turning her head enough to see the three, and to confirm that they had complied.

"Have to try," the vendor said by way of explanation, still showing her his hands, and working in a shrug for added effect.

She looked back at him. "I understand."

"If you want, we can do business now." He smiled hopefully, again revealing his missing teeth.

"Yes, please," Chace agreed, and with her free hand, she pointed to the stack once more, and added, "It's the one sticking out at the bottom."

The vendor nodded, turning to retrieve the gun in question, and as he did, Chace threw the safety back into place on the pistol, and slid it once more into the front of her trousers. She felt as much as heard the tension lift from the market then, and by the time the vendor was showing her the Smith & Wesson, conversations were resuming.

It took the better part of two hours to buy everything she thought she would need, or at least, to buy everything that they had that she thought she would need. When she was finished, the three men who had stalked her helped to carry her purchases back to the Range Rover, where she loaded them into the back. She'd bought three blankets off one of the vendors, and used them to cover the weapons, ammunition, and other equipment. Once everything was squared away, Chace walked back to the vendor with the missing teeth, and paid, in cash. No one bothered her, no one followed her as she returned to the car, poorer, but certainly better armed.

When she returned to the spot where she'd left Javlon, he was gone, and the sun was dipping below the horizon.

Chace waited by the side of the road until darkness came.

The boy never came back.

CHAPTER 15

18 February, 0910 Hours GMT

"Dad!"

"No," Crocker said flatly, in much the same tone and with much the same malevolence he employed on personnel in the Ops Room. In the Ops Room, it was quite effective, and had the desired result of instantly and entirely closing down any further debate.

Here at home was another story and if anything, seemed to have the opposite effect, as his elder daughter, Sabrina, was about to demonstrate. It didn't help matters that he was at the kitchen stove, still in his dressing gown, a skillet in his hand, and more concerned with not breaking the yolks on the eggs he was frying up for the family breakfast than in exerting his authority. It was a position that, he concluded, lacked the appropriate authority.

"I've had the tickets for *weeks*!"

"I'm sure you can find a friend who wants them."

"That's not the point, Dad! *Everyone's* going! Everyone!"

"You're not everyone."

Sabrina slammed her hand on the kitchen counter in frustration, then played her trump card. "Mom!"

From the kitchen table, Jennie didn't look up from her newspaper. "Paul, it's Saturday. She's had the tickets for weeks."

"She also performed abysmally on her mock exams," Crocker countered. "She has lessons, she has that tutor coming, and she's looking at her A-levels come summer. She needs to study."

"I have been studying!" Sabrina complained. "Just because you're never here to see it doesn't mean it isn't happening, Dad!"

I am going to lose this argument, Crocker realized.

"Please don't raise your voice at me," he said.

Sabrina sulked, glowering at him. "I apologize."

"Has she been studying?" Crocker asked his wife.

At the table, his younger daughter, Ariel, in imitation of her mother, didn't look up from her book. "When she's not online chatting with her mates."

"Die," Sabrina instructed her sister.

"She has been studying, Paul," Jennie confirmed. "I already told her she could go. She'll do fine on her exams. Making her miserable every weekend between now and when she takes them won't improve that performance."

"I thought we wanted better than fine."

Jennie glanced up, warning him with her eyes. "I told her she can go."

"Who is she going with?" Crocker tried. "Who are you going with?"

"Friends from school," his daughter answered.

"I'd like names, if you don't mind."

"Are you going to check them?"

Crocker shot her a look. In the Ops Room, it would have sent its target running for cover, or at its best, dropped them in their tracks. Here, it reinforced Sabrina's defiance, and she raised her chin slightly, her mouth tight, daring him to admit that, yes, he kept his family under surveillance. She might not have understood exactly what her father did for a living, but she knew enough to know it was for the Government. He never discussed his work in front of the children, and very rarely with Jennie, but Sabrina was old enough and smart enough to understand what that omission meant. If she thought of her father as James Bond, though, she remained unimpressed. He doubted she actually believed that he would go so far as to keep his wife and children under watch.

Crocker moved the skillet off the burner, began sliding portions of breakfast onto the waiting plates beside the stove. "Is that boy going to be there? Lancelot or whatever his name is?"

At the table, Ariel giggled, then stifled the sound and studiously turned the page in her book. She was reading Brian Jacques' latest, Crocker noted, yet another in a long sequence of novels about noble medieval mice.

"Tristan," Sabrina corrected tightly. "No, I'm not seeing him anymore."

"Who are you seeing?"

"Paul," Jennie warned.

"I'm going with Trinnie, Dad. I'll be spending the night at her place after the concert."

"Trinnie's the one with the spots?"

"It's a mole, and she had it removed."

"When will you be back?"

Sabrina smiled in quiet triumph, sensing the moment of capitulation. "Tomorrow morning."

Crocker finished fixing the plates, moving them to the table. He had to clear his throat twice, loudly, before Ariel and Jennie would lower their respective reading materials to make room for the breakfasts. He set their food in front of them, and watched as each woman set about eating, without so much as the slightest acknowledgment of his culinary efforts.

"I have no authority in this house," Crocker declared.

As if to confirm the statement, he got no response from any of them.

"Right," he told his eldest. "Go. But you're back by noon tomorrow."

Sabrina kissed his cheek lightly, happy once more, and then was out of the room, a "thank you" drifting back toward him in her wake. He heard her feet thumping up the stairs, rushing back to her room. Apparently she had a wardrobe to plan.

Crocker poured himself a fresh cup of tea, then took his seat at the table. Jennie lowered her copy of the *Guardian,* smiling at him. Sometimes he thought his wife read the liberal paper just to annoy him.

From behind her book, Ariel asked, "So I'm supposed to have a broken leg, am I?"

Both Jennie and Crocker looked at her.

Ariel took her bookmark from where it rested beside her plate, set it between the pages, closed the book, and then looked at her parents. Her glasses, Crocker noticed, were smudged. Unlike Sabrina, Ariel went to great lengths not to care how she looked.

"Heard that, did you?" Jennie asked.

Ariel nodded. "I crashed my bicycle?"

"Tuesday," Jennie said. "Yes, you narrowly avoided being hit by a car."

"On Valentine's Day?"

"You were distracted, obviously."

Ariel made a face, disgusted by the thought of the kind of people who cared about things like boys and Valentine's Day.

Crocker looked at Jennie. "Barclay called?"

"One of his assistants," Jennie confirmed. "Last evening, before you got home." She cast a glance to Ariel, then back to Crocker. "Little jugs have big ears."

"Why didn't you tell me this last night?"

"You did get home rather late, Paul. It slipped my mind."

"Did he say why he was calling?"

"The assistant? He wanted to know if Ariel was all right. Said that Sir Frances was quite concerned."

Ariel asked, "Who's Sir Frances?"

"Daddy's boss," Jennie said.

"You lied to your boss? You told him I'd broken my leg?" Ariel asked Crocker.

"Yes."

"Do I get a set of crutches, at least?"

Crocker didn't respond, thinking. Jennie was looking at him, now mildly concerned.

Barclay's checking the story, Crocker thought. *Three days late, but he's checking the story. Why now?*

Crocker rose from the table, finishing his tea, leaving his breakfast half eaten. "I'm going to have to go into the office."

Jennie nodded, which was bearable, but Ariel's look of disappointment was bitter, and not.

"I'm sorry," he told his younger daughter.

"You promised we'd go to the show at the Old Town Hall," Ariel said softly. Like her mother, when Ariel was upset, she wouldn't raise her voice. Rather, she lowered it until it was almost impossible to hear. "You promised we'd see the puppets, the ones from Japan."

"I know. I *am* sorry, Ariel."

"I'll take you," Jennie said. "We'll have fun."

"It's not the same," Ariel said, and then Crocker was out of the room, out of earshot.

The guilt dogged him all the way to London.

Ronald Hodgson was at Duty Ops when Crocker entered the Operations Room, supervising a skeletal staff, as appropriate for a weekend without a major operation in the offing. Crocker thought he did an admirable job of concealing his surprise.

"D-Ops on the floor," Ron declared when he'd recovered, then added, to Crocker, "Didn't expect you to be coming in today, sir."

"No," Crocker agreed, taking a position beside the Duty Ops Desk so he could survey the plasma wall. Lankford's job in Morocco was posted on the map, with a callout designating the operation as "Bowfiddle," and a notation reading, "Running—Joint." Otherwise, there was nothing of immediate interest. Two other minor operations, one in Argentina, surveillance for the MOD, the other in Gibraltar.

Crocker stuck a cigarette in his mouth, lit it, called out to Alexis Ferguson at the MCO Desk. "Have we seen an exchange of signals with Tashkent Station in the last twenty-four hours? Anything at all?"

Alexis tapped her keyboard, quickly bringing up the log, scanning the entries. She was tall and quite thin, with a crown of short black hair, and she had to bend to peer at her monitor. "One exchange, sir, initiated nineteen-twenty-seven hours last night, London to Tashkent, with a reply logged as of oh-thirty-three, local."

"Whose office initiated the communication?"

"The Deputy Chief, sir. Response by Station Number One, Craig Gillard."

Crocker scowled, shook his head. Alison Gordon-Palmer had left the building before him the previous night. Unless she'd turned around and come back—which was entirely possible—the inquiry hadn't been from her office. More to the point, if she was as deep into Sir Walter Seccombe's pocket as Crocker was now beginning to suspect, she wouldn't have risked tipping Chace's run. Which meant that, while the communication appeared to have been initiated by the DC, it most likely hadn't been.

Which left only two others who could make it look like the communication had come from the DC. Either D-Int, or C.

And Crocker couldn't imagine why Simon Rayburn would want to hide any communication with a Station, let alone a communication to Tashkent, something he had both the authority and right to do whenever it suited him.

Which left C.

"We have a copy?" Crocker asked.

Alexis began tapping at her console again, then paused. After a moment, she resumed typing, faster, then paused again.

"I'm sorry, sir," she said, slowly. "I can't find a copy."

"What do you mean?"

"It's not here. It may have been purged to the server already."

I doubt that, Crocker thought. "Who had MCO before you came on shift, Lex?"

"William Teagle, sir. He's forty-eight hours off, due back Monday morning."

Crocker turned back to Ron. "Is C in the building?"

One of the phones in the bank at the Duty Ops Desk began ringing, and Ron moved to answer it, saying, "I believe so, sir, yes."

Crocker grunted, tapping the edge of his cigarette into the ashtray at Ron's desk, waiting for him to finish with the call. Ron listened, murmured an assent, then hung up.

"C most definitely *is* in the building, sir," Ron told him. "He'd like you to join him in his office, in fact."

"Bloody hell," was the only thing Crocker could think to say.

In almost every instance prior, Crocker had entered Barclay's territory to find the other man firmly entrenched, either reigning from behind his desk or in the sitting area, where he would occupy the largest of the leather upholstered chairs arrayed around the coffee table. Barclay, like Crocker, like Seccombe, like Gordon-Palmer, like a thousand others throughout Whitehall, understood the power of the Desk, and the etiquette surrounding its use. Meet an underling while sitting behind it, you demonstrated your superiority in the chain of command; decline to stand upon receiving a guest, you indicated displeasure, or possibly even contempt; rise and move around it to greet, perhaps going so far as to offer a hand for the shaking, you declared anything from camaraderie to gratitude to friendship.

The etiquette of the desk, the ways it could be used, even abused, were legion. Crocker had sometimes thought, in his lighter moments, that the FCO and the Home Office could collaborate on a joint publication to be delivered to all senior civil servants. *Your Desk and You: Strategies in Management,* or something along those lines.

In the imagined publication, Crocker always imagined Barclay writing the foreword.

Entering the office on this Saturday morning, though, Crocker wondered if a new chapter mightn't be in order. Sir Frances Barclay wasn't behind the desk. He was waiting in front of it.

"You wanted to see me, sir?" Crocker said.

Barclay nodded, then gestured vaguely in the direction of the sitting area. Instead of preceding Crocker, he followed. He even went so far as to remain standing until after Crocker had taken a seat on the couch.

"None of my PAs are in, I'm afraid," Barclay said. "Else I'd offer you something."

"I'm fine, sir."

"I suppose we could have a drink from the bar, though it seems early yet."

"A touch, yes."

"Well, then," Barclay said, and stood for a moment longer before almost reluctantly taking his customary seat. He positioned himself sitting on the edge, leaning forward. He adjusted his eyeglasses, then exhaled, resolving himself. "I assume you know that Daniel called your home, and spoke to your wife."

"You didn't believe my daughter had broken her leg."

"It isn't beyond you to employ your family in a deception."

"Why would I deceive you?"

Barclay made a single noise, the start of an abortive laugh. "Paul, I don't think that really deserves a response."

"Perhaps I should rephrase, then, sir. What would I be deceiving you about this time?"

"I don't know," Barclay replied, suddenly frank. "But I do know you've been to see the PUS at the FCO twice in the past week. And I know that when I make inquiries into the purpose of those visits, the answers I receive are, at best, evasive."

"It's as I told you before, sir. Sir Walter has been soliciting my input regarding the fiasco in KL."

"I don't believe you." Barclay finally leaned back in his chair, lacing his fingers together, setting his hands in his lap. He looked at Crocker. "And unfortunately, I seem to have no way to compel the truth from you, considering that you've little over a week left in this job."

Crocker didn't respond.

"You have no interest in the position in Washington?" Barclay asked.

Crocker considered his possible answers, then decided to go with brutal honesty. "None at all, sir."

"Then I suppose the only real thing I can offer you is your job, and my promise that you will keep it if you bring me into your confidence."

That was unexpected, and Crocker did his best to keep the fact from his face, but it answered, finally, the questions he'd been wrestling with ever since meeting with Seale in Hyde Park. For the first time, he felt confident he knew what this was about, if not in specifics, at least in generalities. Something had happened in the last five days to put Barclay not only on the defensive, but under siege. Something that he could not easily avoid or redress.

Something that threatened his career the same way, five days prior, he had threatened Crocker's.

It had to be the MANPADs—there just wasn't any other explanation as far as Crocker could see. And thinking that, it seemed more than plausible, possible even. Barclay on the Joint Intelligence Committee had been in position to authorize the transfer of weapons to the Northern Alliance. He'd had enough clout and seniority to initiate the move, as well as to compel Islamabad Station's silence in the matter, either through intimidation or, more likely, the promise of later reward. Sitting at the head of the JIC, it had been understood that Barclay's next step up the career rung would be as the Chief of Service at SIS. To a Station Number One in Islamabad, Frances Barclay would have been a very good friend to have indeed. But it had gone wrong, the missiles had vanished, and Barclay had spent the last four years looking behind him, wondering when they would return.

According to the CIA, they just had, somewhere in the south of Uzbekistan.

"You know about the Starstreaks," Barclay said finally.

"Yes."

"Seccombe knows about them, too. He's known about them ever since they disappeared into Afghanistan."

Crocker wasn't surprised, and didn't doubt the assertion. "Seccombe's never mentioned them. They've never come up in our discussions."

Barclay frowned slightly, unsure whether or not to believe him.

"They've never come up, sir," Crocker assured him.

"Be that as it may, according to the CIA, these four Starstreaks were sold into Uzbekistan less than a month ago. You know that much from Seale, I'm sure."

It seemed unnecessary to say that the information had come from Cheng at the NCCT, rather than the CIA, so Crocker merely nodded slightly, waiting for Barclay to continue.

"I've been on to the Station in Tashkent, asking them to keep an eye open. I've had to be circumspect, obviously, but I think I made myself clear to them. I want those missiles found, Paul. I want them found, and I want them returned to England. Either that, or I want proof of their destruction."

"They've been in service for over seven years, sir. I'm sure the batteries that power them have run down by now."

"That hardly renders them harmless, Paul. Four Starstreak missiles. If they end up in the hands of our enemies, if they're used to bring down a military, or, heaven forbid, a commercial aircraft . . ."

Barclay trailed off, looking past Crocker, toward his desk.

"I'd hate to be responsible for that loss of life," Barclay concluded quietly.

Not to mention the loss of career, Crocker thought. If the missiles were used, if their use could be traced, then it would be just a matter of time before Barclay would have to claim ownership. There would be no defense for what came next, only the question of how Sir Frances Barclay would conduct his withdrawal from public service.

"The Americans seemed to think it unlikely that the missiles are still in Uzbekistan," Crocker said. "More likely they've been moved farther into Central Asia. They could be in any of a dozen countries by now."

"I know that."

"Without more information, they're impossible to locate."

"I know that as well." Barclay looked at him levelly. "But your aid in the search for them would be invaluable, Paul. And as D-Ops, it's a reasonable directive for you to issue to our Stations. If you took the lead in this search for me, if you worked with Simon, I'd think your chances of success in doing so would be substantial."

"You'll forgive me for saying that I think you're being overly optimistic, sir. We've been searching up MANPADs since the start of the war, and with only limited success."

"But in this instance, you'd have hard intelligence to begin with. A place to start, a direction to head. It would scarcely be fumbling about in the dark."

"Perhaps not, but close to it."

"I'm asking for your help, Paul. Help that I would be grateful to receive. Help that I would reward."

"You'd spare me my job."

"I would see you became my next Deputy Chief."

That stopped Crocker. "The DC is leaving?"

"She could be made to, to ensure your promotion," Barclay rejoined levelly. "And I would, of course, follow your recommendation on the appointment of a new D-Ops. Even Poole, were you to champion him."

Barclay waited, watching him, knowing full well the weight of the offer he had just made. Crocker had been passed over twice already for promotion to Deputy Chief, stalled at the level of Director of Operations. It was the next logical promotion in his career, one he had deeply coveted. As much as he respected, even liked, Alison Gordon-Palmer, Crocker absolutely wanted her job.

Poole wouldn't do as D-Ops, not yet, but if he had to, Crocker could see him as Head of Section. Which would free up Chace, allow him to promote her to fill Crocker's office. Just as he wanted the promotion to DC, he knew that Chace had wanted, eventually, to succeed him as D-Ops.

And with that hierarchy in place, with Crocker positioned between Barclay and Chace, he could do a lot of good, he was certain of it. He could move the Firm fully back into the game, begin correcting the errors of the last twenty years, the compromises, the capitulations.

It was an extraordinarily tempting offer, and looking at Barclay, he knew it was sincere.

"The offer is contingent on the recovery or destruction of the Starstreaks?" Crocker asked.

"Obviously."

He thought again, once more considering it all, everything Barclay had told him. He thought about Alison Gordon-Palmer, and Sir Walter Seccombe. He thought about Chace, still running secretly in Uzbekistan. He thought, for a moment, about Ruslan Mihailovich Malikov and his sister, Sevara Malikov-Ganiev.

Unbidden, he thought about his wife and his daughters, and remembered the bitterness in Ariel's voice, the hurt at yet another of her father's broken promises.

He wondered which of many enemies he'd rather have, and thought it was a luxury to be able to choose even that.

"I'll see what I can do," Crocker told Barclay.

CHAPTER 16

20 February, 0703 Hours (GMT+5:00)

Riess came in early on Monday morning, hoping to use the peace and
quiet of McColl's absence to mow through the majority of the pa-
perwork on his desk. He had yet another in the endless streams of
démarches to prepare, this one regarding conditional subsidies
proposed to support the Aral Sea Project, truly an utter waste of
his time.

The Aral Sea was dying, if it wasn't dead already. The two
mighty rivers that had once fed it—the Syr Darya in the north, the
Amu Darya in the south—no longer actually reached the sea, di-
verted and run dry by irrigation projects devoted to cotton production long before the waterways could reach their onetime
destination. The sea level itself was dropping at a rate of one meter
per year, and what it uncovered as it went could only be described
as chemical crust, a foul mix of pesticides and defoliants that had
run off the cotton fields. So far, over thirty-four thousand square
kilometers of seafloor had been exposed, costing over ten million
hectares of pastureland. All twenty-four documented species of
fish that once swam in its waters were now gone.

It wasn't simply an environmental disaster, it was a humanitarian one. Tuberculosis was endemic to the region, with over two

thousand deaths attributed to the disease each year. Anemia was common. Children suffered from a host of liver, kidney, and respiratory ailments, in addition to cancer and birth defects.

It was a problem that had no solution, and as Riess read the reports yet again, trying to compose the paper that McColl would ask him to rewrite at least twice, he felt his frustration build more. What was the point? The political will to fix the situation didn't exist, not here in Uzbekistan, nor in neighboring Kazakhstan, sharing the northern shores of the Aral. It didn't exist in Turkmenistan or Kyrgyzstan or Tajikistan, all of whom drew from one or the other river to support their own agribusiness.

Yet another situation, another crisis in the long line of crises that Riess had seen in his years at the State Department, that had no solution.

It turned his thoughts dark and made the work harder, and he was so focused on it all that he didn't look up when the door opened from the hall, into the Pol/Econ office. He assumed it was McColl, or the staff secretary, and it wasn't until he heard Aaron Tower's voice that he actually raised his eyes from his computer screen, to see the Tashkent COS standing before him.

"Morning, Chuck."

"Good morning, sir. If you're looking for the Counselor, I'm afraid he isn't in yet."

Tower shook his head, hooking one of the nearby chairs with his foot, drawing it to him. He shoved it with a knee, positioning it to face Riess' desk, then sat down. He had a travel mug in his hand, brushed stainless steel and uncovered, and Riess could see the paper tag of an herbal tea bag dangling over the edge. It surprised him; he'd always imagined Tower to be a coffee drinker.

"Had to give up caffeine," Tower informed him. "Blood pressure."

"Ah."

"Hey, listen," Tower said. "This is one of those things that's a little clumsy to talk about, so I'm just going to come out and say it, all right? And I hope you won't be offended."

"All right."

"You were at the InterContinental on Thursday night."

Riess felt his stomach perform what honestly felt like a back-flip. "I'm sorry?"

"Yeah, it's awkward, see? You were at the InterContinental, and no, I can't tell you how I know it, but I know it, so let's not play the no-I-wasn't/yes-you-were game. You spent the night there. Well, a portion of the night there. In room 615, with a Brit named Tracy Carlisle."

"I'm not sure this is any of your business, sir," Riess countered, trying to channel the embarrassment, rather than the fear. It wasn't very hard to do. He was certain he was blushing, and for a moment was immensely grateful that Tower had chosen to have this conversation while the office was empty, instead of in another hour, when McColl would have been certain to overhear it.

"Maybe, maybe not, but I kind of think that's for me to decide," Tower said. "I need you to tell me who this woman is, Charles, and how you know her."

"I've known her for about twelve years," Riess lied. "She spent a semester at Virginia Tech my junior year."

"Yeah?"

"Yeah. We had a thing. She works for some agricultural firm in England. They do irrigation, I think."

"So she's here on business."

"Much as I'd like to say she came all this way for me, she's here on business."

"This company she works for, you know its name?"

Riess shook his head. "We didn't talk about it. Kind of puts me in a bad position if she starts asking questions about the economy of the region."

"I can see that."

Riess paused, then asked, "Can I ask why this matters?"

"It may not matter at all."

"Yeah, but you're asking me about it."

Tower nodded, took hold of the paper tab on the end of its

string, and pulled his tea bag from the cup. He flicked it overhand, sending it sailing, bag end first, into the wastepaper basket at the side of the secretary's desk. It landed with a loud, wet smack. Tower admired the shot for a second, then turned his attention back to Riess.

"Is there a problem?" Riess asked.

Tower didn't answer, still looking at him.

No, not looking, Riess thought. *Watching.*

"I haven't seen her since then," Riess added.

"I know," Tower said, and lapsed into silence again, continuing to watch him.

The silence turned uncomfortable. The fan on Riess' desktop computer switched on, unnecessarily loud. Outside and down the hall, he heard a telephone begin ringing, then stop, as abruptly as it had started.

"Is there anything else, sir?" Riess asked. "I've got to finish this démarche before the Counselor comes in."

"You've known this woman since you were a sophomore at Virginia Tech."

"A junior."

"Right." Tower stared at him, then rose. "Okay, then. Thanks for your time."

"No trouble, sir."

Tower stopped, a hand on the door. "Chuck—word of advice, okay? Next time you're going to meet an old friend for a quick fuck, bring her to your place, all right? A hotel, that's just tacky."

"It came up unexpectedly."

"Just as long as you didn't." Tower grinned at him.

Riess blinked, then forced himself to laugh.

Tower left the office.

Riess stopped laughing.

He found it very difficult to concentrate on the Aral Sea after that.

CHAPTER 17

20 February, 1326 Hours (GMT+5:00)

According to her math, she hadn't slept in thirty-seven hours, and
Tara Chace was beginning to feel it.

The problem, of course, was that she was alone. If she'd been
able to rely upon some backup, if she'd had Poole or Lankford
with her or, hell, even the Station Number Two, they could have
split the surveillance. She'd have been able to set them in their positions to watch Ruslan Mihailovich Malikov's home, to tell them
what to look for and how to do it, to break the larger job into
smaller ones and, thus, been free to return to the little room she'd
taken at the Hotel Sayokhat and get some goddamn sleep.

But she had no one but herself, and worse, she was running out
of time. Porter would wait until the twenty-fifth, she was certain of
that; he wasn't the problem. At this point, she was reasonably certain Porter was actually the only thing she *could* count on, and
she'd already picked a location for their eventual rendezvous,
seventy-seven kilometers southwest of the city, at the northern
edge of Dzhizak Province. She'd picked the location on her way
back from her shopping trip, off the main highway, along the
banks of the Syr Darya, where it cut through Uzbekistan, joining

Kazakhstan in the northwest and Tajikistan in southeast. Parked by the side of the river, she'd pulled the GPS unit she'd brought with her from London, taken three different readings, all confirming the same set of coordinates, and then spent another minute and a half committing them to memory.

Porter was not going to be the problem.

The problem was back in London, and the problem was here in Tashkent. Crocker had made it clear he wanted—needed—the job done quickly. For that reason alone, time was of the essence. Compounding that was the situation with President Malikov. Since meeting with Riess, she'd had no news of the old man's condition. Local media had resolutely failed to report even a whisper of his illness. She didn't know if the President was lingering, recovering, or already in the ground, but if it was the last, then she felt safe in assuming that the clock was running for Ruslan and his son as well.

So the surveillance fell to her, and it fell to her with an urgency she did not like. Haste made for mistakes, and as things stood, there was already too much room for error, too many things she didn't like.

First, Ruslan and his son were, for all intents and purposes, under house arrest. By her count, there were at least three static surveillance posts devoted to watching the home, each manned by a team of two, each team replaced every eight hours, at five hundred, thirteen hundred, and twenty-one hundred hours. The watchers made no attempts to hide themselves, using automobiles as their staging point, with one person remaining behind the wheel, the second alternately walking up and down the block or lounging against the side of the car. Every other hour of the shift, the two would swap, the walker assuming the seat in the car, the driver assuming the walking post. The occupants of the cars used radios for communication, but from what Chace could see, the walkers did not. She was certain that the drivers not only communicated with one another, but with a central dispatcher as well.

That was just on the outside.

What was going on inside the house was harder to determine, but Chace had been able to confirm a few facts there as well. She knew that Ruslan and his son, Stepan, were inside, because she'd seen them on multiple occasions. Most frequently, she'd caught glimpses of them through the windows of the front room, barely for more than one second at a time. On Sunday afternoon, though, father and son had emerged to play in the backyard, engaging in a game of chase-me-catch-me-tickle-me-do-it-again. Stepan's delight had been loud enough to echo off the walls surrounding the yard, shrieks of toddler joy that had Chace thinking of Tamsin, and what of her daughter's life she was now missing.

When Ruslan and his son had come outside, they'd been accompanied by two more men, and neither of the guards had bothered to conceal the weapons they were carrying. The fact that they were so overt about their weaponry hadn't alarmed Chace; what they'd been carrying, however, had. Each was armed with a Heckler & Koch MP-5K, carried in hand. As far as submachine guns went, they could hardly have chosen better. The weapons, and others like them, were sometimes called room-brooms for their ability to quickly and efficiently clear small spaces of opposition. At close range, the guns would lay down a stream of fire that could only be described as lethal.

And once inside the house, Chace would be at very close range indeed.

In the time she'd been watching, she'd seen the shift change inside the house three times, but had yet to see any of watchers who had entered leave again. Like outside, the interior seemed to be guarded by teams of two, but she was uncertain just how many teams were actually being employed. Her best guess put the number at either three or four, which meant another six to eight armed men inside the house. She found herself praying it was the lower number. Six would be extraordinarily difficult to manage silently, without a fair amount of luck added to what Chace feared were her rusty skills; eight would be impossible, because it led directly to the second complication.

She had no doubt that the guards' orders were very clear: Ruslan and his son were not allowed to leave the building.

Should they try to do so, they would be killed.

Which meant that if the guards thought they were going to lose their prisoners, they were liable to shoot father and son themselves, and be done with it once and for all.

Third complication, then. She had to get inside quietly.

Fourth complication. She had to neutralize the guards just as quietly. Six to eight guards, and they would have to be taken out before they could raise an alarm, before they could react.

Fifth complication. She had to get herself, Ruslan, and Stepan out again. And Stepan, being all of two years old, would have to be carried, because he sure as hell wouldn't be able to keep up if they ran for it. Ruslan would have to carry him, to keep Chace's hands free for the wet work.

Sixth complication. Not only did they need to get out of the house, they had to get out of the *city*, and far enough away that Porter could bring in the helo undetected for the lift, but close enough that it could be managed in a timely fashion.

Seventh complication. She had to do all of these things alone.

Eighth complication. She had to do all of these things soon.

Because the eighth complication was the man named Ahtam Zahidov. His arrival at the house on Monday morning had come as a surprise, as much as to the guards on watch as to Chace, who recognized him from the photograph Riess had shown her, and it had caused an immediate flurry of activity. The arrival had provided an answer to another of her questions, however—Zahidov's presence confirmed for Chace that Ruslan was being held by his sister Sevara's forces, and not by the official NSS.

Zahidov had arrived in a late-model Audi A4, driving it alone, and pulling up to the front of the house. The car was a glossy black, well cared for, and Chace's first thought upon seeing it was that she'd very much like to steal it; the A4 was a good car if one had to get someplace in a hurry, and it would be a much better escape vehicle than the Range Rover, the engine of which was beginning to give her serious doubts.

Then Zahidov had emerged, and two of the guards—one from the house, one of them walking his beat farther up the block—had rushed to greet him, and that was when Chace had given him a second look through her binoculars. Through eyes strained with fatigue and overuse, it had taken several seconds before the recognition had come, and Zahidov had all but entered the house before she'd truly realized who he was.

She was watching, at that point, from a rooftop a block and a half away. It was her seventh or eighth observation post—she couldn't remember how many she'd used any longer, yet another sign of her fatigue—and when Zahidov vanished into the house, she had a moment of panic.

Fucking hell, she thought. *I've waited too long. I've waited too long and now the Big Bad Heavy has come to fix things for his lady friend once and for all.*

And if that was the case, it was over, the whole damn operation was a bust. She wouldn't be able to get there in time. Forget the fact that she wasn't ready, that all she had on her was the Smith & Wesson she'd purchased at the bazaar, forget that the rest of the weapons and explosives were still hidden in the back of the Range Rover. Forget the fact that it was broad fucking daylight, forget all of it. Even *if* she ran and somehow managed to survive a frontal assault on the house, she was certain she'd arrive just in time to find the bodies of Ruslan and Stepan cooling in puddles of their own spilled blood.

It was the broad-fucking-daylight factor that made her reconsider, that calmed her, that allowed her to recognize she was becoming irrational. Zahidov wouldn't execute Ruslan and his son in their home, not in the middle of the day. He had complete control over them, he had armed guards on them. If he was going to murder them, he wouldn't do it there.

No, he'd take them someplace else, use his NSS muscle to bring them to a cell someplace, perhaps, or drive them outside of the city, in the hinterlands, and kill them there.

Chace forced herself to calm down, checking her watch and noting the time. She rubbed her eyes, feeling them sting, then resumed peering through the binos. They weren't the best set of optics she'd used, not even close, but they served. She'd found them at a camera store on Abdukhamid Kayumov Saturday morning, and bought them solely because they were the most powerful set on sale.

Thirty-six minutes later, Zahidov emerged from the house, and this time, Chace was ready, and settled the optics on him immediately, tracking him for the duration of his walk from the front door, down the path to the street, to the car. He stopped before getting into the vehicle, exchanging words with the two watchers who'd exited with him.

Chace put him at five ten, maybe five eleven, perhaps one hundred and eighty pounds, perhaps lighter. His manner was calm, even self-confident, and whatever he was saying, he felt no urge to say it quickly, or with any apparent volume. He was, Chace thought, surprisingly handsome, a fact that Riess' photo hadn't managed to capture.

Then Zahidov finished speaking, climbing behind the wheel of the Audi again, pulling away down Uzbekiston. The two watchers exchanged another few words, then each returned to their posts.

Chace yawned. She'd been sitting in the cold on the tarpaper rooftop for three hours. Her legs ached, and her lower back. When she flexed her fingers, they were stiff.

Tonight, Chace decided. *It'll have to be tonight.*

She broke down her gear, such as it was, stowing the binoculars and its tripod in the duffel bag she'd brought, then making her way to the edge of the rooftop. She checked the drop, confirming that the way below was clear, and then, seeing no one watching her, began her descent to the alleyway, using a drainpipe as a makeshift pole.

It was a twenty-minute walk back to where she'd parked the Range Rover, and she found the vehicle where she'd left it, unmolested. She threw her bag in the passenger seat, and had to try three times before the engine caught and the car started. She made her way back to the Sayokhat.

In her room, she removed her coat and sweater and boots, and then gave up on the rest, collapsing on the bed, the Smith & Wesson close at hand, partially for the security it provided, and partially because of its importance to the coming events. The pistol had been one hell of a find, because it hadn't quite been what she'd thought it was at first blush. Not simply the S&W Mk 39, but rather a modified version of the same, the Mk 22 Mod 0, also called the "hush puppy." It was Vietnam-era, not the most reliable gun in the world, but wonderfully silent, not only equipped with a silencer to eliminate the sound of gunfire, but also with a slide lock, to keep the actual mechanical operation of the gun quiet as well. She'd test-fired the gun at the market before purchasing, and been stunned that it still worked. The Uzbek vendor had offered to sell it to her cheap.

"It's too quiet," he'd explained. "No one wants it."

Chace shut her eyes, half smiling at the memory.

She *really* wanted Zahidov's Audi. The car would be reliable, unlike the Range Rover; she didn't imagine Sevara Malikov-Ganiev's Lover and Head Thug to be a man who drove an ill-maintained car. It would be fast, which was never a bad thing, and would handle well. Best of all, it was familiar to the guards at the house. In Zahidov's Audi, she could drive right up to the front door before anyone became suspicious.

She tried to focus on ways to acquire the car, to think of a plan of attack, but being prone was having an immediate effect, and her thoughts were already splitting into pre-slumber dysfunction. Behind her closed eyes, she saw the hotel room, and then Val, as if she were standing there, at the foot of the bed. Tamsin was in her arms, twisting at the sight of her mother, straining to reach out for Chace.

Chace fell asleep, her last thought not of Ruslan or Stepan or Zahidov's Audi, nor of her daughter, hopefully safe and warm in Barnoldswick, hopefully still able to remember and recognize her mother.

Chace fell asleep thinking of the sheer number of men she would have to kill when she woke up.

CHAPTER 18

London—Vauxhall Cross—Office of D-Ops

20 February, 1356 Hours GMT

"Julian Seale for you," Kate said over the intercom.

Crocker set aside the notepad he'd been working on, flipping it over to keep his writings from prying eyes, taking up the handset on the telephone. He poked the blinking light with an index finger, then answered.

"Crocker."

"Paul, can you come out to play?"

"In the park, you mean?"

"Preferably."

"Regarding?"

"Better in person, I think."

"Ominous."

"Hoping you can answer a couple of questions for me, that's all."

"Thirty minutes," Crocker told him. "Statue of Achilles."

"And I hope there's nothing significant in that," the American said, and hung up.

Crocker replaced the phone, then stowed his papers in his desk, rose, and pulled his coat from the stand by the door. He stepped into the outer office, pulling it on. Kate looked up from her work.

"I'm going out. Should be back within the hour."

"If anyone asks?" Kate prompted.

"I'm meeting Seale."

She affected surprise. "And *are* you meeting Mr. Seale?"

"Does it matter?" Crocker snarled, heading out the door and into the hall. "If anyone asks, that's what you're to tell them."

The door closed behind him before he could hear Kate's reply.

Crocker made his way down the hall, frowning. Seale asking for a meet in short order wasn't necessarily alarming; he could have requested it to address any number of things. It could simply be an after-action debrief between the two of them regarding the Morocco job; Lankford had returned from Casablanca, none the worse for wear, late the previous night, and Crocker had already read and approved his report of the action. It had contained nothing remarkable. The operation had been precisely as Seale had claimed.

But making his way to the lift, Crocker already knew it wasn't Morocco that Seale wanted to talk about.

He hit the button for the lift, waited, and entered the car to find Alison Gordon-Palmer, a single folder tucked beneath her right arm, the only other occupant. The DC flashed him a smile in greeting.

"Down or up?"

"Down," Crocker said.

"As am I. Simon and I are about to have words with the China Desk." She indicated the folder beneath her arm.

"Seale," Crocker said, by way of offering his own destination.

"Probably wants to know why Chace is in Tashkent, I imagine."

"That's my fear as well."

"It was bound to happen. The Americans are more than a little touchy about Uzbekistan. If they think she's tromping through their garden on official business, and if they think we're actively keeping that fact from them, they're going to want to know the reason."

Crocker nodded, canted his head slightly, measuring his tone. "I didn't know you knew it was Chace I'd sent to Uzstan."

"I can count, Paul. And as of this morning, you still had three

Minders in the Pit, one of them affixed to his desk by a chain about his ankle. No one else you *could* send, really."

"But I didn't tell you."

She shook her head, her manner still mild.

"Seccombe did," Crocker said, answering his own question.

"He's very interested in the progress of the operation." Alison Gordon-Palmer smiled slightly, and the elevator came to a stop. As she stepped out of the car, she said, "You'll inform me if Chace stumbles across any MANPADs, won't you, Paul? I know the PUS would be grateful for any such news."

Then the doors were sliding closed, and Crocker was descending again, wondering how much lower he was likely to go.

Seale was waiting at the foot of the statue of Achilles, hands thrust in the pockets of his overcoat, squinting up at the enormous figure. Erected in 1822 and weighing in the neighborhood of thirty-three tons, it had caused something of a stir when it was unveiled as London's first public nude. The statue has been cast from French cannon captured at Vitoria, Salamanca, Toulouse, and Waterloo, and was dedicated to Wellington and the men who had served under his command. At eighteen feet tall, it was one of the more impressive pieces of public sculpture to be found in any of London's parks, at least by Crocker's estimation.

"Don't you love how the only armor he's wearing is on his feet and shins?" the American asked. "Aside from the shield and whatever that is he's got over his cock, I mean."

"He was practically invincible," Crocker said. "He could afford to stroll the battlefield naked."

"Thing is, the greaves, they're only on the front of his shins," Seale mused, staring at the massive bronze. "No protection around the back. You'd think he'd have had something to cover his tendons."

"Pride."

"Before the downfall." Seale turned away from the statue, his hands still deep in his pockets, and motioned with his right elbow to the branching path beyond him. "Shall we walk?"

Crocker almost smiled. When Cheng had said the same thing, his response had invariably been "I'd rather be carried." Somehow, he didn't think his relationship with Seale allowed for that kind of levity just yet, so he nodded, falling into step with Seale as the other man set the pace.

They walked without speaking for almost a hundred yards or so, each giving the other time to check the immediate surroundings for unwelcome eyes or ears, finding nothing. It was overcast, with drops of rain spattering down at irregular intervals, adding to the growing chill and the coming darkness. Not for the first time, Crocker wondered how much longer he'd be permitted to entertain this particular idiosyncrasy before someone from Internal Security or, worse, from Box came to have a chat with him about the dangers of discussing official business in one of Her Majesty's parks.

"Why's Tara Chace in Tashkent?" the American asked him.

And another point for the Deputy Chief, Crocker thought. "I'm sorry?"

"That's her name, right? She's the one Fincher replaced?"

"No, I know who she is. She's in Tashkent?"

Seale glanced at him, annoyed, then went back to watching their surroundings. "Woman named Tracy Elizabeth Carlisle checked into the InterContinental in Tashkent on the sixteenth. Was met that night by an FSO from our embassy, in her room. He was there for several hours."

Oh, for Christ's sake, Chace, Crocker thought. *You didn't.*

"It's a common name."

"I know, and it wouldn't be a thing, but COS Tashkent got wind of it, got a description of Miss Carlisle, ran it back through Langley. And Tracy Elizabeth Carlisle, it turns out, was once-upon-a-time the work-name of Chace, Tara Felicity, formerly your

Head of the Special Section. He got a description as well, and it matches. COS Tashkent wired COS London with the inquiry."

Seale stopped, turned to face Crocker.

"So now COS London is inquiring. The CIA wants to know, Paul. Why didn't you tell us you've got an operation running in Tashkent?"

"Why's your COS Tashkent watching one of your FSOs?"

Seale shook his head. "You first."

Crocker freed his pack of cigarettes from inside his coat, taking his time to pick one, then to light it. Taking the time to think. In all honesty, he was surprised Chace had made it this far before being made; he'd half expected to hear similar news via Tashkent Station, asking the very same thing and more than a little irate at the thought of an ex-Minder in their midst with no forewarning. That it had come from the CIA instead, and through these channels specifically, gave him something else to worry about.

It meant that COS Tashkent, whoever that was—Crocker couldn't remember the name—truly had been watching the FSO in question for one reason or another. His knowledge of American embassy workings was limited, but he was reasonably certain that it wasn't the CIA who was responsible for maintaining the security of the mission staff. So the FSO, whoever the hell he was, had earned the attention somehow.

That couldn't be good news for Chace, not unless Crocker could somehow shut down Seale's inquiry. Which meant giving the Americans something plausible, and that, in turn, meant burning either Seccombe or Barclay. One of the truths would have to come out now. Which one was the only question.

"Paul?" Seale asked. "If you're fucking us in Uzstan, things are about to get ugly."

Crocker hoped to hell that he was reading the tea leaves right.

"It's about the Starstreaks, Julian." Crocker took another drag on his cigarette, meeting Seale's eyes. "The ones you told me about. Barclay lost them four years ago. He's understandably anxious to get them back."

"I told you about the Starstreaks on the seventeenth, Paul. Chace was apparently riding our FSO to the heights of passion on the night of the sixteenth. Which means she left England some twenty hours prior to that, which means you briefed her before *that*, which puts me back to around Valentine's Day. So either you're lying to me—"

"Or I already knew about the Starstreaks when we met on the seventeenth," Crocker said.

"Which is it?"

"You can take your pick, but think about it. Barclay's the one who is ultimately responsible for those MANPADs being lost. Which means if they surface in any fashion that includes civilian or Coalition casualties, he's dead. He asked me to get them back for him."

"He's firing you."

"This is how I keep my job," Crocker said, bitterly. "He doesn't want anyone to know it was he who lost the fucking missiles. That's why I'm using Chace, not one of the Minders. That's why she's running free, without Station contact. No one is supposed to know she's there. I save C's career, he saves mine."

A wind rattled the leaves, followed by another spattering of rain, icier than before. Crocker resumed walking, waiting for Seale to fall abreast.

"And that's why she's using a blown cover."

"I was expressly forbidden to use any SIS assets for the mission," Crocker confirmed. "Barclay's paranoiac, Julian. He's afraid someone will find out, use the information against him."

"A nice, altruistic motive."

"Those are still around?"

"I hear rumors." Seale fell silent for several more long strides, apparently thinking about what Crocker had just told him. "So Barclay offered to let you keep your job. . . ."

"He actually offered me Gordon-Palmer's job, if you want to

know the truth. He seems to think that he'll be getting rid of her soon."

Seale digested that, then said, "Fine, you get made DC. What does Chace get? She's got a kid now, doesn't she? How'd you get her to agree to this lunacy?"

"Chace wants to come back. I told her if she does the job, I'll make her Minder One again."

"And will you?"

"If she does the job? In a heartbeat."

"Then here's hoping she does the job."

"Amen."

"Doesn't explain why she met with the FSO, though."

"I think you have your explanation already," Crocker said, and then, in answer to Seale's look, amended, "Libido."

"You expect me—no, better—you expect the Tashkent COS to believe it was coincidence?"

"No. She probably made your guy as a member of the U.S. Mission, tried to use him for information. Where she picked him up, I can't begin to guess. She's under orders not to make contact with me until she's located the missiles. I would guess—and it's only a guess—that she made your FSO, then got everything she could off him, and indulged herself a bit in the process. That's if she did actually sleep with him; she could have had him drawing her maps of Tashkent, for all we know."

"Regular Mata Hari, this Chace."

"A spiritual daughter, yes."

Seale slowed, then stopped, and Crocker had to stop as well, turning back to face him. He couldn't read anything in the American's expression, no sign if he was buying the story or if he was merely allowing Crocker to dig himself in deeper.

"You have no contact with Chace at all?"

"None."

"Then you don't know where she is?"

"Tashkent, I presume." Crocker frowned. "Why? Do you?"

Seale shook his head. "She checked out of the InterContinental the morning of the seventeenth, hasn't been seen since. COS Tashkent hadn't bothered to put her under hard surveillance—he was more concerned with the FSO."

"It's possible the trail has taken her out of the city, or even out of the country."

"Chechnya, you mean?"

"It's a possibility."

"How'd you guys get on to the Starstreaks, anyway? Angela was sure she was giving you a gift, not confirming something you already know."

"I don't know," Crocker said. "Barclay approached me, remember? I'm assuming he picked up word of the sale from D-Int, or another source entirely."

"That's possible."

"You'd be doing me one hell of a favor if you get a line on where these things are, Julian. I don't know how I can get word to Chace, but if CIA locates these Starstreaks and she can recover them . . ."

"Yeah, I get it." Seale massaged his earlobe with a thumb and forefinger. "You know Malikov's circling the drain?"

"Yes."

"Looks like the daughter is going to take over," Seale said. "She's already had communication with State and the White House."

"And State and the White House approve?"

"We want someone who'll continue the relationship begun with her father, someone who's on the same page about the war. We have to step carefully in Uzbekistan. Malikov's a tried-and-true fucker, no doubt about it, and his daughter isn't much better."

"Then why support her?"

"You know why. We lose Uzstan, we're down to Pakistan and southern Afghanistan as our primary staging areas in the region, and neither is what I'd call secure. We *need* good relations with Uzstan, at least for the foreseeable future. And if we put too much pressure on the country, either by pushing too hard on the human rights angle or by cutting off aid or whatnot, there's a risk of alienating the leadership there. China's awfully close to Uzbekistan, and the last thing Washington wants to see is the PRC replacing us in Uzbek affections."

"There's a son," Crocker said. "Better bet than the daughter, if I recollect."

"No, he's a no-go," Seale said. "Not enough support in-country. If the son tries to take over, it'll get bloody. And since we've now got NATO troops on the ground in Uzstan, nobody wants to see that, either."

Crocker considered, then nodded slightly, apparently agreeing. His cigarette had burned down to its filter, and he dropped it on the path, stepping on it with the toe of his shoe. What Seale was saying was true enough, but it raised a whole new set of questions. If the White House was backing Sevara enough that Seale knew about it, then the Foreign Secretary and the Prime Minister knew it, too. Which meant that either the Prime Minister was willing to oppose the White House covertly—hence his tasking Seccombe with the job of placing Ruslan in power—or Seccombe was playing him.

Correction: of course Seccombe was playing him. It meant that Seccombe was playing him in a very different way than Crocker had imagined.

He checked his watch, saw that it was already eight minutes past five. "I should get back."

"I should, too. I'll contact Tashkent, let them know why Chace was there, what she was doing. Maybe the COS can point her in the right direction."

"If he can find her."

"Oh, he can find her, Paul. Trust me. He can find her."

Seale turned, heading away from him, back down the path, and it wasn't until then that Crocker realized they hadn't shaken hands upon meeting each other.

He wasn't sure what to make of that.

CHAPTER 19

**Uzbekistan—Tashkent—438–2 Raktaboshi,
Residence of Charles Riess**

20 February, 2329 Hours (GMT+5:00)

Riess lived alone, in a semidetached house with a private courtyard. The house had been provided by the Chancery, but not without difficulty. When Riess had arrived in Tashkent, he'd found that the Mission was in the clutches of a housing shortage. As a single FSO, his rank notwithstanding, he found himself on the bottom of the placement list. He'd spent seven weeks in residence at the Sheraton while his belongings had languished in storage somewhere in Belgium, living out of the hotel before everything got sorted out.

When it finally had been taken care of, though, Riess had been pleasantly surprised with his home. It was far more spacious than he'd imagined, a two-bedroom, one with a supplied queen, one with two twins, with a modest dining room, kitchen, and ample living room. Like all Mission housing, it was government-furnished with the standard Drexel pieces, all of them functional and all of them lacking personality. Carpeting was gratis, a vacuum cleaner helpfully supplied to keep things tidy.

It had taken another month for his belongings to arrive, at which point Riess had been desperate to personalize the space. He'd set up his desktop, placed his books on his shelves, erected what he self-mockingly referred to as the Shrine, the three pictures of Rebecca he'd had ever since she'd passed away. He'd put a few photographs and posters up on the walls, and in the end felt he had accomplished the job of making the house more than just a dormitory. Not that he would spend much time there, but it was a matter of principle; he was looking at a three-year tour in Uzbekistan, he damn well wanted to like where he was resting his head at night.

Monday night he returned home a little before eleven from a dinner with three Representatives of the Oliy Majlis. The dinner had run long, and Riess had been forced to stay through the entire proceeding, not because the Reps in question were particularly important to the United States' interests in Uzbekistan, but rather because leaving early would have told them very clearly that they weren't. McColl, of course, had been dining with the DCM, entertaining a more senior group of the same.

The meal had been held at the home of one of the Reps, near the Earthquake Memorial off Abdulla Kodiry. Riess liked the memorial far more than he liked the dinner. A series of granite reliefs depicted the rebuilding of Tashkent, surrounding a central statue straddling a ragged tear in the earth. The statue was substantial, a heroic Uzbek male standing in front of an equally heroic Uzbek female, her hair flying, together shielding a not-so-heroic Uzbek child. A smaller block of granite, this one black, had the face of a clock carved on one side, the hands pointing to 5:22, the hour the earthquake had struck on April 26, 1966. It had been one hell of a quake, 7.5 on the Richter scale, and had devastated the city, leaving some three hundred thousand homeless. The Soviets had rallied, rebuilding the city, giving birth to modern Tashkent.

Riess had taken a walk through the memorial after dinner, stretching his legs and trying to clear his head. Ostensibly, the purpose of the meal had been part social, part an opportunity to discuss changes in the irrigation system around the Aral. But like Riess, the Reps knew a lost cause when they saw one, and so most of the talk had centered on other things: concerns about Islamic extremists infiltrating the country, deteriorating relations with Turkmenistan, and finally, the rumors surrounding President Malikov's illness. Consensus at the table had been that Sevara would succeed her father.

"Not Ruslan?" Riess had asked.

"Not unless you know something we don't," one of the Reps had responded, laughing.

So he'd walked the memorial, thinking about his last conversation with the Ambassador, thinking about Tracy Carlisle. Wondering why it was that she hadn't lifted Ruslan and his son as yet. He didn't know what to make of her, and he still didn't know what to make of his night with her, and the visit from Tower that had come in its wake had only served to cloud the matter further.

The fact was, Riess felt out of his depth.

McColl had come into the office grumpier than usual that morning, about twenty minutes after Tower's departure, and peeved at something the Ambassador had apparently said to S. Whatever it was, it had made its way back to McColl, and McColl, having no recourse, took it out on Riess in the form of busywork. That kept Riess chained to his desk, and it was almost noon before he could manufacture a reason to speak to the Ambassador.

"I can give you three minutes," Garret told him when Riess entered the office.

"Then I'll make it fast. Tower knows something is going on. He knows I was at the InterContinental, that I met with Carlisle."

Riess expected surprise, or at least concern, but Garret exhibited neither. "I figured he might. What'd you tell him?"

"That she was an old friend." Riess hesitated, then added, "I was with her for about four hours."

"In her room?"

Riess nodded.

"Chuck," Garret said. "You dog."

Riess actually thought he might blush, tried to think of something to say, and realized that everything he was coming up with would sound like a double entendre. Finally, he managed, "It wasn't planned."

"No, it wouldn't have been."

"What do you want me to do?"

"About Tower? Not much you can do. There was always a risk of this, Charles. He'll check your story, and when he finds the holes in it—and he will find the holes in it—he'll want to talk to you again."

"What do I tell him?"

Garret looked out the window of his office into the garden, not speaking for a very long time, so long that Riess began to wonder if the Ambassador had heard him or not.

"That's your choice, Charles," Garret said at length, softly. "This thing with Ruslan—if it doesn't work, my career is shot. I knew that going into it. I've got thirty years in, and there are worse ways to leave than being forced into a quiet retirement."

"I'm not going to betray you, sir. I won't do that."

Garret turned from the window, then pulled out the paternal smile. "If Tower already knows, it's not a betrayal, Charles. And if he already knows, you'll have to decide what's best for yourself. I'm not going to hold that decision against you."

Riess shook his head, confused. "Has something happened?"

"Not yet."

"Then you'll forgive me for saying that I think this discussion is premature, sir. Carlisle hasn't even had a chance to lift them yet."

"Lifting them is only half the battle. Getting Ruslan back into play, with support, that's the other half."

"You said there was British support."

Garret nodded. "But that doesn't mean there *is* British support."

"Why else would Carlisle be here?"

"Hell if I know." The Ambassador stared at him a moment longer, then moved to his chair, settling himself behind his desk.

"Go back to McColl before he finds more ways to make your life miserable."

The confusion he was feeling became more acute, and for a second Riess didn't move. Then, almost resigned, he left the office, making his way back through the Embassy to his desk, wondering what was best for himself, and just how long it would take Aaron Tower to find all of the holes in his story about his night with Tracy Carlisle.

As it turned out, it didn't take Tower long at all.

Riess had been home for twenty minutes, long enough to change out of his suit and into jeans and a Virginia Tech sweatshirt, and to brew up a cup of coffee from the beans a friend at home had sent in his last care package. He made the coffee a cup at a time, rationing the beans, and he'd just poured when there was a knock at the door.

He wasn't surprised to find Aaron Tower waiting outside when he opened it.

"Mind if I come in?" Tower asked.

Riess shrugged, turned away, heading back into the kitchen. "You want a cup of coffee? It's good stuff. A friend in California sends the beans to me every so often. Better than the local brew or that nightmare we get at the Embassy."

He heard the door close. "Can't," Tower said. "Blood pressure, remember?"

"Right, sorry." Riess stuck his head back out of the kitchen, saw that Tower was standing in the open living room, taking in the space. "Tea, then? I think I've got a peppermint."

"Sure."

Riess turned to the stove, set up the kettle. He was pulling a mug down when Tower entered and propped himself just inside the doorway, leaning against the side of the refrigerator, watching as Riess went about preparing the cup.

"I've got some cookies," Riess said.

Tower shook his head.

Riess shrugged a second time, set the mug beside the stovetop. "So what can I do for you, sir?"

Tower didn't speak and didn't move, fixing him with a vaguely expectant stare. Riess understood the reason for it, and that, more than anything, made the purpose of Tower's visit crystal clear. He turned away, putting his attention back on the kettle, waiting for it to boil.

The water took a very long time to come to a boil.

Tower didn't say a word.

Riess took the kettle off the heat, filled the mug, watching as the steam rippled off the water, rising toward him, and thinking about the Ambassador, what he had said. He understood now more than he had then, and the feeling of betrayal, of guilt that now settled in his breast was achingly heavy. He hadn't said anything, and he knew that by staying silent, he'd already said far too much. Standing in the kitchen, six and a half thousand miles from home, he felt very much alone.

He handed the mug to Tower, who took it, then said, "She didn't go to Virginia Tech."

Riess picked up his coffee, tasted it. It had gone tepid.

"She's not a friend from college. She's not here working for some agro firm interested in cotton production. She's not a tourist. And her name isn't Tracy Carlisle." Tower toyed with the tea bag, feigning interest in its buoyancy. "You remember who you work for, don't you, Chuck?"

"Of course I remember who I fucking work for." Riess dumped the remainder of his coffee into the sink, suddenly angry. The liquid splashed against the side, slopped out onto the counter. He put his cup down hard, hard enough that he was afraid it might shatter. It didn't.

"I don't think you do," Tower said, quietly. "I think that *you* think you work for the Ambassador. And you don't. You work for the Secretary of State, who works for the President, who works for the American People. So you work for the American People, and those people have elected a leader they believe will make the right decisions for them. And that leader has selected a Secretary of State who will pursue his agenda. And your job is to support that agenda, regardless of whether or not you agree with it."

"Sevara is as bad as her father. If not worse."

"Grow the fuck up. Of course she's worse. I can think of half a dozen ways that she's worse. That's not the fucking point. You think anyone back in Washington likes the way she—or her father—goes about running a country? You think anyone's *happy* that we're in bed with a kleptocrat despot who thinks the words 'secret police' and 'freedom' aren't mutually exclusive? But we need Uzbekistan, and right now, we have to take what we can get."

"I'm so fucking sick and tired of the Kissinger Doctrine!" Riess kicked the cabinet beneath the sink, splintering the door. "I'm fucking sick and tired of expediency instead of doing the right thing! Fucking Dar es Salaam was expedient, and people *died*, dammit!"

"But you, you know what the right thing is, is that it? You and the Ambassador?"

"Maybe not, but it sure as hell isn't a monster like Sevara."

Tower set his mug down on the counter, the tea untasted. "So you and the Ambassador plan a coup to put Ruslan in power instead?"

Riess didn't answer.

"You even think about that? How the fuck is that going to come off, Chuck? We've got *troops* in this country, they're *stationed* here. Ruslan gets himself some guns, tries to seize the Presidential Palace, you think that's going to solve your fucking problem? It's not going to solve the problem. It's going to destabilize the whole fucking country!"

"Not if we support him!"

"We're not *going* to support him, dammit! Don't you get it? Sevara is anointed, she's got the blessing, she's kissed the ring! It's hers for the taking. As soon as Malikov kicks it, she gets the crown. It's a done fucking deal."

Riess stopped himself from kicking the cabinet again, his hands in fists so tight he could feel his fingernails biting into his palms. He wanted to spit, to scream about right and wrong, to say it wasn't fair and it wasn't right.

He didn't want to grow the fuck up.

"Somewhere in Tashkent, right now, there's an SIS Officer on an unsanctioned mission," Tower said, evenly. "The girl you banged, she's here on a job, and you know what it is, you know the why and the where and maybe the how."

"I didn't—"

"No." Tower cut him off. "We're past that now, Chuck. You've got only a couple moves left here, and you need to choose them real carefully. Telling me what you know will go a long way to making sure the skin is still on your career when the dust settles."

Riess closed his eyes, thinking of Dina Malikov and the way her body had been desecrated, then destroyed. The words, when they came, were the betrayal, and the defeat was bitter. "We just wanted to make things better."

If he had hoped for sympathy, Tower's tone dashed it. "This wasn't the way to do it. And I'm still waiting for my answers."

And Charles Riess, standing in the kitchen in his semidetached home in Tashkent, sighed heavily, then gave Tower all the answers he could.

CHAPTER 20

21 February 0001 (GMT+5.00)

She was already bloody twitched. It had started before she'd even
left the hotel.

Chace had woken from her sleep in the dark, disoriented by the
lack of light and the strange noises from the street and the hall,
had come awake alarmed, the hush puppy in her hand feeling alien
and awkward. She'd showered, dressed in the darkest clothes she
had—all black, from turtleneck to trousers, down to the knick-
ers—all the while trying to shake the sluggish feeling that seemed
to have invaded every muscle.

Chace had wondered if she wasn't coming down with something on top of everything else.

She'd left the room and made it as far as the lobby, thinking
that food would be in order, and that was when it happened, the
first real blossom of fear opening in her chest. What was the rule
again? No food before an action—the Rikki-Tikki-Tavi rule was
what the CQC instructor at the School had called it.

*And Rikki-tikki was just going to eat him up from the tail,
after the custom of his family at dinner, when he remem-*

bered that a full meal makes a slow mongoose, and if he wanted all his strength and quickness ready, he must keep himself thin.

Basic, so basic, and she'd almost forgotten, and against her will Chace found herself trying to imagine the pain of her own intestines spilling their contents into her body. Wondering how quickly she'd lose blood from a gut wound. Realizing that, even if she had a catheter, even if she had bothered to precanulate, it wouldn't do a damn bit of good because she'd never be able to replace the fluid loss anyway. She imagined herself in a Tashkent hospital, writhing on a gurney in agony as doctors tried to get a line of what passed for Ringer's solution in this part of the world into her, and how long it would take her to die.

Once those thoughts started, it was hard to stop them again.

It took her fifty-three minutes to walk from where she'd parked the Range Rover off Forobiy, near the Chagatai Cemetery and some seven miles from Ruslan's home, to the apartment building housing Sevara Malikov-Ganiev's penthouse.

The buildings on this part of Sulaymonova were largely residential, older Soviet-style apartments sharing space with more modern condominium complexes, and at midnight on a Monday, the streets were deserted. Everywhere Chace had gone in Tashkent, she'd seen the same signs, architectural proof of Uzbekistan's struggle to claw itself out of its Communist-dominated past into an as-yet-uncertain future. The condominiums at 182 Sulaymonova were the nicest she'd seen in the city, and Chace wasn't at all surprised that Sevara made her home here.

There was an underground parking garage, blocked from the street by a metal gate at the bottom of the ramp, the ramp itself wide enough for two-way traffic. Sodium lights glowed on either side of the slope, serving as deterrent and security in lieu of more practical means such as cameras or guards. Chace took a moment from across the street to check around her once more, then craned her head, and spied lights on in the penthouse. Her angle was bad, however, and she couldn't tell how many, nor how bright, only that there was illumination.

So presumably Sevara was in, and, hopefully, entertaining. Whether or not it was Zahidov being entertained, that was something else entirely. And the Audi's absence in the garage wouldn't be proof that he wasn't, either; Chace had no way of knowing how many vehicles Zahidov owned, nor which he favored when going to fuck the daughter of the President of Uzbekistan. For all Chace knew, he might choose to visit her on roller skates.

It was a gamble, then, like everything else. The car might be there, but it might not. And if it wasn't, Chace wasn't entirely certain how she'd proceed. She'd wasted enough time already getting things into position just this far. If she lost more time on foot, she was looking at not being able to hit the house until almost four A.M., and that was dangerously close to the morning shift change. She'd have to abort for the night.

Which meant another day of exposure in Tashkent, another day that could see Ruslan and son dead before sunset.

Presuming that Zahidov and his NSS crew hadn't already done the deed while Chace was catching up on her sleep.

Too many variables, too many unknowns.

She knew she was wasting time, stalling, and she also knew why she was doing it. That part of the mind—consciousness, or ego, call it what you will—trying to talk her out of going through with it, knowing what she was about to do was dangerous. Knowing what she was about to do could cost her her life.

Time and fear were allies, after all. And the more time she had, the more time to become afraid.

Too late for that, Chace told herself, and with a last look up and down the street, ventured across to the top of the ramp, then continued down without pause, directly to the gate. The bars of the gate were too narrow to squeeze through, and there was no clearance at either the top or the bottom. She peered into the dim-

ness of the garage, barely able to make out the Audi parked between what looked to be a vintage MGB convertible—she didn't
even want to *know* how that had come to be there—and a BMW
sedan.

So Zahidov was with Sevara. Or someone in one of the other
condominiums also owned a black Audi. Or—

Knock it off, Tara, she told herself, and took a closer look at the
gate. It ran on a track, splitting in the center, presumably parting
to the left and right to allow access. Squinting into the darkened
garage, she could see the chain running from the gate to the pulley
wheels, then to the motor, mounted on the concrete wall roughly
fifteen feet to the right.

She pushed the gate, to see if she could get it to part, even
slightly. The metal rattled when she touched it, but didn't budge.

Chace stepped back, glancing around her once more. The gate
was a problem, but the ramp was a benefit, as it hid her from the
street. If anyone came along, they'd be nearly on top of her before
they saw she was even there. She checked her watch.

Three minutes past midnight.

She reached into the outer pocket of her coat. The suppressor
made the gun too long to wear inside her trousers with any degree
of comfort, and Chace had balanced the ease of accessing the hush
puppy quickly with the necessity of being able to move in the same
way. If her luck went so bad as to require the use of the weapon
quickly, then the use of the weapon alone wouldn't be enough to
solve the problem.

The hush puppy in her hand, Chace turned against the gate,
raised the pistol, and fired at the chain. The weapon kicked, its re-
coil made stronger with the slide lock engaged, but the actual shot
barely made a sound. The Mk 22 Mod 0 had been modified for use
by SEAL Teams during Vietnam, to quietly and quickly remove
sentries during covert operations. In particular, it had been used to
silence guard dogs, hence the nickname.

The first shot missed in the gloom, and Chace manually disen-
gaged the lock, pocketing the spent cartridge, then racked a second

round and tried again. This time, the chain sparked, then clanked loose from the pulley, tumbling to the garage floor with an appalling racket, and Chace fought the immediate instinct to run and hide. Instead, gun in hand, she leaned into the gate once more, and this time it slid back on its wheels, just enough to let her through. She twisted through the gap, turning again and sliding the gate closed once more. Each time the door ran on its wheels, it chattered and squeaked, and she winced at the noise, but kept going.

Dropping back into the shadows of the garage, Chace ducked down between the Audi and the Mustang, and again cleared the spent cartridge from the hush puppy. She listened, not moving, until all she was hearing was her own breathing, and then the sound of a car passing by on the road beyond the ramp. Nothing more.

Her eyes finally adjusted to the gloom, and Chace turned on her haunches, checking the Audi's tags to be certain it was the same A4, then peering through the passenger window at the interior. The car was a manual, to her relief; an automatic would have posed a whole new host of problems. Zahidov had parked the car nose in to the wall, and a small red light blinked regularly on the dashboard, indicating that the alarm was set.

That didn't bother her. The alarm was designed to prevent break-ins to the vehicle, arming automatically when the doors were locked. Unlocking the car with the key would disarm the antitheft system. By the same token, starting the car would do the same.

The trick was in starting the car, and thus disarming the alarm, without actually ever entering the passenger compartment.

Hush puppy in hand, Chace made her way to the front of Zahidov's Audi, then crouched down once more. She set the gun down by her right foot, then drew the knife from its sheath at the back of her belt. Like the pistol, she'd purchased the knife at the bazaar. Unlike the pistol, the knife was of local manufacture. She'd found it among the Soviet Army bayonets and cheap knockoffs of combat knives that only seemed to ever be used in the movies. This one had a six-inch single-edge blade that ended in an elegantly curved point, with a bone handle, sturdy in the hand, well balanced, and ultimately far more silent than the hush puppy.

Positioning herself at the driver's-side headlight, Chace slid the flat of the blade along the top of the socket, working the knife in until she felt she had enough purchase to try exerting some leverage. She bore down on the blade, met resistance, pushed harder, and the headlight broke loose of its housing with a resounding crack that seemed to fill the garage and reverberate off the concrete all around.

Chace caught the light in her left hand before it could fall, then sliced the wires running to the lamp. She set the light and the knife on the floor, beside the pistol, then took hold of the wires, touching them to her tongue. A ripple of electricity ran through her mouth.

Thank God for that, she thought, dropping the wires and letting them dangle from the now-empty headlight socket. The current meant that the Audi kept a reserve charge even after the key was removed from the ignition. It meant she was still in business.

Resting one hand against the hood of the car for support, Chace reached into the socket, to the small hole that now gaped, Lear-like, opening into the engine compartment. She pressed her fingers together, tucking her thumb beneath, into her palm, and pushed. Metal scraped her fingers, then her hand, and she felt a sharp pain around her wrist as she shoved farther, finally through the hole. She grit her teeth, twisting, working by feel past the front of the engine block to the rough surface of the firewall. The position was putting a strain on her lower back, and the crouch was starting to make her legs ache.

She almost missed it, working blind as she was, her fingers brushing over the wire once, then twice, before she knew it for what it was, secure in its bracket, grounded in the firewall. Using her index finger, she pried it loose enough to actually manage a grip on it, then yanked. Metal tore at her forearm, and Chace hissed in pain as her hand came free. In the weak light from the ramp, she could see wetness glistening, where she'd stripped skin from her forearm.

But she had the wire she wanted, and she thought that was a fair trade.

Using the knife, she stripped roughly two inches of casing off the wire, then did the same with the leads that had once gone to the headlight. She sheathed the knife, then took the two pieces of wire and twisted them together.

Immediately, the engine came to life.

Chace spared a moment for relief, then picked up the hush puppy and moved around to the driver's side. Like the Range Rover, this was another left-hand drive. Through the side window, she could see the dashboard now dimly illuminated. Better, the alarm light had gone off.

She shrugged out of her coat and wrapped it around her left arm, then, with her right, fired one round from the hush puppy into the driver's window, angling the shot so the bullet would bury itself in the passenger seat. The window spider-webbed, and Chace punched with her left, and then it vanished, falling into minute chunks of safety glass. She tossed the hush puppy through the now-open window, onto the passenger's seat, reached inside, and unlocked the door, then opened it. Using her covered left arm, she swept the glass fragments from the seat until she was certain she wouldn't lacerate herself further, then tossed the coat onto the passenger seat as well, covering the pistol.

To the sound of the engine rumbling through the garage, she sprinted to the gate at the bottom of the ramp, and once more took hold of the bars. Again, she leaned in, pushing, and this time, the clatter of the wheels in their tracks seemed quieter, lost below the sound of the Audi. She shoved the doors apart enough to allow the car through, then ran back to the vehicle. She climbed behind the wheel, put the car in reverse, and pulled out carefully. As soon as she put the car in gear, the remaining headlamp came on, splashing xenon light that turned the garage bright as day.

Chace put the Audi into gear and gave it gas, turning hard at the gate, and narrowly avoiding clipping it with the side mirrors.

She floored it on the ramp, turned again, and shot off, down Sulay-monova.

According to the digital clock on the dashboard, it was seven minutes past midnight.

Four minutes, Chace mused. Not bad.

She slowed to the legal limit after a mile, taking random turns and checking to see if she'd collected any admirers. Once assured that she hadn't, she turned in the direction of Forobiy, to where she'd parked the Range Rover. The air coming through the window was sharp, cutting through her clothes, and it cut through the adrenaline as well, but it didn't diminish her pleasure.

With the Audi, she could drive right up to the house without raising suspicion. Behind its tinted windshield, the guards would never know it wasn't Zahidov at the wheel until it was too late, provided they didn't see her through the missing driver's window.

That was the plan, at least as it stood now, and as Chace drove to where she'd parked the Range Rover, she played it out again in her mind. She pictured her moves, the sequence of events, envisioning what she had to do, envisioning what to do if things went wrong.

The fear was still with her, but not as strong, familiar and manageable once more. It gave her comfort.

The Range Rover was where she'd left it, unmolested off the side of the road, parked by the walls of the Chagatai Cemetery. "Chagatai," best as Chace could understand, meant "Jewish," and she imagined that the cemetery had suffered under the Soviet regime, though it seemed to have been recently repaired and restored. At half past twelve at night, Chace was confident it was one of the quieter places in all of Tashkent.

She swung the Audi off the road, killing the one working headlamp, then backing up so that the trunk of the car faced the back of the Range Rover. She left the car in neutral, set the brake, then took the satellite phone from an inside pocket and switched it on, unfolding the antenna. She punched in her PIN, waited for six seconds that felt more like six minutes before the phone beeped reassuringly, indicating that it was working, and had a signal.

Chace brought up the text message she'd prepared earlier, STAND TO — CONFIRM? and sent it to Porter's pager. She set the phone on the dashboard to await a reply, then began searching the interior of the Audi. In the glove box she found the manuals for the car, as well as a Glock 26, and a white plastic pill bottle. She checked the pistol, found it loaded, and dropped it on her coat, still covering the hush puppy. The bottle was labeled "Magna Rx" in English, and it took a second for her to realize what it was, squinting in the darkness, trying to read the label. Then she saw the words "yohimbe" and "male potency," and was trying to keep from laughing aloud when the satellite phone chimed.

READY.

Chace brought up the second message she'd prepared, with the GPS coordinates she'd picked out for the rendezvous, almost eighty kilometers to the southwest of Tashkent. She checked her watch, added the words PICKUP 0500 to her previously prepared text, and sent the message.

Finished, she folded down the antenna and tucked the phone back into her pocket, this time leaving it on. She switched the dome light on and checked the manuals, not caring for the illumination, but not having any other choice. She had to be able to read. She found the fuse diagram, opened the door, and then, half inside the car, half out, removed the panel to the fuse box. Checking the manual again, she pulled the fuse for the ignition, and the engine promptly died.

She pocketed the fuse in her trousers, put on her coat, stowed the hush puppy and Glock in each of her side pockets, then hit the trunk release. She moved to the Range Rover, lifted the rear hatch, and uncovered the weapons she'd purchased at the bazaar—a box of Chinese hand grenades, a Kalashnikov, the Sarsilmaz pistol, four clips, and two additional boxes of ammunition, one in 9 mm for the pistols, the other in 7.62 × 39, for the AK. She picked up the Kalashnikov, turned back to the Audi, and lifted the trunk, then stopped short as she was about to lay the automatic rifle inside, because she'd then seen what Ahtam Zahidov carried in his trunk, and it stopped her cold.

"Fuck me," Chace said aloud, and then bent, to give it a closer look.

It was a rectangular box, perhaps half a meter wide and thick, and long enough that it had been laid in the trunk at an angle. The markings on the box had been scuffed, as if deliberately obliterated, the paint scarred enough in places to reveal the metal shining beneath.

Chace set the Kalashnikov gently against the rear bumper, and then, with both hands, tried lifting the box. It was heavy, perhaps thirty, maybe thirty-five kilos, and it took some muscling to get the edge of it past the lip of the trunk, propped up enough for her to remove the top.

It was a missile.

If her memory of such things was to be trusted, it was a British missile, made by Thales Air Defense under contract to the MOD. A man-portable air-defense system, called Starstreak.

"Fuck me running," Chace murmured, and then she stepped back until she could sit on the open tailgate of the Rover.

She stared up at the clear sky, and the stars above, and for almost a minute didn't move.

Time to change the plan, Chace thought.

And then she smiled in a way she hadn't in over two years, and if anyone had been watching, they would have become very afraid indeed.

CHAPTER 21

Uzbekistan—Tashkent—182 Sulaymonova, Penthouse of Sevara Malikov-Ganiev

21 February, 0327 Hours (GMT+ 5:00)

They liked to sleep touching, and when the telephone jarred them both from their dreams, it was Sevara pulling away that truly woke him, and not the sound at all. She rolled toward the nightstand, and Zahidov sat up in the bed, groping for his glasses, and by the time he had them on she was answering, her voice husky with sleep.

Then Sevara tensed, responding to whatever she was hearing, and Zahidov felt the change. He switched on the light, turning back to look at her, growing concerned. The phone ringing at three in the morning could not possibly bring good fortune to either of them, he was sure. His first fear was that it was news about Ruslan was quickly dismissed; even if every one of his men knew where he spent his nights, none of them valued his job so poorly that he would call Sevara directly, rather than try to reach Zahidov on his mobile.

Something else, then. Her husband, that potato-shaped coward that Sevara's father had forced her to marry. Or maybe a problem with one of the recalcitrant DPMs, probably Urdushevich.

Sevara concluded the call and hung up the telephone. Her back was to him, and Zahidov couldn't see her expression, and realized that he couldn't read her posture, either. His concern turned to worry.

"What's happened?" he asked.

She took a deep breath, as if steadying herself, before turning to face him. Her eyes were bright, and as he watched, her lips, those lips he never tired of tasting, parted, curling into a smile of purest satisfaction.

"He's dead," she said. "As of two-fifty-seven this morning, my father is dead. The doctor tells me his heart finally gave out."

It wasn't what Zahidov had expected to hear, and it took a second for him to process the news, to move from worry to relief, and then Sevara was in his arms again. She kissed him fiercely, joyously, slipped free from his grip and out of the bed, heading for the bathroom. She left the door open, and Zahidov watched as she slid the door to the marble shower stall back, reaching in to switch on the faucet.

"I have to go to the hospital," Sevara called back to him, over the running water. "Call Abdukhallim, tell him to convene the Oliy Majlis for an emergency session this morning, tell him to introduce the resolution to name me interim President, and to schedule the vote for early this afternoon."

"He knows the terms?"

"He likes being Chairman, Ahtya. He wants to stay being Chairman, he'll do what we want."

Zahidov got out of the bed himself, began pulling on his clothes. "What about your husband and Ruslan?"

"I'll call Denis from the hospital, ask him to join me there, so we can put on a good face for the media. He'll need to be with me for the vote this afternoon, but after it goes through I'll ask for his resignation and then name you to take over the Interior Ministry as his replacement."

He had his shirt on now, tucking it into his trousers. He grabbed his necktie, draping it around his neck, then moved into the bathroom, buttoning his shirt. Sevara was beneath the water, visible behind the glass doors, wrapped in steam.

"And Ruslan?" Zahidov asked again.

"Keep your babysitters on him, Ahtya, nothing more. After the vote it'll be too late for him to do anything."

"I'm worried about what happens before the vote." He managed to look away from her long enough to check that his tie was properly knotted, and when he looked back, she was shutting off the water. He took one of the white towels from the heated stand, wrapped her in it as she stepped out of the shower.

"What's he going to do?" Sevara asked him, taking hold of the towel and passing him, heading back into the bedroom. "You're fretting about nothing."

The cockiness in her voice made Zahidov frown. "I don't know what he's going to do. But I don't want to find out after he's done it."

Sevara moved to the closet, began pulling down clothes from the hangers, a long black skirt, a black blouse, mourning colors. "You have him under surveillance. There's not much more you can do."

"I can bring him in, hold him at the Ministry."

"I don't want to antagonize the Americans," Sevara said. She dropped her clothes on the bed, moved to the bureau, began picking out her lingerie. "I'll have to meet with Ambassador Garret after the vote, and I don't want the first topic of discussion to be how unhappy the White House is with the way we've handled things. I don't want to start that relationship on the wrong foot, you understand?"

Zahidov didn't answer, pulling on his coat, then taking his holster from where it lay on the nightstand at his side of the bed and clipping it onto his belt at his right hip.

"Ahtam," Sevara said, her tone sharpening.

"I think you worry too much about the Americans," he said. "They need us more than we need them."

"You're wrong." It was declarative, and her expression now matched her tone. "It is a mutually beneficial relationship, that's what it's called. I won't antagonize them, not yet. I want this to go smoothly."

"It will go smoothly."

"It *must* go smoothly."

He nodded, trying not to appear reluctant, then turned to the telephone and dialed the number of the Chairman of the Oliy Majlis, watching Sevara continue dressing from the corner of his eye. When Abdukhallim answered, Zahidov spoke quickly, relaying Sevara's instructions. The Chairman didn't hesitate before swearing he would do what was asked.

Zahidov hung up. Sevara was at the makeup table now, and he watched as she quickly traced her mouth with lipstick, then studied herself in the mirror. Her expression fell into one of convincing sorrow, then lifted, and when she turned to face him once more, she was smiling again, satisfied that her mask of grief would be convincing.

"You want me to come with you?" Zahidov asked.

"No, go to the Ministry, start making your arrangements." She stepped closer, fixed his tie, then appraised him. "Deputy Prime Minister Zahidov."

"Madam President."

Her smile was radiant, and he bent to kiss her. She turned her head, sparing her makeup, offering her cheek instead.

The first thing he saw was that someone had stolen his fucking car.

The second thing he saw was that someone had broken the gate to do it.

"What in the hell happened?" Sevara asked.

"Go to the hospital." He turned, taking her arm, guiding her to the BMW. "Go to the hospital, do what you planned, everything as you planned."

Sevara twisted, puzzled, staring at him. "Someone stole your car?"

"Yes, *my* car."

She didn't grasp the significance, he could see it on her face, and he didn't think there was time to explain.

"Go," he repeated. "Just as you planned, please, love."

Sevara hesitated a moment longer, the question in her eyes, then nodded, slipping behind the wheel. "You'll take care of it?"

"Whatever it is, yes."

"Smooth, love. It must be smooth."

"With everything in my power," he promised her, then moved to the gate. He stepped back, onto the ramp, watching as the BMW passed, and Sevara didn't turn to look at him as she drove.

As soon as the car was out of sight on the street, Zahidov went back into the garage, to the chain piled on the ground. He crouched, examining it, finding flecks of cinder block scattered nearby. He rose, peering closer at the motor and the pulleys, running a hand along the wall, until he felt the texture beneath his finger turn from rough to smooth, the scoring left by the bullet.

He stepped back, thinking quickly. Whoever had taken his car, they'd come for it specifically, he was certain, and perhaps for what it carried as well. He didn't know why, he couldn't even guess yet at who, but it was more than just alarming. Malikov finally dead, and someone had stolen the Audi, and worse, the missile.

He pulled his mobile phone from his pocket, hit the fourth number on his speed dial, calling Ruslan's home, waiting for one of the guards to answer. The call refused to connect, and Zahidov thought that maybe the garage was causing the interference, moved up farther along the ramp, swearing as he redialed. Again, there was no connection, nothing, just a radio silence.

Zahidov heard a car coming along the silent street, raised his head to see a Mercedes slowing as it approached. He switched the phone to his left hand, moved his right to his hip, ready to draw his pistol. The car came to a stop, its window hissing down, and Zahidov let his fingers close around the butt of his gun, then released his grip as he recognized the driver.

"Get in," Aaron Tower said, speaking in Uzbek.

Zahidov covered his surprise with suspicion. "What are you doing here?"

"Ensuring an orderly transfer of power. Now get in the fucking car, Ahtam."

"Why?"

"Because Ruslan's being lifted," Tower told him. "And if you don't move fast, you'll have a fucking coup on your hands."

CHAPTER 22

**Uzbekistan—Tashkent—14 Uzbekiston,
Malikov Family Residence**

21 February, 0241 Hours (GMT+ 5:00)

Chace had the Range Rover in position by twenty of three, parked
three-quarters of a kilometer from the house, with line of sight to
the front doors. She'd shattered the rear lights on the car, to keep
the brake and reverse lamps from giving her away, and kept the
headlights off while she worked. When she was satisfied with her
parking job, she twisted around in her seat until she could climb
into the back, to where she'd stored the Starstreak—now un-
packed—beneath the blanket. The Kalashnikov rested beside it,
along with two more banana clips, all loaded.

It took her three seconds to attach the aiming unit to the tube
that housed the actual missile, and then, crouched in the back of
the vehicle, Chace hoisted the Starstreak onto her shoulder. She
sighted the front of the house through the monocular, lining up the
aiming mark. Everything on the Starstreak seemed to be function-
ing as it should, and again it looked like her line of sight was true.

Chace set the missile down again, re-covering it and the rifle
with the blanket, then got out, checking her watch. Almost ten to
three. She removed her coat, checking it a final time to make certain nothing remained in any of its pockets, and swapped it for the

flak jacket. She checked the flak jacket as well, making certain everything was where she had put it. Hush puppy outside right, two spare magazines left breast pocket, two grenades left outside pocket, satellite phone right breast pocket. The Glock she wore tucked into the front of her pants, and the knife, again, rested in its sheath at the small of her back.

Assured everything was where she wanted it, where she needed it, she turned and made her way past the front of the car, heading away from the house. The night was silent and deeply cold, still enough that sound would carry. She hooked a right at the corner, leaving the block, following the route she'd mapped out during her surveillance, one that would bring her around the long way to the back of the house. She tried not to hurry, telling herself that, for the moment at least, time was on her side.

She'd picked the hour carefully. The guards both outside and inside the house rotated shifts, she'd learned that much from the surveillance. Which meant that those working these dead hours of night didn't always work these dead hours of night, but found themselves on day shifts as well. That shot their circadian rhythms all to hell. While the rest of the world was deep in stage four sleep, beyond even REM, those poor six guards on post outside the house had to remain awake, when everything in their biology demanded otherwise. The same would be the case for however many guards were awake inside the house.

It would make the guards weak, put them off their game. They would be fighting off yawns, stretching, pacing, stamping their feet. They would break protocol, meet up for five minutes to share a cigarette and conversation, anything to keep awake.

They would be sloppy.

By her watch, it was eight minutes past three when she came in sight of the house. The wall surrounding the backyard was roughly two meters tall, concrete blocks joined with cement, and certainly scalable if one were so inclined, more effective for preserving privacy than security. There were no streetlights on this side, and the ones along the front were weak, and widely spaced. After almost half an hour of working in the darkness, Chace's night vision was nearly at full.

Parked at roughly the midpoint of the wall was one of the watch cars, a newer-model Volga that seemed an almost luminescent light blue in the darkness. Chace ducked down, moving to her right along the line of shadows growing into the lane. Low, she made her way carefully forward, to the near corner of the wall. The cover was excellent, and put her perhaps eight meters from the back of the car. Exhaust trickled from the Volga's tailpipe, gathering on the ground like some lazy wraith that lacked motivation or energy for actual haunting. The sound of the engine resonated softly off the concrete.

Chace didn't move, watching and waiting. From inside the Volga, she thought she saw movement, and then the flare of a lighter, flame illuminating the driver's face as he started a cigarette. He was sitting alone, and Chace found herself gnawing on her lower lip, needing to find the second guard, the one walking post. She'd hoped he'd be taking a rest in the car as well, but clearly that wasn't the case. He was on his rounds, then, or taking a break elsewhere, perhaps inside the house. When she'd had the house under surveillance, she'd seen all of the exterior guards go inside at one point or another, presumably to use the bathroom. If the graveyard shift used coffee to stay awake, they were probably using the bathroom a lot.

Chace stole another glance at her watch, the barely luminous hands of her Rolex now reading eleven minutes past three, then eased the hush puppy out of her pocket, taking the safety off with her thumb and disengaging the slide lock. Though it would make the gun that much more silent, it allowed her only one shot at a time, and with two men waiting, that just wouldn't do. The timing on this had to be right. As soon as she moved, as soon as she started taking the guards down, there'd be no stopping, no time or opportunity for a real pause until they were out of the city and on the way to the rendezvous with Porter. And even that was suspect, because Chace couldn't guarantee that there wouldn't be a pursuit once they left the city.

The run would start with her first shot.

When and where it would end, she didn't know.

From up the lane came the sound of a man's cough, barely bouncing off the wall and the street, and then she saw him, the walking guard, no more than twenty meters away at the most, emerging from the far corner. He'd been around the front, most likely inside, and Chace took reassurance from that. She was reading the terrain right.

The guard continued in her direction, stopping at the Volga for a moment to lean down and speak to the driver. He was tall enough that bending to the side window of the Volga took his upper body almost parallel to the ground. The pistol in her hand felt solid and even good, and Chace took a deep breath, filling herself with oxygen, then came around the corner, holding the gun flat against her right thigh, her right side to the wall. She started forward, unsteady, bumped into the wall with her shoulder, kept moving forward, almost staggering.

The guard speaking into the car turned his head to her, but didn't straighten, saying something in Uzbek to the driver. She continued forward, and the guard began straightening, turning toward her and now speaking, and Chace bounced herself off the wall again, now almost even with the rear of the Volga. This time, she brought her right arm up as she staggered back, and pulled the trigger twice in quick succession.

The bullets hit the guard in the chest and face, and he toppled in time with the ejected brass pinging onto the ground. Chace straightened instantly, lunging forward and twisting, bringing the gun around to point through the open passenger window. The driver was staring at her in openmouthed incomprehension, not yet having processed what he'd just seen, and Chace fired the hush puppy once more. The driver made a noise between a gurgle and a gag, then slumped back against his door and didn't move.

Chace dropped to a knee beside the first body, running her free hand over his clothes, into his jacket, around his waist, and was unable to find a radio on him. So she'd been right about that, at least; the radios were confined to the cars alone, and not to the walking patrols. So much the better.

Pistol in her hand, Chace came around the front of the car and opened the driver's door, letting the body topple out onto the ground, stepping over it and settling into the seat. The driver had been short, and she had to slide the seat back. The interior smelled of cigarettes and, now, fresh blood. She checked the gauges, saw that there was just over half a tank of fuel still available, and that the engine was still running. Hooked beneath the dashboard on the passenger's side was a radio set, the indicator light glowing a contented green, the frequency visible on a luminescent LCD screen. Chace checked the volume on the set, turning it up, and heard no traffic.

No alarm, at least not yet.

The Volga was a standard, and she shoved the stick into first, easing out the clutch. She kept the headlamps off, accelerating to second, making her way up the lane. She slowed at the top of the road, turning right, then edged forward until the Volga nosed out onto the street enough for her to look down toward the front of 14 Uzbekiston, almost one hundred meters away. There were street lamps on this side, though poorly placed, and they failed to offer enough illumination to reveal her at the corner, at least from this distance.

Some forty meters down, in the glow of one of the lamps, she could see the second watch car, another Volga, its driver's door open and the driver standing outside the vehicle. Another of the walking guards was just now passing the car, heading away, toward the stronger illumination at the front of the house. Beyond that, darkness swelled again, concealing the last car, and, presumably, the last walker.

Chace felt her heart beat so strong it seemed to be thumping in her ears. Her lips were dry, and when she ran her tongue over them, she tasted the tang of her adrenaline. Barely coming off the clutch, she turned her car to the top of the lane. The slope downhill was slight, but enough, and she put the car into neutral, letting the vehicle coast toward the nearest Volga. She stayed off the brakes until she was perhaps twenty feet from the car, then let her foot come down gently, hoping they wouldn't squeak.

They squeaked.

The driver of the second car turned, startled by the noise. Then he recognized the vehicle, or he seemed to, because instead of reacting with alarm, he stepped farther away from his car, raising an arm in greeting. His arm was still raised when Chace came down full on the brakes, stopping beside him. Through the open passenger window, she could see the man's midsection, watched as his arm came down and he began to lean forward, and she pointed the pistol at him and fired twice. He staggered, bumping against the frame of his car, then falling backward into his seat.

Chace dropped the hush puppy on the passenger's seat, came down on the clutch, starting the engine again, and then popped the Volga into first gear, accelerating. Ahead, just beyond the wash of the closest streetlight, she watched as the walker turned, confused and tracking the source of the noise. Chace scooped up the gun, came down on the clutch and the brake together, and this time emptied the gun, firing the remaining three shots as she came alongside. Her first shot caught him high in the chest, below the shoulder, the second in the throat, the third missing altogether. She waited until he hit the ground before dropping the gun once more, then rammed the stick into reverse, and backed up the lane as fast as the Volga could bear it. The whine of the engine was tremendous, and she had no doubt that it would carry down the street, to the remaining car, and the remaining guards.

At the top of the lane she braked, went back into first, and turned, accelerating hard as she came around the next corner, then flooring it. She raced the Volga back down the narrow lane, past the corpses she'd made there. Taking her hand from the stick, she ejected the magazine from the hush puppy, then, using her knees to hold the wheel, retrieved one of her spares and slipped it into place, chambering the first round.

She slowed at the turn, fighting the urge to simply race around the final corner. The radio beside the pistol was still silent, and Chace was beginning to wonder if it really was on. She'd half expected the alarm to be raised by now.

Expected, but not hoped. What she had hoped for was that the sound of the Volga reversing up Uzbekiston would have pulled the remaining walker up the street. He'd find the last body Chace had dropped soon enough, and yes, that would raise the alarm. But he'd do one of three things then. Either he'd run to the next car, to see if it had been hit as well, and perhaps decide to use the radio there; he'd run to the house, and raise the alarm; or he'd run back to his staging vehicle, where his partner was behind the wheel.

Chace was hoping for option three, but one and two seemed just as likely.

She edged her car around the corner, once again going as slowly as she could bear, and saw the last car parked in the shadows up the street. It was too dark to see any sign of the driver.

Inspiration hit her then, and she turned on the Volga's headlights, then started up the street. The lights splashed the remaining car, and she saw the driver of the vehicle opening his door, emerging and raising a hand to shield himself from the glare as he looked her way. She tried to read his expression as she closed the distance, thought she saw there his recognition of the vehicle, but she was closing too fast to take the time needed to process it. Hopefully, this driver was experiencing the same thing.

She kept the headlights on as she came to a stop, and the driver dropped his arm and started toward her, moving outside the spread of the beams. Chace put the car in neutral and set the brake, and it was a reassuring sound to him, she could see it, a sound he expected. Now that she was close enough, she could read his manner as well as his face, and it was clear to her, then, that he suspected nothing.

Why would he? All he had heard was a car reversing up Uzbekiston, nothing else, nothing more.

Chace waited until he was perhaps ten feet from her, then opened the door, and came out firing. She used two bullets this time, because she could use both hands to shoot, and each went where she wished it, and the man fell, his expression of bewilderment clouding into pain, then freezing there.

One left.

Being careful to stay out of the headlights to avoid casting a silhouette, Chace moved up the street, to the last car, in time to see the last walker sprinting toward her. She heard him call out, saw the pistol in his hand, and he called out a second time, and she realized he was shouting the name of the driver. She adjusted her grip on the hush puppy, holding it with both hands, low, breathing through her nose. The cold air burned, and she smelled exhaust and coffee and fried food, and a piece of her mind that had somehow remained detached from everything that had happened in the last two and a half minutes concluded that the driver had been having his dinner before she'd killed him.

When he was perhaps twenty-five feet away, the walker faltered, almost skidding to a stop, and Chace knew he had seen something, perhaps her silhouette, perhaps the body of the last driver. He started to bring his pistol up, but she had been ready, and beat him on the index, firing twice, then twice more. In the distance and the darkness, she couldn't see her hits, but she saw the results, and the man twisted on his feet, a top in its final stages, then toppled.

Chace took a moment to catch her breath.

Then she turned back to her Volga, climbed once more behind the wheel, and drove up to the front of the house, parking at an angle, half on the driveway, half off. The lights on the ground floor were burning, but the lights above were all out. A single fixture burned above the door.

She left the engine running and walked up the path, setting the slide lock on the hush puppy as she made her way to the door. This time, silence would be more important than volume. The light dug at her eyes, killing off the last vestiges of her night vision. There was no peephole on the door, which was a marginal surprise, and no cameras posted above or around, which was not. Chace tried not to think about the men with the room-brooms on watch inside.

She knocked firmly, twice.

She raised the hush puppy in both hands, and waited.

Just need to use the toilet, she thought, and then found herself fighting a giggle, because, in fact, she was sure she did.

The door rattled, parted, and she saw a slice of a man's face. She fired, stepping forward and shoving the door, and managed to catch him before he hit the floor. It struck her that he looked awfully young, and for a moment she was afraid she'd made a mistake and had the terrifying but fleeting fear that she'd done all this work only to enter the wrong house. But as she laid the body down on the carpet, beside the rows of shoes left by their owners, she saw the MP-5K resting on the sideboard.

Chace shut the door quietly, working the slide on the hush puppy and removing the empty casing, tucking it into her pants. She'd dumped the spent shells from the garage at the cemetery, so they wouldn't collide and ring in her pocket. Then she slipped the hush puppy back into her jacket and brought out the knife at her back.

She listened, and for several seconds didn't hear anything.

Then she heard distant waves rolling onto a shore.

She followed the sound, taking each step as its own movement, keeping her progress deliberate. A stairway ran to the second floor, carpeted, but she ignored it for the moment, pressing forward. The sound of waves disappeared, replaced by a man's voice, speaking Russian, and she could make out enough to know she was hearing commentary to a football match. A second voice joined the first, and then both laughed.

She came off the hallway, through an open archway, into a

kitchen, the sound of the television growing gently louder. She passed the light switch as she entered, and threw it, turning the room dark. A dining room opened up in front of her with a view of the backyard, a semidarkened hallway to her left. She took the hallway, still moving slowly, still hearing the television, now finally able to discern its light at the end of the corridor, beyond a half-opened door. Along the left-hand side were two doors, closed; on the right, one, partially ajar, and she could make out bathroom fixtures within.

Halfway down the hall, she heard movement from the room with the television, the creak of furniture springs losing their tension. She retreated as quickly as she could to the kitchen, then turned and put her back to the wall on the opposite side of the opening to the hall as the light switch. She spun the blade in her hand into a stabbing grip, trying to keep her breathing steady, steeling herself.

It was called wet work for a reason.

A man stepped through the archway. She saw him in profile as he squinted in the darkness, then muttered a curse. He half pivoted away from her, the MP-5K on a strap over his shoulder, reaching to turn on the light with his right hand. She saw he was perhaps an inch or two shorter than her, broad-shouldered, and bald.

Chace stepped behind him, bringing the knife up in her right hand, reaching around with her left to cup his chin, pulling it toward her. She stabbed horizontally into his neck, jabbing once, twice, and again and again and again in rapid succession, and blood sprayed out of the man, hot on her hand and face. She stabbed into his neck a sixth time, but he was deadweight on her now, and she had to kneel to avoid dropping him completely. A ragged breath broke through his perforated skin.

That was the last sound he made.

Chace got back to her feet, saw that the knife in her hand was jumping slightly, a tuning fork catching some stray vibration, and that her hands were trembling. She cleaned the blade on the back

of the man's shirt, then stepped over him and back into the hallway, dimly aware that her front, even down to her trousers, was
stained and slick with blood.

She checked the television room first, and found no one there.
Working back, she hit the rooms on the hall, opening each door
with painful care, just enough to glimpse what was inside. Each
room housed two more men, sleeping.

She let them sleep and headed upstairs.

Chace found Stepan first, the toddler curled in a crib in a room
with balloon wallpaper, his bottom thrust up into the air, as if he'd
fallen asleep while preparing to somersault. She hesitated, then
backed out, finally locating the master bedroom after two more
doors.

Ruslan Mihailovich Malikov slept in a king-size bed, but only
on one side, the one nearest the door. The light from the hallway
bled into the room, and Chace recognized him from the photograph Riess had shown her on his digital camera. A positive identification. The way he slept surprised Chace for a second, because
she'd expected him to take the opposite side, that it would have
been his wife who had wanted to be nearest their son. But of
course, that *was* the reason, wasn't it?

Chace wondered if Ruslan had changed the sheets since Dina
had been murdered.

She approached the bed carefully, not wanting to wake him until she could make certain he'd stay silent, mindful of the four
guards and their four submachine guns sleeping below. Reaching
his side, she crouched down on her haunches, then put her right
hand over his mouth, sealing it with her palm, but keeping his nose
free.

He came awake almost instantly, and as soon as Chace saw his
eyes open, she put her mouth to his ear and began whispering,
"Friend," in Russian, over and over. Ruslan surged upward, eyes
bulging, and Chace couldn't blame him for that; if someone had

woken her like this, clapping a gore-slicked hand over her mouth, she'd have tried to scream bloody murder. She shoved him back down, rising up to add her weight to the press, trying to keep him relatively immobile.

"Friend," she kept repeating.

Ruslan's arms came up, straining to break her grip, one going to her forearm, one reaching for her face. Then, abruptly, they dropped to his side, and she saw the confusion come into his eyes, stealing away the panic.

"Understand?" she asked, sticking with Russian.

Ruslan nodded.

"Ruslan Mihailovich Malikov?"

He nodded again.

"I'm here to take you and your son to London."

There was the briefest pause, the confusion again awash in his eyes, before he nodded a third time.

"Quietly," Chace whispered. "Four still asleep downstairs." She removed her hand, stepping back from the bed, showing him her empty palms.

Ruslan Mihailovich Malikov sat up gasping for air, staring at her, half in horror, half in amazement. She couldn't fault him the look; her clothes were covered with blood, much of it still wet, and she stank of gunpowder, sweat, and death. She resisted the urge to touch her hair, to try to brush it back into place, gave him another second to stare, then stepped closer.

"I have a car outside," she said in Russian. "Dress quickly, we get your son, and we go."

Without a word, Ruslan started moving, rising and heading to the dresser on the wall opposite the foot of the bed. He stripped, back to her, began pulling on clothes, and Chace watched him for a half second longer, then stepped lightly back, toward the door, to listen at the opening. There was no sound from downstairs, only the shift of cloth and movement as Ruslan continued to dress. Chace took the time to draw the hush puppy, then shrug out of the flak jacket. When she looked back to Ruslan, he was almost fully, if hastily, dressed in dark trousers and a long-sleeved shirt, now working on his shoes.

"It's cold," Chace whispered to him.

He nodded, finished with his last shoe, moved to the closet. From inside he pulled a thick overcoat.

"You have to keep your son quiet," Chace told him. "Can you keep Stepan quiet?"

He was pulling on his overcoat, and surprised her by answering in English, his accent more Russian than Uzbek, but not so thick as to make him unintelligible. "Yes, he'll stay quiet."

Chace held out the flak jacket for him. "Wrap him in this," she answered, now speaking English, too. "It'll offer some protection."

Ruslan balked for a second, looking at the blood-soaked garment, then nodded, taking it.

"Follow me," Chace said, and slipped out the door, back into the hall. There was still nothing from below, no motion, no noise. She covered the distance to the child's room, feeling Ruslan close behind her, then let him pass her when they entered. Ruslan moved to the crib, scooping up his son and whispering a flood of Uzbek as he did, cradling the little boy against his chest, wrapping the flak jacket around him. The boy barely stirred, and Chace wondered if Ruslan could keep him asleep until they were out of the house.

"Stay close," Chace told him. "The car is out front. When we reach it, get in the back, then lie down on Stepan."

"Yes," Ruslan whispered.

Chace pivoted, moved back into the bright light of the upstairs hall, to the top of the landing. She stole a glance over the railing, down to the floor below, and saw no one but the body she'd left just inside the doorway. She motioned for Ruslan to follow, and he emerged from his son's room. When the light hit Stepan, the boy squawked in soft protest, burying his face further against Ruslan's chest, and Chace thought of Tamsin without wanting to or meaning to, then turned away, leading father and son down the stairs.

She checked the entry hall, looking back toward the darkened kitchen, then turned to the front door and edged it open, the hush puppy held in low-ready, with both hands. No one was outside, and the sound of the unattended Volga, its engine still wheezing, was the only thing she heard.

"Now," Chace said, and she ran for the car, Ruslan with his son still in his arms close on her heels. She reached the car first, whipping her head around, checking the street in both directions even as she pulled open the rear door. The boy was crying now, startled and unnerved as Ruslan bundled him inside, and Chace heard his father's voice, low and calm and constant, speaking in Uzbek. She slammed the door behind them, jumped into the driver's seat, and accelerated out, wheeling the car around into a one-eighty. She floored it, the Volga reluctant at first, then finally catching speed.

From the backseat, she heard Stepan's sobs turn to howls.

Chace slid the Volga to a stop beside the Range Rover, jumped out, saying, "Wait here."

"What—" Ruslan began, almost shouting over Stepan's screams.

She ignored him, moving to the tailgate. Without the flak jacket, the cold was beginning to eat at her, finding the sweat and blood still wet on her skin and clothes. A wind was starting to rise, light, but enough to make her shiver.

Chace pulled the Starstreak from the Range Rover, switched on the power to the aiming unit and ignition, then hoisted it onto her shoulder, settling her right eye against the monocular. Sweat clung to her eyelashes, stinging her, and she blinked, trying to clear her eyes. A new anticipation swelled in her chest, a strange collusion of fear and excitement, almost arousing. She knew the Starstreak from reports, from technical papers and military analysis. She knew the Starstreak academically, what it could do, how it did it. But she'd never fired one herself, never seen the results in person. She lined up the aiming mark, exhaling slowly.

She depressed the firing stud, the small white button resting below her right thumb.

For a fraction of a second there was nothing, no response from the Starstreak, and her thoughts flashed on the possibility that the unit was dead, that the internal battery was incapable of engaging the first-stage motor and starting the launch sequence. Then, on her shoulder, she felt the tube rumble, the missile hissing, the sound of a kettle just before boil. Thrust drove the launcher hard into her shoulder, pressing her down, and she grit her teeth, fighting to keep the aiming mark steady on target. It all took an instant, and then, just as swiftly, the pressure was gone.

It all came back to her then, all of the clinical data, the briefings, the analysis. Starstreak, designed as a high-velocity extreme-short-range MANPAD, maximum distance five kilometers, minimum only three hundred meters. Composed of a two-stage rocket motor, capped with a three-dart kinetically driven payload guidance system. The electronic pulse delivered via the firing stud engages the first-stage motor, propelling the missile from its canister while canted nozzles on the side of the rocket force it to rotate, the rotation in turn causing its fins to deploy, providing stabilization in flight.

Missile clears launch tube, first-stage motor is jettisoned, second stage is engaged, providing full thrust, and accelerating the rocket to speeds in excess of Mach 4. Missile closes to target, the darts fire, each dart with its own high-density penetrating explosive payload, fuse, guidance system, and thermal battery. Dart separation from missile initiates the arming of each warhead, each dart guided independently via a double laser-beam riding system, controlled by the missile operator via the aiming unit.

That was the clinical, the academic, what she *knew*.

What she *experienced* was the roar of the launch, the shock of the missile leaving the launch tube, the flare of light, the wash of heat. White-hot fire streaking horizontally toward number 14 Uzbekiston, her arm shaking, her eye stinging, trying to keep the aiming mark on the door, left wide open in the wake of their flight.

The missile vanished, and for a fraction, nothing, not noise, not light, nothing.

Then the house exploded.

Chace felt the concussion throughout her body, dropped the launch tube, and turned her back to the flames and falling debris. From the back of the Range Rover, she scooped up the Kalashnikov, the spare magazines, and the blanket, then made her way to the Volga, climbing inside. Ruslan was staring at her, and Stepan, for the moment, had gone silent, held against his father's shoulder, staring past him, at the ruins of the house.

She started the car and pulled away from the Range Rover.

In the backseat, Stepan said something in Uzbek, and Ruslan responded tartly. In the rearview mirror, Chace could see the man still staring at her. Stepan repeated the word, and Ruslan responded the same way.

"What's he saying?" Chace asked.

"Again," Ruslan said. "He wants you to do it again."

This time, the urge to laugh was too strong, and Chace didn't bother to fight it.

CHAPTER 23

London—Vauxhall Cross, Operations Room

20 February, 2324 Hours GMT

Crocker came onto the Ops Room floor, shrugging out of his overcoat, demanding, "What's the latest?"

"Tashkent Station now confirms that there was an explosion at the home of Ruslan Malikov," Alexis Ferguson told him from the MCO Desk. "Estimates the blast at twenty past three zone. Several dead, several missing and presumed dead. There's been no indication if Malikov or his kid is among the fatalities. State-run radio has issued a statement, confirming that there was an explosion, and blaming Hizb-ut-Tahir for the blast."

From his inside pocket, Crocker found his cigarettes, then abandoned the coat and crossed the room, heading for Alexis. "Anything more?"

"Station Number Two has a man inside the police department who reports that there's been activity at the NSS, and that both the NSS and the police are engaged in a full-scale search for the perpetrators. Apparently there are two different vehicle descriptions being circulated at the moment, one for a blue Volga, late model, the other for an Audi. It seems they're searching for both cars, though how they're connected to the blast, the Station Number Two can't say."

"The blast, it wasn't a car bomb?"

"Unclear one way or the other."

Crocker nodded, then stepped back, looking up at the plasma wall for a moment before lighting his cigarette. From the Duty Ops Desk, he heard Ron stifling a yawn. He empathized, though only slightly; Ron had relief coming on-shift in two more hours. Crocker, who'd been at home and about to head for bed when the call had come informing him of what had happened in Tashkent, doubted he'd be getting sleep anytime soon.

"You think it's a coup, sir?" Ron asked him.

"No. Not unless someone's gone after the President and his daughter as well."

"No word of that," Alexis confirmed.

"So no, it's not a coup." Crocker frowned, then moved back to the Duty Ops station. "You've informed the DC, C, and the FCO?"

"As per usual, yes, sir. C hasn't arrived yet, but the DC is in her office."

Crocker lifted up the handset on one of the internal phones, held it out for Ron to take. "Inform her I'm coming up."

"Yes, sir."

He turned to face Alexis. "Signal Tashkent, get the Number One on an open line, and tell him to stay there. Inform him that I want updates every twenty minutes, and have him tell the Number Two that I'm especially interested in the pursuit, and any new information about the vehicles, however minor it may seem. Anything they get on those last, they're to inform us immediately. I'll be upstairs."

"Understood, sir."

Crocker grabbed his coat, and headed for Alison Gordon-Palmer's office.

"Would Chace have blown up the house?" the Deputy Chief asked.

"It's not a bad way to cover one's tracks," Crocker told her.

"Creates one hell of a mess, and makes it difficult if not impossible to quickly determine if Ruslan and his boy are missing, rather than dead."

She rested her elbows on her desk, folding her hands one over the other, resting her chin upon them, musing. "So it's possible she did it."

"Yes, it's possible. She's not one to go big if she can get away with small, but if the opportunity and means presented itself, yes, I can see her doing it."

"Presuming that Chace is responsible in the first place?"

"I think she is. I think she's made the lift, and she's on the run to her RV."

"But no way to confirm?"

"Not without informing Tashkent Station that Chace is there to begin with, no," Crocker said. "Though you were right about Seale. I could check with the CIA."

Alison Gordon-Palmer frowned slightly. "No, let's keep the Americans out of it for the moment."

Something in the way she said it struck Crocker as off, but before he could ask the question, the Deputy Chief had continued.

"The blast. Assuming it was Chace, and assuming she did it after getting Ruslan and his son clear, how would she have managed it?"

"Again, I can't say. We don't have enough details about the blast, if the house was leveled or if the reports are exaggerated. She was traveling light, and without support, so anything she's using she must have acquired on the ground."

She raised an eyebrow at him, and Crocker knew what she wanted to hear.

"It is possible it was a Starstreak missile, yes," he conceded.

"Which she acquired in Tashkent somehow."

"She didn't bring it with her from London." Crocker shifted position in his chair, leaning forward. "Isn't it time you told me what you and Sir Walter are up to?"

The Deputy Chief considered, raising her head off her hands, then lowering her arms to lie flat on her desk. Her office, like Crocker's, was spare, sparsely furnished and sparsely decorated. Unlike Crocker's desk, though, hers was almost bare as well, devoid of almost all paper, and occupied with only the barest of office essentials.

"Barclay talked to you," she said after a moment's consideration. "He offered you my job, didn't he?"

Crocker saw no reason to deny it. "Yes, he did."

"And you're willing to burn him?"

"I think that's evident. And he thinks you and Sir Walter are moving to burn him, doesn't he? That's part of what this is about."

"Paul," Alison Gordon-Palmer said, "it's all that this is about."

He needed a second, which was long enough for the realization to both hit and sicken him.

"It's a dummy run?" Crocker asked. "I've sent Chace on a dummy run?"

"Nothing so crude. If she can get Ruslan and his son out, so much the better."

"But you're saying there's no plan for a coup?"

"Not anymore."

"What changed?"

"The CIA got wind of it, and bless their souls, they promptly told the White House. And the White House came back to Downing Street and said in no uncertain terms that Sevara Malikov-Ganiev was to be the next President of the Democratic Republic of Uzbekistan." She straightened in her chair, gauging Crocker's reaction, seeing the distress. "It hardly matters, Paul."

"It matters to Chace."

"What would you have done if I'd told you this four hours ago? You have no contact with her, correct? You wouldn't have been able to get her to abort even if you wanted to."

It was true, but it didn't make Crocker feel any better.

"We'll get her back, don't worry," the Deputy Chief told him. "CIA knows she's there, they'll watch out for her."

"Unless the White House decides otherwise."

"Instruments of government, Paul. If they bend, break, or discard us, it's their prerogative."

"I'm sure that'll be of some comfort to her daughter, though at the moment, I can't imagine how."

The Deputy Chief narrowed her eyes, began to respond, and then her phone rang, so she answered it instead.

It was C, informing them that he was in his office and ready to see them now.

"We'll be right up, sir," Alison Gordon-Palmer told him, then replaced the handset carefully in its cradle. "He wants us upstairs."

Crocker got to his feet. "And what are you going to tell him?"

She shook her head, rising with him. "No, Paul, not me, you. You're going to tell him exactly what you just told me."

"Am I?"

"Yes. And you can tell him that Chace may well have found one of his missing Starstreaks." She opened the door to the outer office, holding it for Crocker. "I think he'll be particularly happy with that bit of news, don't you?"

"I doubt it," Crocker said.

CHAPTER 24

21 February, 0424 Hours (GMT+5:00)

One headlight was enough, it seemed, the xenon beam harsh on the
two-lane highway that ran south from Tashkent to Dzhizak and
then on to Samarkand, a memory of the Silk Road long past. At
the edges of the light, the landscape siding the road glowed like the
surface of the moon, the dirt and dust turning a blue-white. The
wind that had come up on them in Tashkent was stronger south of
the city, howling along the valley, and fingers of dust twirled along
the surface of the road.

Chace drove fast, taking the Audi up to a hundred and forty
kilometers an hour and then holding it there wherever the road
would allow. The sound of the air rushing past the car clogged her
left ear, but the vehicle's aerodynamics were strong, and most of
the wind stayed outside the car instead of climbing inside with
them. Occasionally, a gust would break through, snapping Chace's
hair so hard she could feel it stinging her neck.

Ruslan sat in the front passenger's seat, his eyes fixed on the
road ahead of them whenever he wasn't twisting himself about to
check on his son, asleep in the back, the blanket Chace had taken
from the Range Rover wrapped tightly around him. Chace mar-
veled at it, that the boy could sleep through the racket of the wind

and the car, with all that had happened so far. She envied Stepan. Right now, she wanted sleep, too.

The adrenaline crash was wicked, revealing a soreness throughout her body and a dull ache in her limbs. Her left bicep twinged regularly when she moved the arm, reminding her of the exertion required in holding a man's throat exposed while stabbing him to death. The blood on her hands and arms had dried, and every so often a flake would come loose, caught in the wind, sending it spiraling in one random direction or another, a red snowflake that flipped through the car.

Chace checked her mirrors again, barely aware she was doing it, and saw Ruslan shift in his seat, either nervous, uncomfortable, or both. He'd ridden in silence ever since they'd switched to the Audi, and he hadn't really been talkative prior to that, for the obvious reasons. What little he'd said had been directed at his son, and in Uzbek. But since they'd made the Audi and hit the road, there'd been nothing more from him. Surely he had questions—dozens of them, more than likely—but thus far, he was keeping them to himself.

"My orders are to take you both to England, sir," Chace said, after another reflexive check of the mirrors, thinking that an explanation of one sort or another was in order. "We're on our way to a landing zone where we'll be met by a helicopter to fly us out."

She hadn't expected him to answer, and he surprised her when he did, asking, "Not America?"

"No."

"My wife was working with the Americans." He raised his left hand, rubbed his eyes, wiping sleep from their corners. "Before Zahidov raped and murdered her, she was working for the Americans. You are working with the Americans as well?"

"In a manner of speaking."

"I don't understand."

Chace shook her head, barely. "I wouldn't worry about it, sir."

"But I must worry about it, I have no choice. My son and I are fleeing for our lives with a woman covered in blood in Ahtam

Zahidov's automobile. There is nothing more for me to do now than worry about it."

"My orders are—"

"Yes, you said that," Ruslan snapped, then added something softer in Uzbek, the shape of the words lost beneath the wind rushing past the shattered window. From the corner of her eye, Chace saw him shift in his seat once more, checking again on Stepan, then resume looking out the windshield. "My name is Ruslan, not 'sir.' "

Chace nodded. "Tracy."

"Tracy?"

"Tracy."

Ruslan nodded, and neither of them spoke again for another half-dozen kilometers, and oddly, Chace found herself growing uncomfortable with the silence. She supposed it was because Ruslan's doubts were her doubts, that he was asking questions that she had asked herself. Riess had said Sevara had White House support, and much as she was loath to admit it, she was having a hard time believing that her government would want to oppose the Americans, at least with regard to the future of Uzbekistan.

"How old is he?" She tilted her head to indicate Stepan in the backseat.

"My son is two and two months now."

Chace hesitated. "I have a daughter. Almost ten months old."

Ruslan reappraised her, mildly surprised, before saying, "Ten months was good for Stepan. He was walking at ten months."

"Mine's not walking yet," she said. She considered his reaction to their newly discovered common ground, thought that it might help to put him more at ease if she continued. Tamsin had ignored crawling altogether until only the week before Chace had left Barnoldswick, at which point she'd begun pulling up and the first attempts at cruising. She was adept at it, could make her way around the living room, wobbling wildly, using her hands to find support wherever she could.

Ruslan looked away from the road to study her again. He said, "You are missing her."

"Yes."

"You should be home, maybe, with your husband and your baby."

"I'm not married."

Ruslan considered that, then said, "But the father, he is with your daughter?"

She heard it in his inflection, a wistfulness, and Chace knew Ruslan was thinking of Dina.

"No," Chace said. "No, he died."

Again he murmured something in Uzbek before saying in English, "You have my . . . is it condolence, that is the word?"

"Condolences, yes."

"My condolences, then. I know that pain. Too well, I think that I know that pain. So your daughter, she is without her mother, and there is no father now."

"She's with her grandmother." Chace bit back the urge to become defensive. "She's fine."

"This is not a good job for a mother." Ruslan said it with conviction. "Killing and spying and stealing the cars of rapists and murderers. You should be with your daughter."

"It may not be a good job for a mother, sir, but it's the job I have. And it's a job you want me to complete, I'd think."

Ruslan grunted. "To what end? I will not lead Uzbekistan. Sevara has the Americans, and the British will not oppose the American plan. At the best, Stepan and I are merely being relocated."

"It'll keep you safe."

"No doubt, for a time. But it doesn't help my country."

From where it rested on the armrest, its antenna deployed, the satellite phone chimed, its LCD lighting up.

"It helps you," Chace said, sharper than she'd meant to. Keeping her left on the wheel, she picked up the phone, saw that a message had arrived. She thumbed the menu, bringing up the text.

15 MIN.

"Is there a problem?" Ruslan asked.

Chace dropped the phone in her lap, checking the odometer and doing the math. They'd covered seventy-three of the seventy-seven kilometers to the landing zone. It would be tight, but they'd make it.

"No," she told him. "Everything's fine."

From his expression, Chace saw that Ruslan Mihailovich Malikov didn't believe a word she was saying.

CHAPTER 25

21 February, 0440 Hours (GMT+5:00)

It was a goddamn mess, it was nothing but a goddamn mess, and as Ahtam Zahidov kicked at the broken pieces of the house, knocking burnt wood and blasted tile with his shoe, he swore aloud like a child having a tantrum. He cursed Ruslan Malikov and he cursed Aaron Tower and, most of all, he cursed a woman he had never seen before, a woman he'd never known existed until an hour ago, some bitch called Carlisle who had come to Uzbekistan to make his life miserable, who had come to Tashkent to hurt the woman he loved.

Because that's what this was, as far as Zahidov was concerned. This was an attempt to hurt Sevara, and never in a million years would he stand for that.

"Motherfucking cunt spy," he spat, then kicked again, this time knocking enough rubble clear to reveal the burnt body of yet another guard. From his size, it looked like Ummat, but there was so much damage, Zahidov couldn't be sure. He doubted they'd even find the rest of them; like the house, they'd probably been blown to bits.

This made eight bodies, six of them left on the street, as if declaring their worthlessness as sentries. And they *had* been worthless, Zahidov thought, all of them shot dead dead dead, and only one of them with his fucking pistol even in his hand. Which meant all of the other cocksuckers had been caught entirely unaware. They weren't sentries, they were fucking jokes, and he had hoped to find at least one of them with his pants around his ankles and his prick in his hand, because that, *that* would have explained how this had happened. Six dead outside, two dead inside, and no sign of that cowardly shit Ruslan or his whimpering little abortion of a son.

They'd found cars, for all the good that had done them, but even that was sour because they hadn't managed to find his fucking Audi. No, they'd found a Range Rover that looked like it had been maybe brought into service around the time Khrushchev was getting into a pissing match with Kennedy, and they'd found the missing Volga, parked on the other side of town, outside of the Jewish cemetery, its interior splattered with Kozim's blood and brains and nothing else. And nothing in the Range Rover, either. Zahidov had hoped it was the spy's when he heard about the blood in the Volga, but he knew it wasn't. No, just fucking Kozim the dead and useless, and he had gotten off lucky, in a way, because Zahidov would have done him himself if he'd lived through this.

He glared at the phone in his hand, willing it to ring, and like everything else this night, it defied him, staying silent. All he wanted in the world at this moment was a lead, something, anything on where they were headed in his car—and he was positive they were in his car now. Police and NSS throughout the country had been given the description of his Audi, ordered to find the vehicle and detain the occupants in whatever manner was required.

The border guards had been notified at the crossing into Kyrgyzstan, less than twenty kilometers north of Tashkent; Zahidov had taken care of that as soon as Tower had told him what had happened. But Zahidov knew the spy wouldn't go north—that portion of the border was too closely guarded, too well watched, and if she was traveling with the brat along with Ruslan, they wouldn't go on foot, they would stick to the roads.

So maybe they'd try for Kyrgyzstan via the northeast route, but that would take them into the Chatkal Mountains. The roads that

way were bad, and it would take a lot of time, and time was everything now, both to him and to the spy. By the same logic, he
doubted she'd taken them toward Tajikistan. There were only two
real roads that would lead south to the country, and again, one of
them would wind through the Chatkal. The other would be a trip
of almost one hundred and fifty kilometers, too far. Turkmenistan
was easily eight hundred kilometers by road, would take even
longer. Considering escape through Afghanistan was absurd.

The cunt spy wasn't going to take them out on the ground. No,
she would fly them. Which meant either a plane or a helicopter. If
a plane, they'd need a runway, and he'd already alerted the air-
ports in Tashkent, Dzhizak, and Samarkand, and had heard nothing. No private liftoffs, no private landings, but Zahidov ordered
men to those locations all the same, just to be certain. A helo
would be harder to find, would be able to set down just about anywhere, though he was reasonably sure the landing zone was south
of Tashkent, not to the north. There were too many sets of eyes to
the north, too easy to be spotted.

If the pilot knew what he was doing, he'd come in low, to avoid
radar, and if the helicopter was the right one for the job—and at
this point, Zahidov was positive that it would be, because this
fucking bitch spy knew what she was doing—it would have range
enough to enter the country and then get out again, setting
down just long enough to take on passengers. Coming in from
Kazakhstan more than likely, then.

The police were on the roads now, scouring the countryside and
setting up security checkpoints, but Zahidov didn't hold out much
hope for it. If she tried for Dzhizak or Zaamin or Chichak, they'd nail
the bitch entering the city limits. But for precisely that reason, she
wasn't going to go city. She was going countryside, for a helo pickup.

He looked at his phone again, still resolute in its refusal to ring,
then spun about on his heel, to the six men waiting on the street.
They stood by the cars, engines idling, two of the Toyota Land
Cruisers that the NSS preferred for their ability to go off-road. Six of
his best plucked from the NSS, standing with their M-16s. Zahidov

had even ordered Tozim to pull the two remaining Starstreaks from storage, loading one each into the back of the cars. All these men needed was a direction, a way to go, and he couldn't give them one.

He shouted at Tozim. "Where's the fucking Sikorsky? Where the fuck is it?"

"It's coming, Ahtam! It's coming, it should be here any second. We had to get a pilot out of bed, it's taking—"

Zahidov spun away, waving his free hand to shut Tozim up. He needed to think, he needed to think like this spy. The helicopter, that was the key to it, that was the trick. He'd been hoping Tower would call, tell him where the LZ was for the bitch's pickup, but it wasn't coming, there was no call, and that meant that all of the U.S. forces on the ground and all of their radar and all of their technology and all of their talent couldn't find the bird. Coming in low, coming in from Kazakhstan or Kyrgyzstan.

Coming along the river, Zahidov suddenly realized. Following the Syr Darya in its valley, to stay low.

This bitch, this spy, she would meet her helicopter along the river, somewhere south of Tashkent, that had to be it.

He tucked the phone in his pocket, closed the distance to Tozim, put a hand on his shoulder. Tozim was younger by perhaps two years, tall and strong and faithful and loyal enough that he'd been one of the men he'd chosen to help with Dina Malikov.

"Take three men and head south along the Samarkand highway," Zahidov told him. "Fast as you can. Keep your radio at hand."

Tozim nodded, the excitement visible on his face. "You've got them? You know where they're going?"

"I think so, not exactly, but I think so. Take the road to the M39 bridge, where it crosses the river, start searching there. Take one of the Starstreaks. You see any helicopter that *isn't* the Sikorsky, you bring it down."

"I will."

"Go."

Tozim moved, grabbing the three men nearest, tumbling them into the first car, and they peeled out, the wheels whining as the car

made a tight turn before accelerating out of sight. Zahidov could
hear the Sikorsky now, looked up to see the lights on the helo's
fuselage coming closer.

"You two are with me. Bring the missile."

The two hurried to comply.

Zahidov moved out into the street, raising a hand, and the
Sikorsky settled into a slow descent. Prop wash from the blades
stirred the dirt and dust and debris on the street, making it fly
about. Zahidov turned his head away, to shield his eyes, saw that
his remaining men had their hands to their faces. He heard the
Sikorsky's motor whine, then change pitch as the big machine settled on the ground. He ran for the door, making his way through
the cabin to the cockpit phone.

The Sikorsky was an S-76, a commercial model, not military,
used by Sevara and her father for quick trips in comfort around
the countryside, spacious enough inside for five, plus another two
in the cockpit. There were no armaments, but it did have the one
thing that all Sikorsky helicopters had, from the military Black
Hawks to the civilian S-92: it had speed.

While his men loaded the missile and then themselves, Zahidov
grabbed the handset from the cabin wall. The pilot came on instantly.

"The river," Zahidov told him. "Fast as you can, get us to the
river, and then start following it south."

"Yes, sir."

"Fast as you can." Zahidov repeated, and before he'd even hung
up, the rotors above were again gaining speed, the engine whine
growing louder once more. He helped the last of his men in, slamming
the door shut just as the Sikorsky begin to rise. The helicopter banked
sharply, tilting as it gained altitude, then rocking forward as it gained
speed. Zahidov swayed on his feet as if riding a wave. One of his men
stumbled, falling against the couch and dropping his M-16.

Then the Sikorsky settled on its path, and Zahidov turned his attention to the crate and began preparing the Starstreak for launch.

CHAPTER 26

Uzbekistan—Tashkent—U.S. Chancery,
Office of the Political Counselor

21 February, 0443 Hours (GMT+5:00)

Riess sat, staring blankly at his monitor, not seeing and not much caring for the work that required his attention. He'd been unable to sleep following Tower's visit, wandering around his home in the small hours, unsure of what to do, unsure of how to proceed. He'd tried reaching the Ambassador at the Residence just after two-thirty in the morning, had been surprised when his wife, Michelle, had answered the phone instead, telling him that Garret wasn't in, that she thought he was at the Embassy.

He'd hung up and changed clothes, then headed for the Chancery. The gate Marines checked his pass, let him through, and he'd made his way to the Ambassador's office, through corridors that weren't nearly as empty as they should've been at a quarter to three in the morning. Riess had passed the Press Office, seen the lights on inside, and his mood had soured further. Lydia Straight was burning midnight oil, and the only reason he could see for that was damage control. What damage she was controlling was the only real question, and he hoped it wasn't his or Garret's.

He was stopped at the Ambassador's office by one of the Marines, some kid from Georgia with the accent to prove it. "I'm sorry, sir, the Ambassador is not to be disturbed."

"I need to speak to him."

"Yes, sir. He's not to be disturbed, sir."

"You know what he's doing in there?"

"I believe he's on the phone, sir, but I'm afraid I don't really know. He's not to be disturbed, sir."

Riess wanted to ask what the kid *did* know, if, in fact, the Marine knew anything at all, but he didn't, just turned and made his way to the Pol/Econ office, doing time-zone math in his head. Past three in the morning in Tashkent put it past five in the previous day's evening in D.C. With Lydia Straight in the Media Office and the Ambassador on the phone, Riess was sure that Garret was talking to Washington, getting lashed by either S or D or the White House itself.

Not good. None of it was good, and Riess felt something he hadn't since the days following the bombing in Dar es Salaam. Not just lost, but adrift.

He'd brewed a pot of coffee, started on his first cup, when Lydia Straight came through the door, out of breath and looking like she'd sprinted the halls to reach him.

"There's been a bombing," she said.

Riess lunged for his desk, spilling coffee all over his hand, swearing. He flicked the radio on, hoping to find the news, saying, "Anyone injured?"

"Fuck if I know," Straight said. "It literally just came on, I just heard it on the radio in my office. No idea how long ago it happened."

"Suicide? Car? Both?"

She shrugged at him, and beyond her, down the hall, Riess saw a Marine run past, probably headed out to the gate to double up the watch. He shook coffee off his hand, reached for the secure telecom unit on his desk, started dialing the Operations Center at the State Department.

"The Ambassador's in his office," Riess told Straight. "Let him know what's happened, I'll deal with it here."

"Right," Lydia Straight said, and bolted off down the hall.

The radio babbled Uzbek at him, and he dropped the handset long enough to grab a pen and scrap paper, taking notes as fast as he could. Bomb. Uzbekiston. East part of the city. Unknown casualties. Home of a government official. More to come.

Jesus Christ, he thought. *Ruslan. It's Ruslan's home.*

He dropped the pen and went back to the phone. There was the hiss and ping of the satellite connecting, and the phone rang, or rather, beeped, and then the Duty Officer at the State Department Operations Center came on the line. Riess identified himself, his post, then gave the bullet on what he knew, which was, as yet, too little.

"Any American casualties?" the Duty Officer asked.

"Unknown."

"How many dead?"

"Unknown."

"It was a residence?"

"That's what the radio is reporting. I'm going to head out, see if I can find something concrete."

"Keep us posted."

Riess killed the connection, dialed McColl, waking him with four rings. When the Political Counselor came on the line, he said, "Sorry to wake you, sir, but there's been reports of a bombing on east Uzbekiston. You might want to come in."

"Dammit to hell," McColl grumbled, thoroughly annoyed. "You're in the office?"

"Yes, sir."

There was a pause, then McColl said, "I'll be there shortly."

Riess grabbed his coat, pulling it on as he went out the door, stopping only long enough to close and lock it behind him. He was trying to keep his head clear, trying not to make too much of the news, to not let his imagination run away with him, but all he could think was that it was Ruslan's home, it *had* to be Ruslan's home, and he wondered if this, too, wasn't somehow his fault, the way he felt Dina Malikov's death was his fault.

At least now he had something to do, something he could do, instead of sitting and waiting and dining on his liver.

There were Marines in the foyer, but Riess didn't see any sign of the Regional Security Officer, for which he was grateful. Situations like this, the Department did its traditional two-directions-at-the-same-time dance. The RSO would try to lock down the Chancery as best he could, in case there were further bombings, anything that might be directed against the Mission or its staff. By the same token, staff on the premises would be expected to remain on post, where they could be safely looked after.

Which would be fine, except that a poloff, or at least a *good* poloff—and all the bullshit with Tower and Carlisle notwithstanding, Riess still hoped that he *was* a good poloff, and very much wanted to remain as such—would be expected to actually get out and hit the ground and rustle up some hard facts, instead of relying on state-run radio to feed him its canned version of events. Facts that could be fed back to both the Ambassador and the Ops Center, that would allow both to formulate the State Department response to what had happened. If things went very well, whatever intelligence gathered would be useful enough to offset the requisite ire of the RSO, who was sure to be pissed off beyond belief that the poloff had left the Chancery in the first place.

No sign of the RSO, just the Marines, and Riess blew past them, heading out, raising a hand and saying, "Be right back." One moved, perhaps to stop him, but without the commitment required to do so, and then Riess was outside, smacked in the face by the cold. He ran to his car, a used Toyota he'd bought shortly after he'd been allowed to move into his home, got it started and to the gates. The guards had switched to flak jackets and helmets, and they stopped him, obviously worked up. One of the Marines kept an eye on the road while the other leaned down to speak to him in the car.

"Can't let you leave, sir," the Marine told him. Like all the others, he was young. "RSO wants all personnel to stay on the grounds."

"I need to take a look at the sight," Riess said. "The Ambassador needs to know what's going on."

Which was true enough. And Riess figured that if this twenty-two-year-old on the gate wanted to interpret his words to mean that Riess was acting on direct orders from the Ambassador, so much the better. Certainly, Riess wasn't going to say anything to clarify the point.

The Marine hesitated, looking away, at the road for a moment. A Tashkent police car blew past, blue lights flashing, siren crying.

"It's a short turnaround," Riess told the Marine. "I'll be back in no time."

The Marine grunted, stepped back, waving him through, and Riess hit the gas, turning out onto the street.

He switched onto Uzbekiston as soon as he could, following the emergency lights in the distance, until he hit the roadblock, where the police stopped him. There were two cars, four officers, and one of them stepped forward as he approached, waving him to the side of the road. Riess pulled over and lowered the window. The officer was a stocky, middle-aged Uzbek who looked like he'd much rather be home and in bed.

"Please step out of the car," the officer said.

Riess nodded and shrugged at the same time, stopped the engine, and climbed out.

"Identification."

"I'm with the U.S. Embassy." Riess pulled out his wallet. "What happened?"

The officer took the ID, then motioned to another policemen, telling him to check the car. Riess didn't protest. The first officer used a flashlight, examined his identification, then shone it on Riess' face. Apparently satisfied, he lowered the light, switching it off and handing the ID back.

"Bombing," the officer said.

"Yeah?" Riess watched as the second policeman examined his car, popping the trunk. "Another one, huh?"

"IMU, probably," the first officer told him, sighing.

"Bastards," Riess said angrily.

The officer caught hold of the emotion, tying it to his own frustration. "They went after the President's son, that's how it looks. They've got us out all over the city looking for the bomber. All over the damn city."

"They didn't blow themselves up when they did it?"

"We're looking for a couple of cars, so I don't know. Maybe there was more than one. Maybe it wasn't a suicide bombing. Who knows?"

"So they've got you out here in the cold, just in case."

"Someone got away, one of the fuckers, they're saying. They . . ."

The officer fell silent as a radio in one of the police cars squawked, and he turned his head, listening. The report was from someone on the scene, requesting an ambulance to remove the bodies. There was an answering call, a query, asking how many. Six. Maybe seven, replied the voice, dispassionately.

The officer sighed a second time, pulling a pack of cigarettes from his pocket and putting one into his mouth. "Fuckers."

"May I?" Riess asked. He didn't smoke, he didn't even like to smoke, but it was a universal way to make friends. If it hadn't been a suicide bombing, then it was something else, and for the first time, Riess had hope. After Tower's visit, he'd figured the show was over for Carlisle. But now, now he had to think that maybe she'd actually pulled this off, that somehow she'd gotten Ruslan and Stepan away from the house, was driving them to safety even now.

Whatever she'd picked up at the arms bazaar, it must have been pretty damn big.

"You're with the Embassy?" the officer asked.

"Yeah."

"Out late."

"I heard about the blast on the radio, wanted to take a look. See if it was like last time, in the market. You know, I have to make sure no Americans were hurt."

"No, no Americans. Not unless they were staying at the house."

"My boss will be relieved," Riess said, then looked up, hearing the rotors closing in overhead. He could make out the helo's belly lights, and from that knew it wasn't military.

He flicked the remainder of his cigarette away, thanking the officer. "I should get back to the Embassy."

The officer nodded, bored again.

The helicopter worried Riess. If they were using ambulances to remove the bodies, then the only reason for the helo was pursuit. It meant they had a line on Carlisle, where she was taking Ruslan and Stepan. Either that or they were desperate, and using every means they had at their disposal in their search.

He returned to the Embassy hoping it was the latter.

CHAPTER 27

21 February, 0458 Hours (GMT+5:00)

Chace took the Audi off the road as soon as she could, on the northern edge of the bridge spanning the Syr Darya along the M39, turning southeast to follow the water. The Audi bumped and slid on the ground, spitting out chunks of earth and pebbles from beneath the tires. The Range Rover, for all its problems, had been built for off-road use. The Audi obviously hadn't been, and now Chace was forced to slow in an attempt to keep from catching the car on the rocks and ruts that peppered the path down to the bank of the river. The darkness made the terrain look different, and Chace knew she was close to the LS, but was uncertain as to just how close.

With a free hand, Chace popped open the armrest, pulling the GPS from where she'd stored it, handing it to Ruslan without looking at him. "Turn that on, take a reading."

Ruslan fumbled with the device, then read out longitude and latitude, degrees, minutes, seconds. The information confirmed what she knew, and Chace barely nodded, her focus on keeping the Audi moving in the right direction. She appreciated the fact that he didn't try to hand the GPS unit back to her.

From the backseat, Stepan said, *"Ota?"*

Ruslan turned, answering in Uzbek, and Chace saw the boy sitting up on the backseat, bleary and confused and looking more than a little frightened. He babbled something in response, and Ruslan spoke again, soothingly but it wasn't enough, and in the reflected glow of the one working headlight, Chace saw the boy's eyes growing wet as he started to sob.

"We're close now," she said. "We're almost there."

She saw Ruslan nod, speaking again to his son, and she assumed he was repeating her words, but she had no way of knowing. The headlights caught the water, reflected it, and she downshifted, urging the car forward, feeling the Audi beginning to lose itself in the softer earth fed by the river. Then she saw the bend, a dry wash of shore cut by the water sometime long ago, spreading out in a crescent of river sand. She downshifted a last time, turning the car slowly about in the wash until they faced the way they had come, killing the headlamp as the Audi came to a stop. She left the engine running, put the car into neutral, and hit the trunk release.

"Stay put," Chace said.

She climbed out of the Audi, went around to the trunk. She'd switched from the hush puppy to the Sarsilmaz when they'd changed cars, keeping the pistol at her back, but now she moved it around so it rested at her waist in the front. The Kalashnikov, hush puppy, and grenades were all in the trunk, but she took only the automatic rifle, throwing the strap over her shoulder. She shut the trunk.

The river burbled past on her left, the water sixty feet away at its closest point. To her right, the ground rose sharply, turning into a low cliff, describing the outer edge of the crescent. Chace looked up, saw thin strips of cloud whipping past, obscuring the stars. The wind had risen, both in strength and in altitude.

From inside the car, she heard Stepan sobbing, watched through the rear window as Ruslan contorted himself in the front seat, lifting the boy onto his lap. The crying subsided.

Chace checked her watch and saw it was oh-five-hundred, exactly.

Almost immediately, she heard the first echo of the rotors, the helicopter's rumble bouncing off the Syr Darya. She took the Kalashnikov off her shoulder, racked the bolt, holding the automatic rifle in both hands. The copter's sound was growing louder, but that was all there was—no visual, no telltale lights. She wondered if Porter was flying with NVG, if that had been one of the incidentals her seventy thousand pounds had bought him.

Then she saw the bird, almost skimming the river as it came around the bend, spray flying from the wash of the rotor blades, a big, old, ugly Russian Mi-8 helicopter, and she knew it was Porter. He'd picked a workhorse, one common enough in this part of the world to be easily acquired and maintained, one that would raise no suspicion. She let her grip on the Kalashnikov go to one hand and stepped out from behind the car, to make certain he could see her.

The helicopter altered course, slowing and descending, and now the sand was flying, too, and Chace brought her forearm up to protect her vision, moving to the passenger's side of the Audi. She opened Ruslan's door, and he peered up at her, Stepan wrapped in his arms, the bloodstained flak jacket still around him.

"Our ride's here," Chace shouted. She adjusted the strap on the Kalashnikov, letting the weapon lie against her back, then held out her hands. "Here."

Ruslan nodded, bent his mouth to Stepan's ear, then lifted the little boy to her. Stepan turned his head to her, eyes wide with suspicion and fear, his mouth closed. Chace took him in her arms.

"It's all right," she told him in Russian, and stepped back to give Ruslan room to exit. The Mi-8 was louder than ever, the sand it was throwing up stinging her skin. She put a hand on Stepan's head, pressing his cheek to her shoulder to shield him from the spray, adjusting the flak jacket around him more for protection from the cold and sand than anything else.

Then she heard an echo, what she thought was an echo, the sound of the bird reverberating off the cliff to her right, but the pitch was wrong, too high, and she knew it wasn't an echo. She raised her head from Stepan to the Mi-8, seeing Ruslan emerging from the

Audi in her peripheral vision at the same moment, and caught a glimpse of Porter behind the stick in the cockpit just before the helicopter exploded.

Fire and metal blew through the air, the remnants of the helicopter pitching nose forward, flipping into the earth, and the rotors snapped free, and Chace felt herself knocked off her feet. The world cracked, and she felt pain race along her spine, and she knew she'd landed on her back, on the Kalashnikov. She was dimly aware that she still had Stepan in her arms, and that amazed her.

She opened her eyes and couldn't see anything but the afterimage of the blast. The sound of the second helicopter cut through the ringing in her ears. She forced herself to roll, still gripping the boy, managed to get to her knees. Her vision cleared to pinpoints of dancing white, and she stumbled, turning, disoriented.

Light flared over the ground, blasting daylight into an oblong that skimmed the wreckage of the Mi-8, running over the sand toward her. Chace could barely see the helicopter beyond the flare of its searchlight, hovering twenty-five feet off the ground, and she thought it was a Sikorsky, a civilian model, and she knew that was where the missile had come from, the second Starstreak in the same night, this one used to kill not only Porter, but their chances of escape, too.

Starstreak, Chace thought. *Another fucking Starstreak, and Jesus, but how many of them do these sons of bitches have?*

She was already running for the Audi, clutching Stepan to her with her left hand, using her right to draw the Sarsilmaz from her waist.

"Ruslan!" she screamed. "In the car! In the fucking car!"

She fired as she ran, squeezing off rounds, trying to hit the light, or above the light, and not having any hope of success. The Sikorsky bobbled, turning, and Chace had reached the driver's door, had shoved the boy back into the car, and was yanking the Kalashnikov's strap from her shoulder, when she saw what the searchlight saw, and for a fraction, she froze.

Ruslan was sprawled in the dirt facedown, fifteen feet from the car, his arms splayed out in front of him, one of his legs bent back across the other. The searchlight struck him at an angle, pushing shadows off his motionless body. Chace thought she saw blood, but she couldn't tell how much.

"Ruslan! Ruslan, get up!"

He didn't move.

"Get up! Damn you, get up!"

The searchlight broke away from the body, the Sikorsky swiveling as it hovered, playing its ruthless light across the Audi's hood. The beam struck Stepan inside, then Chace, and she saw the portside door of the helicopter was open, and two men were crouched there, automatic rifles in their hands. She raised the Sarsilmaz in both hands and emptied the gun at them, flinging herself back into the car. One of the men pitched forward and fell.

Chace rammed the car into gear, then stomped on the gas, and the car lurched forward. She floored it, feeling the tires desperate for traction, and beside her, Stepan was screaming, pressing himself to the passenger window. Bullets punched holes along the edge of the hood, and then the wheels caught, the Audi shooting forward. Chace saw the man who had fallen trying to get to his feet and out of the way, and she ran him down before he had the chance, feeling the car jump slightly at the impact. More bullets struck, now hitting the roof, and between her hands on the wheel, Chace saw the dashboard shatter, and wondered fleetingly how the round had missed her.

"Ota!" Stepan wailed. "Ota, Ota!"

She wrenched the wheel, fighting the Audi up the side of the bank, and the car popped onto harder ground. The searchlight flashed on them again, and she saw the orange blossoms of muzzle-flash in her mirrors, and the rear window exploded. The Audi hit the pavement, and Chace slid the car into a right, the rear wheels squealing as they bit into asphalt.

Stepan had slumped, gone silent, and Chace glanced over and for a horrifying second saw only the blood on the flak jacket. She forgot the stick for a moment, reaching for the boy with her right hand, yanking back the fabric, and saw nothing beneath, no fresh blood. Stepan's face was streaked with tears, snot running from his nose over his lips.

"*Ota*—"

"I'm sorry," Chace told him, the ache in her chest sudden, making the words sound like a companion sob.

She put her hand back to the stick, her focus back on the road, trying to think of an escape.

The Sikorsky was fast, faster than the Audi, and she weaved on the road, trying to stay out of the searchlight. They weren't shooting now, and they weren't trying to get ahead of her, and she assumed that meant they liked where she was headed, and wanted her to keep going there. On radios, probably, she decided, maybe a roadblock, but the problem was that she didn't have any other choice. She had to get back to Tashkent, Tashkent was the only option, and Chace cursed herself for not having planned a fallback exfil, no other way out of the country.

She had to get to one of the embassies, either the American or the British, it didn't matter. To hell with Crocker and his secret plans, to hell with keeping things quiet, they'd gotten very loud now, and she'd run out of options. She'd lost Ruslan, she'd blown the mission, but she was damned if she was going to lose the son, too. She'd fucked it up, but she wasn't going to lose the son, too.

Over her dead body would she lose Stepan.

Then she saw the headlights, and she saw the silhouette of the man standing in front of them, and more, saw the silhouette of what he was raising onto his shoulder.

"Oh, fucking hell," Chace said.

Yanking the handbrake, she twisted the wheel, stomping the pedal. The Audi slid, spinning left, and Chace shot out her hand to catch Stepan before the boy could be thrown about the interior of the car. The car screeched to a stop and the engine lurched, then died.

Pulling Stepan after her, Chace shoved her door open and tumbled out of the car, onto the cracked highway. She wrapped her arms around the boy as she regained her feet, felt him clinging to her, whimpering. The searchlight found them both again, and she winced in its glare, half running, half stumbling for the side of the road, desperate to get away from the Audi. The Sikorsky was coming around on her left, trying to block her passage, descending, but keeping distance.

It knows what happens next, Chace thought.

The world split, and she felt heat sweep over her back, pain following after it, her legs knocked from beneath her. Everything turned around, surrounding her in weightlessness and vertigo, and Chace knew her feet weren't on the ground anymore. She tightened her grip on the child, flashed for a final instant on his face pressed against her chest, his eyes squeezed closed, black hair shining in the light of the exploding car.

She saw Tamsin.

Then she saw nothing.

CHAPTER 28

21 February, 0016 Hours GMT

Frances Barclay looked like a man under siege. His shoulders were hunched inward, his hands laid flat on the blotter on his desk, his neck lowered, his chin thrust forward, and his eyes behind his glasses brimming with hatred. And for once, that hatred wasn't being directed at Crocker himself, but rather at the Deputy Chief standing beside him, though Crocker knew it was only a matter of time before he became its focus again.

"You knew about this, you knew about *all* of this, and you failed to inform me?"

"The operation was undertaken in response to a directive by the FCO," Alison Gordon-Palmer said evenly.

"Not an official directive!"

"The PUS acted with both the Foreign Secretary and Prime Minister's blessing, sir. If PUS felt it necessary to omit you from the conops, then you'll have to take it up with him. But D-Ops was acting as ordered, and the paper trail exists to prove it."

"Placed after the fact, no doubt."

Gordon-Palmer didn't respond, and Crocker, for his part, continued standing in silence beside her. Another chapter to be written in his manual of desk usage, Crocker thought. In any other instance, the Deputy Chief and the Director of Operations standing at C's desk while C himself railed at them from his chair would have been the perfect portrait of subordinate reinforcement, more akin to the dressing-down of ill-mannered children than not. Yet this time, with C seated and the two of them standing, it seemed the players were entirely reversed.

Barclay seemed to sense it, as well, because he chose that moment to get to his feet and lean on the desk.

"I know what this is," he told the Deputy Chief. "This is a coup d'état. Don't think I won't fight it."

"If that's how you see it, sir," she replied.

"There's another way I should see it?"

"The disposition of the operation is still in question. Should it be successfully concluded, you'll certainly be entitled, even expected, to take full credit for it."

"Which is your way of saying that, when it fails, I'll be expected to own it?"

Crocker was impressed that Gordon-Palmer managed to sound mildly indignant. "Not at all, sir. Should the operation fail, you have the perfect scapegoats."

"You."

"And D-Ops, yes, sir."

It didn't reassure Barclay in the slightest. If anything, the look on his face hardened further. "So you say. Yet you've also said that the White House is adamant that Sevara Malikov and not her brother becomes Uzbekistan's next President. Even if the operation is successful, it will be a failure."

"Not necessarily," Crocker said. "If Ruslan and his son are lifted, they can be positioned for an eventual return to the country and an attempted ouster of the sister."

"Don't be ridiculous," Barclay snapped. "The operation is pointless, at least as declared. It does nothing but expose Ruslan and force his sister and her supporters to move against him, perhaps overtly, and the results of an overt move will do nothing but damage U.K. relations with Uzbekistan. In the final analysis, it solidifies her power, not diminishes it."

Crocker held his tongue, mostly because he couldn't argue the point. Until three hours earlier, he would have argued that Ruslan had every chance to become Uzbekistan's next President, especially with Seccombe's promised support for the coup. But that was no longer the case. According to Gordon-Palmer, in fact, it never had been.

So he stayed silent and let Barclay and the Deputy Chief continue their bitter dance, all the while struggling with his own guilt. It was one thing to have failed Chace before, in Saudi Arabia, to have been boxed both politically and professionally, and thus prevented from helping her. In that case, he had done everything in his power to protect her, and had, quite simply, been defeated. He had never, however, lied to her.

This time he had, and he had known he was lying when they stood in the Pendle churchyard. A lie of omission rather than deceit, but a lie nonetheless, because Crocker had known—he had *known*—that Seccombe was using him. But he had permitted it, desperate to keep his job. And in so doing, he'd put himself and his career ahead of Chace's safety and well-being.

Espionage was ultimately a game of sacrifice. Truths revealed to protect lies, relationships twisted to steal secrets, lives surrendered in exchange for gains that could range from the incremental to the absurd. But sacrificing Chace had never been in Crocker's plans, and now, more than anything, he feared he'd done precisely that. He would argue until the day he died that what happened to send Chace to Saudi Arabia was not his fault, that Tom Wallace's death, as much as it pained him, was not his to own. Her anger, while righteous, he still believed was misplaced.

But if Tara Chace managed to come back from Tashkent alive, Paul Crocker was sure that she would never forgive him.

And at this moment, standing in Barclay's office, listening with half an ear to Gordon-Palmer's soothing falsehoods and Barclay's rapidly dwindling patience, Paul Crocker knew that if Tara Chace *didn't* come back from Uzbekistan, he would never forgive himself, either.

"And you," Barclay was snarling at him. "I offered you a hand in friendship, and you returned it with betrayal."

Crocker blinked, looking at his C. "As the Deputy Chief has said, I was acting under orders from the FCO. And as for your hand of friendship, if I may be so blunt, you offered nothing of the sort. You were blackmailing me."

The red phone on Barclay's desk began trilling for attention. "And now the both of you are blackmailing me."

Turnabout is fair play, thought Crocker.

Barclay answered the phone, listened, then thrust it out to Crocker. "For you."

Crocker took the phone. "D-Ops."

"Duty Ops Officer," Ronald Hodgson said. "Latest from Tashkent, sir."

"Give it to me."

"It's just come in, sir. State media has issued a statement saying that Ruslan Malikov and his son were kidnapped from their home early this morning by members of Hizb-ut-Tahir, possibly the same cell responsible for the kidnap and murder of Dina Malikov earlier this month. The statement goes on to say that the terrorists used a surface-to-air missile to destroy the Malikov home in an attempt to cover their tracks, but that police and state forces were able to recognize the misdirection and engage in an immediate pursuit along the M39, the main road out of Tashkent toward Samarkand.

"During this pursuit, a second SAM was used to shoot down a state helicopter, killing twelve. State forces surrounded the terrorists and attempted to negotiate. The terrorists then executed Ruslan Malikov, at which point state forces moved in and rescued the son."

Crocker felt his throat constricting, closed his eyes. "Confirmations?"

"None as yet, sir."

"I'm coming down."

He replaced the phone on Barclay's desk. Both C and Gordon-Palmer were watching at him, waiting.

"Ops Room, Tashkent," Crocker said. "State media reports that Ruslan Malikov is dead."

"Paul—" Alison Gordon-Palmer began.

"Later," Crocker said. It was petulant, and he believed it was unintentional, but he slammed the door on the way out.

"Call Grosvenor Square," Crocker ordered as soon as he hit the floor. "Have them wake Seale and get him over here, now."

Ronald Hodgson put his headset over his ears, began dialing, saying, "What do I tell him?"

"Just tell him it's about Chace."

Ron faltered for a second, and all movement in the Ops Room came to a halt as the staffers who knew the name reacted to it, and those who didn't wondered at the sudden silence. At the MCO Desk, Alexis turned in her seat, the same look of confusion now on her face that the rest of the room seemed to be wearing.

"You heard me," Crocker barked at Ron. "Do it."

"Yes, sir."

Crocker strode to the MCO Desk, where Alexis was still staring at him. Her astonishment might have been amusing in any other circumstance. Now it just made Crocker all the more anxious. "Anything?"

She took a second, almost dithering, then nodded and punched at her keyboard. "Yes, possibly related."

"Are you going to tell me or do I have to take you out to dinner first?"

Alexis stiffened. "There are reports that President Malikov is dead, and that both chambers of the Oliy Majlis are being called into session for later this morning. That's unofficial—the Number Two picked it up from a contact in the NSS, who apparently heard it from a man named Ahtam Zahidov."

Crocker swore, moved his glare from Alexis to the plasma wall.

"Name the operation, put it up on the wall, and tag it as pending, bring in a control."

He heard the clattering of her keyboard, scowled as the central quadrant of the plasma screen redrew its picture of Central Asia, a red highlight outlining Uzbekistan, with a red dot now pulsing brightly on Tashkent. On the map, to the south, a yellow dot appeared over Khanabad, marking the Karshi-Khanabad air base, Air Base Camp Stronghold Freedom, where the Americans launched their missions from the country into Afghanistan. The callout came up next, and he watched as the text Alexis was typing at her keyboard translated to the screen, filling the information box.

Operation: Crystalgate.
Status: Pending.

"Allocate Chace."

Alexis stared at him blankly.

"Allocate Chace, she's the agent of record. It's a Special Op."

"But—how? As what? What designation?"

"Don't be a fucking fool, Alex," Crocker snarled. "She's Minder One."

At Duty Ops, Ron called out, "Sir!" and Crocker turned away from the MCO station to see that he was holding out a telephone. He grabbed the phone, pinning it between his ear and shoulder, leaving his hands free to find his cigarettes.

"Crocker."

"Seale. What the fuck is this about?"

"You damn well know what it's about. Get on to your people in Tashkent and find out what the hell's happened there, and find out where my agent is. I've got nothing, I'm getting bits and pieces, and they're no use at all."

There was a silence for a moment as the American digested what he'd said, and Crocker took the opportunity to feed a cigarette into his mouth. Ron held out a light, and Crocker leaned into it, accepting the flame.

"We're on the same page about this now?" Seale asked.

"If you mean the page where I've got an agent caught in the cold and quite possibly dead, then yes, we're on the same fucking page, Julian."

"I'll be there in half an hour," Seale said, and hung up.

Crocker handed the phone back to Ron, pivoted, looking back to the plasma wall. Nothing had changed. Nothing would change, not for a while yet. He could stare at it for another hour, and it would tell him nothing he didn't already know. The anxiety that had propelled him into the Ops Room began to wane, and the seething in his veins began to settle into the familiar queasiness of uncertainty. He tried to think of what else he could do, what else he should do.

"Lex? The line still open to Tashkent?"

"Yes, sir."

"Put me on."

She nodded, quickly plugging in a second headset to her coms station, handing it over to Crocker as soon as he reached her. He settled the earpieces, adjusted the boom.

"Craig? D-Ops."

"Good morning, sir," Craig Gillard said in his ears. There was a hiss on the line, and beneath Gillard's voice a low, regular beeping, indicating the communication was being scrambled.

"Not very," Crocker said.

"No, sir. I'm a little unclear as to what to make of things here."

"I can imagine. You'll receive a proper directive from me later this morning, but for now I need you to proceed as if you've already received the appropriate authorizations, do you understand?"

Gillard hesitated before answering, and Crocker didn't blame him. He was thirty-six, and Tashkent was his first posting as a Number One, after twelve years within SIS. He'd been in-country for eleven months, with another year scheduled on his tour. It was a well-earned posting—Crocker wouldn't have endorsed the placement if he'd felt Gillard couldn't do the job—and one of priority, for all the same reasons the Americans made Uzbekistan a priority.

Gillard was looking at coming back home to a senior desk position under Rayburn's eye, and then possibly further promotion within SIS. All of that incumbent, of course, on his doing his job not just well, but discreetly.

And Crocker had yet to meet a Station Number One who ever was well pleased when things started exploding on his or her watch.

"*Yes, sir, I understand,*" Gillard said. "*What seems to be the trouble?*"

"I've heard the Hizb-ut-Tahir nonsense. Do you know what really happened?"

"*Hayden's been beating the bushes,*" Gillard answered, referring to the Station Number Two. "*Got himself a contact in the NSS he's been working on for the last few months, since November, name of Jamshid Nalufar. Nalufar says that it wasn't the extremists, but Ruslan's people trying to get him out of the country, he thinks in the wake of President Malikov's death. Problem with that, sir, is that Ruslan doesn't have much in the way of people, and those he does have are all in the south, mostly centered in Qashqa Darya Province, cities like Karshi, Shakhrisabz, and Samarkand. It's not making a lot of sense.*"

Crocker exhaled smoke, then said, "No, it's not Ruslan's people, it's ours. The operation is called Crystalgate. You'll get the brief on it in the morning, as I said."

"*Jesus Christ.*"

"Still with me?"

"*Jesus Christ,*" Gillard repeated. "*You're running a bust-out in Tashkent, you didn't bother to notify me?*"

"Believe me when I tell you it was not by choice," Crocker said. "No one was looking to burn you, Craig. The agent has had no contact with either you or your Number Two. The orders were to steer clear of the Station."

"*For all the good that's going to do. The operation's a bust, it's completely blown. Hayden says the NSS shut it all down, they've got the kid, Ruslan's reported dead—*"

"I don't care," Crocker interrupted. "There are two things I need from you, and I need them immediately."

"*Go ahead.*"

"The explosions, the SAM that took down the helicopter and the one that blew up the house, I believe those were both caused the same way, with a Starstreak. I need you to confirm that, and then get that confirmation to me, that's one."

"*We're arming the Uzbekis with MANPADs now?*"

"That's one, Craig. Second, I need to find out what happened to the agent. I need to know if she's dead, if she's been captured, or if she's still running."

"*She?*"

"Tara Chace. She's running under the name Tracy Elizabeth Carlisle. It's vital I know what's happened to her."

"*Yes, sir, I understand.*" Gillard paused, then added, "*All right, Hayden and I will get on it right away. I'll have him hit his contact again, though God knows he'll resist communicating with him twice in the same night.*"

"Soon as possible, Craig."

"*Yes, sir, that's understood as well. I'll contact you as soon as we learn anything.*"

"London out." Crocker pulled the headset off, dropped it back on the MCO Desk, then dropped his cigarette to the floor and ground it out with his toe, frowning. He had to get back upstairs, to inform Barclay and Gordon-Palmer what had happened, and he needed Seale to arrive, and soon. But that was it for the moment, that was all he could do. If Chace was dead, the Station would confirm it soon enough.

"I'll be with C," he told Ron. "When Seale arrives, ring me. Have him escorted to my office, I'll meet him there."

"Yes, sir."

"And find me the number of Valerie Wallace, Barnoldswick, Lancashire." Crocker hesitated, then added, "I may need it later."

He headed back upstairs to rejoin the battle in C's office.

CHAPTER 29

Uzbekistan—Tashkent—Yunus Rajabiy, Ministry of the Interior

21 February, 0955 Hours (GMT+5:00)

Something stabbed Chace in the nose, rising sharp and hard into her sinuses, and it tugged at her mind, trying to pull her awake. She moved her head, trying to escape, and the pain stopped, and she felt her hair being pulled and then it returned, stronger, and she gagged, coming fully conscious with a start. She tried to raise an arm and bat the offense away, but her arm barely moved, and a fresh ache tore along her shoulder.

Chace blinked, tasting blood and dust. A man in a suit was stepping back from her, looking at her, tossing aside the ammonia ampoule he'd held beneath her nostrils. Her vision was blurred, and one of her eyes, she couldn't tell which, was seeing nothing but a milky white haze. The right side of her face felt tight, as if encased in dried wax, and when she moved her mouth to lick her lower lip, she felt it crack, and guessed the dried wax was blood, and probably her own. A pain ran in a circle from temple to temple, as if someone had wrapped her skull in wire and then decided to pull, just for the fun of it.

She wondered how badly she'd been hurt when the Audi exploded, if anything had broken.

It was cold in the room, very cold, and Chace saw her breath, and she shivered, and heard chains rattle as she did so. They had taken most of her clothes, her boots and socks and pants and jacket and sweater and shirt, everything but the underwear. They'd left those for later, she knew, the threat implicit.

She was sitting in a chair in what she thought at first might be a basement storage space or perhaps a boiler room. She tried moving her arms again, more carefully, and felt metal around her wrists and heard the clink of the handcuffs on the chair. They'd used two sets, one for each wrist, twisting her hands up to the middle of her spine before securing the other end of the cuffs to the back of the chair. The chair was metal, too, and conducted the cold from the concrete floor. Her feet felt like they'd already been soaked in ice water, and she realized they hadn't bothered to restrain them, and she wondered if that's where they would start, first.

Chace turned her head, taking in the room, trying to catalogue it, trying to find a means of escape. She saw a bathtub in the corner, and a tripod with a video camera. The camera appeared off. Lightbulbs hung naked overhead, high wattage so bright she winced when she looked at them. There was only one door into the room that she could find, metal and rust-stained, and she'd been positioned directly in line of it, just to make sure she could see how close it was, and how far away.

And so she could see that between her and the door there was a table, and at that table sat Ahtam Zahidov, looking at her like she was meat on a butcher's hook, and he was deciding where to begin cutting.

He'd brought two others with him to wherever this was, both dressed in similar suits, both looking tired and angry. One of them lit a cigarette as she watched, staring at her the whole while. He was tall, looked young, perhaps mid- to late-twenties, broad-shouldered and big-handed, and there was nothing approaching sympathy in his expression. She guessed the beatings would come primarily from him.

The other one, the one who'd roused her with the ammonia,

looked to be at least ten years older, shorter and fatter. Now he was ignoring her, more concerned with the contents of the red toolbox that rested open on the table, by Zahidov's left elbow.

Chace tried not to be afraid, and found it impossible.

Zahidov stared at her without speaking, then removed his glasses and held them up to the lights, making a grimace of displeasure. He took a handkerchief from inside his coat and, leisurely, began cleaning the lenses. By Chace's guess, it took him over a minute to complete the job.

Then he replaced the glasses on his face and nodded slightly, and the big one, the bruiser, moved forward, toward Chace in the chair, while the older one removed a short length of pipe from the toolbox.

"Don't," Chace warned.

Zahidov barely shook his head, and the bruiser came closer, bending as he reached for her legs. Chace twisted in the chair, feeling the cuffs trapping her arms, lashing out with a kick. The bruiser had expected it, blocked it with his forearm, then tried to grab her ankle again, and she kicked with her other foot, and caught him in the face. The bruiser grunted in anger, and the cold and the impact with bone made pain ride up Chace's leg like fire. She kicked again, but this time he caught her, trapping her calf between his chest and arm.

She brought her free leg up, firing off obscenities without realizing she was even speaking, not hearing herself, and thrust with her toes into his crotch. He tried to catch the foot, missed, and groaned as she felt the kick sink into him. He lost his grip on the leg he'd been holding.

"Don't you fucking touch me!" she yelled, hearing her voice rebounding off the concrete. "I'm a British citizen, don't you fucking touch me!"

"You're a British spy," Zahidov answered in English.

The bruiser was trying to right himself, gritting his teeth, and Chace planted her feet on the floor and pushed off, taking the chair with her, lunging at him. She hit his nose with her head, felt the collision snapping cartilage, the ache in her head expanding. She staggered back, bending and turning as fast as she could, striking him with the legs of the chair. Her arms felt like they would tear free from their sockets.

Suddenly she saw red, even through the eye that wouldn't work, and she heard a scream. Her air left her, blowing out over her lips, and she felt her gorge rising to follow it, and then she was hit again, and she knew she was on the floor. Something pressed down on her neck, and her vision swam, then cleared, and she was being righted in the chair. Another blow struck her stomach, and she pitched forward, and then another blow, higher, and again, and she skipped consciousness for a second, swimming in icy darkness. She felt hard hands grabbing her ankles, lifting her legs, and then forcing her thighs apart, and she struggled against the grip, but didn't have the leverage or the strength or the air.

Vision returned enough for her to see the bruiser licking at the blood running down over his lips from his nose. He held her ankles at his waist, her calves pinned at his hips. The posture was obscene, and the bruiser knew it, and when he saw that she was seeing him clearly now, he rocked his pelvis toward her in a mock thrust, fucking the empty air between them. Chace saw the lump in his pants, realized he was aroused, and the fear and the disgust expanded inside her, and she wondered if she would be sick.

Zahidov's chair scraped back on the floor, and she saw him come around, between the older man and the bruiser. The older man offered him the length of pipe, and Zahidov took it, his eyes fixed on Chace.

"That was stupid," he told her. "Now Tozim wants to hurt you."

She tried to free her legs, failing.

"Of course, I want to hurt you, too," Zahidov continued. "That's interesting, because mostly what I want in this room is information, and pain and humiliation, those are only tools to get it."

"So ask your questions already," Chace spat.

"No, you don't understand. Mostly I want information, and you'll give it to me, because everyone eventually does. But right now, I want to hurt you."

He swung the pipe at the bottom of her right foot, almost casually. The pain that shot through Chace's leg was extraordinary, and brought tears to her eyes.

"Where is he?" Zahidov asked.

The question didn't make sense. She shook her head, choked out a response. "What?"

He hit the right foot again, twice, the arch and the base of her toes. Chace tried to stay silent, but it hurt too much, it hurt more than anything, and she heard herself whimpering, and that made it even worse.

"Where?"

She managed to shake her head, saw his arm draw back, tried to work her feet free and failed. He hit her left foot this time, four times along the arch, each blow harder than the one that preceded it. She screamed, struggling, and he struck the right again, and she was trying to move, to break free, anything to stop it, and nothing worked.

He had stopped hitting her, letting the lingering pain do his work for him. She was out of breath again, her lungs aching. She heard herself sobbing, fought to control it.

"There are other places that will hurt more." Zahidov said when he thought she had calmed enough to hear him. "Places that will tear, places where bone is barely covered by skin, places that will rip and scar. Where is he, where is Ruslan?"

Chace blinked back tears of pain, trying to clear her vision from the eye that still worked, and trying to keep what she was thinking off her face. Either Zahidov was toying with her, or Ruslan hadn't died by the Syr Darya. She didn't know which to believe—if he was asking her a question she could never hope to answer satisfactorily because Ruslan was dead, or if he'd escaped.

Both seemed just as likely.

"Dead," she managed to say. "You killed him."

Zahidov frowned, examining her leg, then running his fingers along it, over her shin to her knee, stopping at midthigh, close enough that she could feel his breath on her face. She fought the shudder caused by the touch, not wanting to give it to him. He lifted his hand, then brought it down again on her bare shoulder, tracing the strap of her bra with a finger.

"Where is he?" he whispered in her ear.

Chace pulled her head away, again struggling against the bruiser's grip on her ankles, again to no avail. Despite the chill in the room, she felt herself beginning to burn with the humiliation of the posture, the helplessness, the touch.

"I told you, you killed him, he's dead. The last I saw of him he was lying in the dirt by the river."

"You planned the escape." Zahidov continued to stroke her shoulder. "Where did he go? After the river, where did he go?"

"There was no after the river, he fucking died at the river. He died, I ran, you caught me and his son." She turned her head, meeting his smiling eyes. "Where is he? Where's Stepan?"

"With his aunt."

"She likes them that young, does she?"

Zahidov swore at her in Uzbek, bringing the pipe down on her shoulder once, twice, then a third time, and Chace screamed from the pain of it, swearing in return, thrashing against the cuffs and the chair and the fingers gripping her. She kicked herself free, felt her foot hit the bruiser again, and screamed louder from the impact. Something hit her alongside the head, a fist, and her vision went again. There was cursing in Russian, in Uzbek, and she was struck alongside the head this time, and this time both she and the chair went over onto the floor. She felt blood leaking from her mouth.

And she wanted to laugh. They were going to torture her, and they were going to do it until she was dead, Zahidov had said as much. They were going to rape her and beat her and mutilate her, do everything in their power to destroy her entirely. She had no illusions, she knew the purpose of this room, and she knew she couldn't resist. At the best, one survived torture, but no one ever endured it. It was why torture was ultimately useless as an interrogation technique; hurt someone enough, and they will tell you that, yes, they murdered Kennedy, Princess Diana, and Thomas More, just please, God, please, make it stop.

Chace was terrified, but that was all right, because she'd have to have been insane not to be. Yet in the midst of her terror, she'd found her anger, and that was what she wanted to hold on to now, what she needed now. To be angry, and to stay that way. To stoke it and fuel it and tend it so that when the worst came, she could still find it.

This ends only two ways, she told herself. *You tell them everything and then they kill you, or they kill you before you can.*

She didn't want to die. She absolutely didn't want to die. At that moment, more than anything, what Tara Chace wanted was to live, to go home, to *her* home. Not Barnoldswick and its alien world but Camden and London, and to have her daughter there with her. She wanted her job and her life, and to find a way to make them both work together. She wanted to be Minder One again, Head of the Special Section again, and then one day to leave the field and become D-Ops. She wanted to watch Tamsin grow and learn and live, and to see Tom Wallace in her every time she looked her daughter's way.

She did not want to die being tortured in Tashkent.

But if she had to, she would. And if Ruslan *was* alive, if he was on the run, she hadn't failed. The more Zahidov and his brutes stayed focused on her, the better it was for Ruslan, the farther away and safer he would become.

Zahidov had given her a way in, had shown her the exposed nerve. All Chace had to do was keep her anger alive long enough to fully ignite his.

The bruiser came around, righting her in the chair once more. Chace shook her head, trying to clear it, then spat out a mouthful of her own blood. Zahidov watched her, the older man still at the table, waiting by the toolbox. When the bruiser came around to grab her legs again, Zahidov motioned him back with the pipe.

He extended his free hand again, running his fingers over her shoulder, then down across her chest, tracing the edge of her bra along the swell of her breasts. He kept the touch light, watching her for a reaction, and Chace stared back at him. The bruiser laughed, said something in Uzbek.

"He says you like this," Zahidov remarked. "That it's making you wet."

"No, but clearly it's how you get your rocks off." Chace met his eyes. "What's the matter, Ahtam? Not getting any at home, you have to keep feeling me up?"

He backhanded her across the face, striking near her wounded eye. She saw blood on the back of his hand as he brought it around again.

"You really think Sevara's going to let you keep fucking her after she's President?" Chace taunted him. "What's the endearment form—Sevya, is that it? You think little Sevya's really going to let you bang her in the big house in Dormon?"

His expression flickered, and she saw the hand coming up again, the one without the pipe, and Chace turned her head to roll with the blow. It hit hard, rocking her in the chair, and she realized he'd pulled it at the last moment, that he'd almost lost it. The pipe would do it, she realized. If she could get him to hit her in the temple with the pipe, that would do it, that would end it.

"We're not talking about her," Zahidov said. "We're talking about Ruslan. You're going to tell me where he went, who his contacts are."

Chace tried to laugh, a sound that came out like a croak. "Little Sevya, she'll find two dozen more just like you but younger, ones that don't need yohimbe to keep them going at night."

He brought his fist up again, and she braced for the blow, but he didn't strike. "Where did he go? What was the route? Was there a second helicopter?"

"Maybe he went to see his sister."

"Why? Why would he do that?"

Chace grinned at him, feeling blood rolling off her lower lip. "To get shit on his dick."

It took him a second to parse the language, and then Zahidov roared, throwing down the pipe so it clattered on the floor, ringing throughout the room. He punched her in the side, grabbing hold of her hair, shouting in Uzbek. Chace tried to shift forward, to get to her feet again, and this time he shoved her, and she went down face-first, feeling the cement ripping her skin. He was still shouting, and she saw the bruiser's—Tozim's—feet coming around, the Adidas sneakers he was wearing navy blue and new. There was a clattering of keys, and Chace tried to rise, then felt the air being crushed out of her as someone, Tozim or the older one or Zahidov himself, bore down on the chair.

They freed one of her hands, then twisted it, cuffing it to her other wrist before unlocking the second set. The chair was knocked away, she heard it bounce, then slide, and the bruiser jerked her to her feet, then dragged her to the table.

Zahidov was still swearing at her in Uzbek, yanking off his jacket. The older man had moved around to the other side of the table, and he grabbed her wrists by the chain of the handcuffs, yanking her forward. Chace twisted, trying to roll, and felt Tozim's hands on her shoulders, pinning her down.

She felt another pair of hands on her skin, Zahidov's, and they ran along her sides, down to her hips, and she howled in outrage, kicking back at him. Through her blurred vision she saw the metal door past the older man slam open, two figures, out of focus. One stayed outside, turning away, but the other entered, big, blond, out of focus, in a suit like the others but somehow not like the others.

The man said something in Uzbek, and everything in the room froze. The blond man spoke a second time, more bite in the words, and the hands holding her down left her body. First the bruiser, Tozim, then the older man, and then, finally, Zahidov.

Chace tried to right herself at the table. She heard herself wheezing for breath.

The blond man cast his eye around the room, and through the distortion of her vision, Chace thought she saw naked disgust on his face. He pointed in the direction of the video camera, speaking once more. Zahidov came past Chace, caught in her periphery, smoothing his shirt and tie. He spoke to Tozim, and Tozim moved to the camera.

Chace pushed herself upright, trying to stand, and the pain of using her feet was too much to bear, and she dropped again, trying to catch the table to arrest the fall, and missing. She hit the floor on her side, rocking back and forth.

More words in Uzbek, the new man speaking to Zahidov, furious. Zahidov responded, his voice rising, and then the man shouted, and whatever the debate was ended then, because there was nothing more said. Chace lifted her head, trying to see what was happening, watched as Zahidov stormed out of the room, the other two men following in his wake.

Leaving the new man, the blond man, to kneel down beside her as he removed his coat. He wrapped it around her shoulders, and Chace's mind flickered on the thought that this, too, might be a trick, some mind game played by Zahidov. She tried to pull away, but the man took hold of her upper arms, then closed the coat around her front.

"You're a fucking mess," the man said. "Do you think you can walk?"

Chace blinked at him, perplexed, then realized he'd actually spoken in English, his accent American.

"I don't think so," she said.

The man frowned, drawing creases along his face.

"You're going to need to try," he said.

Chace nodded, and the man slipped an arm around her waist, helping her to her feet. The pain was as intense as before, and Chace gasped and faltered, but he caught her, pulling her upright again. It felt like she was walking on a thousand splinters of glass, but somehow she managed to stay on her feet this time, using the man as a crutch. Slowly he began walking her to the door.

"I've got a car outside. Just make it to the car, hon, you can do that, can't you?"

Chace nodded again.

They entered a hallway, now empty, then reached a flight of stairs. The stairs were hard, and it seemed to Chace it took them an eternity to climb them together, coming through a door and into another hallway. Like the one below, this one was empty.

It took another eternity to make it down the hall, turn, and then reach the exit of the building.

The sun was out, shockingly bright to Chace's eyes, and it was cold, colder than it had been in the basement, and she felt it sinking through her bare legs, striking for bone. The car was a Mercedes-Benz, old and dented along the front panel, and the man guided her to it, then opened the rear door and helped her inside. He shut the door, and Chace lay down on the backseat, shivering. She heard the driver's door open, then slam shut, and the engine started, and she felt the vibration through her whole body. The car started to move.

Chace forced herself upright, catching a glimpse of herself in the rearview mirror and not recognizing the woman she saw there at all. The right side of her face was scraped and caked with dried blood, and her eye had swollen closed. Her lower lip had split, and a bruise of angry purple and red was glowing on her left cheek. Her hair was stringy, matted with blood and dirt.

She looked out the window, at the Interior Ministry, wondering how she'd gotten out of there alive.

Standing in the entrance, watching her go, she saw Ahtam Zahidov, and it looked to her like he was wondering the same thing.

CHAPTER 30

London—Vauxhall Cross, Office of D-Ops

21 February, 0649 Hours GMT

Crocker was sitting at his desk, watching a cigarette burning down in the ashtray, when the red phone rang. He looked across to where Seale was sitting, waiting with him, then answered the call. He listened to the Duty Ops Officer, asked him to repeat, then thanked him and hung up.

"She's alive," Crocker told Seale. "Your man found her at the Interior Ministry, brought her to the British Embassy. A doctor is tending her now, they'll fly her home as soon as they think she can make the trip."

Seale nodded, clearly sharing Crocker's exhaustion, if not his immediate sense of relief. "They were working her over?"

"I believe the term they use is 'interrogation.' "

"How bad?"

"Bad enough that she won't be traveling until tomorrow at the earliest, according to the Station Number One."

"Could've been worse. My guy could have gotten there too late."

They were each silent for several seconds, then Seale sighed and leaned back in his chair. "Paul."

"Hmm?"

"We have to figure this thing out, what you and I are doing, how we're going to trust each other."

"We don't have to trust each other, Julian."

"Look, I know you were tight with Cheng. And I know you don't trust me. But if you'd come to me at the start of this, told me you had an agent running in Tashkent, it would have saved a shit-load of grief."

Crocker shook his head, then stubbed the half-dead cigarette out and started a new one, this one to actually smoke. The relief he felt regarding Chace was beyond words, and maybe, because of that, he was less inclined to be combative, or even antagonistic.

"It was never about Tashkent," Crocker said.

"You were jockeying for Ruslan—"

"You think Ruslan was *our* idea? You're the ones with an air base in the south of the country, you're the ones who negotiated the overflight and land-use deals, not us. The last member of our team to speak out about Uzbekistan got canned, remember? McInnes was out of his job within a week of his outburst."

Seale frowned.

"This didn't start with us," Crocker said. "It started with you, in your house."

"You should have come to me with it anyway."

"As Barclay has been anxious to point out to me in the past, I don't work for you."

"No, but you don't work against us, either."

"Not if I can help it. The plan was never to screw you or yours, Julian." Crocker picked up his internal line, punched a key, waited for a response. "Escort out for Mr. Seale."

"I'm leaving, am I?"

"For the time being." Crocker indicated the ceiling with his cigarette. "It was never about Tashkent, Julian. Tashkent was the excuse."

Seale looked up, toward the sixth floor, then looked back to Crocker, then shook his head. He put his hands on the arms of his chair, pushed himself to his feet.

"I'm glad your girl is okay."

"Her name's Chace." Crocker tapped ash into the tray. "I owe you for this."

Seale smiled. "I know you do. And I know you'll be good for it."

"I will."

"You mind if I ask? What're you going to do with Fincher?"

"We'll find a Station for him. He was fine as a Station man. He just wasn't made to be a Minder."

"The Thousandth Man."

Crocker raised an eyebrow. "Kipling?"

"Yeah, you know the poem? 'Nine hundred and ninety-nine can't bide the shame or mocking or laughter, but the Thousandth Man will stand by your side to the gallows-foot and after.' I had to memorize it in the Boy Scouts."

"You were a Boy Scout?"

"I was an *Eagle* Scout, mister, so don't fuck with me."

"Never again. Neither you nor I would count Fincher in that number."

"No," Seale agreed.

There was a rap on the office door, and then it opened, revealing one of the wardens from downstairs. Crocker nodded to him, then got to his feet and offered Seale his hand. Whatever the reason, it was clear then that he and COS London had reached a mutual understanding.

"When I get Chace's after-action, I'll let you know," Crocker told him.

"It'd be appreciated." Seale turned for the door and the waiting warden. "Should've been called 'The Thousandth Woman,' huh?"

He left, the warden closing the door after them.

Crocker turned his chair, opening the blinds to look out at the dawn over London. The sky had already begun to lighten, and the clouds were low, and behind the tinted windows, they looked a gangrenous green. He snorted, swiveled back around to his desk, wondering when Kate would arrive and how long after that he could coerce her into preparing a pot of coffee, and there was a knock on his door.

"Come," Crocker said, then got to his feet as Sir Walter Seccombe entered the room, umbrella and hat in his hand and a smile on his face. "Sir. Can I offer you a seat?"

"No time, I'm afraid. I have to brief the Foreign Secretary so he can inform the Prime Minister and the Cabinet. But I wanted to stop by and let you know how things are shaking out. You still have your job, Paul."

"I'm relieved."

"Sir Frances will be tendering his resignation this morning, with no explanation given. Best that way, for all concerned, I should think. Certainly he has no desire to explain how it was that four Starstreak MANPADs ended up in Uzbekistan. Nor does HMG wish to see a public inquiry into the same."

"And our involvement in Uzbekistan?"

"Will be kept quiet as well."

"I see."

Seccombe lifted his chin slightly, regarding him with a smaller smile this time. "Any news on Chace?"

"She was taken by the Interior Ministry, but we've got her back now. She should be home in the next few days."

"And you'll reinstate her?"

"If she still wants it." Crocker ran a hand through his hair. "The irony is, she's going to come back thinking she blew the mission. She doesn't know that she did exactly what you wanted."

"This wasn't solely about Barclay. It began exactly as I presented it."

"When did it change?"

"When the Prime Minister thought better of antagonizing the White House. And as Chace was running without contact, we couldn't rightly abort the op, could we?"

"We could've," Crocker said. "If I'd notified the Station."

"Hmm," Seccombe said. "I'm afraid I didn't think of that."

Liar, Crocker thought.

"It all worked out in the end, regardless, Paul. I think you'll get along well with your new C. You share a great many traits."

"It's confirmed, then?"

"Not officially. Alison will step up as acting C following the resignation. Should confirm the posting by the end of the week."

"She'll need a Deputy Chief."

"Yes," Seccombe said, nodding. "You should probably talk to Alison about that."

FOR INTERNAL USE ONLY—DO NOT DISTRIBUTE—KK/49877-08-03-06

To: DEPUTY CHIEF OF SERVICE
RAYBURN, SIMON;
DIRECTOR OF OPERATIONS
CROCKER, PAUL;
From: DR. ELEANOR CALLARD
Date: 3 AUGUST 2006
Re: ANNUAL EVALUATION OF THE SPECIAL SECTION
(ref KK/49836-07-28)

Gentlemen,

With all due respect, I believe D-Ops is missing the point. Yes, I *did* clear all three members of the Special Section for duty. Their psychological defects notwithstanding (and D-Ops will argue that in the case of the Minders, these traits are not, in fact, defects at all) the Section is entirely capable, and more, willing, to perform whatever tasks assigned to them.

Rather, I am concerned that Minder One has not been given adequate time to reacclimatize to the job, and, more important, I believe she has been given no opportunity to properly address and resolve those issues arising out of her capture and torture at the hands of the NSS in February of this year.

Her experience is still very much at the forefront of her mind, and she has admitted to me that it still preys upon her. While Dr. Clark's examination of her at Tashkent Station concluded no rape had occurred, clearly she was sexually assaulted. From our conversations I have concluded that she has not been physically intimate with anyone since her return from Uzbekistan, and that she has had little desire to be so; this is a marked change in her personality. When questioned about her drinking, she claims to have all but stopped, citing the presence and proximity of her daughter, as much as the demands of the job.

She also admits to having taken it upon herself to identify each of her assailants, so that she may "know them when the time comes." Her humiliation and shame at her ordeal are second only to her anger at the experience, and she shows no intention, nor even a desire, to release her hold on these feelings.

While D-Ops' concern revolves around the question of whether or not Minder One can be counted on to act as required should a similar circumstance or threat arise (i.e., will Minder One hold back if she fears she may once again be subjected to capture and torture? The answer, of course, is no; were it anything otherwise, D-Ops would never have returned Minder One to Active status), my concern is perhaps less pragmatic, but no less valid, especially given my above findings.

D-Ops will confirm that the Special Section views itself as a separate, if not an elite, part of SIS. They view themselves as beholden to D-Ops first and foremost, to one another second, to SIS third, and to the Government only inasmuch as SIS is responsive to the needs and desires of Government. What is done to one Minder is done to all. So, yes, I am forced to agree with D-Ops when he argues that the Minder will "get the job done, regardless"— provided the job is one that D-Ops *wants* done.

Beyond that, however, the ethic of the Special Section is that they look after, and take care of, their own. That Minder One was not considered an active member of the Special Section at the time of her capture in Tashkent is irrelevant. *All* three Minders view her experience with the same eye, and all three of them feel that the situation must be redressed.

I do not believe I am overstating the situation when I say that, given the opportunity, any one of them would cheerfully go to Tashkent *right this moment* to murder those people responsible for what happened to Minder One. That they haven't is due *only* to the fact that the opportunity has not arisen and nothing else.

While D-Ops maintains that this is to be expected, and is even requisite for members of the Special Section, I remain unconvinced that this desire for vengeance can be controlled.

In conclusion, I can only reiterate my previous point: until the situation with Minder One is resolved one way or another, tasking *any* Minder to a special operation in the Central Asian Theatre runs the risk of turning that mission into an opportunity for the Minders to pursue their private vendetta.

Minder One especially.

Thank you for your attention.

E. Callard, M.D.

CHAPTER 31

London—Vauxhall Cross, Office of D-Ops

18 August, 0858 Hours GMT

Time didn't heal all wounds, not for her, but in some cases it helped. Chace had come back from Tashkent thinking she was repeating her return from Saudi Arabia, expecting to find Crocker and another trip to the Farm, and then an uncomfortable and unceremonious discharge, this time once and for all.

Instead, she'd returned home to find Crocker acting as if she'd never left; not for Tashkent, not for Saudi, as if she'd been Minder One all along. He'd given her two weeks leave to recover and get her things in order, and to move from Lancashire back to London. So she'd continued on to Lancashire as she'd done for over a year and a half, taking the GNR to Leeds and then changing to Skipton, finally hiring a cab to take her the rest of the way to Barnoldswick.

People either stared at her as she went or studiously avoided looking at her. The bruises on her face had swollen, and she'd been given an ointment for the scrapes, which made the wounds appear still wet and fresher than they were. The sight in her right eye was beginning to return, clearest when she stood upright, worse when she lay down. The doctor who'd tended her at the British Embassy, hovered over by a concerned Station Number One, had explained that there was blood in the eye, and that was what was occluding her vision. It would stop and be reabsorbed soon enough, he assured her. As for her feet, luckily nothing had been broken, but the blunt trauma was severe enough that he'd advised her to stay off them as much as she could. He'd given her a set of crutches.

When Chace finally hobbled through Valerie Wallace's door in the late afternoon of the twenty-fourth of February, she found Tamsin and Val in the front room, playing with a sorting set, plastic pyramids, spheres, and cubes that could fit into an elbow-shaped tube. Val came to her feet quickly, unable to completely hide the dismay and concern on her face, or the sharp inhale she made at the sight of Chace.

Tamsin merely looked at her blankly, eyes wide and blue and curious.

Chace thought her heart would break then, that her daughter couldn't remember her. But Val saw it, too, and understood.

"It's your face, love," Val told her softly. "She doesn't recognize you."

Chace propped her crutches against the side table, nodding, still drinking in the sight of her daughter. Ten days had passed since she'd seen her last, and Chace was stunned by how much Tamsin had grown.

"Hello, Tam," she said. "I've missed you."

Tamsin dropped the ball she was holding, struggling to her feet, her face lighting with an openmouthed smile. She wobbled like a drunk, then lurched forward, arms out, a miniature Frankenstein's Monster, babbling happily.

Chace knelt and caught her in her arms, and held her until she was certain her heart wouldn't break.

She stayed in Barnoldswick for the week, and one night, after putting Tamsin to bed, sat with Val at the kitchen table, and explained her intentions. She was going to return to work, and that required her moving back to London, and she wanted Tamsin with her. She would hire a nanny, someone to live in and take care of her daughter during the day and sometimes the night, if need be.

Valerie nodded, failing to hide her disappointment or her hurt. "If you think it's best, then."

"It's what's best for me, and in the long run, I think that makes it best for Tam as well," Chace said. "I'll be traveling again, though. I don't know how much, and I'll never know when. But if you're around, I'd like it so that Tamsin stayed with you while I'm away."

"Here? Or in London?"

"Whichever you'd rather, Val."

"Don't much care for London."

"Then here, by all means."

Val considered, then nodded. "She's my granddaughter, and far as I'm concerned, Tara, you're my daughter-in-law. You'll always have me, the both of you."

"You've been generous beyond reason, Val, and I can't tell you how grateful I am."

Val reached for her hand on the table, resting beside her mug of tea. Her touch was warm and soft and dry, and the look she gave Chace was grave.

"And this is what you want? What you truly want?"

"It is."

"And it's the same work, the same work you and my Tom were doing before?"

"Yes."

"Either you're good at it, or you're a glutton for punishment, Tara. For Tamsin's sake, and for yours, I hope you're good at it."

"I'm very good at it," Chace told her.

And so she returned to London.

Her feet had recovered enough that she could walk on them without the crutches for short stints. It made it easier to go about the shopping, the acquisition of those things that would be required to turn her bachelorette's house into a home for a single mother. She contacted a service, set about interviewing nannies, and before the end of the second week had spoken with three she liked the looks of, forwarding their names to the Firm's Security Division for the appropriate checks. Two of them came back clean, and Chace hired them both, a young woman from Salisbury named Missi, twenty-one years old and studying art history, and an older girl who'd grown up in Bristol, named Catherine, who was planning on a career in early childhood education.

Then she called Val and asked her to bring Tamsin down to London, to be with her mother.

By the time she reported for work on the thirteenth of March, the shakeout had already occurred, and she entered the Pit to find Lankford and Poole already there, greeting her with applause. The Minder One Desk had been cleared of the previous occupant's personal belongings, and a bouquet of flowers sat at its center, waiting for her. Chace had brought her go-bag, and as she felt her cheeks redden with the applause, turned and put it up on the shelf, beside Poole's and Lankford's.

"Like your bouquet?" Lankford asked.

"His idea," Poole said. "He's a romantic."

Chace moved to the desk, took a closer look, then burst out laughing. They weren't flowers at all, but rather an artfully arranged display of condoms in red, purple, yellow, green, and blue, most of them out of their wrappers, folded and tied to appear as blossoms. A card was taped to the vase, reading, "For God's sake, be careful!"

"We got you the extra-big bouquet, boss," Lankford told her. "Forty-eight, jumbo-size."

"She'll go through them in a week," Poole said.

"I'm not like that anymore," Chace said, mildly. "I'm a mother, I have to set an example."

"Half a week, then," Poole said.

The internal circuit on her desk rang, the same infinitely annoy-
ing bleat she remembered, and all of them, Chace, Lankford,
Poole, stared at the phone.

"Minder One," Chace said when she answered, and she felt
herself smiling, and saw Lankford and Poole quietly laughing at
her as a result.

"Come and see me," Crocker said, and hung up.

So she'd gone to Crocker's office, and he'd given her a seat, and
had redrawn the map of the Firm for her. There was no Frances
Barclay, there was Alison Gordon-Palmer. Simon Rayburn was
no longer D-Int, but instead was awaiting confirmation of promotion to Deputy Chief. Paul Crocker was D-Ops, Tara Chace was
Minder One, and Kate Cooke still believed she ran SIS.

"I'm sorry," Chace told him when he was finished.

"For? You did your job, you did it damn well, and you didn't
even know what the bloody job really was."

"About Rayburn. I know you wanted the promotion."

Crocker took out a cigarette, then offered her the pack. Chace
hesitated, then accepted.

"I can live with it," he told her. "Besides, you're not ready to
take over for me yet, and if I move on, I want you to fill this desk."

"I'm flattered," Chace said. "I think."

"It's not because I like you," Crocker said. "It's because you
can't be any worse at it than Fincher would have been."

"And where is Mr. Fincher now?"

"Out at the School, taking a refresher before his reassignment."

"He's being reassigned?"

Crocker pulled a face. "Our new lady mistress on the floor
above feels he is a damn fine officer. For that reason, he'll soon be
off to parts unknown to head up the station there. As long as he
doesn't end up as the new D-Int, I'll be content."

"Is that all, sir?"

"No." Crocker shoved the stack of folders on his desk toward her. "This is homework. You've got a lot of catching up to do, Minder One."

Chace laughed, taking the stack and getting to her feet. "Then I'll start reading. You know where to find me."

"Yes," Crocker agreed. "I do."

So it was that, six months after she'd returned from Tashkent, Tara Chace waited in D-Ops' outer office, two blue internal distribution folders in her hand, joking with Kate Cooke and waiting for Crocker to see her for the morning brief.

"It's a new perfume," Chace said. "There's a boy."

"There is not a boy," Kate responded, indignant, offering her a cup of coffee.

Chace took the cup, sipped at it, grinning. "It's Lankford, isn't it? You've got a thing for my Minder Three."

Color crept into Kate's cheeks, and she settled at her desk, putting her attention on the files she'd been sorting before Chace had entered. It seemed to Chace that she was trying very hard to avoid eye contact.

"I do not."

"Well, it's not Poole, and it's not me, and I can't much figure who else comes through this office that you'd try to capture with a new scent. So I'm thinking Lankford."

"It's not Chris."

"Oooh, Chris, is it?" Chace moved toward the desk, reaching for the internal phone. "I'll call down to the Pit, shall I, see what he thinks of that?"

Kate swatted at Chace's hand. "Don't you dare."

Chace stopped, looked closer at Kate, who held the stare for a fraction before again turning her attention back to her work. The younger woman's expression had tightened, the joke taken too far, and Chace realized three things in quick succession. First, Kate wasn't trying to catch Lankford; she'd already caught him. Second, Kate Cooke had been in this office long enough to know the directorate's opinion of staff/Minder fraternization. Relationships weren't forbidden between most SIS staff, but between SIS staff and members of Special Section was a different story. One thing to tandem-couple with the new lad on the Argentine Desk, another thing entirely to tandem with an agent who might be asked to kidnap a general from his home in Tehran, a job he or she might not come back from, ever.

Third, Chace realized that she was living in her own glass house, that there was nothing she could say to dissuade either Lankford or Kate. Even if her affair with Wallace didn't strictly fall into the same category—Wallace had left the Section at the time, to teach at the Field School—she'd done the same herself with Minder Three Edward Kittering when she'd been Minder Two. In the rankings of sin, Chace was the winner, and both of them knew it.

"Just keep it quiet," Chace told Kate. "You don't want D-Ops getting wind of it."

Kate's expression was a mixture of gratitude and hope.

"Don't look at me like that. I don't approve, but I won't obstruct."

"You did it."

"Yes, I did." Chace finished her coffee, moved around to the pot for a refill. "I was astonishingly stupid."

Kate started to respond, but the door from the inner office opened, and Simon Rayburn emerged, bearing a folder of his own, this one red. He smiled at Chace.

"Tara."

"Good morning, sir."

"All well?"

"For the moment at least, yes, sir."

"Very good." Rayburn made for the exit, back onto the hall. "You can go on in, I think."

"Thank you, sir," Chace said, and went through to the inner office, to find Crocker seated behind his desk, as ever he seemed to be, scribbling his signature at the bottom of the memorandum he was reviewing. Chace stood, waiting while he shuffled the memo back into the stack, and when he looked up, she held out the folders she was carrying.

"Report to the FCO on the viability of recruitment in Guangdong Province as prepared per your request with input from the China Desk, with notes. And request for operational oversight regarding travel and incidental expenses to operational theater, prepared for submission to the Finance Committee. I almost handed it to the Deputy Chief on his way out, but thought it'd be better coming from you."

She dropped the second folder on the first, and Crocker reached for it, flipping it open. "Sit."

Chace barked, once, sounding less like a dog than like a woman trying to sound like one, then pulled up the chair. She leaned forward and lifted his pack of Silk Cut, freed a cigarette, and Crocker slid his lighter across the desktop absently, without looking away from his reading. Chace lit, exhaled, and sat back, waiting for his verdict.

Crocker closed the folder, then reached for his pack and lighter, sitting back himself. "You were diplomatic."

"I thought honey rather than vinegar."

"Probably wise. All right, I'll send it up to C. If she approves it, she'll have Rayburn present at the meeting."

"He'll sell it? We need more money."

"We always need more money, Tara."

"On Operation: Lanyard, Mission Planning couldn't secure seats for Poole and me on the same flight, sir. We ended up flying into Hanoi sixteen hours apart, and that put me sixteen hours in theater without backup. The last time Lankford went out, he flew economy because Budget wouldn't authorize a first-class ticket."

"He did all right."

"He did, but that's hardly the point."

Crocker lit his own cigarette. "C will give it to Rayburn, and Rayburn will bring it to Finance. It'll be taken care of."

"Nice to have a Deputy Chief we can trust."

"Let's not get carried away," Crocker told her. While he didn't actually grin, he came close.

Tara laughed, then reached into her jacket pocket and removed the printout she'd been carrying there, folded widthwise. "You see this?"

"I'm still working through the 'Urgents,' so unless it was graded 'Immediate,' no, I haven't. What is it?"

"It's about Tashkent."

"Will it make me happy?"

"It's not about the last Starstreak, if that's what you're asking, no."

Crocker took the next paper waiting for him at the top of his stack, readying his pen. "You're still certain they only used three of them?"

"Technically, they used two of them, I used one," Chace clarified. "And yes, I am certain, as certain as I can be considering that I was unconscious for a time."

"I don't like loose ends."

Chace grunted agreement. In the past sixth months, there'd been no sign nor whisper of the fourth of Barclay's four missiles, and try as Tashkent Station might, they'd heard nary a whisper of its whereabouts. If it was still in Uzbekistan, in Ahtam Zahidov's possession, perhaps, there was no proof of the fact. If it wasn't in Zahidov's possession, then God only knew who had it, and what they were planning to do with it. Neither Chace nor Crocker nor the DC nor C doubted it would come back to haunt them. Where and when were the only questions.

Chace handed the sheet over, watched as Crocker unfolded it. It was a simple printout out of a news piece Chace had pulled from online earlier that morning, a Reuters story carried on the wire, with a photo. The printer in the Pit was a cranky old laserjet, and incapable of color, though it had tried its best to reproduce the graphic. The photo had been taken in Tashkent the previous week, outside the Bakhor Concert Hall in Tashkent, and showed President Sevara Malikov-Ganiev speaking to the American Ambassador, a man named Michael Norton.

Crocker skimmed the article, examined the photo, then sent it back to her across the desk. "I do not see the missing Starstreak."

"As I said, this isn't about the missing Starstreak."

"Then please explain the operational significance of this photograph."

Chace pushed it back toward him, this time tapping an index finger on the photograph. "There."

Crocker looked again, and either didn't like what he saw or didn't like where he suspected Chace was going with this. "That's the boy?"

"Stepan, yes." Chace took the paper back. In the photo, Stepan was in the background, in the cluster of bodyguards behind Sevara. The boy had been dressed up, wearing what passed for formal clothing for a two-and-a-half-year-old. Chace had looked for, but hadn't seen, Zahidov in the shot. "I'm wondering if she knew they'd be photographed."

"It looks unstaged," Crocker said.

"So maybe the Ambassador didn't know the camera would be there. But maybe she did."

"You think she's parading the boy? Why?"

"I don't know." Chace put out her cigarette. "But you read my after-action, you know what I was asked during the torture. If Zahidov was trying to play psychological games along with the physical ones, that's one thing. But if Ruslan actually escaped, that's something else. Sevara brings his son out for a photo op, that's a warning to him. 'Hey, look—hostage.' "

Crocker scowled, tilting forward in his chair. "You could just be paranoid."

"There's that, too." She smiled thinly, to show that she didn't think she was. "But no one ever confirmed Ruslan's death, boss. I didn't get a good look at him, and no one from our team ever saw the body."

"There were two state funerals held in Uzbekistan the week after you got home. One for President Malikov, one for his son."

"Closed casket," Chace pointed out.

"For Ruslan, yes. And if he died the way you thought he died, that would make sense, because he would have caught a faceful of shrapnel."

"You don't think he's alive?"

Crocker exhaled smoke. "I don't know. There's been no sign of him, there's been no word of him. What I do know, however, is that Ahtam Zahidov tortured you and intended to kill you. And you've never been the type to forgive and forget."

"I've forgiven you."

"I'd like to think you don't group me and Zahidov in the same class."

"No, of course not." Chace leaned forward again, serious. "I'm not trying to make up an excuse to go back to Tashkent, boss. That's not what this is."

"I don't think you are," Crocker said mildly. "But you're not beyond finding an excuse for me to send you there."

Chace fell silent, thinking, then sitting back once more and looking away, to the bust of Winston Churchill that Crocker kept atop his document safe. It was one of the few appointments he kept in the office, the bust, a bookshelf filled with the latest in Jane's titles, and a Chinese dragon print on one wall. He'd had the dragon for as long as Chace had known him to occupy the office, and she sometimes wondered at its significance, but she'd never asked.

He had her number, of course—but that didn't mean that Chace was wrong about the possibility Ruslan had survived.

Since returning from Uzbekistan, she'd made a point of staying informed about what was happening in the region, and as much as she could claim the interest was operational, it clearly went to the personal. She'd spent dozens of hours reviewing files, viewing photographs, in particular attempting to identify the two men who had helped Zahidov torture her. She knew their names now. Tozim was Tozim Stepanov, the older man with the tools Andrei Hamrayev. She remembered them.

There were nights when she dreamed about Tozim Stepanov

and Andrei Hamrayev and, worst of them all, Ahtam Zahidov. Memory had blunted nothing, and Chace recalled him perfectly. Zahidov's thin-lipped smile and his insistent fingers, and the practiced nonchalance with which he'd hurt her. She remembered Zahidov's hands burning on her as he had moved to strip the last of her clothes, his eagerness to rape her.

Chace didn't just want Zahidov dead. She wanted to be the one to kill him. There would be a reckoning, she was certain. The only question was when.

And no one in the Firm who knew what Zahidov had done to her could expect her to do anything less when the opportunity came.

Crocker said, "I do understand, Tara, you know that."

"I know." She looked back to him, then got out of the chair. "I'll be down in the Pit."

"Tara."

She stopped at the door, looking back.

"It's been six months," Crocker said. "You're going to have to let it go."

Chace thought about the terror of that room and the cruelty of the men who had filled it. There were still times, six months after the fact, when she would lift Tamsin or reach above her for a high shelf, when her right shoulder would send fire down her arm. When she touched the skin around her eye, she could feel a spur of bone, floating just above the orbit. And, condom bouquet notwithstanding, the only people she'd allowed to touch her in any way but the most formal or accidental since Tashkent had been her daughter and her physician.

"No," she told him. "Really, I don't. And you wouldn't, either, boss."

Time didn't heal all wounds, not for her.

Especially not this one.

CHAPTER 32

20 August, 0621 Hours (GMT+5:00)

Zahidov stood in the dawn light at the foot of the bridge beside an
Uzbek army captain named Oleg Arkitov, took the offered binoculars from the man's hand, and looked into Afghanistan. Across the
Amu Darya River, past the newly built Customs houses and immi-
gration offices staffed by the Afghanis, the Salang Highway joined
the road that ran parallel to the tracks, cutting straight to Mazar-i-
Sharif, and then on to Kabul, winding through the red hills in the
distance. A train was rumbling up the tracks toward them, returning empty, Zahidov suspected, having been emptied of the UN relief supplies it had delivered earlier in the day. It would be stopped
by the border guards on the Uzbek side and thoroughly searched
before being allowed to proceed.

"You look upriver, Minister, you can see the barges coming,
too," Arkitov told him.

Zahidov swiveled, turning east to follow the river. The Uzbek
side of the border was lined with a 380-volt electrified fence, and
beyond it, land mines covered the banks down to the water. The
fence and the mines had been laid in the late nineties in response to
incursions from the extremists who then ruled Afghanistan. The
bridge, at that time, had been all but permanently closed, reopened

only in late 2001. Since then, the border operated almost at random, the Uzbek side shutting down whenever the government responded to a security alert or a bombing. Despite continued American insistence to keep the border open, there were still times when the border was ordered shut.

Zahidov lowered the optics, handing them back to the captain. "They hit before the bridge?"

"Last night, just after three in the morning, sir. We could see the muzzle-flashes and the rocket grenades."

"How many trucks made it?"

"One."

"And how many were coming?"

"Three."

Zahidov felt his frustration well. This was the fourth time the heroin had been hijacked before reaching the border. Twice in May, once in July, and then again this morning. Four times, and there could be no doubt in his mind any longer. He was being persecuted, he was being targeted specifically.

When it first happened, he'd been angry, but willing to accept the loss. The north of Afghanistan was populated by warlords and drug lords, each leading a private army of Pathan soldiers eager for nothing more than a chance to fight. The Pathans' favorite sports, the saying went, were dog racing, horse racing, and fighting each other, not in that order. If Zahidov's heroin was lost in this cross fire, it wasn't ideal, but it was survivable, it was the cost of doing business with the Afghanis.

But when it happened again, less than two weeks later, and the replacement shipment had also been lost, he had become immediately suspicious, and just as quickly considered the possibility that it was Ruslan Malikov behind it all. No proof, of course, except for the fact that the man had escaped him in February, and when he thought back to that, all of his rage returned. He'd been a fool, so filled with hatred for the bitch spy he'd ordered the Sikorsky in immediate pursuit of her, instead of commanding the pilot to set down first, to allow him to finish what they had begun with Ruslan.

The fact was, he'd been so eager to catch and kill the spy that he hadn't even considered the possibility that Ruslan wasn't dead. It had been almost two hours later, after he'd brought Stepan to Sevara and was making his way back to the Ministry to begin the interrogation, that he'd received the call. Ruslan had vanished, there was no sign of him.

And there had been no true sign of him since then, Zahidov's suspicions notwithstanding. But there was logic to the idea that the President's son had gone south. His support had always been strongest there, in Bukhara, Samarkand, Qashka Darya, and Surkhan Darya provinces. He would have been able to find some aid, some shelter, at least enough to provide for his immediate needs. It was even possible he had jumped aboard a UN relief shipment, either hiding in one of the train cars or riding in one of the trucks that traveled the thousand meters across the river alongside the tracks.

Why he'd gone to Afghanistan was the question, and it wasn't a terribly difficult one to answer. There were few places better in the world for a man to hide, the terrain placed by God, it seemed, only for that purpose and no other. Add to that the central government's lack of actual power in the outlying regions, the scores of bickering warlords and tribesmen, all of them bound by their peculiar code of honor, what they called Pashtunwali, the Law of the Pathan. And first among the laws was the demand that they provide sanctuary and hospitality to any and all who request it. It was how bin Laden's people had survived when the Coalition had come for their blood.

Sanctuary was given to any and all who asked for it. The Pathans would shelter Ruslan, if the bastard asked. They would have to: their culture allowed them no other choice.

So Zahidov had become convinced it was Ruslan persecuting him, stealing his heroin. And it wasn't simply to hurt him or Sevara, no, though that was certainly an added benefit. Zahidov was certain Ruslan was selling it, perhaps to the same Moscow buyers that Sevara and he dealt with. Ruslan was selling it, and making a lot of money. Money he could use to pay the warlords and their men, money he could use to raise an army.

It wasn't far-fetched. In 2000, *taleban*-backed extremists had poured over the border from Afghanistan in an attempt to overthrow the country. They had closed to within one hundred kilometers of Tashkent before they'd been stopped by Uzbek forces. If Ruslan tried to do the same, he stood an even better chance. He knew the land, and if his support in Uzbekistan still held, if those in the military rose to join him, it would be either a coup or a civil war.

These were Zahidov's fears, and watching as the rising sun turned the already red hills of Afghanistan bloody, he gave them their due. A coup, or worse, a civil war, would destroy Uzbekistan, and at the end of the day, despite everything he did or had done—or perhaps because of it—Ahtam Zahidov was a patriot. He saw no conflict in wishing to do himself well in the process of serving his county, he saw no fault in the viciousness he showed his enemies. He wanted what was best for his nation, and he did what he did to ensure it. All his love for Sevara notwithstanding, it was why he had supported her as President in the first place. It was why he continued to serve her, despite their troubles.

It was why he was in Termez now.

The problem was—or had been, until that morning—there was no proof at all it was Ruslan behind these attacks.

Then Andrei had woken him before dawn, rousing Zahidov from a lonely, fitful sleep. He'd told Zahidov that the Ministry had received a call from Captain Oleg Arkitov in Termez, that the captain had in his custody a Pathan who swore he'd seen Ruslan Malikov to the south of Mazar-i-Sharif, enjoying the hospitality of General Ahmad Mohammad Kostum, an ex–Northern Alliance commander and one of the more notorious warlords of the region. That the Pathan in question, a man using the name Hazza, had successfully identified Ruslan Malikov from a set of photographs.

Proof, at long last, but Zahidov needed to hear it for himself.

He turned to Arkitov, saying, "I want to speak to Hazza."

They went by armored personnel carrier from the bridge to the barracks, Zahidov riding with Arkitov and four of his rangers. The soldiers sat on their benches, their automatic rifles in hand, bored. After the extremists had tried to overthrow the country in 2000, the Uzbek Army had been redeployed and remodeled, breaking away somewhat from its Soviet antecedents. Now the soldiers here in the south, the rangers, imitated the Americans, in training, unit composition, and tactics.

Zahidov looked back at the bridge, the only ground route joining Afghanistan and Uzbekistan. Friendship Bridge, the Soviets had called it, although the Americans had tried to rechristen it "Freedom Bridge" once their war against the *taleban* began. It was the Soviets who had built the bridge, who had established this sole land crossing of the 130-mile-long border between the two countries, formed by the Amu Darya. It was over this bridge the Soviets had invaded Afghanistan in 1979, and it was over this same bridge that they had limped back ten years later, defeated. It was a refugee bridge, had seen thousands of Afghanis cross it, fleeing both the *taleban* and the Coalition. It was a terrorist's bridge, one of the ways al-Qaeda foot soldiers used to infiltrate his country.

When the Americans had secured the rights to use Karshi-Khanabad, they'd argued for the bridge to be reopened. The UN kept offices in Termez, both for UNICEF and UNESCO, and the organization continued to use the city as a staging point for distribution of humanitarian aid to Afghanistan. The International Security Assistance Force, ISAF, resided in Termez as well, its efforts more focused on the military than the humanitarian. Staffed by the Germans, Airlift Detachment 3 had supported Operation Enduring Freedom since the war's start. The Germans had renovated the old Soviet airfield, built their own infrastructure, pouring millions of euros into Uzbekistan in the process.

The APC jostled Zahidov as it made its way back into town. He was sweating already, could feel beads of it trickling down from his hair along his spine, inside his cotton shirt. Nowhere in Uzbekistan got hotter in the summer; the temperature today was liable to hit 49 Celsius, over 120 degrees Fahrenheit, and that was cooler than it had been for a week.

Just another of the thousand reasons that Zahidov hated Termez.

They disembarked at the Border Watch HQ, a cluster of Soviet-era buildings that had served as command post, once upon a time, for the ground soldiers being deployed into Afghanistan. Now it was staffed by Arkitov and his rangers.

The captain led him from the garage into the air-conditioning of the dormitories, entering a common room with television and tables. The television was on, broadcasting the news, but the room itself was unoccupied. They moved into a hallway, and Arkitov led him to a door, knocked once on it, then opened it.

There were three men inside, two of them rangers, and both of them were coming to their feet before the door had fully opened. Both snapped salutes to Arkitov, and he dismissed them, then nodded to Zahidov and stepped out after them, closing the door once more, leaving Zahidov alone with the man who remained.

"Hazza?" Zahidov asked.

The man nodded to him, eyeing him with blatant suspicion and fingering the Kalashnikov resting across his thighs. Zahidov guessed him to be in his late thirties, perhaps older, but with the Pathans, after a certain age, it was hard to tell. They were the ethnic Afghanis, sometimes called the Pashtun or Pushtun, a collection of peoples that together constituted the largest patriarchal tribe in the world, and a fierce enough enemy to have driven the Soviets out of their homeland.

"When do I get paid?" Hazza asked.

Zahidov pulled out his PDA, brought up the picture of Ruslan he'd stored there. "This is the man you saw with General Kostum?"

Hazza squinted, and Zahidov wondered if his eyes were bad, if his ID would be useless. In July, Zahidov had ordered Arkitov to begin circulating rumors of a reward, paid to anyone who could prove he had seen Ruslan Malikov. If it was greed that had brought Hazza here, then his information was, by necessity, suspect.

"Looks like him," Hazza said, after a second. "But he has a beard now, and covers his head."

Zahidov considered, tucking the PDA back into his coat. "When did you last see him?"

"Yesterday. He took tea with the General." Hazza's suspicion had not eased. "When do I get paid?"

"When I believe you."

Hazza's expression clouded with anger, and he gripped the handle of his rifle. "You insult me."

"Prove to me that you've seen the man."

"My word is not enough? You insult me again."

"You will get paid after I have proof."

Hazza scowled, scratched at his beard with a filthy fingernail. "He limps. His left leg, it has a brace. I asked once how he was wounded, and he said it came trying to protect his son from the godless."

"More."

"I asked about the battle, and he said Allah smiled on him but also turned away, because he lived, but his son was taken from him. He said his wife and his son both were taken from him by a godless man."

"He speaks like a good Muslim. Is he a good Muslim?"

"He tries to be."

Zahidov ran his tongue along the back of his teeth, measuring the words. It sounded possible, it sounded like Ruslan, self-righteous and simpering, taking shelter in religion in the face of his losses.

"And Kostum?" Zahidov asked. "What is his relationship with Kostum?"

"Kostum has Uzbek blood, they are brothers. They talk as

friends, and the money Kostum gets makes him like Ruslan all the more. He will not betray your man, he has given him sanctuary. If Kostum betrays him, his life is worth less than a goat's."

Zahidov digested that. "Thank you. I'll see that you are paid."

"Soon," Hazza said. "I must return before they can learn where I have been."

"You're going back there?"

"Yes, as soon as I can."

"I will see you are paid immediately then," Zahidov said, and stepped out of the room, to find Arkitov and the two soldiers waiting in the hall.

"He had what you needed, Minister?" Arkitov asked him.

Zahidov nodded, then indicated over his shoulder at the closed door. "I don't want him warning Malikov or Kostum. Kill him."

Arkitov nodded, and signaled to the soldiers, then joined Zahidov walking down the hall. They heard the shots before they were back in the common room, and neither of them looked back.

"He's building an army, I'm more sure of it than ever, Sevya," Zahidov said. "He will wait until he has the men and the guns, and then they will come over the border, and they will come here, and they will try to kill you."

"You believed this man?"

"Yes, I did."

Sevara frowned, shook her head slightly, then waved past him at the secretary standing in the doorway of the office, dismissing the man. Zahidov watched him go. The secretary was in his mid-twenties, and far too attentive to the President for Zahidov's comfort.

"Could there be another reason?" she asked him when they were alone.

"Why else take the heroin, Sevya? He's selling it and keeping the money, using it to fund his eventual offensive. There is no other explanation."

She shook her head again, this time with more certainty. "No. It would be too foolish."

"Why?" He struggled, managing to keep the frustration from his voice.

"In 2000, there was no ISAF, no Coalition. In 2000, it was possible to come from the south and meet little to no resistance. Now if you come from the south, you meet the Germans in Termez and the Americans in Karshi. No—it makes no sense."

"It makes perfect sense," Zahidov countered. "For just those reasons. Think how such a move would humiliate you, think how it would look to the rest of the world. It would make us—you—look insecure, even incompetent. And if Americans or Germans died as he came north?"

"Then the Americans and the Germans and all the rest, they would join us in destroying him."

"And every extremist from Pakistan to Chechnya would come and join him. There is no way this is good, Sevya, there is no way we can continue to ignore this! We must act."

"How? How do you suggest we do that, Ahtam? You let him get away once, and now he's in Afghanistan. Are you going to send one of your men after him? You think that man would stand even the slightest chance of success, assuming he could find Ruslan, assuming he still is somewhere around Mazar-i-Sharif? If you know all these things about his plans, then surely Ruslan must have considered that. No. As long as he remains in Afghanistan, we cannot touch him."

Zahidov stepped closer to where she stood by the windows of her office, looking out at the courtyard of the Presidential Residence in the Tashkent suburb of Dormon. It was late afternoon, the sunlight slanting through the glass and making her hair burn like copper.

"If we wait for him to leave Afghanistan, it will be too late," Zahidov said. "You could use Stepan."

Sevara shot him a look of warning. "No."

"Just take him out in public with you, have pictures taken of the two of you together. The President and her beloved nephew. Ruslan will get the message."

"I won't use the boy that way," she said. "Bad enough that he was photographed at the concert last week."

"It does him no harm—"

"He wakes crying every night, Ahtam! He has nightmares, he still calls for Dina, he calls for my brother! I won't hurt him any more, I can't do it. He's my nephew, he's the only family I have left."

It struck at Zahidov, and he spoke before he meant to, saying, "So divorce Deniska instead of promising me that you will. Let me give you the child you want, let us make the family we talk about having! It's been three months since you were elected, you can do it now, no one would dare say anything!"

"Soon, not yet."

"When?"

"Soon," she repeated sharply. "And we will not discuss using Stepan again, Ahtam. Is that clear?"

"Then we have nothing to hold over Ruslan."

Sevara moved away from the window, nearer to him. "There must be a way to remove him."

"If you had let me, I would have removed him long ago," Zahidov reminded her. "You would never be threatened like this. I could remove Denis, too."

She slapped him, and the blow surprised more than it hurt, knocking his glasses askew, and he stepped back, shocked.

"Don't even think of it," she hissed at him. "Do you know what trouble you have made for me already? Do you know how the Americans watch me now? Watch us? You cleared the way for me to sit in this office, but you left a mess behind you, Ahtam."

He touched his cheek, feeling it burn. The first time she had touched him in weeks, and it was to strike him, and for a moment, he thought he felt tears trying to rise, and that both shamed and enraged him.

"I did it for you, Sevara."

She took a breath, then spoke to him again, her voice softer. "The man from the American Embassy, the one who took the woman spy away. Do you know what would have happened if he had arrived five minutes later? Or ten? Or an hour? Can you imagine the nightmare for me that would have been? The Americans and the British both, can you imagine it?"

She touched his cheek where she'd struck him, her fingertips light on his skin. He could feel the cool of her enameled nails against the burning of his cheek.

"You pick your targets badly, Ahtam," Sevara said. "It makes you look like a thug."

She pulled her hand away. "Go back to work," she told him. "I'll find a way to handle Ruslan. I'll speak to the Americans; they don't want to see him opening the south to extremists."

Zahidov stood for a moment, reeling, in the grand space of her office, then did as she'd instructed. He looked back to her as he went through the door, hoping she would raise her eyes to his, that he would see some forgiveness, some sign of her love.

But Sevara never looked up.

CHAPTER 33

London—Victoria Street, Number 75b, Pret a Manger

22 August, 1301 Hours GMT

"Salmon or Thai chicken?" Seale asked.

"Salmon," Crocker said.

"The salmon's for me."

"Then why'd you offer?"

"I was being polite." Seale handed the Thai chicken sandwich over, along with a can of Coke. "You want to eat here?"

"We could find a bench."

"It's air-conditioned in here."

"You're offering me choices where you've already determined the response," Crocker observed, following the American to one of the square metal tables in the corner of the eatery.

The table had just been vacated, and Seale swiped crumbs from its surface with his left hand, holding his own sandwich and soda together in his right. Satisfied the surface was now clean enough to eat off, he sat, spreading a paper napkin like a small tablecloth, then unfolding another onto his lap before tearing open the plastic container that held his meal.

"You keep making the wrong choice," Seale said.

"Story of my life." Crocker sat opposite, cracked open his soda. "What's up?"

"Ruslan Malikov is in Afghanistan, somewhere in the northern part of the country, we think near Mazar-i-Sharif."

"You're sure?"

"Pretty sure."

"Chace will be pleased," Crocker said, tucking into his sandwich. It wasn't bad, just not what he'd have chosen for himself.

"She won't be for long," Seale said, around his own mouthful. "We've got a problem, Paul. It looks like Ruslan's recruiting and arming his own militia in an attempt to overthrow his sister. He's been cozying up to one of the local warlords, Ahmad Mohammad Kostum, as well as working with some of the dope peddlers, selling heroin for financing."

"Someone should tell him to knock it off."

"Yeah, we're thinking the same thing." Seale wiped his mouth with the napkin from his lap. "So who are you going to send?"

"Me? You found it, it's yours. Besides, you've got your set crawling all over Mazar-i-Sharif."

"And we've worked long and hard to earn the trust and cooperation of the people there, so we're not looking to foul it up. Besides, we didn't turn Ruslan loose, that was you."

"Foul it up how?"

"Telling him to knock it off is the nice way to put it, Paul. Ruslan's got to be firmly dissuaded, if not permanently."

Crocker stopped his can halfway to his lips, staring at Seale. "You want him removed?"

"Me, I don't know the guy. But, as has been said twice already, he's got to knock it off. He charges at his sister, he's going to be kicking the door into Uzbekistan wide open for every extremist in the region to follow. And despite Tashkent's eagerness to blame everything that goes wrong in their country on terrorists, there *is* a legitimate threat there."

Crocker thought, then took the drink he'd paused on, set the can down, shaking his head. "I'm not going to get authorization to hit Ruslan."

"You don't have to hit him, you just have to get him to—"

"—knock it off, yes, I understand. But you've just told me it's going to have to stick. Which means we're not talking about possibly removing him, we're talking about definitely removing him."

Seale tucked the last bite of his sandwich into his mouth with an index finger, chewed, swallowed. "Dammit, these are good. I love this country—you get salmon and butter sandwiches as fast food."

"Julian."

Seale wiped his mouth again with the napkin, crumpled it into his fist, making it vanish. "I know you don't like it, Paul, but I'm getting stick from Langley. The sentiment there is that this is your mess, you guys need to clean it up."

"How legitimate a threat is he?"

"Legitimate enough that it has to be addressed." Seale checked his watch, then rose. "I've got to get back to the office. Call me when you've got good news."

Crocker watched him go, threading out of the little restaurant through the lunch hour crowd. He thought about finishing his lunch, but discovered he'd lost his taste for it.

No, he's right," Alison Gordon-Palmer told him. "It is our mess, and we do have to clean it up."

"We're talking about putting an agent into Afghanistan to kill a man under the protection of Ahmad Kostum. A man whose life, six months ago, we were trying to save."

C nodded. "And if Chace had been successful, we wouldn't be in this situation."

If she had been successful, Crocker thought, *you wouldn't be sitting in that chair right now, either.*

"We can hardly blame Chace for this," he said.

C rose, capping the pen in her hand as she did so and dropping it on the blotter. "I'm not blaming Chace, Paul, nor am I blaming you. But the fact remains, the situation with Ruslan Malikov would not be what it is if we hadn't become involved. The Americans expecting us to clean it up isn't an unreasonable request."

"I think that it is. We've had to clean up plenty of their messes."

"Don't be petulant. You're my Director of Operations, not some pubescent teen. You've spoken to Simon?"

"I brought it to the Deputy Chief first, yes."

"And?"

"And his assessment agrees with yours."

"Then why are you here?"

"In the hope that you would disagree with him. It's a betrayal."

"A betrayal it may be, but it's now also a directive," C said. "Consider it a Special Op, and task a Minder for it, two if you think it's necessary. I'll contact the FCO, speak to Seccombe about authorization, but for the moment, you may safely assume the mission has Downing Street's blessing."

"The Prime Minister will authorize an assassination?"

"The mission objective is not to assassinate, but to dissuade by all means necessary. Conops will be very clear on that."

"It's a dodge."

She raised an eyebrow at him, the kettle returning the look from the pot.

"Well," Alison Gordon-Palmer said, "I suppose you'd know."

CHAPTER 34

London—Vauxhall Cross, Operations Room

22 August, 1519 Hours GMT

Crocker was waiting for them when Chace led Poole and Lankford into the Ops Room, and she thought he looked more than his usual unhappy. He was standing—actually, Chace thought it was closer to slouching—with his hands thrust deep in his pockets and his cigarette burning between his lips, glowering at the plasma wall. Behind him, at Duty Ops, Bill Teagle was in the throes of mission planning with Danny Beale. She nodded to them both and they acknowledged her, then continued poring over the map unfolded between them.

Chace glanced to the wall, feeling more than seeing Lankford and Poole doing the same behind her. There was a highlight around Afghanistan, which immediately struck her as a bad thing, and Mike Putnam at MCO was busy typing up the information that would go onto the screen.

"Who has the control?" Putnam asked.

"I'll take it," said Beale.

"The operation is designated Sundown."

"Boss?" Chace asked.

Crocker ignored her, still looking at the plasma wall, and then he turned sharply to face Beale, saying, "Minders One and Three allocated."

"Yes, sir," Beale said.

"They'll need to connect through a military flight," Crocker said. "Put them on the ground as close to target as possible. What do we have in the area?"

"NATO activity is primarily focused on the hinterlands, sir, but there's a forward support base at Mazar-i-Sharif staffed by our troops."

"Get onto the RAF, see what they have headed that way and when, and if that doesn't give us anything for the next twenty-four hours, work your way through the rest of the Article Five powers."

"Yes, sir."

"They're to draw weapons. If travel is via RAF, they can draw them before departure; otherwise we'll have to arrange for a delivery by the Station in Kandahar when they hit the ground."

"Kandahar's been having communications difficulties," Putnam said from the MCO Desk. "We may not be able to get the cable to them in time."

"Islamabad, then. But they're not wandering around the countryside unarmed. Clear?"

"Absolutely, sir."

Crocker finally looked to Chace. "You and Chris are going to Afghanistan."

"So I'd gathered," Chace said.

"Not me, too?" Poole asked.

"You get to stay here and look after the store, Nicky." Crocker motioned them toward the map table. On the plasma wall, the word "Sundown" had appeared in a callout over Mazar-i-Sharif.

Chace couldn't help but notice how close the city was to the Uzbekistan border.

"Ruslan Malikov has been found in Afghanistan," Crocker told them, stabbing out his cigarette in the tray on the table. He focused on Chace, and she saw in his expression the acknowledgment that she had been correct, that Ruslan was still alive, and that Crocker also didn't need her going on about it here and now.

Chace couldn't argue with that. It didn't seem the time for an I-told-you-so.

"Ruslan's cozied up to one of the local warlords," Crocker continued. "There's a fear that Malikov is gathering troops and matériel for an attempted coup in Uzbekistan. I'm sending you two to deal with it."

"Deal with it how?" Chace asked.

He ignored her. "Warlord's name is General Ahmad Mohammad Kostum, he's an ethnic Uzbek from the region, fought against the Soviets and then against the *taleban* with the Northern Alliance. He's got a stronghold somewhere south of Mazar-i-Sharif, in the Samangan region. Intelligence is that Malikov is staying with him there."

"Warlord's stronghold, there's going to be a lot of guns about," Lankford observed.

"It's Afghanistan," Poole said. "The babies have AK-47s—I think they get them for their first birthday."

Lankford snorted, and Chace shot Poole a look, silencing further comment from the peanut gallery, before turning her attention back to Crocker and repeating, "Deal with it how?"

"How do you think?" he snapped. "Find him, make contact, do what you need to do to ensure he won't stir things up north of the Afghan border."

"Wait a second—"

"I'll be in my office," Crocker cut in. "Minder One to see me on completion of briefing."

He headed out of the room, leaving her to stare after him. And she knew already how she was supposed to "deal" with Ruslan Malikov.

Kate buzzed Crocker the moment Chace entered the office, and Chace heard the answering buzz immediately, and Kate said, "You can go on in."

She pushed into the inner office, let the door slide shut behind her, and then said, "You can't really expect me to go and kill him."

"That's why I'm sending two of you," Crocker said, eyes on the papers on his desk.

"Boss . . ."

He looked up, angry. "If you can't do the job, Tara, you shouldn't have come back."

That stung, and she let him know it. "It has nothing to do with my ability to do it, it's my willingness. It's a bad op."

"If you're twitched—"

"It's not mission twitch! Jesus Christ, Paul, it's my bloody fault Ruslan's there to begin with!"

"I'm not certain I agree."

"If I'd gotten him and his son out of the country as planned—"

"You did everything you could."

"I didn't have a fallback!"

"A fallback wouldn't have helped, and you know it."

"Why send me? Why aren't you sending Nicky with Chris?"

"You've met Ruslan, you'll be able to get close to him."

"I've met him, he'll see me coming, and he'll know exactly why I'm there! Chris and I'll end up shot before I get a word in edge-wise. Aside from the fact that Western women don't just wander around the Afghan countryside."

"Find a burka."

"I don't find that remotely amusing."

"I don't find *any* of this remotely amusing, Tara," Crocker snarled, slamming a hand down on his desk. "As the CIA has so eagerly pointed out, and as our dear new C has cheerfully con-firmed, the Powers That Be consider Ruslan Malikov *our* problem, and they want it swept under the carpet, and they want it swept there now."

"He won't be convinced, sir. I won't be able to talk him out of anything."

"You're authorized to use any means necessary to dissuade him."

"I heard the conops—I *was* present for the briefing." Chace paused, caught her breath, realizing that her heart was pounding. She didn't mind being worked up over this, but she was vaguely embarrassed to find that she wasn't even bothering to try to hide the fact.

"You realize that if he's under this warlord's protection then he's more than likely protected by Pashtunwali?" she asked. "You know what that means?"

"Yes, I seem to recall that particular issue of *National Geographic*, Tara. December '03, was it?"

"The mocking is good, I like that a lot. Ruslan's been granted sanctuary. It's why bin Laden got away in the first fucking instance, boss, it's the same bloody thing."

"Bin Laden was trying to stay hidden. It's quite obvious Ruslan isn't. Besides, Kostum is ethnic Uzbek, not Pashtun."

"Which doesn't mean he isn't beholden to Pashtunwali! If he was fighting the Soviets, he's an Afghani, not an Uzbek, he's going to be part of the culture. And if Kostum has given Ruslan Malikov sanctuary, then Kostum and all of his men are now duty-bound to protect him. That means that if I so much as try to harm a hair on Ruslan's head, they'll kill me."

"Then let's hope it won't come to that."

"I'm not seeing any other option!"

Crocker shot out of his chair as if on a wire, sending the seat banging back into the wall, beneath the window. "Then you'd damn well better find one!"

Chace caught herself, turned away, as embarrassed by his outburst as by her own. She heard Crocker moving, the chair being righted and replaced at the desk. She looked out the window at the late-summer afternoon, the traffic on distant Lambeth Bridge.

"This stinks," she said. "And it's wrong."

"No," Crocker said. "What was wrong was sending you into Tashkent in the first place so Seccombe could spring his MANPAD surprise on Sir Frances Barclay. That was wrong. What this is now is the endgame, it's the resolution of something that started in February—hell, of something that started five years ago. So, yes, maybe it's wrong, but it's not a different wrong, Tara, it's the same wrong it always was. And it's come home to roost, and I'm sending you to deal with it because I can't send Chris alone and because you know Ruslan."

"We exchanged perhaps five hundred words," Chace said.

"That's five hundred more than Nicky and Chris combined."

"Shit," Chace said emphatically.

"I concur." He held out his pack of cigarettes.

After a second, Chace grabbed one, then his lighter. She dropped the lighter back on his desk, then began pacing around the room.

"You have time to get Tamsin squared away?" Crocker asked.

"There's a Tristar scheduled out of Brize Norton at oh-four-twenty tomorrow morning, troops and supplies," Chace said. "Two stops before landing in Mazar-i-Sharif to resupply the support base there. Mission Planning is checking with MOD, and you'll have to get onto the Vice Chief of the Air Staff most likely, but unless someone suddenly comes to their senses, it looks like Chris and I will be on the flight. I've already called Val, Missi will stay with Tam until Val can come down to stay with her."

Crocker didn't speak for several seconds, then said, "I was thinking. If you ever need a sitter in a hurry, Jennie could watch her."

Chace stopped her pacing, staring at him in disbelief. "Did you just offer your wife as a babysitter for my daughter?"

"She taught nursery school for twenty years," Crocker said, lamely. "And there's Sabrina and Ariel, they'd be glad to help."

She narrowed her eyes at him. "Is this your way of apologizing for handing me a bag of shit?"

Crocker considered, then said, "I suppose."

"You realize that it's still a bag of shit?"

"Yes," Crocker agreed. "Yes, it most certainly is."

CHAPTER 35

23 August, 1055 Hours (GMT+5:00)

It had taken him a while to decide what he should do, how it was he could regain her favor, but when Zahidov hit upon it, the idea seemed so simple and so correct and so *right* that he was certain Sevara would have approved. He understood what she had tried to tell him in her office, that things had changed, and that he would have to change, too. She had accused him of being a thug, but if he could find a way to take care of her problem with Ruslan, and to do it right, to do it clear, without anything that could be laid at her feet, she would be able to forgive that. It wasn't simply a question of how he picked his targets, as she had said, but of where.

The fact was, Sevara needed him to be a thug. But she was also correct in that he could have been more discreet in the past. Before her father had died, discretion had been unnecessary, even counterproductive. It diminished fear, and Zahidov had always felt fear was his most powerful tool. Now, however, Sevara Malikov-Ganiev was President of the Republic of Uzbekistan, and discretion was more than required, it was mandated. Whatever he did to remove Ruslan would have to remain far away from her, and far from the prying eyes of the Americans and their allies.

In Tashkent, Zahidov couldn't be a thug. In Termez, perhaps. But in Afghanistan, where thugs were called soldiers or warriors and were as common as rocks, that was a different story.

So that was the solution, and it was all so very simple. He would take care of Ruslan for her once and for all, the way he should have done back in February, when he'd removed Dina. With the information he'd learned from Hazza, it wouldn't be that hard to find Kostum's stronghold, or that difficult to wait until Ruslan exposed himself enough to be killed. It could be done quite easily, he was sure of it.

What was harder to reconcile was his own participation in the matter. His preference was, of course, to go and do it himself. As a general rule, he preferred to handle these kinds of things personally. He told himself this was not because he enjoyed it, but rather because he was a perfectionist and wanted these sorts of things done right. It was why he participated in the most important interrogations, such as with Dina and, after that, the British spy.

But it was Wednesday morning before Zahidov resolved that, this time, he would have to delegate the task in its entirety. It would demonstrate to Sevara that he was *not* a thug, that he could keep his hands clean while still doing what needed to be done. Perhaps more important, it would allow him to remain in Tashkent, and close to her.

He remembered all too clearly the male secretary who had attended Sevara in her office, and he remembered, too, the way the man had looked at her.

So Zahidov would stay in Tashkent, close to Sevara, just in case she needed him. He would send Tozim and Andrei and some of Captain Arkitov's men to go south of Mazar-i-Sharif, to murder her brother.

He briefed them in his office at the Ministry of the Interior late Wednesday morning.

"Get yourselves to Termez by tomorrow morning," Zahidov

said. "I'll let Arkitov know you are coming. Take four of his men, whatever weapons and ammunition you will need, and then head south tomorrow night."

Andrei pinched his nose, cleaning his nostrils, thinking. Unlike Tozim, he was a deliberate man, more of a thinker, and it was one of the reasons Zahidov liked him. Smart, but not so smart as to be a problem, and with an easy handle for Zahidov to grab and control him. Andrei had money problems, most of it lost to online gambling, the rest to women.

"The crossing won't be easy," Andrei said. "They watch the border closely."

"Leave it to Arkitov to arrange," Zahidov answered, dismissing the concern. "He'll be able to bribe your way across."

"Where are we going?" Tozim asked.

"Someplace south of Mazar-i-Sharif. There's a warlord there, Kostum. He's harboring her brother."

Andrei and Tozim swapped glances, then looked back to him, nodding in understanding.

"This is the General? The one with Uzbek blood?" Andrei asked.

"That's him."

"If the brother's with him, he'll be well protected."

"That's why you'll take some of Arkitov's rangers with you."

"How much time do we have?"

"Not enough," Zahidov said. "So do whatever you need to."

Tozim sighed. "I wish we had one of those missiles. That would help."

"There were only the three, and all of them have been used," Zahidov said. "Arkitov will be able to give you explosives, anti-tank weapons, even, if you think they will help. As I said, use whatever you need, but make damn sure he's dead. I don't want a repeat of the river."

"We'll bring you his head," Tozim vowed.

Ahtam Zahidov thought he might like that, then shook his head.

"No, Tozim," he said. "We are not thugs."

CHAPTER 36

24 August, 1707 Hours (GMT+4:30)

It meant "Tomb of the Chosen One," the city named after the Great Blue Mosque that had been built both as a house of prayer and as a tomb to Hazrat Ali, the Fourth Caliph of Islam, son-in-law and cousin of the Prophet Mohammed. Sometime in the thirteenth century, as Genghis Khan had ravaged his way through Central Asia, the mosque had been buried in dirt in an attempt to preserve it— no small undertaking—and apparently those who'd buried it had been slaughtered and Mazar-i-Sharif razed, because the mosque remained hidden for over two hundred years. In the late fifteenth century, reconstruction of the city began, the ancient mosque was rediscovered, excavated, and restored.

It was, to Chace's knowledge, the first great slaughter in the city's history, but by no means the last. Much as Mazar-i-Sharif was known for its Afghan rugs and its fine horses, it was known mostly for death.

In the years leading up to Operation Enduring Freedom, when the *taleban* had been opposed solely by the Northern Alliance, Mazar-i-Sharif was a Northern Alliance stronghold. Or at least it was until 8 August 1998, when the *taleban* finally succeeded in sacking the city. By many accounts they came into town shooting anything that moved, including women and children, before deciding on a more systematic approach. They targeted the male members of the various ethnic groups that had lived in the city, specifically pursuing the ethnic Tajiks, Uzbeks, and Hazara. The Hazara saw the worst of this persecution—they were a Persian-speaking Shi'a sect, and thus anathema to the *taleban* regime. When all was said and done, at least 2,000 people had been murdered.

Compounding this infamy came another incident, this time at the Jala-i-Qanghi prison on 25 November 2001, where *taleban* and al-Qaeda fighters were being held by members of the Northern Alliance. What has been alternatively described as both an uprising or a riot broke out, and the prisoners engaged in a pitched battle with their captors, one that lasted several days until U.S. and U.K. Special Forces arrived on scene and brought with them air strikes that resulted in the deaths of over four hundred. Among the Northern Alliance forces had been two CIA officers. One of them, Johnny Michael Spann, was killed in the riot.

Chace remembered that fact especially, because it was the first time that the CIA had disclosed to the media the death in the line of duty of one of its officers. There was still some question as to whether the Company had actually *wanted* that information disclosed, or if it was released as the result of an overzealous White House Press Secretary. Spann became a martyr, the first American casualty of the War in Afghanistan. Apparently, there was now a memorial marker at the site of the prison, commending his soul to God.

These were the things Chace knew about Mazar-i-Sharif, the things she remembered about the city as she stepped off the RAF Tristar transport and onto the airport tarmac. The sun was already up, as was the temperature, yesterday's heat rising from the concrete beneath her feet. She heard Lankford cursing softly behind her as he fumbled for his sunglasses.

Mazar-i-Sharif, Chace thought. *An appropriate place to come for a murder.*

She'd traveled in the Islamic world enough to dress for it, with long sleeves and long pants, and a tan ball cap she could tuck her hair into to preserve her modesty. There were places where it wouldn't have been enough, and God knew that before the *taleban* had gone, Afghanistan had been one of them.

Just before 9/11, there'd been a job to come up in the south, in Kabul. Operation: Morningstar, and Crocker had refused to send Chace, dispatching instead Wallace and Kittering. Chace had been bitter about it at the time, but Crocker had been right; she'd have been useless on the ground then, a woman surrounded by the *taleban*.

It struck her as vaguely ironic that here she was now, herself Minder One as Wallace had been then, with Lankford, Minder Three as Kittering was at the time. Even the operation names— Morningstar and Sundown—seemed to parallel one another. She wondered if there was a significance in that, some subtle computer error back at Vauxhall Cross that needed to tie stellar phenomena and time of day with the word "Afghanistan."

With Lankford beside her, Chace fell in with the cluster of personnel moving off the airfield, toward the collection of prefab buildings and huts assembled in support of the military's operations. Mission Planning had arranged cover for them as a BBC team, with the MOD in on it, of course, just to make their entry into the country that much easier. They went through without a hitch, the RAF Staff Sergeant who reviewed their papers finding them both appropriately permissioned and permitted.

"First time to Mazar-i?" he asked as he handed Chace's passport back.

"Yes, it is."

"You've arranged for a guide?"

She looked accusingly at Lankford, who said, with convincing defensiveness, "I tried, I did, but everyone I contacted fell through on us."

Chace snorted, looked back to the sergeant, leaning forward slightly over his desk. "Do you think you could recommend someone? Or someplace to hire someone, perhaps?"

She watched the man struggle, trying to decide if he would focus on her chest or her face. Her chest won.

"If you'll wait a moment, miss, I'll see what I can do." He raised his gaze, earnest and helpful.

Chace gave him her friendliest smile. "I'd be very grateful."

The sergeant mumbled something unintelligible, then rose from his desk and headed around the corner, calling for one of the other soldiers. Chace glanced to Lankford, saw that he was looking at her, grinning.

"Wish that trick would work for me," he said.

"Try a tighter shirt," Chace suggested.

An hour and twenty minutes later they had not only a guide but a guide with a car, or more precisely, a taxi and its driver. They negotiated a fee of sixty pounds per day with a long-faced Pathan named Faqir, whose English was weak but "improving," and whose French was not quite as good. The first thing Faqir did was drive them to his home, to meet his family, and offer them dinner. There were seven, including Faqir, living beneath one roof in a modest but well-kept new house. As Chace stepped out of her boots, she found herself wondering how much of a windfall the British troops in the region had been for Faqir.

They accepted the hospitality offered them graciously, mindful of where they were and of the customs of the land, sitting around a low table with Faqir's wife, his younger brother, his father, and his three children, two boys and a girl. Chace let Lankford do most of the talking, remaining modestly silent, and from Faqir they got what was, without a doubt, a better briefing on the lay of the land than they had received in the Ops Room. She used the camera in her photo bag to take pictures, with permission first, of course, trying to get used to carrying the thing and using the bag. In it she had several rolls of film, as well as a loaded Walther P99 with two spare magazines.

The conversation was lively, Faqir and his brother, Karim, doing most of the talking. Faqir's eldest son was missing his left arm below the elbow, replaced with a prosthesis that didn't quite fit. Faqir explained that the boy had lost the arm during the Northern Alliance assault on the city post-9/11. The prosthesis had been courtesy of the British, though clearly the boy needed a new one.

Lankford used English and French alternately to eke out more and more information, little by little, until finally, as the meal was finished, he slid up to the name Ahmad Mohammad Kostum and gave it a nudge into the open.

"Have you heard of him? An Agence France Presse team spoke with him a month or so ago, and said he was quite friendly."

Faqir and Karim exchanged hasty words.

"I know this man," Faqir told Lankford. "But he is not . . . not . . . *très amiable*? Yes?"

"Perhaps it was someone else, then. The one we're looking for, he's not Pathan, but Uzbek."

"No, that is Kostum."

"We're hoping to interview him."

Faqir ran his fingers through his beard, pulling at it, apparently deep in thought. "Kostum is south, Samangan. Up in the mountain, Kargana, I think. Far away. Very dangerous to travel there."

"Hmm," Chace said. "Perhaps we should hire some guards?"

Faqir looked at her and smiled, putting an arm around Karim's shoulder. "My brother would make excellent guard."

"When can we leave?" Lankford asked.

"Oh, tomorrow, *in'shallah*," Faqir replied almost absently. "Tomorrow, yes. You can stay here, *dormez*. Tonight. Please stay with us here."

The table was cleared, leaving Chace and Lankford alone. Outside, they heard a muezzin call from one of the nearby mosques for the last prayers of the day.

"What do you reckon?" Lankford asked her.

"He knows where he is," Chace said. "Kostum isn't trying to hide. Few of these warlords do. It's just a matter of finding someone who can take us to him. Either Faqir can, or Faqir knows how to reach someone who can."

"He's just figuring how much to charge us, then."

"That, and how dangerous the trip is. There's still a lot of banditry about. Weighing his options."

"As long as they're not planning on robbing us."

"The least of our worries, I should think," Chace said.

Chace slept in the daughter's room that night. The girl was perhaps eleven years old, maybe twelve, and very shy. When Chace removed her ball cap, she made friends with her by leaning forward and letting the girl touch her hair.

The next morning she woke early, the daughter still asleep, and took the momentary privacy to open the camera bag and retrieve the Walther. She tucked the weapon into her pants, again at her waist, covering the butt with her shirt, then ventured out to find that Lankford, Faqir, and Karim were already up and waiting for her. They shared a quick breakfast, dried fruit and goat cheese, then made their way out to Faqir's cab, which was in actuality a rather sad and beaten Jeep Cherokee, dented and bruised by use. Karim and Faqir both carried Kalashnikovs, and Karim brandished his for their benefit, demonstrating his effectiveness as a bodyguard, before they climbed into the vehicle and set off.

They drove out of Mazar-i-Sharif, heading south on a freshly repaired road that served them well for fifteen kilometers before beginning a steady deterioration that ended some thirty kilometers after it began. They passed herds of goat and sheep, watched over by shepherds with Kalashnikovs dangling from straps at their shoulders. The lowlands surrounding Mazar-i-Sharif fell away behind them, and they began to climb. The greenery disappeared and the heat intensified, and the earth around them grew hard and yellow, as if baked one too many times. Chace supposed that it had been, at that.

Faqir switched over to four-wheel drive, and they began a torturous series of switchbacks, alternately climbing and falling, so Chace felt her teeth rattling in her skull. They passed clusters of houses, seemingly built of the same stone as the mountains. Once, Chace looked out her window into a valley, saw a shock of green below, dotted with buds of red and pink, small figures moving among the poppies, collecting the opium from the still-closed buds. A chatter of Kalashnikov fire rose up at them, warning them to mind their own business and move on.

The mountains began to rise around them, and beside Faqir in the front passenger seat, Karim fingered his own rifle, hunching forward, peering out the windows on all sides, leery of an ambush. Beside her, Lankford mirrored the action, and she was tempted to follow suit, but then saw no point in it. This was what Afghanistan was known for, this terrain, this unforgiving land, with its thousands upon thousands of places to hide, cliffs and ravines and canyons. If there was an ambush coming, they wouldn't see it until it was upon them.

After four and a half hours and perhaps eighty-odd kilometers of travel, the road ran out on them altogether. Faqir slowed, exchanging words with his brother, and beside her, Lankford leaned in to whisper in her ear.

"There're tracks," he said. "You see them?"

"Problem is telling how recent they are."

"Too right."

The Jeep stopped abruptly, and Chace looked up to see both Faqir and Karim raising their hands. Twenty feet ahead, four men had emerged from the boulders, all with their Kalashnikovs pointed at the car. All wore white knit prayer caps to cover their heads, some with vests over their heavy shirts, some with robes. For a moment, Chace feared they'd wandered into an ambush by *taleban* remnants, but their garb was wrong, for lack of a better word, not *devout* enough, or at least she hoped so.

One of the men, his beard beginning to show gray, shouted at them, and Faqir and Karim opened their doors slowly, and Chace and Lankford followed suit. Chace caught Lankford's eye as they moved to their own doors, shook her head slightly, warning him to keep off his weapon.

Fariq and the graybeard were speaking, the remaining three watching them, their weapons still leveled, but casually now, as if they'd quite forgotten they were doing it. That Karim hadn't been asked or ordered to drop his own gun gave Chace hope they were on the right track, and then she heard the name "Kostum" in the litany of Pashto spoken between them. Fariq gestured back in her direction with his right hand, then at Lankford.

"You want to speak to Kostum?" the graybeard asked Lankford. "For BBC?"

"That's right," Lankford said.

There was more conversation in Pashto, this time between Fariq, the graybeard, and two of the others. Finally the graybeard pointed to one of the gunmen, a younger one that Chace couldn't imagine as older than eighteen. The young man set off nimbly, up the trail, disappearing behind the boulders almost immediately.

Fariq looked at Chace, then at Lankford, saying, "We are waiting now."

"Will it be long?" Lankford asked.

Fariq shrugged, and the graybeard asked a question, then laughed at Fariq's response. The tension abated somewhat, muzzles dipping lower. Chace leaned against the Jeep, looking around, then down, examining the tire tracks in the dust. There'd been enough traffic along the path to make discerning different sets difficult, but at a guess, she had to think that at least four or five different vehicles had come this way fairly recently.

The heat had climbed past uncomfortable to sweltering, and she watched as Lankford removed his hat long enough to wipe the sweat from his brow. Minder Three was as fair-skinned as she, almost as tall, with straight black hair that added to his pallor. She thought he was already turning pink, and wondered if she was doing the same.

A pebble broke loose from above them, bounced down the

mountainside, and the graybeard and the others with him all turned, bringing their rifles up, only to see the young man they'd dispatched as a messenger returning. He popped out from behind the rocks higher on the ridge, calling down to them and raising his arm, and immediately, Chace saw both Fariq and Karim relax.

"You can go with them," Fariq said, addressing both her and Lankford. "We will go back now, before it is dark."

"You're leaving us with them?" Chace asked.

"Kostum sees you," Fariq said. "Safe."

He and his brother climbed back into the Jeep, starting the car once more.

The graybeard approached them, speaking and smiling at her, the others following, then coming around to get behind them. The graybeard indicated a direction, roughly the way the younger man had gone, then began leading the way.

With no other choice, Chace and Lankford followed.

They walked for another two and a half hours, and Chace suspected that the graybeard was setting an easy pace for their benefit, or more precisely, for hers. The narrow trail weaved around the rocks and scrub, summiting and then again descending. She wondered how the messenger had traveled the distance so quickly, then realized that he couldn't have, that he must have used a radio or a satellite phone instead.

Either that or this was one hell of a setup, and she and Lankford were about to find themselves truly in the middle of nowhere, in the dead wild on the western edges of the Hindu Kush mountains. If they were going to be done here, no one would ever find their bodies.

She doubted that was how this would end up—at least, not until journey's end. The graybeard had promised them safety, and she had to take him at his word. Al-Qaeda or Coalition, it didn't matter who; once the promise was made, it was kept until death.

Finally they descended to a ravine, following a narrow trail midway along its side until it opened to a canyon floor. Below, a walled stronghold—it was the only way Chace could think to describe it—rested at the bottom of the way, built back against the side of the mountain, almost built into it, in fact. A cluster of trees grew in the yard, their leaves shockingly green against the deadened tan, and beyond that, in the shade cast by the mountainside, a large, almost sprawling house. A minaret rose up from the corner of the wall, and Chace could see movement inside, a man with an RPG launcher on guard.

Along the sides of the canyon, Chace saw more guard emplacements, more of the vested and robed men, sitting or standing in what little shade they could find, rifles to hand. A mortar had been positioned high on the south side, far enough away that Chace couldn't readily identify the make and model, but it was a safe bet it had been recovered from the Soviet occupation. Chace didn't doubt the weapon was in working order, though she wondered where Kostum found the rounds for it.

They reached the canyon's bottom, approached the gates at the wall. The earth down here was hard-packed, and Chace could make out tire tracks, the signs of heavy vehicles that had traveled along the canyon floor. She hadn't seen a garage on their descent, and wondered where the vehicles were stored.

"Bloody hell," Lankford murmured to her as they approached, and she knew why he'd said it and what he was thinking. If they were going to kill Ruslan Malikov, they'd have one hell of a time getting out again after the deed was done.

"They're going to search us," Chace said. "Don't fuss."

"We're heavy."

"I know. Don't fuss."

Lankford nodded, his lips tightening, and then they had reached the gates. The graybeard called out in Pashto, and a response came back from behind the wall, and the man laughed, rested his Kalashnikov against the gate, and turned back to face them. He spoke pleasantly as he approached, holding out his hand, gesturing for the bags they were carrying on their shoulders.

Chace handed hers over, watched as Lankford did the same. The graybeard was joined by the others who had accompanied them, one of the others taking Chace's bag from him. For a moment, everyone's attention was on the bags, and Chace took the opportunity to smooth the front of her shirt, and in so doing, to shove the Walther fully down the front of her pants. It was uncomfortable but not intolerable, and she feigned shifting impatiently, trying to move the gun into a more concealed position.

The graybeard laughed, brought out the pistol Lankford was carrying, a Browning, showing it to him. Lankford shrugged, and the graybeard laughed again, then spoke to the man who'd been helping him. The man approached Lankford, clearly apologetic, and gestured for him to raise his hands. Chace watched as Lankford did so, submitting to the search. It was brief and efficient, but Chace noticed that the searcher avoided checking Lankford's crotch too carefully.

The two men searching her bag had finished, and were now looking from her to the graybeard, clearly uncomfortable. Graybeard indicated one of the two, then Chace, and the man sighed heavily, then approached her, shaking his head slightly as he did so. He gestured for her to raise her arms, and the discomfort on his face was blatant and so acute, Chace almost felt sorry for him.

He took all of six seconds to check her, doing her arms and legs first, before stealing himself to check her torso. He avoided actually touching the front of her body, and barely touched her back, more mime than actual search. He touched her hips, but nothing more, before stepping back and speaking to the graybeard.

Chace and Lankford were each handed their bags, and the gates opened, and they were allowed through into the courtyard.

"Kostum?" the graybeard said to them, directing his words primarily at Lankford. "Speak Kostum?"

"Malikov," Chace said. "Ruslan Malikov."

There was a sudden stillness in the yard, and the graybeard stared at her.

"No Ruslan."

"Stepan," Chace said. "Tracy."

"Trahcee?"

Chace pointed to herself. "Tracy."

From the shadow of the house stepped Ruslan Malikov, dressed in the vest and loose pants worn by so many of the others. Dirtier, wearier perhaps, wearing a white knit prayer cap and armed with a Kalashnikov of his own in his hand. He stared at her, as if trying to remember her face. He'd barely seen her in the light before, Chace thought, and a lot had been going on that night.

"It's good to see you, sir," Chace told him in English. "There are some matters we need to discuss."

CHAPTER 37

Uzbekistan—Tashkent—Residence of the U.S. Chief of Mission to Uzbekistan

25 August, 2011 Hours (GMT+5:00)

On 31 August 1991, Uzbekistan declared its independence from the disintegrating Soviet Union, following in the wake of the other newly forming independent states that surrounded it on all sides. In the grand scheme of nations and their histories, it hadn't been that long ago at all, and for that reason, the Uzbek Government still made a deal of the day, and of the event. This year, the thirty-first fell on a Thursday, and for that reason, the Ambassador's Reception in honor of Independence Day was scheduled at the end of the week prior, a Friday night.

Riess, who had been in the doghouse for so long now he'd almost grown accustomed to it, hadn't expected that his attendance would be required, or, for that matter, welcome. Ever since Garret had been relieved of post, Riess had existed in a sort of semiexile, under McColl's spiteful eyes. That Riess, too, hadn't been shipped back to the States continued to surprise him.

It had been Garret who'd spared him, of course, a last act of gratitude before departing public service. The Ambassador had taken sole responsibility for opposing the White House and supporting Ruslan Malikov, and in the end, even if Garret hadn't shouldered the load willingly, he'd have been made to bear it anyway. Garret was the Ambassador, and there were more than enough people back at State who had been willing to excuse Riess his indiscretions as a result. It wasn't an uncommon thing for a poloff to be taken under an Ambassador's wing, after all, and there had been some question as to how much of what had occurred had been of Riess' doing, rather than Garret's. FSOs were hard to come by, anyway. Measured against the difficulties in replacing Riess on post versus leaving him on station, it was easier to let him stay. His service record would reflect his involvement in Garret's plot, and Riess knew that his next posting would be a junior desk back in D.C.

He would live in the wilderness for a long time to come.

For that reason, Riess had thought he'd spend Friday night working late in the Pol/Econ Office, finishing up the cables back to State, and putting the final report on the latest in the stream of démarches. It had been midmorning before McColl had corrected his assumption.

"It's black tie," McColl had said, passing by his desk without stopping.

"Sir?"

"The reception tonight, at the Residence. It's black tie. I hope your tuxedo is clean."

"I wasn't aware you wanted me to attend."

"I don't, but the Ambassador does." McColl sniffed, pulling a handkerchief from his trousers and wiping his nose. "See if you can resist the urge to play spy this time, all right?"

Riess had nodded, hiding his anger and his frustration. The wound was still open, the sense of failure profound. Not one of the things he and Garret had set out to do had come to pass, after all. While Sevara had done an exceedingly good job of keeping her nose clean and of working with the U.S. in the past six months, Ahtam Zahidov was now DPM at the Interior Ministry. She kept him on a short leash, but the country's human rights record was still a far cry from anything that would earn kudos from Amnesty International or HRW.

Sometimes, Riess wondered if it had been an ill-conceived venture from the start, if Garret hadn't been totally unrealistic in his dreams of what they could do, what they might accomplish. Nations rarely changed overnight, and even when they did, there was always a price to pay in blood and pain. He had come to doubt that Ruslan would have made a better President of Uzbekistan than his sister. In all likelihood, for all of Ruslan's best intentions—if indeed his intentions had even been true—very little would have changed.

Things were improving in Uzbekistan under Sevara, little by little. There were still drugs coming up from the south, out of Afghanistan, but less and less seemed to be getting through these days. The new President had eased off the dictatorial enforcement of the government's version of Islam, permitting slightly more freedom of religion. The election that had seen her confirmed into office had been fixed, of course, but not so blatantly or arrogantly as her father's had been in the past. For the first time, the Oliy Majlis now seated an opposition party as well as Sevara's own. It was small to the point of being entirely ineffective, but it was more than her father had allowed. There was even an opposition newspaper available on the streets of Tashkent and Samarkand—overseen by government censors, but again, more than before.

So maybe it was the best Riess could have hoped for. This was the way diplomacy was supposed to work, incrementally and out in the open. Not behind the scenes.

He had grudgingly come to accept that, and in so doing had found a measure of peace that allowed him to sleep better at nights.

At least until those few times he saw Stepan, either in a photograph or in video footage, and he remembered the boy's mother, and what Zahidov had done to her. What Zahidov had done at Sevara's order, he was certain of it.

Maybe it was because Riess had known Dina Malikov, but he couldn't forgive that.

He couldn't let that go.

———

He arrived at the Residence forty-five minutes after the reception had started, showed his ID to the Marines who were pulling double duty as guards for the event. Since Michael "Mitch" Norton had taken over as CM for Garret almost five months back, Riess had had no reason to visit the Residence. In fact, the last time he'd been here was back in mid-February, in the wake of Dina Malikov's murder. Most of the lights had been out then, Riess remembered.

This time, though, the house was ablaze, as if it had caught what remained of the sunset for use indoors. Music reached him as he went through the doors and entered the enormous two-story entry hall. A string quartet from the Bakhor Symphony had set up about twenty feet from the door, playing an Uzbek piece Riess didn't recognize. The sound was amplified in the space, mixed with the voices speaking in Russian, Uzbek, and English. There were almost three dozen people in the hall alone, and Riess wondered just how many had been invited. The Residence, if he remembered right, could entertain somewhere in the neighborhood of one hundred and fifty before the RSO went into fits about lack of security.

Riess saw several faces from the Mission, moved through the hall exchanging brief but polite greetings. He made his way through to the salon, weaving through the crowd. The doors into the back garden were open, and he could see tables set up outside, more people seated there, dining on appetizers. He saw a couple of the DPMs, too, the Head of Consumer Goods and Trade standing with the DPM for Foreign Economic Relations, and McColl was among them, his wife chatting with their wives. Riess tried to move through unseen, edged his way out into the garden.

It was cooler outside, and quieter, though the noise from inside the Residence was still audible. Riess got himself a drink from the banquet table, a plastic bottle of mineral water, twisted off the cap, and drank half of it down. There were things he could be doing inside, things he should be doing. At a function like this, his place was to mingle and chat with the junior officials in attendance, to keep his eyes and his ears open for news that might be useful to the Ambassador and Political Counselor later.

He didn't want to. He didn't really want to be there at all. It had been at a party like this that he'd first met Ruslan and Dina, and it brought back memories, and again, he felt like a failure.

He sighed, steeling himself. What he wanted to do was irrelevant; what he needed to do, right now, was his job. He turned around to head back inside, then stopped, seeing Aaron Tower coming toward him.

"Chuck," Tower said. "Standing outside all alone?"

"I was about to head back in, sir."

The CIA man continued approaching, reaching out to the banquet table and snagging a bottle of water for himself. His smile was easy. Like almost all the men attending, Tower was in a tuxedo, though somehow he'd already managed to rumple it.

"How you doing?" Tower asked.

Riess pondered the question for longer than he intended. They'd spoken in passing a handful of times in the last few months, confined it to greetings and social pleasantries. If Tower had harbored ill will for what had happened, there'd never been any true sign of it. He'd been angry about the Ambassador's two-step behind his back, of course, but none of it had come back to hit Riess, at least not that Riess knew.

"I was thinking about Dina Malikov," Riess said.

Tower sipped from his bottle, nodded slightly. "You heard anything from Garret?"

"No, sir. Not since he went back home. I understand he's in the private sector now."

"Got himself a job as president of some college on the West Coast," Tower confirmed. "You look tired."

"McColl's keeping me busy."

Tower grinned. "I'll bet. Well, you're doing a hell of a job for him, Chuck. He might make DCM yet. Not here, of course, but on his next posting."

"Good for him," Riess said.

They drank their water in silence, looking back toward the Residence, through the open doors. More people were making their way outside from the den, drinks in hand.

"Coming out for the fireworks," Tower said. "Soon as it gets dark."

"Right."

A cluster of people emerged, surrounding the Ambassador and his wife as they escorted Sevara Malikov-Ganiev and her husband, Denis, the former DPM of the Interior, outside. Sevara looked stunning, Riess had to admit, the gown she'd chosen for the event just managing to straddle the line between alluring and reserved, but her beauty lay far more in the way she carried herself. She was supremely self-confident, and when she laughed at something the Ambassador's wife said, it carried over the grass to him. Riess wondered if Sevara had left her nephew at home for the evening.

"She didn't bring the kid," Tower said, reading his mind.

"Yeah, I was just wondering."

"She takes good care of him." Tower took another pull from his bottle, watching the Ambassador's party advance. "It's called guilt, Chuck."

"I don't think she feels guilty about anything, sir."

Tower turned slightly, looking him in the eye. "Never forget that they're patriots the way we're patriots, Chuck. They believe in their country the way we believe in ours."

"Not all of them."

"Most of them, then. Sevara Malikov-Ganiev is the first CIS leader who didn't cut her teeth under the Soviets, Chuck. Think about that. All the others, the old men, either they're former Communists or they came up under the Communists. But that woman's the new breed."

"It's not where she is now that bothers me," Riess answered. "It's what she did to get there."

"Don't think it doesn't bother me, too." Tower's eyes were on the Ambassador's group, now being seated at the largest table.

Riess didn't say anything.

"You know Ruslan's alive," Tower said, softer. "In Afghanistan."

Why are you telling me this? Riess thought. "No, I didn't."

"Somewhere in the Samangan. Or maybe the Bámiyán region."

Riess stared at Tower, who continued to watch the Ambassador speaking with Sevara. "Nice place to hide."

"If that's all he's planning, yeah," Tower said. "Let's hope that's all he's planning."

Behind them, they heard a series of cracks, then a hiss, and both of them looked up to see the first of the fireworks streaking into the sky. The explosives shrieked as they climbed, then went silent before bursting into a cascade of green, white, and blue, the colors of the Uzbek flag. Green to represent Islam, but officially said to represent nature and fertility, the life of the young country. White to represent purity in thought and deed. And blue for the waters that fed the cotton and the land, and to recall the fourteenth-century flag of the ruler Timur, who had claimed an empire from Samarkand, controlling the heart of the Silk Road.

The crowd broke into polite applause, and a second volley of fireworks started, chasing the first into the air.

"Come on, Chuck," Tower told him. "Let's enjoy the show."

It was when Riess was leaving, shaking hands with the last of the junior Reps, that he saw Zahidov. The Deputy Prime Minister of the Interior stood alone at the edge of the den, looking out into the garden. He had a drink in his hand, but it was untouched, and Riess followed his gaze to see that Zahidov was watching Sevara, still seated outside, now talking animatedly with the DCM.

Riess headed outside, wondering about Zahidov, thinking about the other color in the Uzbekistan flag, the one color that hadn't been represented in the fireworks display. On the flag, between the strips of blue and white and green, ran thin red lines. Red for blood.

He was sure that Zahidov had noticed it was missing, too.

CHAPTER 38

Afghanistan—Hindu Kush Mountains—
Samangan Region

25 August, 2105 Hours (GMT+4:30)

They were allowed to freshen up, which gave Chace the opportunity
to move the Walther into a less uncomfortable position at her
back, and then were given refreshment, food and drink. Ruslan
and Kostum watched them while Chace and Lankford ate, the two
men speaking quietly to each other in Uzbek. Both she and
Lankford were hungry and very thirsty, and they took the meal
eagerly, thanking their host.

Kostum seemed to approve of their manners and their gratitude. He was a short man, broad-faced, and like everyone else in
Samangan, had his own Kalashnikov ever close at hand. He asked
Ruslan what sounded like some very pointed questions at one point
while watching her and Lankford, and Chace had no doubt the
questions were about them, why they had come, what they wanted.

When the meal had been cleared, Ruslan said something to
Kostum that started a brief argument. Lankford cast a quizzical
glance her way, and Chace shook her head. Nothing in either
Ruslan or Kostum's body language indicated imminent violence.
Beyond that, she had no way of knowing what was being said.

"Your friend," Ruslan said in English. "He will go with Kostum."

"I'd rather stay," Lankford said.

Kostum spoke up, also in English. "No, tour, please. I give for you a tour."

"It's all right, Chris," Chace said.

"How you figure?"

"We're under protection, isn't that right, General?"

Kostum grunted. "Protect you, yes. But." He raised his right hand, index finger pointing down. "But my brother Ruslan protected also."

"We understand," Chace said. "Go with him, Chris."

"Right." Lankford unfolded his legs, getting to his feet. "Holler if you need me."

"Will do."

She and Ruslan watched as Lankford left, escorted by Kostum. They could hear his broken English as they went, explaining how he had come by the home, how it had been used by the Soviets first. Then Kostum's voice faded to nothing, leaving Chace and Ruslan looking at each other in silence.

Ruslan sat down opposite her at the table, refilled her glass of tea halfway, using the silver pot on the table, then poured a half glass for himself.

"Have you come to kill me?" he asked her casually.

In answer, Chace pulled the Walther from behind her back, then set it on the table between them. Ruslan reacted at the draw, then relaxed fractionally as her hand left the gun.

"It's an option," Chace told him.

Ruslan moved his eyes from the gun back to Chace. "You saved my life and my son's life, and now they send you to undo that. Why?"

"There are people, sir, who think you are planning to make trouble for your sister. That your intention is to gather men and arms and launch an attack, to try to force Sevara from power."

"And you, Tracy? You think this, too?"

"Kostum looks to have a lot of men, sir, and a lot of equipment. Whether or not he could move those men and that equipment north without being stopped by either the Afghan Army or the NATO forces between here and Termez, that's another question."

"You are not answering my question."

"No. It's not what I think."

Ruslan seemed surprised, tilting his head as he regarded her. "Then what do you believe I want?"

"Whether you wish to live out your life here in peace or whether you're planning something else, I can't say. It doesn't matter."

"No? Why does this not matter?"

"Because there are people who believe you threaten Sevara. Unless they're given a reason to think otherwise—and a compelling reason—they will continue to believe it."

Ruslan nodded thoughtfully, drank his tea, then asked, "How is your child?"

Chace smiled. "Very well, thank you."

"I hear my son is well also. You saved his life."

"I'm not sure that's true."

"It is true. You saved both our lives. If you had not taken us from Tashkent, Zahidov would have killed us. Perhaps not that day, but on a day to follow it. The way he killed my Dina."

Chace nodded, waiting.

"I do not want to be the President of Uzbekistan," Ruslan said. "In truth, I never did."

"You told the Americans—"

"My wife had been murdered, and my son and I were in peril." He was studying her, as if trying to measure her understanding of his motives. "You have a daughter. Is there anything you wouldn't do to protect her?"

"No," Chace said immediately. The question didn't merit any thought.

"If I went to the Americans and I said I would be their man, I thought perhaps they would protect me and my boy. Instead, they went to the British, and they sent you. If we had escaped Uzbekistan, I would have been content."

"You wouldn't have wanted to return?"

"Why would I?" He seemed perplexed by the question.

"It's your home."

"I would make a new home. Would it have pleased me to leave Uzbekistan forever? No. But that is a small loss to bear if measured against the loss of one's child."

"You want Stepan back," Chace said, realizing. "This is all about your son."

"I want Stepan," Ruslan agreed. "And I trust you to bring him to me."

Chace laughed softly, pulled the ball cap from her head, ran a hand through her hair.

"You are amused?" Ruslan asked.

"At myself. At them." She gestured vaguely in the direction she thought was the West. "My understanding is that Stepan has been well looked after by your sister, that Sevara takes very good care of him."

"That is my understanding also."

Chace looked at him, and for a moment saw the man as he had been when she'd found him in Tashkent. Sleeping alone in a bed made to be shared, on the side nearest his son's room. She felt the familiar ache in her chest that came with the reminder that Tom had died never knowing they'd made a daughter, never seeing Tamsin's face. She thought of how much she missed Tamsin at the best of times, when she wasn't traveling, when she wasn't away from home for days on a job. She wondered how much more it hurt to be Ruslan Malikov, unable to see his son for almost seven months now.

And he trusts me to bring him his son, Chace thought. *But we're not in the business of reuniting families, certainly not this one. Not unless the reunion could serve not just SIS' interests, but the Americans' as well.*

"Is there a phone?" Chace asked, finally. "A satellite phone?"

"Kostum has one. He does not like to use it, because the CIA, they can detect it. They send the Predator drones out, believing he is a terrorist. Kostum does not wish a missile shot into his home."

"No, I can see why he wouldn't." She leaned forward. "Could I use it? It wouldn't take long."

"I can ask him."

Chace nodded, fell silent and into her thoughts once more. Ruslan watched, frowning, as if trying to read her thoughts.

"Does Zahidov have another missile?" Chace asked. "Like the one I used, like the one that brought down the helicopter?"

"I do not know. Why?"

"There were four missiles in the set. Three have been accounted for, but the fourth is still missing. They were stolen here in Afghanistan, then sold again, probably several times. We think the last buyer was Zahidov, that's how they came to be in Tashkent."

"And you want this fourth missile?"

"We want it back."

Ruslan scratched his chin beneath his beard, turning away in thought. "Kostum might know something of this."

"Any information on the whereabouts of the last missile would be very helpful."

He arched an eyebrow at her. "Yes, but for whom?"

"We want the missile. You want your son. There may be a way to get both."

"You will help me?" Chace saw hope flicker across Ruslan's face.

"If I can."

"Why?"

Chace thought of the best way to answer the question, of all the things she could say, all the ways in which she could appeal to him, convince him. The plan stirring in the back of her mind was ill formed at this stage, but it had potential, she was certain. The problem was, it required not only her participation, but that of Ruslan, a two-year-old boy, and the Americans as well.

"Because you're not the only person that Ahtam Zahidov has stolen something from," Chace told him.

The name had an immediate effect on Ruslan. His expression darkened with encroaching memories. He looked at Chace again, and the realization was there, and then it was replaced with understanding.

"He had you? Tortured you?"

"I was fortunate," Chace replied. "Someone came for me in time."

"My wife was not fortunate."

Chace was silent.

"And you think there is a way to return my son to me, to appease my sister, and to punish Zahidov?"

"Perhaps."

"I would like to see them pay, Tracy. More than you can imagine." Ruslan Malikov bit back a laugh, more bitter than incredulous. "All right. I will listen to what you have to say."

CHAPTER 39

London—Vauxhall Cross, Operations Room

25 August, 1709 Hours GMT

Crocker blew into the Ops Room, cutting off Mike Putnam before he could announce his presence on the floor.

"What's happened?"

"Minder One on Sundown, sir," Danny Beale said, turning at the Mission Control Desk. "Satellite link, duration seven seconds. Open code, says she needs to speak with you, that she'll be calling back in . . ." He looked to the plasma wall, checking the clock there. "One minute, eighteen seconds."

"No idea where she is?"

"Presumably still in Afghanistan, sir."

"Is it a flap?"

"Didn't sound like it, sir."

"Then what the bloody hell is she calling in for?"

Putnam, Beale, and, at Duty Ops, William Teagle shrugged in unison.

"You're all useless," Crocker told them.

"Yes, sir," Beale agreed cheerfully. Bill Teagle snorted.

Crocker scowled, then moved to the coffeemaker. The coffee was foul, had probably been sitting on the burner since the shift had begun, seven hours earlier. He crossed back to Communications, took the headset Putnam offered, settling it over his ears just as the call came through.

"Crocker."

"*Hello, Dad,*" Chace said. "*There are birds in the air and they make big droppings, so I have to be brief.*"

"Understood."

"*Long-lost brother has been found, but he's not the big bad we've been led to believe. He misses his family and has been trying to get his sister's attention enough to talk about arranging a reunion. He assures me he has no interest in moving back home. In fact, he'd like to move to a different neighborhood altogether, one much farther west.*"

"You believe him?"

"*I do, yes, I think it's all about his little boy. And the fact is, he's staying with some overprotective relations. It's limited our options.*"

"You still have company?"

"*Baby brother is with me, yes.*"

"What do you want to do?"

"*The long-lost is only one part of it. The other concerns the four candles.*"

The reference was oblique enough that Crocker needed a second to translate. Then he said, "You know where the missing one is?"

"*According to our host, the set was sold intact. Which means the man who bought the first three still has the fourth.*"

"You trust your host's information?"

"*Apparently our host was interested in buying the candles himself at one point.*"

"Go on."

"*I'm wondering if a reunion between long-lost and his son couldn't be engineered to somehow bring that last candle out of its box.*"

"It's no use to us if it gets lit."

"*No, it's a delicate situation. But I think it's doable. Grandmother might be able to get a message across to big sister.*"

"I'm not certain our cousins are going to care for this," Crocker said. "It's not the definitive solution they wanted."

"If we can convince big sister, she can talk to the cousins. And I'm sure the cousins want all of the candles blown out as much as we do. Might be a way to make everyone happy."

"I'll talk to Grandmother. If we can arrange the reunion, we'll set it up through our house there—"

Chace cut him off. *"Long-lost has been very clear on one point, Dad. I'm to babysit. Seems he's reluctant to trust anyone else, especially after last time."*

"That complicates things."

"It does. I have your permission to proceed?"

"All right," Crocker said. "You'll be traveling north?"

"Soon as I can."

"I'll contact the family in Tashkent, let them know you're coming."

"Very good, sir. Have to go, I can hear the birds in the trees."

"Take care," Crocker said, but the line had already gone dead. He removed the headset, handing it back to Putnam absently, thinking for several seconds before saying, "Mike? Signal Tashkent, let them know Minder One is on her way there and should arrive in the next twenty-four to forty-eight as part of Sundown. Stress to Fincher that it's a Special Op, and that he's to follow her instructions. I'll want confirmation of receipt of signal."

"Very good, sir."

"Ask the Deputy Chief to meet me in C's office, Bill."

"Right away, sir."

Crocker headed upstairs.

"I'm not sure I like this," Alison Gordon-Palmer said.

"It gives the Americans what they want, just not in the manner they requested it. And if Chace is right, it'll bring us that missing Starstreak."

"Which would delight me to no end, Paul, if I felt there was the remotest chance that Kostum's intelligence on its whereabouts was in the least bit reliable."

"Chace reported that Kostum had been interested in buying the Starstreaks himself. It's plausible that he tracked their sale in the hopes of acquiring them at a later point. And if there had been four available, I can't imagine that Zahidov would have only purchased three of them."

"Plausible is not proof." She frowned, thinking. "We know that, as of February, Zahidov had three of the four missiles. Is it reasonable to think he's been holding the fourth?"

"Chace thinks so."

"I'm asking you, Paul."

"I trust her assessment."

"And all of this is contingent on whether or not Ruslan Malikov can be trusted to begin with. Simon?"

Rayburn, seated beside Crocker, closed his eyes for several seconds before opening them once more. "I think Malikov may be on the level, ma'am."

"Why do you say that?"

"There was never any intelligence to indicate that Ruslan had ambition to become President of Uzbekistan. It was only after the murder of his wife that he contacted the Americans to express interest. My understanding is that, prior to that time, it had been *Dina* Malikov who made contact with the U.S. Mission. So if he was running for President, he'd have been making a very late start, to say the least. I think Ruslan's overtures read more as an insurance policy for himself and his son than a legitimate grab for power."

C frowned at him, then at Crocker, weighing the decision. "And you want me to contact the Foreign Office, have them communicate with our Ambassador and pass along the message to Sevara Malikov?"

"It seems the best way to arrange things," Crocker said.

She nodded, reached for her phone, tapping the intercom to her outer office. "Danny?"

"Ma'am?"

"Contact PUS at the FCO, ask if he's available for a meeting soonest. I'll come to him."

"Very good, ma'am."

She tapped the intercom again, then looked back to Crocker. "What's Chace going to do in the meanwhile?"

"She'll proceed to Tashkent, then stand by for word as to where and how to collect the boy. Assuming it all goes through, she'll deliver Stepan to his father, then she'll arrange transport for both of them out of Central Asia to the West."

"Here?"

"It's unclear. But Ruslan's informed Chace that he has no desire to remain in the region."

"Have you spoken to Seale?"

"Not yet."

Rayburn nodded, already ahead of the conversation, and apparently in agreement with what C was about to say. "Probably best you let the CIA know Chace will be in Tashkent, and our suspicions about the fourth Starstreak. You don't want their COS getting jumpy."

"I'll speak to Seale right away," Crocker said.

The phone on C's desk rang, and she answered it swiftly, listened, then said, "Have my car brought around, please, Danny." Finished with the call, she rose, and Crocker and Rayburn followed suit.

"Seccombe will see me if I head over now," C said. "If he likes the sound of it, he and I will bring it to the Foreign Secretary."

"You'll sell him on it?" Crocker asked.

"The way you've sold it to me," she answered. "Paul, this'll be the second time Chace has tried to get Ruslan and his son out of the region."

"I know."

"Let's hope she gets it right this time."

CHAPTER 40

**Afghanistan—Hindu Kush Mountains—
Samangan Region**

26 August, 0623 Hours (GMT+4:30)

They were ambushed before they came out of the mountains.

The fact of the ambush didn't surprise Chace. What surprised Chace was who was doing the ambushing.

They'd departed Kostum's stronghold before dawn, the sky just beginning to lighten enough to show the blue behind the black, and the last hard stars starting to vanish above. Kostum had insisted on guiding them back to Mazar-i-Sharif himself, leading the convoy, and leaving Ruslan behind in the stronghold, to limit his exposure. Lankford would wait in Mazar-i, and Chace would continue on to Tashkent. Once everything had been confirmed, Ruslan would join Lankford and proceed to the exchange, to be reunited with the boy.

Kostum assembled a convoy for them of guards and vehicles, three of the seven automobiles that he kept in a substantial garage. Chace and Lankford traveled in the middle vehicle of the convoy. The car was a four-wheel-drive Jeep SUV, like Fariq's had been, but unlike Fariq's it was in much better condition. Kostum drove, with Lankford beside him, Chace seated in the back. In the bed of the SUV, the graybeard who had escorted them to Kostum's rode with them, Kalashnikov cradled in his lap.

They drove out along the base of the canyon for just over a kilometer before turning uphill, the vehicles following one another in a weaving incline that, to Chace, seemed impossibly steep. In the moments before they crested onto the road, she was certain their vehicle would topple over backward, and she envisioned herself being bounced around the interior of the car like a pinball as it fell, end over end, back to the canyon floor. It didn't happen, and after a moment spent to allow the follow car to catch up, the convoy resumed its journey, wending along the mountainside, descending again.

Then they were hit.

The explosion came first, just as the lead car began around a bend. Dirt and stone rained upward from the road, and the lead SUV veered wildly, fishtailing, then falling sideways, skidding to a halt, its wheels spinning uselessly in the air. Kostum slammed on the brakes, cursing. Chace didn't have to turn around to know that the same thing was going on in the car behind them; it was why the lead vehicle had been hit first, to stop the convoy dead in its tracks.

She lunged for the passenger-side door, shouting, "Out! Get *out!*"

An RPG streaked down from above, fired from higher along the mountainside, and as Chace tumbled out of the car she heard the lead vehicle exploding, and she thought she heard the screams, too. Then the chattering of weapons fire began, the sounds of glass breaking and metal tearing, Kostum's men desperate to exit their vehicles to return fire. Chace had been riding behind Lankford, and both had exited the Jeep along the downslope side, and she figured the drop had to be nasty, but it couldn't be nastier than staying on the trail, exposed. She leaped over the edge just as she heard another explosion, quieter than the RPG blast, what she thought was a grenade.

It was a good drop, almost fifteen feet on the vertical, just enough of an incline that she could get her feet down and lie back, sliding on the rough terrain, feeling the rocks and earth tear at her clothes. When she came to a stop beside Lankford, he was already up, with his Browning in hand. Chace struggled to her feet, reaching around for her gun, and discovered it was missing. She looked up, saw the Walther snagged on the rocks above her, where it had been stripped from her back during the slide. She started to curse, then heard a third explosion, and above, on the road, another blossom of flame rolled skyward as the follow car took another RPG.

"Well, this isn't good," Lankford remarked.

Chace ignored him. It was a turkey shoot above, she was sure: Kostum's men trapped in their vehicles, exposed as they exited, and the ambushers using the higher ground of the mountainside for cover. She couldn't see any movement, but she could hear the weapons fire, and it didn't sound right. Whoever had hit them wasn't using Kalashnikovs. The bursts were becoming more controlled, more measured. Whoever was up there killing off Kostum's men knew what they were doing.

"We can't stay here," Chace said.

Lankford nodded, checked around them, then indicated a direction farther downslope that would wind back around in the direction the convoy had come. Seeing no better route and no immediate reason not to take it, Chace began leading the way.

"Who do you think?" Lankford murmured, keeping his voice low. "Bandits?"

"Sounds too precise," Chace answered, eyes on the slope. Calling the terrain treacherous was generous, and the last thing she wanted was a broken ankle. "Sounds more like a military strike."

"Maybe the Americans? Removing another warlord?"

"Christ, let's hope not."

The gunfire from above had stopped, the last echoes bouncing away from them, off the mountains. Chace moved behind a substantial boulder, dropped down flat behind it.

"Sevara?" Lankford asked, dropping down beside her.

Chace shook her head. The timing didn't fit, it wasn't right. If this attack was courtesy of Sevara, she'd have had to move damn fast to make it happen. It hadn't been twelve hours since Chace had spoken to Crocker in the Ops Room. Even if C had gone straight to the FCO and the FCO had agreed and gone straight to the U.K. Ambassador in Tashkent, there hadn't been enough time. Not to mention that the Ambassador wouldn't have wanted to bother the President of Uzbekistan in the middle of the night about this.

"It's not Sevara," she said. "Got to be someone else. Question is who?"

"It's fucking Afghanistan," Lankford muttered, peering around the side of the boulder, the Browning held in both hands. "Take your pick."

For several seconds, neither of them moved, listening hard for more sounds of gunfire or combat. Nothing came back to them.

They couldn't just sit and wait. Two of the convoy vehicles had been taken out, which meant, as far as she knew, the third was still intact. If it was a robbery, even if it wasn't, whoever had sprung the ambush wouldn't just leave it there. If they decided to withdraw, they'd take the vehicle with them, leaving Chace and Lankford stranded.

And if they weren't withdrawing, it meant that it was a hunting party who had no intention of leaving the job half done.

She cursed the fact that she hadn't moved the Walther to a front-carry this morning. She still had her knife, a folding Emerson blade she'd scored off Kittering in a bet years before, but it required getting very close, and from the sound of the weapons they'd heard, she didn't think close would be terribly likely. She needed a gun of her own.

"We need to get back up to the road," she said. "And fast. Come around behind them."

"Don't want to get stranded," Lankford agreed. "Figure another hundred yards or so back the way we came, then up again?"

Chace nodded. "I lost my gun. You'll have to lead."

Lankford slid around her, swapping places. "Now," he said.

They broke from their cover, Lankford leading, running low and as fast as they could along the mountainside. The ground was covered with a layer of loose earth and rocks, and the footing remained dangerously uneven. Another chatter of weapons fire bounced off the mountains, but the echo made its direction impossible to determine, and Chace couldn't tell if the shots were targeted at them, at someone on the road, or at someone else, somewhere else altogether.

Lankford slid to a stop at the edge of a ravine running down from the road at almost ninety degrees, looked back over his shoulder to Chace. She nodded to him, and he wedged himself into the narrow space, using it to climb. Chace pushed herself into the crevice, trying to keep in cover as much as possible. She looked up toward the top of the ravine, saw Lankford disappear back onto the road, waited for him to reappear, to give her the signal that it was safe to climb.

Her heart was pounding, and she could feel perspiration running down her back, stinging the skin scraped during the downhill slide. Her mouth was dry from dust, it had filled her nostrils as well, and as soon as she realized that, she had to fight the urge to sneeze.

A pebble dropped down from above, bounced off her hand, and she looked up quickly to see Lankford sending hand signals her way, telling her to come up, and to stay quiet.

Chace pulled herself farther into the ravine, chimney-climbed her way to the top. Lankford pulled her the last three feet, onto the narrow road, and she rolled past him, then came up. They had backtracked far enough to be beyond the bend. Black smoke drifted from farther down the trail.

Lankford tapped her shoulder, started with the hand signals again. Three, no, six men, all armed.

Jesus Christ, six, Chace thought. *We'll have to draw them out.*

She pulled out her knife, unfolded it, and Lankford raised an eyebrow at her, as if to question her sanity, and the look she gave him in return begged for a better option. Lankford inhaled, then pointed to himself, then down the trail, to the bend. Chace shook her head, indicated herself and the same direction, then indicated Lankford and the rising mountain slope. He saw the wisdom of it immediately, nodded, and began climbing again.

Chace took a moment to give Lankford time, watching the bend in the road, where she was certain that, any moment, a member of the ambush team would appear. She risked a glance away to track Lankford's progress. He climbed swiftly, and as she looked he stopped ascending and began making his way alongside, following the bend.

There'd been a time, when Lankford had first joined the Section, that Chace had thought he wouldn't make it, that he wouldn't last. They'd done a job in St. Petersburg together, and he'd blown it, but then again, so had she, and Crocker had been quick to point that out when she'd returned to London complaining about Lankford's performance. She'd wanted him out of the Section, and Crocker had refused to terminate him.

At this moment, she was very glad for Crocker's refusal.

Lankford crouched down, working himself into cover behind another cluster of boulders, and she saw him glance back her way. She gave him a wait signal, then started along the road, the knife in her right hand, gripped for an upward thrust. She went as quietly as she could manage, which meant going slowly.

She heard voices as she approached the bend, and it took her a moment to understand the words being said as Uzbek, and not Pashto. So it hadn't been just a robbery, just an ambush. Whoever this was, they'd come looking for either Ruslan or Lankford and Chace. But Chace was positive it couldn't have been Sevara who had sent them; it didn't make sense. The timing simply made it impossible, not unless Sevara had somehow known that Chace and Lankford were with Kostum.

Just shy of the bend, Chace held up. She took two deep breaths, filling herself with as much oxygen as she could, adjusting her grip on the knife. One of the voices sounded close, and she hoped it was very close indeed.

She looked up above her, to where Lankford crouched waiting, watching, and gave him the go signal. He returned it, began moving again, this time much more cautiously. The idea was that he'd take a position around the bend but well above the road, preferably one in strong cover. As soon as he had position, he'd open fire, and Chace would move. She licked dust from her lips, waiting. He didn't have a lot of bullets. He'd have to make them all count, and she would have to work fast.

Then the Browning spoke, two shots, and someone cried out, and immediately upon that, there was shouting in Uzbek, and a barrage of return fire. Chace shoved off the slope and sprinted, the knife in her right held low and ready.

The lead and follow cars had been the ones to burn, their carcasses still smoldering on the trail as Chace came around the bend. There had been six in the ambush team, but Lankford had dropped one with his opening shots, and the man's death had achieved the desired result. Along the trail, the remaining five were all facing the mountainside, looking up, three of them with M-16s at their shoulders, laying down a spray that chewed the rocks and earth above. Their clothing was closer to Chace's and Lankford's than to what Kostum and the others sported, and it confirmed it for her that these men had come from Tashkent.

The nearest of them was fifteen feet away when she made the turn. He was firing furiously at the mountainside above, and Chace made straight for him. He caught her motion in his peripheral vision at the last second, too late, trying to turn toward her and bring the rifle down at the same time. The result was that he turned into her knife as she drove the blade into him, punching above his stomach, then thrusting up with all her might. His eyes bulged and his arm came down, and Chace yanked both her knife and the M-16 from the man, then dropped her blade, turning the automatic rifle in her hand.

There was a shout from down the road, one of the gunmen spotting her, and the firing stopped abruptly, and in that split second the scene seared itself into her mind. She tasted her sweat and the cordite and the acrid smoke from the two burning vehicles, saw the man she'd stabbed doubled over, facedown. She saw the others, the bodies of Kostum's men burnt and shredded by the RPGs or the M-16s, and the gunman that Chris had hit, flat on his back, his left leg tucked awkwardly beneath him, his blood sucked up by the thirsty earth. She saw Kostum himself, slumped against the rear wheel of the Jeep, bloodied and beaten, in the shadow of two men, each with pistols in their hands.

Two men she knew in her nightmares, one young and big who had grown erect at the sight of her pain and fear, the other older and shorter and disinterested to the point of inhuman. She saw Tozim Stepanov and Andrei Hamrayev, and they saw her at the same moment the other gunmen saw her, and perhaps they recognized her then, perhaps they didn't, but Chace had no doubts, and she understood it all in that fraction of a second; this hadn't been Sevara's doing, it had been Zahidov's, and that explained everything.

Then Lankford sprang up from behind his cover and laid down another three shots from the Browning, and another of the gunmen flailed and fell. Chace ducked low, scurrying behind the wreckage of the last car in the line. She brought the M-16 up, butt into her shoulder, and she fired. Tozim was turning and trying for cover but Andrei wasn't as fast, and the burst caught both of them, cutting across the big man's thighs and then tearing into the older man's belly. Both went down.

Chace advanced around the side of the wreck, M-16 still to her shoulder, and she saw the last gunman crouching in the road, by the Jeep, fumbling to reload his rifle, and she put a burst in his chest. He flopped back, gagging, as the M-16 went dry, and she dropped the rifle as the man fell silent.

The gray-bearded guard lay on his side near her feet, face half-missing from shrapnel, Kalashnikov still in his bloodied hand. She took the AK, began walking through the bodies, checking for life.

"All clear?" Lankford called from above.

"Clear," Chace shouted back.

She heard him begin to descend toward her, rattling more rocks down the mountainside.

Kostum stared at her from where he was slumped against the wheel, holding his right hand in his left, and she saw that one of them, Tozim or Andrei, had put a bullet through it. As she dropped to her haunches beside him, the General smiled at her weakly, saying something in Pashto through bloodied lips, and she nodded, then looked past him.

Andrei Hamrayev was dead, eyes wide and mouth opened, saliva visible at the corner of his mouth, mixed with his blood. But her eyes were on the bloody smear on the ground, tracking the path of a wounded man as he tried to crawl away.

"I'll be right back," she told Kostum softly, then stood, adjusting her grip on the Kalashnikov.

Tozim had made it halfway to the ruins of the lead car, dragging himself along, and from the amount of blood he was losing, Chace figured he didn't have much time. He was sobbing in pain, trying to keep the noise to himself, and she saw a pistol in his right hand, and she almost laughed. It was a Sarsilmaz, maybe the same one they'd recovered from her over six months earlier.

She watched him crawling, and his progress steadily degraded, less and less ground covered with what seemed greater and greater effort. Finally she set the Kalashnikov silently on the ground at her feet, then moved to him. She kicked him hard in the face with her boot, snapping him onto his side, then brought the same foot down on his gun hand, stomping. Tozim cried out, lost the grip on the gun.

She picked the pistol up, still looking down at him. There were tears of pain in his eyes. There was recognition on his face.

Chace thought of all the things she wanted to say, as she checked the pistol, and she was almost positive it was the same Sarsilmaz, and it was loaded and ready, so she pointed it at his right foot. She decided there were no words to say.

She pulled the trigger.

Tozim screamed.

She pointed it at his left foot and fired again.

He screamed again.

She tucked the pistol into the back of her pants, leaned down, and searched him. She found his wallet, a pack of American cigarettes, and a plastic lighter. She took all of them, shoving them into her coat pockets. Tozim was babbling at her, a torrent of Uzbek, and when she began dragging him, he tried to break her grip with his bloodied hands. There was almost no strength to his efforts, and when he did finally succeed in grabbing Chace's wrist, she punched him in the face before she resumed pulling him.

"You don't ever touch me again," she told him.

She was aware of Lankford watching her, crouched beside Kostum, trying to tend his wounds, as she manhandled Tozim to the side of the trail. The slope was severe here and she looked back down at Tozim Stepanov, and she knew he was begging her not to do it, not because she understood his words, but because she heard the garbled desperation in them.

It was another sound from her nightmares, and she would have relented then, she would have spared him then, if only, in her dreams, it hadn't been her doing the begging.

"Try to land on your feet," Chace told him, then pitched him over the edge.

They reached Mazar-i-Sharif seven hours later, and three hours and fifty-four minutes after that, Chace was on a NATO-staffed helicopter bound for Termez.

CHAPTER 41

Uzbekistan—Tashkent—438–2 Raktaboshi, Residence of Charles Riess

27 August, 0917 Hours (GMT+5:00)

Riess answered the door in his T-shirt and boxer shorts, the day's first cup of coffee in his hand. He'd have been better dressed if he'd been expecting a caller, but it was Sunday morning, there was no need for him at the Embassy, and he'd been up late the night before, watching the better part of a television series he'd ordered off of Netflix, concerning cowboys with extraordinarily foul mouths. He'd dreamed of saloons and the Wild West, and perhaps because it was still so fresh in his mind, the first words out of his mouth when he saw Tracy Carlisle at his door were "Cock-sucking motherfucker."

"Delighted to see you, too," she replied, and then Tracy Carlisle, whose name wasn't really Tracy Carlisle, smiled at him like they were old friends. She smiled like she was happy to see him. "May I come in?"

Riess thought about that for a moment, wondering what in hell he'd tell Tower when he was no doubt asked about this, then sighed. He moved back and waved her in, then looked out over his tiny yard to the street, seeing nothing that alarmed him. He almost laughed.

As if I'd know what I'm looking for, he thought.

"Coffee's fresh," he told her as he moved past, heading back to the kitchen. "I get it from a friend in San Francisco. The beans, I mean, not the coffee."

"Coffee would be delightful," Tracy Carlisle said, following him.

"You take cream? Sugar?" Riess opened the cabinet, pulled out a mug.

"Black, like my heart."

"Uh-huh."

He set the mug down, filled it from the pot, handing it over. She was looking at him with what he interpreted as vague amusement, and as he stood there, she ran her eyes the length of him, down, then up, then smiled again.

"I just woke up," Riess explained.

"So I see."

Riess returned the look, and had to admit he liked what he was looking at. She wore jeans and a black T-shirt, a loose linen jacket, tan. He could smell the hint of soap, saw that her hair appeared to still be damp. Fresh from the shower, he assumed, and straight to his doorstep, but God only knew why. Then he saw what looked like dried blood on the toes of her boots, and had to wonder if the shower had been about more than just hygiene.

"You probably shouldn't be here," he told her.

"I need a favor."

"I don't do those kinds of favors anymore."

"This one won't cost you anything. You might even like it."

Riess laughed tersely. "You'll forgive me if I don't believe you."

"It's a favor for Ruslan, Charles."

"Ruslan's in Afghanistan."

"At the moment, yes. He wants his son back. I'm here to fetch him."

"Oh, God," Riess said, his mind filling with visions of the Dormon Residence, where the President lived, erupting in flames, collapsing from a missile strike. "The way you fetched them the first time?"

Carlisle laughed. "You really think I'm a monster, don't you?"

"I don't know what to think of you," Riess answered honestly. "You show up on my doorstep with bloodstains on your boots, telling me that you need a favor but it's okay because it's semiofficial, and it's about Ruslan, and it's about Stepan, and the last time I saw you, you were headed for the shower and I was headed out the door. So, no, Tracy, I don't know what to think of you."

"My name's Tara," Tracy Carlisle said.

"What's this favor?"

Tara-not-Tracy tasted the coffee he'd poured for her, and he saw her expression brighten in pleasant surprise. She took a second gulp before saying, "Late yesterday afternoon, the U.K. Ambassador met with President Sevara Malikov to discuss the possibility of returning Stepan Malikov to his father's care. The Ambassador carried a message from Stepan's father, the details of which are largely unimportant, but the gist was this: Ruslan gets Stepan back, Sevara never has to worry about her brother again. Ruslan will stay far away from her and Uzbekistan, and that will be that.

"President Malikov, after some deliberation, agreed. The exchange is set for the day after tomorrow, early Tuesday morning, to take place at the border crossing in Termez. Sevara will make the visit ostensibly to examine the security at the border and to meet with the United Nations staff for the relief effort. Ruslan will await on the Afghan side of the bridge, and Sevara will deliver Stepan on the Uzbek side. A third party will escort the boy across the bridge to his father."

"Sevara's agreed to this?"

"So I've been told. You seem surprised."

Riess shrugged. Nothing about Uzbekistan surprised him anymore. "So far I'm not hearing anything about a favor."

"I'm coming to that." Tara-not-Tracy finished her coffee, then placed the mug on the counter. She reached into an outside pocket of her coat, removing two wallets, both leather, one black, the other tan. She set them beside her empty mug. Riess noted that the tan one was spattered with dried blood, too.

"I took these off two men in Afghanistan," she told him. "They were reluctant to part with them."

Riess hesitated, then picked up the black wallet, flipping it open. An ID card stared back at him, printed in Uzbek, and declaring the bearer an officer of the NSS. The officer in question's name was Tozim Stepanov. He glanced up from the wallet to her, and she inclined her head, indicating that he should examine the second one as well. He did so, reading the ID of a second NSS officer named Andrei Hamrayev.

"You got these off two men in Afghanistan?"

"About eighty klicks south of Mazar-i-Sharif, in fact."

"What were two NSS officers doing eighty klicks south of Mazar-i-Sharif?"

"I believe they were leading a hit squad in an attempt to kill Ruslan Malikov. The hit squad consisted of four Uzbek Army soldiers in addition to these two."

"You have proof of this?"

From the another pocket, Tara-not-Tracy removed a zip-top plastic bag. She jiggled the bag before handing it over, causing the metal contents inside to ring lightly. Riess took the bag.

Four sets of dog tags.

"The question is, of course, whether or not President Malikov authorized this hit squad or not," she told him. "Given that this was an armed incursion by one sovereign nation upon another, I find that doubtful, especially considering Uzbekistan's cozy relationship with your government, not to mention your government's relationship with Afghanistan. I find it very doubtful indeed."

"She didn't," Riess said. "Not in a million years, not just to kill her brother."

"Then someone else must have initiated the action. And considering the nature of the IDs in those wallets, I think we both know who that someone would be."

"I should bring this to the attention of my Ambassador."

"I'm certainly not about to tell you how to do your job," she said cheerfully. "But if you were to ask me, I'd say that was a fine and proper course of action."

Riess considered her again, her smile, her manner. "You're setting up Zahidov?"

"Am I?"

"At the least, President Malikov demands Zahidov's resignation. At the most, he disappears and the body is never found."

Something flickered behind her eyes, almost like a shadow moving from one darkness to another.

"That would be a pity," Tara-not-Tracy said. "That would be a great pity indeed."

Ambassador Norton was reluctant to meet with Riess on such short notice, but the mention of an Uzbek incursion into Afghanistan dispelled that reluctance quickly. They met in the Ambassador's office at the Embassy, and while it certainly wasn't the first time that Riess had been inside it since Norton took over for Garret, he was again surprised by how little things had seemed to change. Only the photographs on the glory wall and the desk, and even those were remarkably similar to the ones that Garret had hung.

Aaron Tower attended the meeting as well, which surprised Riess initially, but in retrospect he thought it really shouldn't have. Tara-not-Tracy was SIS, he knew that, and this time the Brit was here on official business. COS Tashkent would have been notified, if not via London, possibly via Langley. It helped Riess in making his case, because Tower was able to provide some missing details— namely, about the Uzbek soldiers, where they'd been stationed, and how Zahidov most likely arranged things.

"And we're positive that President Malikov didn't authorize the action?" Ambassador Norton asked when Riess and Tower had each finished their respective reports. He gazed at them over the top of his glasses.

"As positive as we can be," Tower answered. "It flies in the face of everything President Malikov's done since winning the election, Mitch, especially the steps she's taking to improve relations with the Afghanis. Add to that the fact that she's been working extremely hard to stay on our good side, easing up on the religious restrictions and press issues, even reining in the NSS."

"She still has a long way to go," the Ambassador pointed out mildly. "But I take your point. It'd be a hell of a risk for her, sending troops into Afghanistan, at least like this."

"I think we're safe in assuming that it was done without her knowledge or permission."

"Then I'll put a call into her office at once, see if she isn't available to discuss this potential diplomatic incident." The Ambassador sat back in his chair, removing his glasses. He folded them closed, but held them in his hand. "Mr. Riess."

"Yes, sir?"

"You're aware the British have brokered a deal between President Malikov and her brother?"

"I am, sir."

"Have you been to Termez before?"

"Three times, yes, sir, though not in the last eight months or so."

"You're about to make it four times. I want the handoff audited. Anything goes wrong, I'd like to have an American eyewitness to what transpired. Get yourself to Termez by tomorrow night. The exchange, as my colleague at the British Embassy has informed me, is set for eight o'clock Tuesday morning. I want you there."

"How close should I get?"

"Close enough that if anything goes sour, you'll be able to give me an accurate report, son." The Ambassador seemed vaguely annoyed. "You know both Ruslan and the boy, or so I understand."

Riess glanced to Tower, who shot him a grin in return. "I'll recognize them, yes, sir," he replied.

"That's all I need. I'll make sure McColl knows where you're going and why; you won't have to worry about him." The Ambassador swept the hand holding his glasses across his desk, indicating the wallets and dog tags. "Thank you for bringing this to my attention so promptly."

Riess took that as his cue to exit, said, "Thank you for your time, sir," and started out of the office.

"Mr. Riess," the Ambassador called after him. "One more thing."

"Sir?"

"No cloaks and daggers for you." It seemed to Riess that the Ambassador was rather pointedly not looking at Tower. "I've got enough people with those running around this country already."

"I understand, sir."

Tower hefted himself from his chair, saying, "I'll walk Charles out, if you don't mind, Mitch."

The Ambassador grunted assent, already reaching for the phone. Tower settled a hand on Riess' upper arm, guiding him the rest of the way out of the office and through the secretarial bunker, into the hallway. They cleared the security doors, and Tower dropped the hand, walking alongside Riess silently until they reached the entry hall.

"Didn't get a second roll in the hay?" Tower asked him.

"I don't think she was that interested."

Tower stopped, tucking his hands into his pockets. The CIA Chief of Station was looking toward the exit, brow creasing, apparently in memory.

"No, I don't imagine that she was," he said after a second, then moved his look back to Riess. "Mind if I ride down to Termez with you?"

"You need to audit the handover as well?"

"Something like that."

"But not quite like that."

Tower grinned by way of answer, then said, "DPM of the Interior Zahidov's going to have a very bad day tomorrow, I think."

"Couldn't happen to a nicer guy."

"If you knew half of what I know, Chuck, you'd be drinking a toast."

"You think she'll do it? Have him killed?"

"President Malikov? He was useful to her before she won the election, but he's a major liability now. Her problem is, he knows too much. All of her dirty laundry. What do *you* think?"

Charles Riess remembered the videotapes Dina Malikov had passed to him of the NSS interrogations, of the men and women, young and old, beaten and brutalized to coerce confessions. He remembered Dina Malikov, the photographs of her naked body, the burns, the shattered bones, the blood. He remembered the story, that Zahidov had sent for Ruslan so he could identify his wife's body, a request that might have been interpreted as Zahidov warning Ruslan, but was in truth nothing more than pure sadism.

"I think it couldn't happen to a nicer guy," he said.

CHAPTER 42

Uzbekistan—Tashkent—488 Chimkent

27 August, 2022 Hours (GMT+5:00)

He didn't sleep at the penthouse on Sulaymonova any longer, not since Sevara had become President. She kept the penthouse, of course, and Zahidov knew she still used it on occasion, but now she lived in the Residence in Dormon, and it had taken him time to understand that she had no intention of letting him join her there. Not unless he could convince her otherwise, convince her that the love between them was still strong, and still served their nation's best interests.

It bothered him no small amount that Ruslan's brat slept there instead. Sevara doted on the child, inasmuch as she had the time to dote on anyone. But why she seemed to focus on her nephew, on the boy's comfort and happiness, he didn't understand.

So Zahidov lived alone, in his apartment on Chimkent, an apartment appropriate for a man who was both the Deputy Prime Minister of the Interior and the Head of the NSS. It had everything he could want, all the finest fixtures and appliances and electronics, from a flat-panel television to a mighty stereo and a king-size waterbed. It had an eighteen-hundred-dollar secure refrigerator made especially to hold his collection of fine wines, and even a secret room with a cabinet safe, where he kept those things most important to him and his job: the documents used for blackmailing other members of the Government, his favorite handguns, some of his money—half of it in gold, the other half in American dollars.

It had everything he could want, except her, and Zahidov knew he was lovesick, and despised himself for being so weak. But he couldn't change his heart.

He hated coming home.

And this was why he was inattentive when he parked his newly purchased Audi TT in the lot that night, returning from the Interior Ministry, where he'd spent the day, waiting for word from Tozim or Andrei. This was why he didn't notice that the lights at the entrance to the stairwell from the car park seemed to be out, and why he wasn't as careful as he perhaps should have been when he exited his car and then leaned back in to reach across to his briefcase, sitting on the passenger's seat, to retrieve it.

"What is it with you and Audis?" a woman asked Zahidov softly, from behind.

He reached for the pistol at his hip, trying to straighten as he did so, but before he could even begin the move, he felt pain slicing across the backs of his legs, the Audi's door slamming closed on him. He cried out in surprise as much as in pain. Then the door opened and slammed a second time, and this time there was only pain in his cry.

Then he was being pulled from the car, felt the cement of the garage floor on his face and a dull pain from his front teeth, and he knew he'd been pulled free, that he'd hit the ground face-first. A flower of light bloomed behind his eyes, blinding him with its intensity, and he tasted blood in his mouth and felt its warmth running over his face. Hands stripped the pistol from the holster at his hip, then his other gun from his ankle.

Nausea surged through him, rising from between his legs, and he couldn't breathe, and the blossom of light faded to points that swirled and weaved in front of his eyes. He saw the woman then, and despite his disorientation and his suffering, he made the connection. This woman here and the British bitch spy then, the cunt that Tower had stolen from him, the one Sevara blamed him for. She had him by the throat, yanking him toward her, and he saw the flash of her hand, his pistol in it, and she struck him across the mouth with the barrel. His front teeth, already loosened from his impact with the garage floor, broke free in his mouth, and he tasted a new flood of blood.

She slammed him back against the Audi, still holding him by the throat, choking him. With her other hand, she shoved the end of his pistol against his lips, pushing hard, harder, until he had no choice but to open his mouth. The barrel cut across his raw gums, and he couldn't keep himself from voicing his pain.

At that, her face came in close to his, her hands gripping him, and he felt her hair brush his cheek. He lost track of his pain in the swell of sudden fear, certain from her expression alone that she was about to pull the trigger.

"Remember me?" she asked. "Remember what you did to me?"

Zahidov stared at her, his vision still swimming with light and, now, with tears.

"Answer me," she said, softly.

He nodded.

"Good," she said, sounding satisfied. "Tozim remembered me, too, just before he died. Andrei, though . . . Andrei never had the chance before I killed him."

She paused, to let her words sink in. The barrel of the gun was cutting into the roof of Zahidov's mouth, and he felt his gag reflex trembling, and he was afraid what would happen if he couldn't control it.

"Ruslan's alive," she whispered. "He wasn't even in the convoy, you dumb fuck. You blew it, and anytime now, sweet little Sevya's going to know you blew it, too. The President's going to know you sent soldiers into Afghanistan to murder her brother, and that you did it without her permission. And what do you think she's going to do?"

The urge to gag was unbearable, and Zahidov's head came off

the roof of the car involuntarily, and she slammed him back down with the gun. He couldn't breathe, her figure blurring from the tears in his eyes.

"What do you think she's going to do with an embarrassment like you, Ahtam? With someone as crude and stupid as you? You're way past your expiration date, mate. What do you think she's going to do now that she's found a way to make peace with her brother?"

The spy, the British cunt spy, smiled at him then. She smiled.

Then she pulled the gun from his mouth, and at the same time, drove her right knee into his crotch.

Zahidov crumpled, pitching forward to the floor once more. This time he managed to get an arm in front of himself to cushion the fall.

"I don't need to kill you, Ahtam. Do you know why?" The woman's slightly husky voice came from above him. "Because your little Sevya's going to do it for me. You're already dead, Zahidov. You just haven't stopped breathing yet."

Then he felt his ribs threatening to break, and the little air he'd recovered fled, and the bright light consumed his vision a second time. This time it grew, and he heard the roar of a river, deafening in his ears.

When he came back to himself, he was on his side beside his car, still in the garage, still in darkness. He didn't know how much time he'd lost, and, for a moment, he didn't know how he'd come to be there, like this.

Then it came back to him, the pieces falling together, and he remembered the woman. He remembered the pain she'd given him. He remembered what she'd said, and he knew it had been true. Tozim and Andrei had failed, and Sevara did not abide failure.

Instead of proving Sevara wrong, he'd proven her correct. Worse—he wasn't merely a thug. Now she had no choice but to see him as a dangerous and out-of-control one as well.

He pulled himself to the side of his car, then used the open door to struggle to his feet. Halfway up he had to stop, doubling over and emptying the contents of his stomach onto the floor and his shoes.

Zahidov caught his breath, ran the back of one arm across his eyes. He'd lost his glasses, he had no idea where they were. He wiped the tears and blood from his face, touched his leaking gums with the tip of his tongue. He hurt more than he'd ever before, not just his body, but his heart.

It was over between Sevara and him. Everything else crashing down, and the finality of that, more than anything, took root and sparked his rage. He could surrender to her and face what would happen next, or he could run.

He fumbled around inside the Audi, found his keys and his briefcase. He shut the door, staggering toward the stairs.

He would run. Leave the country, go far away. He had connections, he could disappear. Moscow first, Paris after. He would leave and recover and then, when he had the strength and the people, he would repay this British spy. He would repay her in kind, and he would make her wish with all her soul that she had pulled the trigger on him, and he would make her know what he'd done to her in the interrogation room at the Ministry had been a mercy.

He reached his apartment, moved to unlock the door, then realized the lock was broken and the door itself ajar. He pushed inside, then stopped cold, staring at the wreckage. His apartment had been tossed, as viciously and thoroughly as any search he himself had ever performed. The lock on his wine refrigerator had been smashed, the bottles shattered, and even the cabinet in the secret room had been opened, his weapons strewn across the floor, his money gone.

Zahidov felt the rage boiling through him, and he thought about all the things he should have done to the British spy when he'd had the chance. All the things he would do to the cunt if the opportunity ever came to him again.

He heard her voice again in his head.

She's found a way to make peace with her brother.

Zahidov steadied himself against the broken gun cabinet, turning slowly, then sinking to the floor, the pain in his body momentarily forgotten. What had that meant? Sevara had made peace with her brother? Would she do such a thing?

And how? Would Ruslan be returning to Tashkent? Would Sevara allow him back into the government? Why would she? It made no sense; to do so would make her vulnerable.

The brat, Zahidov thought. *It must be the brat, she's giving the boy back to her brother, that must be it.*

Somehow, Ruslan was playing on his sister's sentimentality, on her guilt. Somehow, Ruslan had convinced Sevara to return her nephew to him, and she had foolishly agreed.

He had to find out how.

He had to find out how, and when, and put a stop to it, once and for all. A stop to all of them, to Ruslan, and Stepan, and the British spy who had been so very, very stupid in leaving him alive.

CHAPTER 43

Uzbekistan—Tashkent—U.K. Chancery, Commercial Section

28 August, 1034 Hours (GMT+5:00)

"He's in motion?" Andrew Fincher asked Chace.

She flopped into the chair opposite his desk in the tiny office that served as the heart of Tashkent Station, then nodded. Officially, Fincher was listed as Vice Consul of Trade Development to the Mission, which would have earned him a larger office, if it had been true. Instead, he was shunted off into a ten-by-ten room that Chace suspected had initially been used as a closet. It made the Pit back at Vauxhall Cross look spacious.

For all that, though, she was surprised to find that Fincher appeared to be remarkably at ease with himself.

"You have the documentation?" she asked him.

"Everything'll be ready by this evening, before you leave for Termez. They had some trouble finding a picture of the boy, as you might imagine." He slid an envelope across the desk to her, thick with paper. "Tickets for the four of you."

"Routing?"

"RAF from Mazar-i-Sharif as far as Turkey, from there commercial, Frankfurt, then London."

"Roundabout."

"Best we could manage on such short notice. Easier if you're willing to fly out of Tashkent."

"That's not an option."

"No, I know it isn't. I've spoken to the COS here in Tashkent, a man named Tower, you may remember him."

"Should I?"

"Tower remembers you. He's the one who pulled you from the Interior Ministry last February."

"Then I owe him a very large drink."

"I suspect you owe him a case's worth of very large drinks," Fincher said, opening one of the drawers at his desk and producing a small radio set and wireless earpiece. "Anyway, Mr. Tower is now at speed regarding the search for the Starstreak, and he'll be present in Termez, with support, ready to move on Zahidov if he shows up. London is officially viewing it as a joint operation."

Fincher handed the radio and earpiece over to Chace, who took them, examining both quickly.

"Frequency's been set. Your call sign for the operation is Shere Khan, Stepan's is Mowgli, Tower's is Baloo, Lankford's is Bagheera, and the Uzbek team's is the Ikki. You can guess who's Kaa, and no, before you ask, I didn't pick the names."

Chace laughed, making note of the frequency being used so she could share it with Lankford, before tucking the set away in the pocket of her jacket. "Seems like we're all covered, then."

"I can come down to Termez, if you'd like."

"I appreciate the offer, Andrew, but if it all goes to hell, I'd rather have you here." She considered him for a moment, then added, "Head of Station seems to suit you."

"Or I suit it," Fincher agreed. "Took a while to warm to it, though. Hard not to view it as a demotion."

"I understand."

Fincher tugged his right earlobe. "I'm better here. A better fit, I think."

"It wasn't personal, Andrew, you know that."

He shook his head. "Not with you, no. But I'm not looking forward to seeing Nicky or Chris come through here anytime soon."

"They'll behave themselves. I'll make certain of it."

"Yes, I know you will." Andrew Fincher smiled. "And you? You're doing well?"

"Well enough at the moment."

"I still think pushing Zahidov is a mistake. You're taking an awful risk bringing him into play like this, especially if he does have that last Starstreak."

"There was no sign of the missile when I tossed his apartment," Chace replied. "Which means he's hiding it someplace else. I had to do something to force him to bring it out into the open."

"All the same, you can't be certain of what he'll do next. And Ahtam Zahidov angry with a MANPAD is an extremely risky proposition."

"I am aware." Chace cocked her head, brushed hair out of her eyes. "You're keeping an eye on him?"

"Until an hour ago."

"What happened an hour ago?"

"Hayden says he went to the airport. He lost him there."

"Zahidov shook Bobby?"

Fincher shrugged. "Bobby can't say if it was intentional or not, but given that President Malikov has the entire NSS out looking for him, I'd suspect so."

"Which means that if your Number Two lost Zahidov at the airport, Zahidov certainly didn't leave from the airport," Chace said.

"On his way to Termez, then?" Fincher asked.

"Let's hope." She smiled at him, then leaned forward. "Can I use your coms, Andrew? I need to contact Minder Three, tell him we're still running."

"By all means." Fincher turned in his chair, reaching to the side of the desk, to the cabinet that seemed to run the length of the wall, opening the center doors. He rose, switched on the secure telephone unit inside, then edged his way between the cabinet and the desk, passing Chace. "I'll wait outside."

"Thank you."

She waited until he'd left and shut the door after him before rising, moving to the cabinet. The space was cramped enough that she ended up perched on the desk to use the phone. She dialed into the Ops Room first.

"MCO."

"Chace. I need a patch to Lankford in Mazar-i-Sharif."

"Stand by."

Chace waited, listening to the regular click of the secure line as Alexis Ferguson put her on hold. She imagined her at the MCO Desk, trying to connect with Lankford via satellite phone to the FSB in Afghanistan. It would take several minutes, and Chace tried to be patient, but waiting led to thinking, and right now thinking too much would lead to second-guessing, and she didn't have time for that.

But as one minute folded into the next, and she waited for Alexis or, preferably, Lankford to come on the line, she couldn't stop herself. It wasn't the fact that Sevara had agreed to the exchange that bothered Chace. She had been dutiful enough in following the news of Uzbekistan back in London that she had months ago noted President Malikov's attachment to the boy; it didn't take a degree in psychology to understand that it was guilt as much as affection that kept her nephew in Sevara's care. It wasn't even that the Americans had agreed to allow the exchange to proceed; in the final analysis, Sevara Malikov's decision was the only one that mattered, certainly in matters of Uzbekistan's security.

Winding up Zahidov, though, that was the gamble, just as Fincher had pointed out. The goal had been to drive Zahidov out in the open, Starstreak in hand, by giving him a target too irresistible to ignore. But if Zahidov could actually make it to Termez with the missile, the variables increased again, because all he would need to do was wait until she, Ruslan, and Stepan were all together in the exfil vehicle, whatever it might be. As long as Zahidov had clear line of sight—and she'd seen the bridge from the air, coming across the border from the British FSB, just three days prior, and there was plenty of clear line of sight—he could park anywhere within five kilometers and easily take them out from there.

She prayed to God that Tower would find Zahidov before Zahidov found his shot.

There was a click on the telephone, and then Lankford's voice. *"Tara?"*

"I'll make it quick, Chris," Chace said. "Delivery is set for oh-eight-hundred in zone tomorrow morning. Father is to present himself at your side of the bridge for eyeball verification by big sister's team, then I take the package across."

"And where am I?"

"With the father, as planned."

"Then we have a problem," Lankford said.

"What?"

"Kostum told Ruslan about the ambush. He's afraid his sister will have someone take a shot at him if he comes to the border."

"It's his son, he needs to be there."

"That's what I told him, but he's adamant. And he may have a point. All President Malikov needs is one warm body who knows what he's doing with a rifle and her brother is a thing of the past. He's planning on staying in Mazar-i-Sharif until we reach him with his son. Kostum's supposed to ride out with me in his stead."

Chace chewed her lower lip for a moment. "I don't like it."

"Didn't think you would, but I've been trying to convince him to change his mind since he informed me of the decision when he got into town last night, and he won't budge."

"Where is he now?"

"With Kostum and some fourteen of Kostum's men, holed up in a house about twenty minutes from the FSB. You want me to, I can bring him back here, you can try to talk to him."

"That'll take you an hour, at least."

"And he may not come. He's twitched, Tara. He's certain Sevara has it in for him."

Chace cursed softly, then said, "Right, can't be helped. But he needs to be ready to move as soon as we hit town. And you'll need to arrange transport to and from the Afghan side of the bridge."

"Already taken care of it."

"You'll need a radio from the FSB as well." Chace gave him the frequency and the call signs, and Lankford repeated the information without comment.

"I'll contact you as soon as we're in position." The line crackled slightly, whispering static into Chace's ear as Lankford took a moment. *"And the other factor that's now in play?"*

"He's been given a nudge in the right direction."

"Risky."

You don't know the half of it, Chace thought. "Too late to turn back now."

"Understood. See you tomorrow."

"I sure as hell hope so," Chace replied.

CHAPTER 44

Uzbekistan—Surkhan Darya Province—Termez

29 August, 0319 Hours (GMT+5:00)

Zahidov held a handkerchief to his mouth, then checked the white cloth, seeing spots of blood mixed in with his saliva. His gums were still leaking, raw to the touch of his tongue, raw like the rest of him. It gave him resolve, made him all the more certain of what he had to do.

Not for her any longer. This was for him now.

Captain Oleg Arkitov was watching him with both suspicion and concern. "Tell me again?"

"One helicopter and a pilot, that's all I need. Everything else, I've already taken care of it. But I need the pilot and the helicopter quickly, Captain, I must be in position before dawn."

"And at dawn—"

"It may not be at dawn, but I think soon after, certainly before noon. Then I do what I have been sent here to do, and your pilot, he takes me in the helicopter east, drops me in Tajikistan. Then he returns to you. That's all."

"I am hesitant, Ahtam." The yellow light shining from the ceiling of the captain's office made Arkitov's expression seem even more troubled, his frown more profound. "Even if everything is as you say, it puts my pilot at great risk."

"My risk is far greater, Oleg. This is for our country. I'm appealing to you as a patriot."

"So you have said." Captain Arkitov motioned to the radio resting on the shelf beside the door. "But you can't be here officially, Ahtam, the President replaced you this morning with her husband. It was on the radio."

"I've explained that she needs to preserve her deniability." Zahidov ran his handkerchief across his mouth a second time. "That's why she did it. You know the President's relationship with me, how close she and I are. Think about it."

"I had heard you were no longer as close as you had been."

"The President of Uzbekistan must be discreet."

Arkitov nodded slightly, accepting that. "But if what you're telling me is true, Ahtam, why haven't I received orders from my superiors? Or from the President herself?"

"Deniability. The fewer who know about this, the better."

"But surely, after it's done, the whole world will know. You'll be a wanted man."

"Which is why your pilot must take me to Tajikistan. You see how I look?" Zahidov indicated the bruises on his face, his injuries. "I had these wounds done to me by my own men, Oleg, to build my cover. If I am willing to lose my front teeth for this, you think I would not sacrifice even more for our country's future?"

Arkitov studied him, and Zahidov knew he was marking all of his many bruises and cuts and scrapes, and he tried to keep anything from his expression that might betray him.

"No, you are a patriot, Ahtam, you always have been," Arkitov agreed. "I accept that, I accept what you are telling me."

"Then you know what I need. We must get moving, I don't have much time."

Zahidov rose from his chair, stopped as he realized that Arkitov had made no move to follow.

"I don't have much time, Oleg," Zahidov repeated.

"Yes, I understand that. And I understand that you are willing to sacrifice yourself for this, that Uzbekistan's future is more important than your own. But I now must think about mine, Ahtam. If I do this, I will be blamed, accused of aiding and abetting you."

"You do this for your country."

"No, *you* do this for your country. I need more."

"You don't deserve that uniform," Zahidov spat, furious.

"Perhaps not, but I am the one wearing it, and you, as you have said twice already, do not have much time."

"How much do you want?"

"For this? For an act that will end my career and possibly shame me and my family? A million American dollars, I think."

"I don't have a million dollars."

"Of course you do. Just wire one of your banks in Switzerland or the Cayman Islands to transfer the cash to my account."

"We don't have time for this!"

Arkitov folded his hands across his stomach, then stared patiently at Zahidov. "I do."

Zahidov swore, thought about killing the man right there, where he sat, but knew that if he did, he would never get what he needed. And the money, he would need the money if he was to run and to stay hidden, he would need the money to survive. One million dollars, that was perhaps an eighth of what he had hidden away, but it rankled, being blackmailed in this way.

Arkitov pointedly looked at his wristwatch.

Zahidov cursed a second time, then moved to the desk, grabbing the telephone and dialing quickly, from memory.

"Give me the account number," he spat at Arkitov.

Arkitov leaned forward, pulling a piece of paper from the yellow Post-It pad on his desk, and taking up a pencil. He scribbled out a sequence of numbers, and the name of his own bank in Bern.

It took Zahidov another twelve minutes to arrange the transfer, and three minutes more for Arkitov to confirm that the funds had made their way to him. Satisfied at last, the captain hung up the phone, rose, and smiled at Zahidov.

"Now, my friend," he said, "let's see about that helicopter for you."

CHAPTER 45

Uzbekistan—Surkhan Darya Province—
Termez, "Friendship Bridge"

29 August, 0747 Hours (GMT+5:00)

One journalist had labeled it the "Checkpoint Charlie of Central Asia," and as Riess rode with Tower out toward the bridge in a filthy white Daewoo van, he thought the description both appropriate and painfully ironic. Termez itself had seen recent construction and renovation, attempts to repair and bolster its infrastructure in support of both the relief and military operations that were staged from the town. But as they left the city and followed the road down to the river, the already sun-blasted landscape dropped around them, flattening out as it ran to the water. Patches of scrub and weeds clung to the land, barely surviving.

The van rattled as they crossed the railroad tracks, continuing down toward the foot of the bridge. Approaching, Riess could see concrete slabs painted white and black positioned as roadblocks, in an attempt to channel and control approaching vehicle traffic. The bridge itself was ugly, pure Soviet in execution, white-painted steel and concrete, and the paint was faded and peeling. On the Uzbek side, the final access to the crossing was blocked by a gate, closed and electrified, another part of the fence that marked the border. Armed guards in camouflage uniforms patrolled the immediate perimeter.

Tower parked the Daewoo some fifty feet from the bridge, off the side of the road, and killed the engine. Riess wanted to question that decision. Not yet eight in the morning, and already the temperature had passed miserable and was well on its way to kiln. The air conditioner would be a relief.

"It'd overheat the engine," Tower said, answering the unasked question, and then lowering their respective windows. The scent of fouled water wafted into the car.

Riess turned around in his seat, reaching into the rear for the backpack he'd brought along. From within he removed his binoculars and his camera, a Konica Minolta digital camera with telephoto lens. Tower had brought his own binoculars with him, but when Riess turned back, he found the other man had also brought a radio with him, and was raising it to his mouth.

"Ikki, this is Baloo, over," he said, and Riess stared at him, because Tower had transmitted in Uzbek, not English.

"Baloo, this is Ikki."

"How do you read?"

"Five by five."

"Over and out," Tower said, and then set the radio on the dashboard, above the wheel.

Riess continued to stare, and Tower seemed not to mind, now producing his own set of binoculars. The CIA man raised his optics and looked out toward the bridge.

Seeing no explanation for his behavior forthcoming, Riess followed suit, pointing his lenses down to the foot of the bridge. There was movement from the guards, what he read as agitation, and two of the soldiers were beginning to make their way toward the Americans, slipping their rifles off their arms. But as Riess watched, he saw the pair turn even as the distant shouting made its way to him through the still air. An officer was running toward the soldiers, waving an arm angrily. The officer pointed at them in the van, and the soldiers snapped to attention, then ran hastily back to their posts.

The officer watched them go, then cast a glance back in the

Americans' direction. Through the binoculars, Riess could make out the man's expression, the confusion and displeasure. Whatever he'd been told, whatever orders he'd just passed on to his men, he was uncomfortable with them.

Riess looked away to check his watch. Nine minutes to eight. He was raising the binoculars again when Tower spoke.

"West side. Blue Lada approaching, along the fence."

Panning swiftly right, along what Riess thought of as a service road running parallel to the fence, was a late-model Lada, its wheels kicking up clouds of dust. He lost his view of it for a moment as it passed between him and one of the squat bunkers near the shore, but reacquired it immediately as it emerged, slowing to a stop. He could make out the driver behind the wheel.

"Hell," Riess said. "I should have seen that coming."

"Yeah," Tower agreed, raising his radio once more. "You probably should've."

CHAPTER 46

Uzbekistan—Surkhan Darya Province— Termez, "Friendship Bridge"

29 August, 0753 Hours (GMT+5:00)

Chace had left Tashkent just after midnight, arriving in Termez on a flight run by a charter service contracted to the British Embassy. The Lada had been waiting for her at the airfield, and Chace didn't want to know who Fincher had bribed to get it for her, and she made a mental note to thank him when she had the chance. He may have stunk as a Minder, but she was rapidly gaining new respect for the man as an HOS.

She'd spent the night in the car, which wasn't to say she'd slept in it. Rather, she'd driven out to a vantage point overlooking the bridge and parked there for almost an hour, watching the floodlights on the Uzbek side as they ran along the length of the fence and shone off the water, trying to understand the terrain. She'd emerged from the car a few times to smoke the cigarettes she'd taken from Tozim's body, to stretch her legs, to try to calm her mind. Neither the nicotine nor the movement had done the trick.

Before dawn, she'd started the Lada up again, easing it back into Termez proper, such as there was a Termez proper, and then made her way west, out of town, watching the odometer and counting out five kilometers. She'd passed the airfield the Germans were using, then turned back again, toward the Amu Darya, until the fence had once again become visible in her headlights, then reversed the direction. She'd passed plenty of places where a man could hide with a MANPAD, and it didn't give her much comfort that she'd seen no signs of the same.

The sun had been rising by then, at which point she abandoned the hunt. She had no guarantee that Zahidov was going to make a play to begin with, and searching for him in the dark had been just shy of foolish. Had she found him, there would have been a very good chance that he'd have seen her coming first. And if he did have the MANPAD, she suspected that both herself and the Lada would have ended in a fireworks of light and flames.

For the best, then, that she lie low for the time being.

She'd driven down to the river, parking in time to watch the remainder of the sunrise. The warmth had reached her through the car's windows, and despite herself, she'd dozed off, thinking of home and Tamsin and wondering for how much longer she could expect Val to come when called. If it was hard on Tamsin for Chace to go away, it was, in its fashion, harder for Val. Val knew just enough to be aware that, like Tom, Chace might not return.

She'd started awake with a panic then, afraid she'd blown the pickup. By her watch, she'd slept for all of two minutes. She'd gotten out of the vehicle again, smoked more of Tozim's cigarettes, and by then it was time to get moving. She'd climbed back behind the wheel, turned the nose of the car east, and found a dirt track used by the border guards that took her back to the bridge.

She saw the van, parked on the slope, before she stopped the Lada. Her watch read exactly nine minutes to eight, and when she looked south, across the river, she could see the Afghan checkpoint. She shut off the engine, leaving the keys in the ignition, then pulled out the radio set, fitting the earpiece into place before switching the unit on and slipping it into her pocket. She climbed out of the car, and had to fight to keep herself from gagging. The air was rank from the river, fouled with a mix of chemical runoff and human waste, an odor that invaded the sinuses and clung to the back of her throat. The heat augmented it, and Chace hoped the stench wouldn't be quite so strong from the bridge, but expected that it would be worse.

There was a crackle in her ear, and then a man's voice, gravelly and American. *"Shere Khan, this is Baloo, respond."*

She keyed her radio, watching the activity of the guards on the Uzbek side of the bridge, walking their patrol along the concrete roadblocks. "Go ahead."

"Proceed as planned."

"You have a location on Kaa?"

There was a hiss in her ear as the CIA man, Tower, paused while keeping the line open. *"We have overwatch on Kaa. You may proceed as planned."*

Chace moved around to the hood of the car, only marginally relieved by the news. She glanced again to the van parked off the main road leading to the bridge, saw the flash of a lens. She wondered who was in the vehicle with Tower, handling the camera. Perhaps it was Riess, and she liked that idea. Riess had been a part of it the last time; it seemed right to her that he participate again now.

"Should I say cheese?" she asked. "Where's Bagheera?"

Lankford's voice broke in, choppier than Tower's had been. *"We're in position, holding."*

She turned her attention back to the bridge, following it across the river to the Afghan side, over a kilometer away. She could see movement at the checkpoint, vehicles, but without optics had no hope of making out Lankford and Kostum's position.

"Understood," Chace said.

"Here they come," Tower said.

Chace heard the cars coming along the main road first, the helicopter second, coming from the center of Termez. The helo looked like another Sikorsky, or perhaps it was the same Sikorsky that had pursued her when she'd run in the Audi, she couldn't be certain. She watched as two Uzbek Army Jeeps led a black Mercedes-Benz, a third Jeep following, off the main road at the summit of the slope, where the helicopter was lovingly settling to the earth, blowing clouds of dust as it came in to land. For a second time, she wished she had optics, could confirm that the boy was in the helo.

The Sikorsky's rotors slowed, then stopped, and she saw activity around the Benz, figures moving, passengers shifting from the helo to the car. She imagined, rather than heard, the sound of the vehicle doors slamming, the engines starting, and then the convoy was moving again, the two Jeeps again taking the lead back to the road, the Benz close behind. The line of cars started down the road, past the parked van, toward the foot of the bridge.

Trying to ignore the stench from the river, Chace began walking toward the checkpoint.

CHAPTER 47

Uzbekistan—Surkhan Darya Province— Termez, "Friendship Bridge"

29 August, 0754 Hours (GMT+5:00)

The windows on the Benz were tinted, and Riess couldn't see who rode inside as the minor motorcade passed them, making its way down to the bridge. He'd switched to the camera, and as soon as the last Jeep passed, put the lens back on Tara-not-Tracy, now walking slowly along the access road to the foot of the bridge. She was wearing the same clothes he'd last seen her in, right down—he suspected—to the blood-spattered boots, but with the addition of sunglasses.

"You going to tell me what's going on?" Riess asked as he took another two shots, then moved his focus to the Benz, now coming to a halt perhaps ten yards from the checkpoint.

"You know what's going on," Tower said.

"What's with all the code names? Who's Bagheera?"

"He's with Shere Khan, on the Afghan side. Take a look across the bridge."

"And Kaa? Ikki?"

"Just take a look at the Afghan side, Chuck, tell me what you see."

Riess panned the lens from the Benz, its doors still closed, to the foot of the bridge, then followed its line across the muddy water of the river to the Afghan side, settling his view again on the cluster of newly painted buildings there. He'd maxed the telephoto and could make out figures, but not much detail. There was a fair amount of activity, Afghan border guards at their posts, and an SUV of some sort, what he thought might be a Jeep Cherokee, parked near the gate at the far side of the bridge. A thin black-haired man in civilian clothes was speaking to one of the border guards, another man with him, Afghani from the way he was dressed. Riess could make out a smear of white around the man's right hand, as if it was wrapped in a scarf or otherwise bandaged.

"I've got two men, one of them could be Ruslan if he's gone native," Riess said.

"It's not Ruslan," Tower told him. "He's in Mazar-i, lying low."

Riess lowered the camera slightly, puzzled. "He thinks it's a setup?"

"He's got a reason to be paranoid."

"*Is* it a setup?"

"Yeah, but Ruslan's not the target."

"Who's Ikki?"

Tower grinned. "Uzbek military. I was talking to an Army captain named Arkitov."

"About?"

"Security. Eyes on the road, Chuck, c'mon. You're supposed to be documenting this for the Ambassador."

Riess bit back more questions, brought the camera up once more, locating Tara-not-Tracy again, still strolling toward the Uzbek checkpoint. He snapped off three pictures in quick succession.

"One for the scrapbook?" Tower asked him.

"Bite me," Riess said. "Sir."

Tower laughed.

Riess next moved the camera to the bridge, where the border guards had all come to attention. The soldiers in the Jeeps had already leaped down, fanning out to form a perimeter. For a second, it seemed vaguely silly to him, until Riess remembered where they were, and that to the right sniper with the right rifle, one thousand meters could be considered an easy shot to make.

An aide jumped out from the front of the Benz, running around to the passenger door and opening it, and Riess snapped another set of photographs as he watched Sevara Malikov-Ganiev emerge from the vehicle. She'd adopted a more conservative style of dress since ascending to the Presidency, wearing a tailored business suit that Riess guessed was linen, her hair up, sunglasses hiding her eyes. She took the man's offered hand, and Riess saw that she was holding a small, plush lion in her other. Once she was out of the car, she turned back to help Stepan out of the vehicle.

The boy looked confused, Riess thought, and frightened. Stepan had been dressed in what Riess supposed were his best clothes, very Western, and for a moment he had to wonder if Sevara ordered from Baby Gap or the like. Stepan sported toddler chinos and a blue button-down shirt, and he tugged after him in one hand a backpack, made for a child at least five years older than he, with the image of a Disney character large on its outward side.

As Riess watched, Sevara crouched down on her haunches, setting her free hand on the boy's shoulder, speaking to him, and he could tell she was trying to reassure the boy. She clasped his hand and began walking him toward the bridge.

Riess moved his view back toward the Lada, trying to find Tara-not-Tracy, and saw that she was already halfway to the checkpoint. Her pace hadn't increased. Three soldiers were heading toward her, and they intercepted her with twenty feet to go, two of the three leveling their weapons at her.

"What the hell . . . ?"

"Easy, Chuck. It's a search, that's all."

Tower was right, and Riess snapped off another half-dozen shots, filling the camera's data card, as the third soldier searched Tara-not-Tracy, hands efficiently running over her body. He swapped cards quickly, and when he brought the camera back up again, she was continuing toward President Malikov and Stepan, the soldiers following after her.

Tara-not-Tracy slowed, then stopped, leaving ten feet between herself and Stepan, President Malikov, and the foot of the bridge.

"Moment of truth," Tower said.

CHAPTER 48

29 August, 0758 Hours (GMT+5:00)

Chace stopped, keeping her hands loose at her sides, palms open.
She could see that the boy had been crying, and she thought about
how often she'd seen him cry, and she sincerely hoped that this
would be the last time. He held the oversized backpack by its
strap. It only made the child seem smaller, more vulnerable.

She smiled at Stepan, and, without looking away from him,
said, "Madam President."

"You're the one taking him across?" President Malikov-
Ganiev's English was flawless.

"Yes, ma'am."

President Malikov tilted her head, issued an order in Uzbek.
One of the soldiers, an officer, stepped forward, and she spoke to
him again. The officer saluted, then sprinted back to the foot of the
bridge, calling out. Chace looked away from Stepan long enough
to confirm what the officer was doing, watched as he was handed
a set of binoculars and then climbed up onto one of the checkered
cement roadblocks to get a better view of the Afghan side.

Chace put her attention back on the child, the boy still watching her warily.

"Hello, Stepan," she said to him in English. "My name's Tara. I don't know if you remember me."

Beside the boy, President Sevara Malikov-Ganiev tilted her head slightly, her eyes hidden behind her sunglasses. Then she looked down to Stepan and spoke in Uzbek softly, and the contrast between the voice she'd used to issue her orders to the soldier and tone she used on the boy was stark.

Stepan stared up at Chace, then spoke in response, so softly that, even if it had been in English, she doubted she'd have understood it.

President Malikov turned back to Chace, saying in English, "My nephew says he remembers you. You're the one who tried to take Stepan and his father out of the country back in February?"

"Yes, ma'am."

"You're the one that Ahtam tortured."

Chace looked at President Malikov-Ganiev, trying to read her expression behind the sunglasses, her tone. There was nothing in it one way or another to indicate approval of what had been done to her, or disapproval.

"One of the many," Chace answered, and her voice was flat.

From the bridge, the officer came jogging back, delivering another salute and then speaking quickly. President Malikov-Ganiev frowned, and the officer stepped back.

"Where is my brother?" the President asked Chace. "Why can they not find him?"

"He's waiting in Mazar-i-Sharif, Madam President. He was afraid of another attempt on his life."

President Malikov-Ganiev's frown went from annoyance to anger, and she hissed softly, cursing. Chace caught the name "Ahtam," but nothing else.

"So you bring Stepan across, and then you two join my brother in Mazar-i-Sharif," the President said to Chace.

"Yes, ma'am."

For a moment, President Malikov-Ganiev didn't move, and

Chace was certain the woman was staring at her from behind her sunglasses. Then she bent back down to Stepan and spoke to him again. Stepan responded, just as quietly as he had the first time, and President Malikov-Ganiev seemed to repeat herself, her voice gaining an edge. The boy looked up at her with wide eyes, then to Chace, and then to the bridge.

The President turned to Chace. She held out the stuffed animal in her hand. "Take him and go."

"Thank you, Madam President," Chace said. She took the stuffed lion, and then she reached out for Stepan's hand.

The boy hesitated, and President Malikov-Ganiev snapped at him, and the anger in her voice was unmistakable. Stepan flinched, then offered Chace his hand, and she took it, felt it small and a little cold in her own.

"It'll be all right," Chace told Stepan.

"Go," President Malikov-Ganiev said. "Go, and never come back. Tell my brother, he never comes back."

Chace turned away without answering, holding the boy's hand. After a half-dozen steps, she stopped and took his backpack, slipping her arm through the strap, hoisting it onto her shoulder. She offered Stepan her hand once more, and this time he took it without hesitation.

Ahead of them, the border guards stepped aside, watching them advance. Chace heard the clack of a switch being thrown nearby. Another guard moved to the gates, pushing them apart.

Walking alongside the railroad tracks, Chace and Stepan stepped onto the bridge and began the thousand-meter walk into Afghanistan.

CHAPTER 49

Uzbekistan—Surkhan Darya Province— Termez, "Friendship Bridge"

29 August, 0800 Hours (GMT+5:00)

It wasn't perfect, but it was better than he had hoped.

Zahidov had thought he would get Ruslan and his turd off-spring, but Ruslan was nowhere to be found on the Afghan side. That had disappointed him. He'd wanted Ruslan to witness what would happen, to see it with his own eyes.

But then he'd seen the blond woman, the British spy, the woman who had given him nothing but pain, physical and more, and it drove away the disappointment, replacing it with a joy he hadn't felt since he'd last been in Sevara's arms. This was justice, and if he had believed in God, he would have offered a prayer of thanks.

Perhaps Ruslan wouldn't bear witness, but the bitch would, and maybe, if everything went very well and he was very quick, he could kill her, too. For a moment, he even toyed with hitting her first, but discarded the idea. The woman meant nothing to Sevara; it was Stepan who mattered to her. So it had to be Stepan first, and that was fine with Zahidov.

From his vantage point, lying in the dirt a half-kilometer or so from the bridge, just over one and a half kilometers from Afghanistan, watching through the spotting scope mounted on its squat little tripod, he felt no fear. Through his scope he could see the vehicle on the Afghan side, could see the pale black-haired man pacing beyond the closed gate. Every so often the man would stop, then raise a set of binoculars to his eyes, never once looking Zahidov's way, simply tracking the progress of the British bitch and Stepan across the bridge. Then he would lower the binoculars and resume pacing.

Zahidov moved off the spotting scope, sliding to his right in the dirt, to where the weapon waited for him. He brought it to his shoulder, used the line of the bridge to guide his view, settling the crosshairs between the woman and the small boy. He would wait until they crossed, until they had stepped into Afghanistan.

All he needed now was a little more patience.

Behind and below him, the Mi-24v helicopter he'd bought from Arkitov—and that was how Zahidov viewed it, he had paid a million dollars for it, after all—waited, nestled in the bowl made by this series of hillocks, its pilot behind the stick, waiting for his word. The pilot had made no sound since they'd landed, apparently understanding the seriousness of Zahidov's undertaking. His presence, a guarantee of escape, reassured Zahidov. Once his work here was done, he would board the helicopter, order the pilot to fly low and fast to Tajikistan. And if the pilot resisted or offered protest, then Zahidov would put his gun against his neck, to end that dispute.

Once in Tajikistan and on the ground, Zahidov would kill the pilot, something that he was sure Arkitov had understood was part of their transaction. He would have to; he couldn't risk the pilot returning to tell the Americans where he had gone, or worse, have the pilot turn the helicopter's guns on him.

Zahidov blinked, clearing his vision, then settled again behind the sight. The morning sunlight had been heating the weapon steadily since dawn, and it was already hot to the touch, burning against his cheek, waiting to be used.

The spy was still walking with the boy, walking so slowly, and Zahidov felt an almost unbearable frustration in his chest. They

weren't even halfway to Afghanistan yet, and what patience he
had left was swiftly being stripped away.

Pick him up, he thought angrily. *Just carry him.*

But no, the spy, this bitch who had beaten him, this bitch who
had hurt him, mocked him, humiliated him, she walked, letting a
two-and-a-half-year-old boy's legs set her pace. Holding his hand,
and every so often her head turned to the boy, and he could tell she
was speaking to him, and that infuriated him even more.

Then, to his horror, midway across the bridge, they stopped.

They stopped.

CHAPTER 50

Uzbekistan—Surkhan Darya Province— Termez, "Friendship Bridge"

29 August, 0802 Hours (GMT+5:00)

"Good God," Riess muttered, "why doesn't she just carry him?"

Tower didn't speak. Instead, it was the radio that squawked, as if in response, and then a voice came on, speaking in Uzbek, the same voice Riess had heard before.

"Baloo, Ikki, respond."

Riess came off the binoculars, watched Tower grab the radio, then glare at him. Tower stabbed his free hand out the front of the van, in the direction of the bridge.

"Keep your eyes on them, dammit! I need to know if anything changes."

"What's going on?"

"Watch the fucking bridge, Chuck!"

Riess went back to looking through the binoculars, finding Tara-not-Tracy once again, still gripping the boy's hand, still walking steadily along with him. Their progress was painfully slow, governed by the little boy's inadequate stride.

"Baloo, this is Ikki, please respond."

"Go ahead, Ikki."

"We are in position and holding. Status?"

"Shere Khan and Mowgli are making the crossing, stand by."
Riess heard Tower move slightly. "Where are they?"

"Halfway," Riess said. "They're halfway—Shit!"

"What?"

"They've stopped!" Riess came off the binoculars again, looking to Tower. "They've fucking stopped!"

Tower raised the radio. "Ikki, Baloo. Direct me."

"North point two kilometers, then east. We will meet you."

With his free hand, and much to Riess' distress, Tower turned the key in the ignition, starting up the van. "En route. Out."

"What the hell are you doing?" Riess demanded.

"What we came here to do, Chuck."

Tower pulled the gearshift, dropping the van into drive, and they lurched forward, accelerating and turning all at once. Riess felt himself pulled to the left, twisted around against his seatbelt, trying to keep an eye on the bridge.

"We can't just—"

"Sure we can," Tower cut in. "What are we going to do—drive out onto the bridge and pick them up?"

"They're out there, they're just *hanging* out there!"

"Relax, it's in hand."

Riess fell back into his seat, started to open his mouth again, then shut it. She wasn't moving. Tara-not-Tracy wasn't moving, and Tower hadn't at all been surprised she wasn't.

"It was a signal. Between you and her, it was a signal."

Tower hit the brakes, hard, and the van slid into a turn, then hopped off the road onto a thread of dirt trail. The road and the van weren't a good pairing, and Riess grabbed at the dash, trying to keep himself stable in his seat.

"You're learning," Tower told him.

Then the van hit a slope that came out of nowhere, and the vehicle pitched forward, and suddenly Riess was looking at two Uzbek Army APCs, and Tower was slamming on the brakes again, slowing them. Even as he did, the APCs started up, and the radio spoke once more.

"Ikki, Baloo. Standing by."

"Let's do it," Tower told the radio.

The APCs rolled forward, accelerating, and Tower slid in behind them, and Riess' mind raced, trying to fit the pieces together, and then suddenly he saw it, understood why Tower had come. Stepan, Tara-not-Tracy, Sevara . . . none of them had anything to do with it.

"Zahidov," he said. "Zahidov is Kaa."

"Bingo."

"Why's he here, what's that bastard doing here?"

"Unless I'm wrong, he's going to fire a missile into Afghanistan."

"He'll start a fucking war!"

"Nah, it'll just be a messy diplomatic incident. Don't overstate it, Chuck."

Riess shook his head, half to clear it, half to try to dispel his disbelief. "Where'd he get the fucking missile?"

Tower, still concentrating on driving the van over the rough terrain, started to answer, but then the van burst over the crest of the hill. Riess saw the helicopter, an Uzbek Army bird, covered with camouflage netting, and past it, the man sprawled on the ground, looking down at the river and the bridge and Afghanistan.

Zahidov turned at the sound of their approach, his expression empty in its confusion. The van came down and skidded to a stop, and Riess was thrown against his door, but he didn't feel it, because his whole world had become one man, what that man held in his hands.

Zahidov was twisting about, back to face the bridge, and from the APCs, Uzbek soldiers were pouring forth, and there was gunfire, all of it together, and everything happening together. Zahidov flopped and flailed, hit by several bursts at once, his body trying to follow each bullet and instead able to follow none. He fell, and the weapon he'd held in his hands tumbled free.

"Motherfucker," Tower said, reaching for his radio.

CHAPTER 51

No-Man's-Land—Amu Darya River—
"Friendship Bridge"

29 August, 0803 Hours (GMT+5:00)

Chace had stopped not so much because the boy needed her to carry him, but because she needed the signal to be clear. It was a game of trust now, trust that everyone would do what they were supposed to, be where they were supposed to, when they were supposed to.

She could see Kostum and Lankford at the far end of the bridge, standing in Afghanistan, five hundred meters away. When she turned and looked back, she could see Sevara's little motorcade, the President standing where they'd left her, watching their progress.

Then she heard the radio chatter in her ear, Tower's voice speaking in Uzbek, and another's, answering him in the same language. She saw the plume of dust spurt from where the van had been parked on the slope, and she knew it was on, and as a result, she knew several other things. The first was that Ahtam Zahidov was somewhere within five kilometers of their position, within the maximum range of the Starstreak. Second, that he planned on using the Starstreak to kill not just Stepan and Ruslan, but Lankford and herself as well.

And third, that she now needed to make certain Zahidov stayed so focused on what she was doing that he didn't decide to fire early, that he wouldn't see what was coming.

Stepan was looking up at her, confusion painting his small face, and he asked her a question in Uzbek, and she smiled at him, then crouched and hoisted him in her arms, positioning him on her left hip.

"How about a song?" she asked him. "Shall we sing a song?"

Stepan's confusion remained, and Chace resumed walking along the bridge. Most of the songs she knew by heart, she realized, were entirely inappropriate for children, whether Stepan could understand them or not. Instead, she pointed with her free hand down toward the southern end of the bridge, and used the one Uzbek word that Stepan himself had taught her.

"That way," she told the little boy. "*Ota.*"

The boy twisted in her arm, looking, and she felt him tense with excitement, and for a second, she was afraid she would lose her grip on him as he tried to lunge forward. Then, not seeing his father, he sagged and turned an accusing look at her. She couldn't blame him. That Ruslan's fear had been greater than his desire to see his son, to be present when the little boy came across the border, confused her. If it had been Chace waiting for Tamsin, she'd have stood naked with a bull's-eye painted over her heart, just so her daughter would know she was waiting.

From the southern end of the bridge, Kostum shouted something in Uzbek at them, and Chace didn't understand a word of it, but it got Stepan's attention, and he squirmed in her arm. There was a crackle in her ear, and a second transmission in Uzbek, followed by another response, and now Tower sounded more agitated, more urgent. Chace tried to keep her progress as slow as before, buying time, but Afghanistan was coming closer. She thought about stopping again, but to do so a second time would be too risky—Zahidov would see it for what it was, a stalling tactic.

Look at me, she thought. *Look at me, hate me, look at me. Just don't hate me so much you lose your patience.*

Stepan was speaking in her arms, apparently in response to

Kostum's words. Chace wondered just how much of what the little boy was saying was actually Uzbek versus toddler babble. Kostum was gesturing toward himself, then the vehicle, parked and waiting for them. Lankford now stood by the open driver's door, the tension on his face, the anxiety. She shared it.

The trap hinged on denying Zahidov the optimum shot, on keeping Chace, Stepan, and Lankford apart for as long as possible. Once they were all together in Afghanistan, once they were at the vehicle, that would be when Zahidov loosed the Starstreak. They had to stay separated long enough for Tower and the Uzbeks to close in on Zahidov. But they couldn't be obvious about it, because if Zahidov for an instant thought he was being set up, he'd take whatever shot he could.

And Chace knew whom that shot would be targeted at, and this time, she was sure there'd be no narrow escape for her and little Stepan Malikov.

She kept walking, measuring her pace, trying to guess at the time. How long had it been since she'd given the go signal? Thirty seconds? Forty? A minute? How fast would they be able to move overland, how far away was Zahidov?

The Afghan border guards were raising the gate now, she saw the two bars of white-and-red-painted metal lifting and separating, clearing the way. Chace felt her stomach contracting, knowing that her next few steps would take her and the boy into the kill zone, the blast radius of the Starstreak when it hit the Cherokee. Any instant now, Zahidov would fire.

Any instant now, he would kill them all.

Then Chace heard the echo of gunfire as it rolled down the hills out of Uzbekistan and across the water, the chorus of automatic rifles as they made certain that the man who had tortured her, who had murdered the mother of the child in her arms, could never hurt anyone ever again.

CHAPTER 52

Uzbekistan—Surkhan Darya Province— Termez, "Friendship Bridge"

29 August, 0803 Hours (GMT+5:00)

Finally, the bitch had done what she was supposed to be doing all along. And carrying the little shit, that was even better—she'd be wearing his blood by the time he was through.

Zahidov felt his heart pounding in his ears, his pulse making his very palms vibrate. He adjusted his position slightly, pressing the sight more firmly to his eye, settling the crosshairs on little boy's head as it rested on the blond bitch's shoulder. If he did it right, he'd take them both together.

He heard engines, car engines, or engines larger than cars, and for a moment the sound confused him. They were far from the road, far enough that the sounds of the vehicles traveling it wouldn't carry. He pulled his eye from the sight and half turned, trying to find the source of the noise, and then he saw the vehicles coming, two APCs and, of all things, a white van, a Daewoo, and they were roaring toward him, cresting the hill above where the helicopter waited.

And in that moment, Ahtam Zahidov knew he had been had.

Swearing, he twisted back around, to face the bridge and Afghanistan, trying to reacquire the bitch and the boy in his sights. But he'd shifted, he was looking at the water, not at the bridge, and it took him precious seconds to reacquire the target, and then he could see them, the two figures about to come off the bridge, the gate on the Afghan side being raised.

He heard the shouts and the gunfire together, the rattle of automatic weapons, and he knew that they were too late, all he needed to do was pull the trigger, such a little gesture, such a tiny act. But his chest felt suddenly heavy, as if filled with cast iron, and his legs felt brittle, and he couldn't see the target anymore, only sky. He felt a thousand blows raining down on his body.

He saw his rifle on the ground.

Then a last blow shattered his head, and he never saw anything else.

CHAPTER 53

29 August, 0806 Hours (GMT+5:00)

Lankford drove the Cherokee, taking them out along the newly paved road that paralleled the Amu Darya, Chace seated beside him. In the backseat, belted in, Stepan sat numbly beside Kostum, who, Chace thought, was doing a wretched job of trying to reassure the boy.

She was looking back over the river, to the Uzbek side, when Tower's voice crackled once again in her ear, the transmission distorted with interference from the border posts.

"We have Kaa but negative on the candle. Baloo to Shere Khan, do you copy?"

Chace glanced sharply to Lankford, saw from his expression that he'd received the transmission as well, was just as bewildered by it as she was. She twisted in her seat, looking past Stepan, back toward the bridge spanning the ugly river.

"Shere Khan, do you copy? I repeat, negative on the candle, the candle is not *here."*

The binoculars that Lankford had used were on the dashboard, and Chace took them up, used them to look back toward the Uzbek checkpoint. She could feel Lankford slowing the Cherokee, and that made it easier to find what she was looking for, the cluster of soldiers and vehicles that formed President Sevara Malikov-

Ganiev's motorcade. They were still parked as before, and she could see the figures that made up her retinue as the President made nice with the guards, taking her promised tour of the border crossing before returning to the Sikorsky and a quick trip back into Termez.

How long until she got aboard her helicopter once more? Three minutes? Five?

There was another transmission from Tower, this one so distorted as to be unintelligible, but it didn't matter, she knew what he was saying. Zahidov hadn't had the missile, maybe had never had it, and that meant it was in someone else's hands.

She lowered the binoculars, and saw Kostum watching her, and then she understood, and the humiliation and betrayal that burst open inside her at having been played so well and so effectively was sickening. It all made sense, then, what Ruslan had done and why he had done it. Why he had demanded that she be the one to bring Stepan across, why Ruslan had claimed that the fear for his own life was greater than his concern for his son's. Chace understood it all, and worse, understood just how effectively Ruslan had found her blind spot and exploited it.

She saw it all, and she saw the reason for it, but Kostum had seen the realization coming, too, and the pistol was coming out from the folds of his shirt, held in his left hand. With his other, Kostum held Stepan with an open palm on the little boy's chest, pressing him against the backseat, keeping him still. The bandage around his hand was filthy and stained, and looked like a tumor where his hand pressed against the little boy's breast.

"Chris—" Chace started to say, but the pistol was already pressing into the back of Lankford's head, and it was too late for any move.

"Stop," Kostum said.

Lankford stopped the Cherokee in the middle of the road.

"I take son to him now," Kostum said. "You both out."

"Where is he?" Chace asked. "Where's Ruslan?"

"Out."

"He's going to kill his sister. That's it, isn't it?"

Kostum pushed the barrel of his pistol harder into the back of Lankford's head, and in her peripheral vision, Chace could see Minder Three wince, his hands still tight on the wheel. The gun was a Makarov, a Russian pistol, and from the looks of it, acquired during the Soviet invasion of Afghanistan. Not the best gun in the world, and not the most accurate outside of fifteen meters or so, but here and now, perfectly suited for its job.

"Out," Kostum repeated, then slid his eyes to Chace, and his expression softened, almost to a plea. "Please."

"Where'd he get the Starstreak? From you?"

Kostum's mouth tightened, but he didn't move, and neither did the pistol, and Chace could see him struggling with the conflict. She and Lankford had saved his life on the road to Mazar-i-Sharif, when Zahidov's men had ambushed them, after all. There was a debt to be paid.

"You're the one who sold them to Zahidov in the first place, aren't you?" Chace persisted. "Kept one for yourself?"

"Please." Kostum spoke through clenched teeth. "I take son now."

"You gave us protection. Pashtunwali."

Kostum turned his head to Chace. Trapped beneath his palm, Stepan seemed frozen in place, staring straight ahead, at nothing, young eyes dead, a witness already of too much violence. Beneath their voices, the engine idled softly, waiting.

"He asks my help for his revenge. You do not understand—"

Lankford twisted his neck to the left, wrenching himself about in the seat, the Makarov slipping from his head, and when he did, Chace lunged. The interior of the car exploded with the sound of the pistol's report, the windshield shattering, and Chace felt something slap her face, a hot line burning across her cheek. She bore down on the weapon, hearing Stepan's screams as if her head were inside a bucket of water, her ears ringing from the gunshot, and she kept her grip on the Makarov, twisting it with both hands, turning it away from Kostum's finger trapped inside the trigger guard, refusing him a second shot.

Then Lankford had his Browning out, pointed at Kostum's face, and Chace had the Makarov in her hand, and Stepan was wailing, and Kostum was falling back against his seat, shaking his injured left hand. The look on his face was devoid of anger, even of pain, just an acknowledgment of his failure, and already Chace could see him finding his resolve. This wasn't what Kostum had wanted, but in its way, it satisfied his obligations. He had tried, and he had failed.

Lankford was saying something, but Chace couldn't hear him. She saw Kostum start slightly in his seat, glance down at his shirt, then look back to them. With the pistol in one hand, pointed at him, Chace leaned forward, digging into the folds of his shirt with the other. Kostum's expression tightened with anger, but he didn't move, and she found the phone nestled near his hip. When she pulled it out, her hearing had returned enough that she could dimly make out the trill of an incoming call.

"Get him out of the car," Chace said to Lankford, then turned her attention to the phone.

It was another satellite model, not unlike the Iridium she'd brought with her to Tashkent in February. She set the Makarov in her lap, pulling the earpiece from the radio free while using her teeth to extend the antenna on the phone. She punched the receive button with her thumb and put the unit to her ear.

"Hello, Ruslan," Chace said, and she hoped she wasn't shouting.

There was a moment's pause. "You have my son with you?"

Chace looked at the boy, his face stained with tears, snot bubbling over his upper lip, miserable in the backseat.

"I do. Where are you? I'll bring him to you."

"In a few minutes. After Sevara has boarded her helicopter."

"Now," Chace disagreed. "Or I don't bring him to you at all."

There was a second pause, Ruslan hesitating, trapped between conflicting desires.

"You kill her, you'll never see your son again, Ruslan. Even if you do manage to disappear into Afghanistan for the rest of your life, you'll never see Stepan again."

"You will kill him?"

"I'll take him back to Uzbekistan. Your sister's husband is still there."

His muttered curse came over the line.

"You're running out of time, Ruslan."

"Come toward the water," he told her. "Quickly."

He hung up.

Chace shifted the Makarov to her coat pocket, then opened her door and moved around the hood to the driver's side, to climb back in. Lankford stood with Kostum, now at the side of the road, the Browning still pointed at him.

"Where are you going?"

"Ruslan's down by the river. I'm going to get the missile."

Lankford didn't look away from Kostum. "You're taking the kid with you?"

"He wants his son."

"And Ruslan will just hand the Starstreak over in trade, will he?"

"For the boy's sake, let's hope so," Chace said.

He'd taken a position another half-kilometer away, along a dried wash at the edge of the water, and Chace saw him from a distance, and thought that he'd picked a fine place to stage an assassination. She'd expected him to take higher ground, but instead, he'd gone for lower, using the shelter cut from the earth by the water long ago. It was a good spot, not unlike the one Chace had picked for the failed rendezvous with Porter nearly seven months earlier, and well within the maximum range of the Starstreak.

He had the MANPAD deployed, resting on his shoulder, nose to the ground. Chace guided the Cherokee toward him along the river's edge, closing the distance as quickly as she could manage without giving him the impression she would run him down. When he thought she'd come far enough, he lifted the missile and pointed it at the car, indicating that she should stop.

Chace killed the engine, stared out at Ruslan through the shattered windshield. Behind her, still belted into his seat, she heard Stepan snuffle as the latest bout of his tears finally subsided.

"Step out of the car," Ruslan called to her.

From the backseat she heard Stepan cry out, surprised and frightened and delighted all at once, hearing his father's voice. Chace could hear the child moving, straining against the lap belt, caught a glimpse of the little boy's reflection in the rearview mirror as he struggled against the safety restraint.

Chace got out of the car, slamming her door, then looking again to Ruslan. He was dressed much as he had been the last time she'd seen him. About two meters past him, resting in the dirt, was the crate for the Starstreak, opened and empty, and propped against it, a Kalashnikov. She wondered idly how he'd gotten himself and the missile into position, then realized there would have been a thousand ways to do so, that all it took was money to bribe the right people and the will to make it happen.

"You killed Kostum?" Ruslan asked.

She shook her head. He was still holding the Starstreak as before, the launch tube roughly parallel to the ground, but skewed away from her, his eye clear of the aiming unit. Chace turned, looking in the direction Ruslan faced. Across the water, the Uzbek minefield sloped upward, toward the electrified fence. She could see the bridge in the distance, and a couple of vehicles parked near the checkpoint, but not the Sikorsky.

"You're waiting until she takes off," Chace said.

"If my son had not been aboard, I would have shot her down before she landed."

Stepan called out from inside the Cherokee, his voice climbing in volume and pitch. Ruslan didn't answer, but she saw him look to the vehicle, and for a moment thought he might actually lower the Starstreak and go to his son.

But he didn't.

"Then what?" Chace asked him. "You and Stepan disappear into Afghanistan, never to return?"

"It is a country made for hiding," he answered.

"Zahidov's dead."

"A good start, but not enough."

"Put it down, Ruslan."

He shook his head. "I must do this."

"Forget that she's your sister. She's the President of Uzbekistan."

"She killed my father. She killed my wife!"

"Zahidov killed your wife."

"At her request! At her pleasure! She is a monster, you know this!"

His voice was shaking now, churning with anger and desperation, with his need for Chace to understand. And she did understand—too well she understood. Blood cried for blood.

"She's the President of Uzbekistan," Chace repeated. "I can't let you kill her. Please, put it down, Ruslan. You have your son, let that be enough."

"It isn't enough!" He glared at her, then turned his head slightly, suddenly, and she knew he was listening for the rumble of the helicopter lifting off from across the river. So far, there was only the running water of the Amu Darya and their own voices.

"It isn't enough," he repeated.

Chace turned, walking around the rear of the vehicle to the passenger side. She looked back toward the bridge as she did, thinking again that Ruslan had done an excellent job of picking his spot. The helo would be visible in the air as it turned back toward Termez. Fired from here, the Starstreak could hit it in mere seconds, and there was even a chance that the missile would never be seen coming.

When she reached Stepan's door, Ruslan snapped, "Leave him inside."

Inside the Cherokee, Stepan was looking at her, wide-eyed. Chace turned.

"Put it down."

"I cannot."

She opened the passenger door, reaching across the little boy to unfasten his seatbelt.

"Please," Ruslan pleaded. "Leave him in the car!"

Chace finished unfastening the boy, caught him beneath the armpits, and swung him out of the vehicle. She set Stepan down on the rough sand, facing his father.

"Don't do this!"

"*Ota,*" she told the little boy. She needn't have said anything.

As soon as her hands left him, Stepan was off, a full toddler run, arms flailing, legs pumping, making straight for Ruslan. Chace straightened, watching the little boy as she pulled the Makarov from her pocket. She followed after him, slower, the gun in her right hand.

"For pity's sake, Ruslan," she said, "put the damn thing down."

She thought she saw him consider it, saw the launch tube of the missile dip toward the earth once more just as Stepan reached him. The little boy threw his arms around his father's legs, and Ruslan looked down at his son, then up at Chace, and there was no escaping the pain on his face.

"Put him back in the car! I am begging you!"

Chace continued to approach, shaking her head. From across the river, she could hear the Sikorsky, the echo of the rotors spinning up. She saw Ruslan's head jerk to the right, hearing it as well.

"You have to decide what's more important, Ruslan," Chace told him. "Your son or your revenge."

"She raped and murdered his mother!"

"And you're about to murder his aunt."

"Tell me! You tell me! Tell me that you wouldn't have killed the man who murdered the father of *your* child."

Chace brought the Makarov up, holding it in both hands, placing the sights high on Ruslan's body, as far away from his son as she dared.

"I did kill him," she answered.

He wasn't looking at her now, looking instead past her, focusing on where the Sikorsky would rise into sight. The noise of the helicopter went from faint to suddenly much louder, and without needing to turn and look, Chace knew it was off the ground. The window was open for his shot, would only remain so for a few more seconds.

Ruslan looked down at his son, still clinging tightly to his legs, then to Chace. He hoisted the Starstreak back into firing position on his shoulder, turned his face to settle his right eye against the sight.

"You are the mother of a child," Ruslan Mihailovich Malikov reminded her. "You will not shoot me in front of my son."

"You're wrong," Chace said, and then she shot him four times in the chest.

CHAPTER 54

London—Camden—Chace Family Residence

1 September, 0033 Hours GMT

She'd sent a message from Mazar-i-Sharif before she and Lankford
had caught the transport to Turkey, telling Val that she was on her
way home, and that she hoped to see her and Tamsin in London on
her return. It was a break in protocol to send any such communication while on a job, and if Crocker had known about it he'd
have gone into fits, but after seeing Stepan back to Uzbekistan and
returned to Sevara Malikov-Ganiev's care, Chace didn't really give
a damn. They had the last Starstreak back and Ruslan Malikov
was no longer a problem for anyone except perhaps his son.

If that didn't make Crocker happy, Chace had no interest in
performing whatever task would.

The little boy had looked at her with eyes devoid of any comprehension or soul when she'd pulled him from his father's body.
There had been no more tears and no more sobs, there had been
no sound at all. There had been nothing because, Chace suspected,
Stepan Malikov no longer had anything.

She told herself that he would forget, that he would recover,
and on the plane to Frankfurt, Lankford tried to tell her the same
thing.

Both of them knew it for the lie it was.

———

Her house was quiet and still and the lights were all off when Chace came through the door, and she wondered if Val had received the message. She shut and locked the front door behind her, hung her coat on the stand, dropped her go-bag at its foot. She would have to replace its contents, substitute clean clothes for the dirty, replace those things she had used.

Then she saw her mail piled neatly on the table beside the couch.

She checked in the guest room, parting the door just enough to confirm that Val was indeed asleep there, then made her way to the bedroom. She stripped, changed into pajamas, and then went to look in on Tamsin, finding her sixteen-month-old daughter awake and on her feet in her crib, waiting quietly in the darkness.

"Mama," Tamsin said.

"That's right," Chace agreed, taking the child in her arms. "Mama."

ABOUT THE AUTHOR

GREG RUCKA has worked at a variety of jobs, from theatrical fight choreographer to emergency medical technician. The author of *A Gentleman's Game*, *A Fistful of Rain*, and five previous thrillers, he resides with his family in Portland, Oregon. He is currently working on the next Atticus Kodiak crime novel, *Patriot Acts*, which Bantam will publish in fall 2006.